Sometimes There Were Heroes

Sometimes There Were Heroes

Douglas C. Jones

The University of Arkansas Press
Fayetteville
2000

04   03   02   01   00   5   4   3   2   1

Designed by Liz Lester

⊛   The paper used in this publication meets the minimum requirements of the American National Standard for Permanence of Paper for Printed Library Materials Z39.48–1984.

Library of Congress Cataloging-in-Publication Data

Jones, Douglas C. (Douglas Clyde), 1924–
    Sometimes there were heroes / Douglas C. Jones
          p.   cm.
        ISBN 1-55728-610-8 (alk. paper)
      1. San Antonio (Tex.)—History—Fiction.   I. Title.
    PS3560.O478 S58 2000
    813'.54—dc21   00-008996

Printed and bound in Canada

For Swampy
And all the old brotherhood know who he is.

This story is fiction.

But there's a lot of fact in here, too.

That's so maybe you can feel some of the melody and rhythm of the Texas-Mexican-Commanche frontier.

A long time ago.

Contents

Acknowledgments

In appreciation:

Although it is impossible to credit all the sources one uses in historical fiction, there are always a few that demand recognition. So . . .

For the big historical stuff regarding Mexico, Texas, and Comanches, highest on the list are the three works by T. R. Fehrenbach: *Fire and Blood; Lone Star,* and *Comanches.*

The University of Oklahoma Press deserves acknowledgment for all those excellent publications on North American Indians. So does John Upton Terrell's *American Indian Almanac.*

A whole herd of small publications touches on the minutiae of life and love the big scholars often ignore. Like Mary Ann Noonan Guerra's history of Market Square; *The Texas Germans* from the University of Texas Institute of Cultures; *The German Texans,* by Glen E. Lich; Eldon Cagle Jr.'s *Quadrangle;* Mary V. Burkholder's *Down the Acequia Madre;* and *Pioneer Flour Mills,* by Ernest Schuchard. To all of these for providing the historical footnotes that create the basic rhythms for this kind of novel, *muchas gracias.*

But most of all, to Colonel H. T. Marsh, an old comrade at arms, *danke.* The first time I sat at his board was in Germany, and the last time it was in San Antonio, for he has now become a resident of Bexar and is perhaps that area's most vocal, and certainly its most enthusiastic booster. So, sort of, I can think of him along with all the Germans in my story who immigrated to Texas more than a century ago.

Prologue

Once Old Eben Pay was sitting in his law office, where it smelled of dust and sealing wax and cigar smoke and everything around him was the same color. He called the color legal brown because that was the color of the leather bindings of his library of law books presented to him a long time ago by the Bar Association, when he was appointed United States Attorney for the Western District of Arkansas with Jurisdiction in the Indian Territory.

He was looking down on Garrison Avenue, watching the new contraptions called automobiles going along scaring good horses and creating a horrid-smelling blue haze. And like all people of his age, he wondered where the good days had gone.

And perhaps sang under his breath a song his Cherokee wife might have sung to their son if she hadn't died before the boy was old enough to appreciate such things:

> Oh where, oh where has my little dog gone?
> Oh where, oh where can he be?
> With his tail cut short and his ears cut long,
> Oh where, oh where can he be?

A lot of things were gone, all right, like the old federal court where he'd tried so many cases. Well, the federal court was still there, in one of these brand-new, columns-at-the-front marble monuments to what somebody thought the Greeks once built.

But jurisdiction in the Indian Territory, that part was long gone. In fact, the Indian Territory was gone. Where it had been was now called Oklahoma. Like all old folks, Eben Pay thought about the good times past and ignored all the bad stuff, of which there had been plenty. Sometimes in larger than comfortable doses.

Maybe some of the old times were a lot older than even Eben Pay. Maybe his grandson's question had started his thoughts back on a trail of generations.

The grandson's question had been why everyone they knew came from the East. Old Eben Pay, who had been thinking about something else and was a little irritated at being interrupted in his thoughts, had snapped something like, "Where the hell did you expect them to come from?"

3

Whereupon his grandson had stomped out of the office and left Eben Pay feeling like a sour puke.

Now he thought about that question, and he said to himself, Well, they all *did* come from the East. Not from the West. Many folks during one period were going through Arkansas to Texas. Sam Houston, the Austins, Bowie, and Crockett. There was no other place west of Arkansas where you could go legally. The only alternative in that direction was the Indian Territory, which was supposed to be off limits for the white man.

So people in Arkansas went to Texas.

You never heard about anybody going the other way. It was as though a lot of people were trying to get into Texas but nobody ever tried to get out. Or maybe people who left Texas didn't talk about it because they were ashamed they left, or maybe they didn't talk about it because they were ashamed they didn't leave sooner.

But there had been one! He was the best United States Deputy Marshall ever to serve Isaac Charles Parker, the Hanging Judge, so-called by the jingo, sensational eastern newspapers, which meant all of them in that day.

Yes sir! Oscar was from Texas.

Part One

Paco

Chapter One

A long time ago, a man named Hernando Salazar stood with an official of Spain on a post oak plain just west of a little winding river. They were surrounded by about fifteen other men, eyes shaded from the fierce summer sun by wide hat brims.

The Spanish official had some papers in his hand. These papers were like a book. Sheets of paper were held together by string tied through the holes in the margins of the papers, so they looked like a book although they were only pieces of paper, tied together.

The Spanish official was wearing a small leather cap with a bill, like a soldier's hat. He said something, then took the hat off. The wind blew his black hair across his forehead. It was short hair. The fifteen men standing in the circle had long hair, tied in queues in back, so it hung down under their wide hat brims.

Hernando Salazar had short hair, unlike all the other men standing with big hats, but like the Spanish official. However, he did not remove his hat as the Spanish official had done.

Now the ceremony began. Hernando Salazar bent to the ground and pulled a handful of weeds, and maybe a few Indian pipes, with their pale blossoms turned down like they were trying to eat themselves. Then he pulled another handful of weeds. As with the first, he dropped them back on the ground.

Next, the men in the circle watched alertly to avoid being struck by a stone, for Hernando Salazar bent to the ground, took four rocks, and threw them in the four cardinal directions. North. East. South. West.

The Spanish official returned the leather soldier's cap to his head, wrote something on the booklet of papers in his hand, using a piece of charcoal, and everybody began to walk back toward a bend in the river where there was a considerable scatter of adobe and thatch houses.

Across the river was a whitewashed mission in a grove of cottonwood trees. These were very tall trees. Closer, there were a few sycamores that turned the bottoms of their white leaves up to the sun. Beyond that, across gentle swells of land, there were groves of oak and walnut trees, making a dark shade that looked purple in the distance.

There was the smell of dust and a little of rain, as though maybe there had been a thunderstorm out along the Balcones Escarpment far to the northwest. It was a smell of late spring, or early summer.

During the ceremony, no one except the Spanish official had written anything on the papers he held that looked like a book. Mostly because the Spanish official was the only one among them who could write. Except for Hernando Salazar, and he had already written on the paper.

With the ceremony and the witnesses and the *alcalde's* charcoal markings on the paper, Hernando Salazar officially had taken possession of the approximately eight acres of land-granted to him by King Carlos IV in gratitude for the thirty years of faithful service Hernando Salazar's father had performed in the armies of Spain.

It might be interesting to note that shortly after this ceremony, King Carlos would be forced by Napoleon to abdicate. He would be replaced on the Spanish throne by Joseph, one of Napoleon's brothers.

It was probable that Hernando Salazar knew this when it happened but didn't care. He had the land, and he doubted if Napoleon's brother would take it from him.

It wasn't Napoleon's brother he had to worry about. What he had to worry about was the Holy Office of the Spanish Inquisition.

When Ferdinand and Isabella had set out to conquer the New World at the end of the fifteenth century, they told Don Francisco Vasquez de Coronado and other *conquistadores* that they expected to vanquish this land and all its peoples and that the soldiers of Spain must do this. Further, the soldiers were to find many riches of silver and gold and send them back to the treasuries of Castile and Aragon, which had been joined in marriage, like Ferdinand and Isabella had been, to form Spain.

Of equal importance, they said, was to bring all those vanquished peoples to Christ.

These two missions continued under all the rulers of Spain for the next two hundred years. Mostly, the first mission of sending home silver and gold, and later sugar, would finance all the Spanish wars in Europe.

The second mission continued as it had begun, out of consideration for the souls of all native peoples and the obvious duty of the Most Christian Monarchs, which is how Spanish kings characterized themselves, to save these souls.

As you would expect, then, when the conquerors came, they brought armies for the first job and a few Franciscan and Dominican priests and monks for the second.

Now obviously you would not use soldiers of Spain or priests and members of the Holy Orders to dig in the earth and do other very hard labor to produce or procure the riches of silver and gold, so naturally, the vanquished peoples did this, under the careful eye of the soldiers.

You might consider them slaves under such a system, but the *conquistadores* said the *indios* had a pretty good deal because after all, as the vanquished peoples worked, their souls were being saved.

A great many priests and monks didn't agree that the natives had such a good deal and made a lot of fuss about it and wrote long letters to the king or various bishops, which you can still read, and there was much lip service given in Madrid to making things better.

But nothing much ever came of it except more lip service, which developed into an exercise in which everybody blamed everybody else. This came to be called covering one's ass.

Maybe one of the great ironies of this was that the priests likely killed more *indios* than the soldiers. Their line of work required close contact with the natives, and it was from this kind of contact that small pox, measles, and a host of other diseases were passed to a population with absolutely no built-up immunity to such European maladies.

Anyway, the Spaniards found precious metal in the high country of the Aztecs, which was now New Spain or Mexico, but beyond the river of the north, which they called the Rio Bravo, they didn't have any luck at all. After a while, they gave up in that quarter, which they were calling Tejas, or Texas.

If they could find no silver and gold in the north, they could at least save the souls of some of those savages who lived there. A soul was a soul, no matter where found. But in the northern provinces of

New Spain, the savages willing to be saved were rare indeed. Most of them, in fact, took violent exception to the Spaniards being there for any purpose whatsoever.

But many of the priests and monks, with modest support from the various army commandants, stubbornly continued to try.

Early in the eighteenth century, a group of Franciscans marched about fifty leagues northeast of the Rio Bravo, across the Nueces, to near the headwaters of a stream they had named after Saint Anthony, the Italian divine who was patron of the poor.

The San Antonio River was what geologists would one day call an old river, which meant it had a very slight gradient, so the current was slow. Such rivers form what are called meanders, or very abrupt bends that are shaped like the Greek letter omega. These bends are also called ox-bows.

In an area of beautiful rolling hills and scattered hardwood stands of timber, plenty of water, and good soil, the padres found one of these ox-bows, and at the open end of the omega, on the west side of the river, they located a new mission.

They named it for the same patron saint of the poor, and they added the name of the Marques of Valera, the viceroy of New Spain, who had sent them there in the first place.

Hence, the mission of San Antonio de Valera.

Marching with them, as you might expect, was a contingent of the Spanish army of Mexico. They located their fort just west of the mission. Naturally, they named it for the same saint, adding the name of a great hero who had been brother to the viceroy of Mexico and had died fighting the Moslems in Spain. He had been the Duke of Bexar.

Hence, the presidio of San Antonio de Bexar.

The most beautiful thing about this location, which padre or soldier likely didn't know, was that it attracted little attention in Comanche lodges because it was outside any of the big buffalo ranges.

The Franciscans had brought some Christianized Indians from Mexico who spoke the language of a few local tribes. So these began to come in to be saved, too, and to work in the surrounding fields, which had all been allotted the mission by the viceroy, de Valera.

Wichitas, the Caddo, a lot of pumpkin-growing tribes nobody ever heard of. There were maybe even a few who came hoping the mission might protect them from Comanches consolidating gains, having just driven the Apaches out of the Southern Plains.

A few settlers from below the Rio Bravo actually came to locate around the mission. There was enough optimism for the friars to establish other missions up and down the river. Mission Concepción, Mission San Jose, San Francisco de la Espada.

But before that, there had been friction between the mission people and the soldiers. The friars complained that the soldiers were low class. They were not married, mostly, and those who were had left their wives in Mexico. So they paid too much attention to the *indio* women whose souls the padres were trying to save.

The viceroy, even though the mission was named in his honor, did not send any high-class soldiers as the priests requested. Maybe he didn't have any high-class soldiers to send.

Obviously the rigid medieval Spanish caste structure that had always characterized Iberians had not died crossing the Atlantic; it was still recognized and used by the clergy.

To get their *indios* away from the low-class soldiers, the padres moved their mission across the river. So the San Antonio River now stood between cross and sword.

The Christianized Indians built a new mission under the close supervision of the padres, who complained in letters to Spain that these *indios* had to be whipped often to remind them of the beauty of hard work and the glory of God.

They built anew at the western edge of a large grove of cottonwood trees. They called it *la alameda*, which means poplar grove, so maybe there were some poplars there, too.

Between the mission and the river, and on the far bank in the "U" of the ox-bow, there were only a few trees, post oak and cedar elm and some black willow along the riverbank at the ford at the top of the "U." From the presidio, the soldiers could clearly see the mission.

But before long, settlers from the Canary Islands came and built around the presidio. Their buildings were of log or adobe, many with windows, and some two stories high. One was a limestone church they would call the cathedral of San Fernando. So now from the west side of the river, a view of the mission was often obscured.

As time passed and more people came to Bexar, which the whole area was being called, the wandering trails along the river and between the buildings became streets or roads, and were named.

At last, at Plaza del Presidio, or Military Square, farmers appeared sometimes with wagons and carts and produce for sale to each other or to the mission or the army garrison. There were not many farmers. They grew their crops close in to the settlement for protection from hostile Indians.

There was an adobe house for the *alcalde* of all Bexar, which was now much more than just the settlement, so the *alcalde* would be an important official, although none had yet arrived. They started to build a jail. It was beginning to look like a town, they said.

It was the soldiers who did the building outside the missions. The *indios*, with the friars overseeing, and the Canary Islanders built all the mission structures. A few businessmen from south of the Rio Bravo built stores and *cantinas*. The farmers put up their huts and sheds around all the rest, like a ragged lace on the edge of an old pillowslip cover.

The viceroy thought it must look like a town, too, although he never saw it. What he saw was the garrison commander's letters describing it.

The viceroy then proceeded to send a man who had learned engineering skills from the Moslems in Spain, and *indios* began digging irrigation ditches. *Acequias*. To water the land all around the presidio and the mission, and as far south as Mission Concepción, about a mile downstream, where San Pedro Creek flowed into the San Antonio.

The viceroy secularized most of the land originally allotted to the Franciscans, leaving them only enough to grow vegetables for their flocks and themselves. He sent an *alcalde* to live in the *alcalde* house that had already been built by the soldiers. He sent in bureaucrats to administer the land.

It was one of these officials from whom Hernando Salazar received the king's patent for the plot in the *labores del sur*, the southern work fields of Bexar.

Hernando Salazar had never imagined he'd come to be a farmer on the raw northern edge of New Spain. Nobody was ever sure what

Hernando Salazar did imagine he'd come to be because he didn't confide in anybody. In fact, he didn't talk at all to most of his neighbors.

The record is pretty spotty, but there is no doubt about why Hernando Salazar's father, Old Paco Salazar, came to Hispanic America. He was a sergeant in the Spanish army, and his unit was sent to Mexico as part of the contingent keeping order around the silver mines.

It was hard, hot duty, when it wasn't freezing cold, and in all kinds of weather there were sometimes heated gun battles between the soldiers and *indio* bandits looking for silver somebody else had dug out of the ground, or Yaqui raiders looking for hair to decorate Sierra Madre lodges.

In all of which Old Paco acquitted himself well.

Old Paco was not *un caballero*, a noble who rode around on a horse all day, but a foot soldier made into a dragoon on a mule, along with all his company. But he was Spanish-born, which placed him at a high notch in the caste system.

Had Old Paco been interested in such things, he could likely have traced his bloodline back to some of those Visigoth tribesmen who invaded the Iberian Peninsula after the Romans left. He was fair in complexion, not swarthy, his eyes were blue, and he had light brown hair.

He had married a woman of his class, as most Spaniards did, and when he came to New Spain, he was of sufficient rank to bring her with him. And when they arrived in the New World, she was pregnant.

Things were looking good for Old Paco. Although a number of families named Salazar were still being hounded by the Inquisition as possible Jews, he was lucky not to ever have been suspected by the Holy Office.

But now, in America, Old Paco's luck started running out. Instead of being posted with his regiment in the high plateau area, near Mexico City, he was detailed for harbor duty in Veracruz.

This place was a pest hole. All most people could recall of it was mud flats, flies, and stink. The young Señora Salazar lived long enough in this place to give birth to a healthy boy, but then she died in less than a year, probably of yellow fever.

Old Paco raised such a dismal howl that his superiors immediately moved him off the coast and back to his regiment near some of the larger silver mines. There wasn't much of a town in the vicinity. In fact, there wasn't much of anything, except what you could find in the one *cantina*.

A mission with half-a-dozen Franciscans so busy among the army of slave-labor *indios* they had little time for anything else, so the school was pretty bad.

At least the climate was healthy, and there were plenty of young *indio* women who were excellent mistresses and could even pass muster as stepmothers to a growing boy like Hernando, named obviously for the conqueror of Mexico.

Yet the boy was never happy. In fact, he was the most irritated boy anyone had ever seen in that area, and as he became a man, he was the most irritated man. And irritating as well.

Maybe he had good cause. He was caught in the caste squeeze. His parents had been Spanish, so he was, too, but they were peninsular Spaniards, meaning they were born "at home," and the boy was "New Spain," or born in Mexico.

Amazingly enough, there was a difference in the hierarchy of privilege and prestige between the two. Hernando was the kind of boy and then man who was particularly infuriated at such a thing, and he made it worse by constantly harping on it and refusing to fit himself into society at the position for which his caste suited him.

As a result, he grew to be a bitter young rebel, refusing to get in step with his culture and making no bones about his distaste for it. He even said a few bad things about Pope Pius VI, to his old father's dismay.

Some people said Hernando's attitude went a long way towards killing Old Paco, who had a stroke and died just a week after retiring from the army with thirty years service.

If his general demeanor and his comments about the Pope were not enough to attract the attention of the Inquisition, there was at this time the likelihood of a few people he'd made angry taking their revenge by whispering to the priests of the Holy Office about the ways in which Hernando Salazar was such a dolt, a dolt who by this time had grown to be a man.

Surely such a man must be at least a heretic, they likely said, and maybe even a practicing Jew who drank the blood of Christian children, trained black cats to become witches, and of course, copulated with goats.

Finally awakening to the reality of the world in which he lived, Hernando began to fear being trundled away in the night to be racked and scourged and maybe tried and convicted for treason by the civil authorities, who made it a practice to cooperate with the Inquisition. So he sought safety in distance.

Figuring that Texas might be a good place to escape the scrutiny of the Holy Office, he went to Bexar and, as we have seen, took possession of eight acres of land to become a farmer. He wasn't much of a farmer. Before he struck hoe into ground the first time, after that ceremony where he threw the rocks, he noted that the settlement was enlarging before his eyes and would soon engulf his field completely.

All this while, from local *indios* and Mexicans, he heard about this place he had taken as his new home. Some of what he heard was not reassuring. At that moment, everybody still nervously watched the pecan and cottonwood groves on moonlit nights and thought about what had happened at San Saba.

Just a few leagues northwest, on a branch of the Colorado River, about fifty years ago, the friars had started a mission like San Antonio de Valera. Many Indians came and learned about the cross and how to rotate crops like pumpkins and maize to make the soil healthy and strong.

Everything was fine. The Comanches were only watching, and staying away.

Then the Comanches decided they'd watched and stayed away long enough, and they rode in and destroyed the mission. The ones who didn't run, they killed. Some of the ones who ran, they rode down on their ponies and lanced.

From Mexico City came cries of rage. Soldiers and a very brave officer and a punitive expedition went into the High Plains to punish the Comanches. After a while, they returned. Well, a few of them returned.

It was the last time the Spaniards sent a punitive expedition against the Comanches. After San Saba, it was pretty much just trying to hang on to what you had. Until the Gringos came. But nobody knew that yet.

So everyone waited at San Antonio de Valera for the Comanches to come. But they never did. They rode close and watched sometimes, eighteen or twenty of them on painted ponies, blood lances streaming decorative scalps.

Sometimes three or four of them rode into the streets to trade. Usually buffalo robes for whatever the Mexicans or friars or soldiers had to trade. They were arrogant but caused no trouble, and everybody gave them a wide berth.

They didn't get credit at the time, but these Comanche robe traders were the forerunners of the San Antonio de Bexar hide business, which became a big thing, indeed.

It was pretty obvious that the Comanches figured San Antonio de Bexar belonged to them and that it sat in Comanche ground at their forbearance. There were some pretty grim signals that they felt this way about it.

Sometimes a farmer would wander too far from the town fields or a soldier would get drunk and walk too far out toward the Balcones Escarpment. They'd be found in the morning, naked and mutilated in imaginative ways. Always it appeared the victims had been killed quickly. Something for which you could be thankful was, when taken by the wild tribes, being killed quickly.

At least, they said, the government in Mexico City was no longer quivering and squealing about a French invasion from Louisiana, and hadn't been since the French gave all that land to King Carlos. Then took it back again and sold it to the Gringos.

They said you might not have seen a Frenchman on the Guadalupe, but you could bet your rosary beads you'd soon be seeing plenty of *hombres* from Norte Américano. Just as they were already coming from Louisiana and taking land along the Trinity and even as far west as the Brazos. And they'd be here soon, everybody said.

It was good, those Gringos, because then maybe there could be some trade from Bexar toward the east, toward New Orleans and Saint Louis.

The king's appointees in Mexico City had always been so skittery about the French or the British or somebody coming from the east to conquer Texas that they had put all kinds of restrictions on traffic in that direction.

"We can trade only with Mexico and Mexico can trade only with

Spain or Portugal. I would like to get some French brandy in here. Don't you want a change now and then from all this port and Madeira?"

"Si! And I would like some British gunpowder. Aren't you tired of this Cadiz shit that does nothing but sizzle like a wet firecracker half the time!"

Hernando not only came to know all this but was beginning to tell it as well, and when newcomers appeared, he was one of the best at explaining to them how things used to be when you could still stand at the presidio and see the mission, San Antonio de Valera, across the river.

Well, there wasn't really a mission there anymore. Just the building, since now the padres had moved back to the west side of the river because the new cathedral was there, having been built between Military Plaza and Main Plaza.

The padres were leasing the old mission to the army for storage space. They were calling it the Alamo now. A name taken from a garrison compound in Mexico called Alamo, where these soldiers had been previously been stationed.

There were few houses on that side of the river, and the old mission with its main building facade and the walls and the long monk-cell barracks stood out starkly.

Most of the big cottonwoods that had attracted the priests to that spot originally had been cut. Along the rear of the mission walls a line of ragged black willows and persimmons showed dark green. They'd grown up near the main irrigation ditch that had been dug behind the mission.

There were usually canvas-covered carts or army wagons and some mules in what had been a closed-in cloistered garden. This was now being called Alamo Plaza. It wasn't very pretty.

Salazar may have grown with the settlement, but not as a farmer. He became what could best be described as a maintenance man on the elaborate irrigation system around the presidio of San Antonio de Bexar, and on a major trunk-line ditch on the east side, the one behind the Alamo.

"All this work requires," he said, "is a little common sense and a lot of respect for the laws of gravity."

He sold off his land by lots, saving enough on which to build two

17

houses, one house for himself and a second one for renting. He was a man of the town, known as a hard worker. Maybe he was aware that irritating behavior could attract the Inquisition, but for whatever reason, he had become calm and not disruptive.

He married a mestizo woman, which meant her father was a European of some kind and her mother was an Indian. Her name was Maria. In less than a year, a son was born and they called him Paco, in honor of the old soldier whose grant from the king of Spain was now their home.

These circumstances of race made Paco Salazar a Creole in the New Spain caste system. Such things, as it turned out, did not mean as much to the boy as they had to his father.

The boy was like his grandfather, fair of skin, gray of eye. But he had the sharp nose, high cheeks, and raven black hair of his mother's *indio* people, who were Karankawa, a splinter of some Coahuilan tribe that had moved from the main body of Karankawas in Mexico a long time ago and settled along the Gulf Coast from Matagordo Bay to Louisiana.

For all practical purposes, by the time this Maria Karankawa became Paco Salazar's mother, her people already had been made extinct by European diseases and Comanche war parties.

She was proof that the Spanish system worked with some *indios*. When Hernando Salazar married her, she considered Spanish her mother tongue, was a Catholic, and ran a home like any good mestizo housewife, but was Indian to the core.

At the rear of the house where they lived, there was a patio, a kitchen in the open, except for the rear wall of the house, and a roof of pole shingles. There was a low shelf on one side, with a small alcove, . and she hung a blanket there, and the child Paco would sit with the blanket wrapped around his shoulders and watch his mother cook tortillas and frijoles.

With long supple fingers she would drop the cornmeal pancake across the hot stone on top of her adobe oven and in a few seconds flip it, still with her bare fingers, never burning herself, then lift the browned tortilla. Holding the corn cake cupped in one hand, she would ladle into it a spoonful of brown beans, cooked long and black with beef suet, salt, white pepper, and a pinch of sugar, and roll it as men rolled cornhusk cigarettes, yet with only the one hand, then pass it to the boy, his little hand always ready to take it, reaching from the folds of the blanket.

"That child, he can eat more tortillas and beans than anyone I have ever seen," she would say proudly to her husband.

It was a happy time, but it didn't last very long. All sorts of trouble and revolution were brewing in the south.

Chapter Two

When his father sent him away from Bexar to get him out of the line of fire, as it were, Paco Salazar was about ten years old, give or take a year. The record isn't clear.

Paco's father, having lived near the center of New Spain until the Inquisition began sniffing around, was much more politically astute than most of his Bexar neighbors, and he knew that if the revolution came, San Antonio would be the center of *mucho* activity north of the Rio Bravo.

"In a revolution," he told Paco's mother, "especially a revolution with Spaniards involved, you never know which way the rooster will jump. So it would be better to have Paco visit his family, away from this place."

"I don't want to send him," Maria said. "If we send him, we will never see him again."

"Of course we will see him," said Hernando. "He will only be in Goliad, not the other side of the world. Your brother-in-law will have plenty for him to do."

"I don't want to send him," said Maria. "We will never have him living in our *casa* again if we do. I feel it in my bones."

"Those are *indio* bones, and this is something such bones know nothing about," he said. "Besides, we must think of the boy's safety. Do you want some crazy general to have him taken out and shot?"

"They would never do that to my Paco."

"Like hell they wouldn't!"

It was good that he had this insight; otherwise it might have been the end of Paco Salazar, and there wouldn't be any story left to tell.

Paco Salazar's aunt in Goliad had learned her lessons on being a good Spanish Catholic wife from the same priests and monks who taught her younger sister Maria, Paco's mother, and gave them both their Christian names.

The two of them, sitting side by side on a pine lumber bench in some adobe mission school dedicated to Saint Francis, were taught the catechism of the Mother Church and that the old heathen religion of their people was false and must be cast out. And they were taught the language of conquistadors and of the *yanqui*. And how to sew with a steel needle. And how to refry brown beans—in good white lard.

Now, the sister of Maria Salazar was Señora Lena Pujanza, her husband Diego a respected businessman of the town. He was strong in spirit, which is what his name meant. For he had fought and struggled to establish himself in an atmosphere not conducive to such things for a mixed-blood mestizo. Married to a full-blood *indio* besides.

They had been blessed with four children who had survived infancy. They'd lost two, but now their oldest was the proud Francisco, whom they called Cisco and who was seriously looking at girls. Then came Lirio and Lila, who showed with these names their mother's joy in flowers, in this case lilies and lilacs. And then Juan, the youngest, only two years older than Paco.

These two became inseparable. Paco was rather tall and light complected, with gray eyes. Juan was coffee colored and short like his mother. Nonetheless, she called them *los gemelos mios*, her twin boys.

Diego was *un pescadero*, or fishmonger, and a cart master.

Goliad was on the road from Bexar to Matagordo Bay, a long stretch of coastline protected by the Matagordo Islands; it was the location of all the towns where goods for Bexar were unloaded from ships. These materials included textiles, metals, gunpowder, and all such plunder, and were shipped north by ox cart along the San Antonio River trace.

These Mexican two-wheeled carts were some of the most extraordinary vehicles on any frontier. Wood wheels, six feet across, stake-and-slat flatbed cargo space where loads could be stacked high, covered with canvas, and lashed down. Thus loaded, an ox cart was like a two-story house grinding along the pathways called roads. With a heavy oak axle, a two-wheeled Mexican cart could carry better than two tons.

A double brace of oxen was usual, but if guns and lead and black powder for the army garrison at Bexar were in a consignment, as many as four brace might be necessary for the heavy load. A man walked alongside with a bullwhip. An ox train could be heard from some distance off and sounded like a serious gunfight, with all the popping of whips. Closer, it sounded like a barroom brawl, with the colorful language of the bull whackers and the grunts of the beasts.

Ten miles a day was good. Fifteen was exceptional and possible only with light loads and mule teams. If it rained, everything took twice as long. Maybe more.

Ox trains between the coast and Goliad had to make one overnight camp stop. Between Goliad and San Antonio de Bexar there would be as many as five. So depending on how long a train paused at Goliad on a haul from Lavaca Bay to Bexar, the trip took more than a week, one way, with clear weather, no breakdowns, minimum outlaw activity, and animals staying hale and healthy.

In the night camps there were occasional raids on the livestock by local *indios*, fragments of once large tribes, pretty much beggar Indians now. The raids were a nuisance, not much else.

More serious were the times when bandits thought they might take guns or ammunition being shipped to the presidio at Bexar, or the silver Diego Pujanza had been paid for a shipment just delivered.

So everyone went armed, there were always two or three outriders on good horses, and at night sentries were posted, as in any military encampment. The Pujanzas had four large black mastiff dogs as well.

These trains had a reputation that tended to discourage anybody with evil intent. No one would try to rob a Pujanza train unless they'd been smoking hemp all day and chewing too much loco weed along with it, the locals always said.

Maybe so. There is no record of a Pujanza train being successfully robbed.

Uncle Diego believed in teaching at a tender age, so he always took Paco along on these trains. The boy learned a lot, and quickly, about horses and dogs and *indios* and maybe seeing in the dark. He learned pistols and muskets, too. And he loved it all.

There was another good thing. On each trip to Bexar, Paco saw his mother and father before going back to Goliad and the coast with a load of hides or some such thing.

A few more Anglos were coming into Bexar, Paco's father told him. Maybe as many as fifty were in San Antonio now, about half with their families. In the east, along the Trinity and the Brazos, there were a great many *norteamericano* colonists, coming across the Sabine from Louisiana or the Red from Arkansas. Everybody wasn't happy about it, either.

"They are of a different religion," Hernando Salazar explained. "They do things differently. It's good to have them here for trading. But they are always in a hurry. They like to work hard enough to sweat all the time."

They called them *yanqui*, or Gringos, which meant foreigner; neither of these was a kind word.

"The *yanqui* men from the United States do not like us, either. They do not make too many bones about that," Paco's father said. "But we can get along together. Just don't ever marry one of them."

Almost all the ships that came in to Matagordo Bay were flying the flag of the United States, because oceangoing vessels usually docked at New Orleans, and anything coming to Texas was transshipped by smaller coastal schooners. A lot of this trading was illegal, for the government in Mexico City had many rules about with whom you could do business. More and more of the storekeepers were Anglos either in Texas illegally or, in some cases, with permission of the government in Mexico City. Some of these *yanqui* men had become citizens of Mexico, and some had even converted to the Mother Church. But most of them still looked and acted suspiciously like Anglo-Celtic Presbyterians or Methodists, and it was always hard for the local padre to remember the last time he'd seen any of them in the confessional.

"A Gringo will do anything to make a little money," Salazar told Paco on one of his visits. "Even change the way he prays."

Diego Pujanza had a serious face all the time. He said to his own sons and to Paco Salazar, "There will be trouble because of the Gringos. They are everywhere now, more every day. And to encourage them, our government allows them to do things we are unaccustomed to doing in Tejas."

"Why do they come?" Francisco asked.

"To get land. To make money," said Diego. "They come because our own people, south of the Bravo, will not come. The Mexicans you see here were born here. Their fathers came a long time ago. But now, nobody comes north, and there is much empty land."

But if our people do not want the land north of the Rio Bravo," asked Paco, "why can't the *yanqui* take some of it?"

"That's what our government said for a long time. They invited Gringos, like Steven Austin. But now, our government thinks it was a mistake and will try to stop them coming."

"Because of the religion?" Juan asked.

"It's because of the slaves some of them have," Francisco said. "Slavery is against the law in Mexico."

"No, Cisco," Diego said. "It's more than that. The *yanqui* want to run the government. No. That's not it. The *yanqui* want to *be* the government. And our people are not accustomed to such a thing. They don't know how to do it.

"Our people are accustomed to having the rules made by someone they trust, an aristocrat they trust, in Madrid or Mexico City, with the rules enforced by *agentes de policía* and judges. The Gringos want to make the rules and say how they will be enforced. And how the government officials conduct their business."

"They tell judges about justice?" asked Juan.

"Yes. Maybe judges most of all."

"How do they do such things? If the *alcalde* doesn't suit them, do they shoot him?" Juan asked.

"No, they do not shoot him," said Diego, smiling at their perplexed expressions. "They have an election and put somebody else in the judge's seat."

There was a long silence until Francisco broke it.

"Father, if these *yanquis* in Texas fight the Mexican army from south of the Bravo, on whose side would we stand?"

Now it was Diego Pujanza's time to think for a long while before replying.

"I do not love Gringos," Diego said. "But I love tyrants less. Now the government in Mexico City can take any of you and throw you in jail without giving a reason and without telling your family. Some commandant *mierda* doesn't like you, he can have you placed against a wall and shot."

It was unusual to hear Diego Pujanza use such language in speaking with his children, even though they were practically grown men.

To call someone a shit would have been shocking but for the serious nature of this talk. As it was, no one paid any notice.

"Yes," said Cisco. "Because the men who make the laws are men we are supposed to trust and admire, but they grow more corrupt and selfish every day."

"Good. I hope you will all think on it and understand," said Diego. "If we had a part in trouble, and I don't think we could stay clear of it forever, then we would stand with the people of Texas. Whether our own blood or the Gringos. Whoever is against the tyrants who could shoot my children without trial, that's where we would stand."

Talks like these came infrequently, but when they did, Paco Salazar tried to remember what was said. At first, he understood little of it. But he was growing, and he was understanding more and more.

In the off season, the two coolest months of winter, when ships did not arrive at the Gulf ports so often, Diego Pujanza loaded his entire family in one of his giant carts and moved to Isla del Ganzo on Matagordo Bay. As the name implied, this place was a wintering marshland for geese, great flocks of them. Mostly, these were snow geese.

For the first three years of Paco Salazar's stay with the Pujanzas, everybody went to the coast. But then, with Paco clearly able to handle a man's work there, Francisco was left in Goliad to care for stock and do local hauls, which they had always hired someone else to do until now.

The program at the Island of Geese was the same each year. They'd shoot geese for two days, then the harvest of their hunts would be carried on horseback to Goliad or Victoria overnight, arriving at the meat markets at about dawn in whichever town they chose, in time to sell the geese to the butchers for their daily trade.

Señora Pujanza, Lirio, and Lila cleaned and dressed the birds before the rider departed the coastal camp, so when a butcher in the towns got the geese, they were ready to hang on display in the street outside his shop.

Paco and Juan alternated riding the Goose Run, as they called it, going in the dead of night at the end of the second day's shooting, going at a good pace, well armed, with one or two of the dogs accompanying them.

The arrangement was that butchers in Victoria and Goliad didn't pay them anything but kept a tally. At the end of the season, Diego Pujanza would pick up the money. Thus, there was no cash being carried back and forth, a fact well publicized, so nobody ever worried much about robbers.

Besides, there were the dogs, and the rider always carried a long rifle and two pistols. Buckshot loaded. That was well publicized, too.

After the two-day goose shoot, the entire family took to big flat-bottom boats and fished the bay for two days. Catches went back to the same markets in the same way the geese did, except that with the fish, they had to run them to market at the end of each day they fished.

Diego Pujanza would not work on Sunday if he could avoid it, so what all this meant was that one or the other of them, Juan or Paco, was flogging a horse back to Goliad or Victoria four days, or rather nights, each week.

It was good that Diego Pujanza had half-a-dozen good horses and two couriers who loved the ride. In the dark. Alone. Maybe with all those dangers that are supposed to be out there in the dark. And if the dangers are not really there, then imagine them.

Paco liked the geese shooting best. Lying in the boat and listening to the watery world, waking and smelling the salt scent of the sea in the grasses that grew up along the shore where they concealed themselves, and waiting to hear the first geese take a morning fly-around, as they supposed, stretching their wings, then coming back down to feed again, storing up fat for the long fly back north in a few weeks.

The geese flew in twos or maybe three at a time. The hunters had to be fairly close, and they used only buckshot. None of the smaller shot would penetrate the feathers.

There were two flintlock double-barrel guns, and so altogether, on each chance, they had only four shots. If they got two birds, they felt extremely lucky.

The black mastiffs were not bird dogs by training or blood, but they had learned to leap into the water and retrieve the big geese that floated like rumpled pillows on the surface of the bay after they plunged, their noisy flight interrupted by the blast of shotguns.

Years after he was no longer a little boy, Paco Salazar felt a little-boy security each year they returned to Goliad from the Gulf Coast. The same safety as his dry alcove and blanket and his mother's warm tortillas and beans had given him.

His mother and the place she prepared food had been the center of that safe world, and now as he grew older, the center again was a woman in the same circumstance, his Aunt Lena in her kitchen.

Maybe some of it was smell. Hot oil and garlic and red sauce boiling. Lena Pujanza's kitchen was a feast for the eyes, too. All along one adobe wall were strings of dried peppers. Green, yellow, red, black. Along another wall, brass pans and ladles and spoons. It was the kitchen of a woman whose husband knew how to make money. The Pujanzas had two goats, another sure sign of financial well being. Lena made goat cheese, and on early spring nights when it was raining, she made *chili con queso*, melting the cheese with dried tomatoes, ground chilies and jalapeños, white pepper, red vinegar, brown sugar. A little beer.

The family would sit at the round oak table, and Lena would toast tortillas until they were crisp, break them into small pieces. They would dip these in the cheese and eat them. It made their mouths just hot enough for the cool, damp night.

Paco liked it best when the *con queso* had cooled and had the consistency of butter.

"There's an art to making *con queso*," said Diego. "And *la* Lena *mia* has the method. *Comprende?*"

There was a mission school in Goliad. At first, Paco Salazar attended. Until he grew a little old for being rapped across the head with a stick by a Dominican monk. One of the mission converts was a Lipan Apache who taught Paco the Comanche tongue.

It was at the mission school that Paco Salazar met Rosalinda Molar. Discovered would be a better word. Of course, they were not in class together. Boys and girls, and most especially young men and young women, were kept apart by church and state, as much as it was possible to maintain such an unnatural condition.

But there were times and places, even under the most severe kinds of chaperoning. Such as the party at the Molars, celebrating something or other. All the young men of the town, about six of them, were invited to come and have pecan pralines, made, of course, by the delicate hands of Señorita Rosalinda Molar, daughter of the hostess.

Nobody was ever fooled by such things. They were simply putting an innocent face on a family showing off a daughter who was about to come of age.

Lena went to great effort to have Paco presentable. She got him into a white linen shirt, and she combed out his long hair and pulled it into a tight braided queue down the back of his neck. He bought a new sombrero, which he told Jaun was not for Rosalinda's party but because he needed it anyway, and was teased mercilessly about it for a week before the day he would spend in the Molar living room, holding the hat instead of wearing it.

"Don't worry about them teasing you," said Aunt Lena. "You look like *un caballero*. That girl will be so happy to see you."

Paco wasn't too sure about that. There was one chance for talking with Rosalinda alone in one of those big bay-window alcoves the Spaniards loved to build into their houses. He stood with a melting praline in one hand, his new sombrero in the other.

"I don't think we could ever be friends," she said. Her eyes didn't say that, and Paco was sure she'd offered him the platter of pralines more often than anyone else there. Which, he assumed, had to mean something.

"I thought we could," he said lamely.

"My father says we could never be associated with anyone who was in trouble with the Holy Office," she said.

She had a very impertinent nose, Paco thought, which made it even more tempting to touch her mouth with his own.

Then what she'd said finally struggled through his haze of adoration.

"Holy Office?" he asked, maybe a little too loudly. "What has the Inquisition got to do with anything here, anyway? Nobody ever hears of the Inquisition anymore."

"Uh huh," she murmured. "My father said your father had to leave Mexico to escape the Inquisition."

"That was a long time ago," he said, again too loudly, and he saw Señora Molar coming toward them, smiling and showing her gold tooth.

What was all that? he wondered for days afterward. He didn't dare tell Juan anything about it. He'd have been razzed terribly. So he tried to figure it out himself.

Rosalinda still smiled at him. More than ever, she seemed to appear in the wagon of her father when he came to get hay for his burros. Paco talked to her, being very nonchalant. But their hands always touched. She asked him to help her pick out faces in the clouds or some other absurd thing Juan and Cisco would have razzed him out of his head about if they'd seen any of it. He felt like a fool.

When he was at Market Plaza, she always just happened to pass by, and she'd wave and come up to him and act as though she was surprised to see him. As though it was an accident they'd met like this.

Her eyes were trying to encourage him; he knew it, he was sure of it. Well, maybe almost sure. Sometimes he felt as though she was trying to eat him alive with her eyes. He'd never been so completely confused. Here he was, no longer a boy, no longer a child, and confused by some skinny little girl with beautiful white teeth and big eyes that were so moist and clear. Looking at him. Even when he was trying to get to sleep at night.

He knew he was supposed to be moved to some action which would require appearing in the confessional for a recitation of the terrible things he'd done with a girl, and he wondered wildly if the priest would make him name the girl and if she, on her own trip to confession, would be obliged to name the man. In other words, him! Paco Salazar!

It was so embarrassing. And terrible. He had Hail Marys floating around in his brain, and he hadn't done anything yet. How bad would it be after he'd actually done something?

But he couldn't, simply could not think of this girl in connection with anything he might do with her that he'd want to do, that he'd know how to do, that would require penance.

He'd even checked that through to see, grabbing her one day when she wandered into his Aunt Lena's kitchen and Aunt Lena wasn't there. He'd taken her quickly with both hands, yanked her against his chest, and kissed her for what seemed a long time. Then stepped back, both of them flushed, and her without a word wheeling and dashing out.

He certainly hadn't felt any pinch of guilt about *that*. But he knew it didn't prove anything.

She was purity and grace and fine as the little innocent white sandpipers that flew up from the Gulf and daintily marched back and forth in her father's barn lot, keeping company with her mother's domesticated ducks.

God, it was maddening. But he certainly wasn't going to ask Juan about it.

It wasn't as though he was born yesterday, he said to himself. After all, just a few months ago, Francisco and two of his friends had taken him to this little farm south of Goliad where they would stay a few days and catch some of the wild horses that ran on the grassy sand dunes and in the short pines and black jack oak groves bordering the salt marshes of the coast.

Closer to Goliad, too, along the Arkansas River, where there were many wild horses. They spent three days chasing and roping wild horses and bringing them in to the corrals and snubbing them to the posts and getting them saddled and gentled. All the things that must be done to make wild horses ready to sell in Victoria.

But that farm where they'd stayed. Just down the road a short distance was another house and there a woman who made a few pesos now and then selling herself to horse ropers or anybody else who might be passing. And Francisco and his friends, knowing all about this, and like all older men with a younger one whom they suspected was a virgin, arranged to have the young man be entertained by this woman.

So Paco Salazar was not completely in the dark about what a man and woman could do with one another when they were alone and the proper spirits moved them, and Paco Salazar could not picture himself doing with Rosalinda Molar the things that he did, or should we say was encouraged by Cisco and his friends to do, with the woman in the little house near the sand dunes off the Gulf Coast, where they went to capture wild horses.

He concentrated on learning English, and Juan did as well. Nobody could explain this interest in language, least of all Paco. But it was here that once more he learned the wisdom of his Aunt Lena, maybe not recognizing it at the time, but recalling it later.

"El sabrino mio," she said to her nephew, "if you can talk to every farmer who comes down the road in his own mother tongue, you will always get the best cantaloupe at the lowest price. Do not be as Comanches and Gringos are, too proud to learn how others speak because they believe their own language is the best!"

Paco began to see that his aunt and probably his mother, as well, were a lot closer to their old culture than anyone imagined.

Once, because he slept in a patch of poison ivy on one of their Bexar trips, Paco broke out in a painful rash.

"Maybe if you had our dark skin," Juan teased, "you wouldn't be bothered with such bullshit."

Of course, Juan didn't say such a thing where his father or mother could hear.

Lena Pujanza looked at Paco's rash and walked out to an oak grove not far from the southern edge of town, where she had marked some wild spotted touch-me-nots. She brought home a basketful of these and crushed stems and leaves with her ever-ready pestle and mortar until she had a paste that looked like her melted goat cheese. She rubbed this on Paco's rash to the accompaniment of his protests and Lila and Lirio's giggles.

The next morning the itching was not so bad. With a few additional applications of the touch-me-not juice, the rash began to retreat, and after four days it was gone.

Now they had stopped taking ox trains into Bexar. Too unstable there, Uncle Diego said, too much happening. So they fished more and made more trains to Victoria and other short-haul destinations.

Paco missed seeing his father and mother. But Goliad had become home and the Pujanzas his family. He had spent all these years with them, now almost a full decade. He would always say later that Goliad was his home.

From time to time, Paco heard of the turmoil of revolution south of the Bravo and how it affected the people of Bexar. Often, he thought that perhaps he should say goodbye to the Pujanzas and return to his father and mother, but each time he hinted at such a thing, Diego reminded him that his being where he was had been Hernando

Salazar's idea and that to return to his father's house now would be a direct affront to his father's authority as head of the family.

Sometimes, when he thought of these things, Paco's face grew hard and he looked much like his mother's *indio* people, with his lips a grim slash beneath suddenly more prominent cheekbones.

Then came the dreadful time. Diego and Lena Pujanza put it off as long as they dared. Then, to keep him from hearing in other places, Diego told him. It was at the end of a haul to Gonzales, and Paco was dusty and tired, going toward the tubs at the well, when his uncle stopped him under the awning of the rear veranda.

"Paco," he said softly. "I must tell you something."

"All right, Uncle Diego," he said. He was sixteen years old, but his uncle had to look up into his face. He stood slouched and tired, dusty, with his trail clothes wrinkled and, draped over his shoulder, a bullwhip.

"There have been many revolutions in the south," said Diego. "Always, some of it spills over and there is trouble in Bexar. One army takes the presidio, then the other army takes it. It is very confusing"

"I've not paid too much attention."

"Good. You aren't supposed to," Diego said. "But now. Well, in the last exchange of Bexar between armies, a royal army, one putting down uprisings against the regime in Mexico City, came and won the Alamo. The general of this army, a man named Arrendondo, went through the town, arresting people."

Suddenly Paco had become tense and was listening.

"Arresting who?"

"Anyone this general thought was a rebel," Diego said.

"Who told you this, Uncle Diego?"

"An old friend. We disagree on politics. But he is a friend, in Bexar. He was not arrested, and he told me."

Diego drew a deep breath and continued, talking faster now. Wanting to finish it.

"There were more than a hundred men arrested. They put them in a room in an adobe house on Military Plaza. No water. It's August, as you know, and by morning about thirty of the men had suffocated."

He drew a deep breath, but in the pause, Paco did not ask a question as Diego had expected he might. So he hurried on.

33

"Your father was one of those arrested, but he was strong, and he was alive the next morning when General Arrendondo's men unlocked the door. They marched the survivors out along the street a short distance, halted them. And shot them."

Paco's face did not change, and his body trembled just enough for the bull whip to slide off his shoulder, but he caught it in his hand and held it.

"Then," Diego started, then he stopped and had to cough and clear his throat and wipe his eyes with the bandanna around his neck. But finally he went on. "They took most of the women of the town, saying they were rebels, too, and the general gave them to his army. Your mother . . ."

Paco choked and started forward. He was gripping the whip now, and his knuckles were white.

"What did they . . ."

"The women were to go along with the army and make tortillas for them and mend and wash clothes and . . ."

Diego had no way of telling it, so he spoke in short, hurried sentences.

"We don't know where your father was buried," Diego said, already knowing that most of the bodies had simply been thrown in the river. "Nobody has heard of your mother since then. If she is alive, she is in Mexico probably. But Paco, I don't think you should expect that she is alive. Paco? Paco?"

Paco Salazar didn't move for a long time, only stood trembling, eyes staring. But Diego Pujanza knew Paco was seeing nothing before him now.

With what sounded like a dog's growl, Paco wheeled and dashed into the center of the lot and with the whip began lashing savagely a snubbing post set in the ground, then screamed, not words, only incoherent shrieks. The dogs began to bark and rush about, and the donkey brayed, and the horses whistled and kicked their stall slats.

It stopped only when he'd beaten the leather whip into a thousand thread-thin fibers against the post. Then he threw what was left of the whip onto the ground and stalked past Diego into one of the barns. Diego would never forget the terrible light in his nephew's eyes.

Nobody in the family saw him again until morning, when he came out of the loft where he'd slept. As though nothing had happened. Diego Pujanza shook his head and muttered about crazy *indios*.

When Paco was eighteen, his Uncle Diego had a small ceremony. It didn't concern anyone else, and it was held in one of the ox sheds. Everything important seemed to happen near the animals.

"Today, you are a full man," Diego said. He handed Paco a cured goatskin leather money belt. "Now you have this, which comes from my hand, and I tell you to wear it and keep important things in it."

Diego kissed Paco quickly on the lips, holding his face in both hands.

Paco knew something was already in the money belt. He could feel it, even as his uncle handed it to him. So now, alone in the stable, away from everyone, he looked.

There were a number of coins, two of them more striking because they were the largest. He recognized them both from all his dealings with patrons and clients of Uncle Diego in the hauling business. They were Spanish coins, minted in Mexico and very heavy because the Spaniards always put plenty of precious metal in their money and not much tin. That's why Spanish coins were so popular. They were worth something.

One was a piece of eight, an old silver coin still in use all around the Gulf. There was the profile of Charles III, the king of Spain when the Spaniards threw in their lot with the French against the British during the American Revolution. He was also father of the man who had granted Paco's father the land in the *labores del sur* at Bexar in honor of Old Paco's service in the Spanish army.

The other was of gold, a doubloon, old Phillip V with his handsome Bourbon profile gracing the reverse side. He'd been the first Bourbon on the Spanish throne, grandson of Louis XIV of France, the Sun King.

Phillip, coming to the throne, had kicked off the War of the Spanish Succession, one of those conflicts Spain was trying to pay for with sugar and gold and silver from places like the mines where Old Paco Salazar was sent to keep order and prevent slave rebellions.

Of course, the War of the Spanish Succession had been a long, long time before Old Paco Salazar came to Mexico, but Spain was still trying to pay for it, along with a few even earlier wars.

Paco figured the gold coin was worth about twenty-two *yanqui* dollars and the silver piece of eight about seven. That was just their monetary worth, not their value to Paco.

He almost missed the most important item in the money belt. He thought it was the lining in one of the belt pouches, but it wasn't. He pulled it from the pouch and was very careful then because it was something obviously old and brittle.

It was a document. Not very big. A small plat, with survey marks. The signature of one Viconde Anador and also the signature of Paco's father. At its bottom, the red crust of sealing wax and in that the imprint of a seal, probably from the *alcalde's* ring. And beneath that, Hernando's handwriting again, "This property belongs to my son, Paco." And another red sealing wax mark.

It was the original patent. And it was a deed. To the Salazar property in Bexar. Later, Paco was told by his Uncle Diego that Hernando Salazar had given Diego this document to be handed to Paco on his majority.

So it was a bequest, father to son, and it was more, too. That it had been given into Diego Pujanza's hand at all was pretty hard evidence that Hernando Salazar did not expect to survive to see his son return to Bexar.

And each time this came to mind, Paco took on what Juan came to describe as Paco's Indian mask. Maybe so. Maybe to hide the difficulty of talking with the hard lump in his throat.

Slavery had been abolished in Spain. But there were those who said the system of peonage wasn't any improvement. And nothing had changed in the structure of a caste-system society. Or an autocratic government.

One thing was certain. All this made for a state with a few elite ones at the top running things and a whole pot full of nobodies at the bottom doing the sweating with not even a small chance of bettering themselves. And no one in the middle.

And if that was what the Spanish did at home, you can imagine how it was in one of their colonies, a colony managed as though it was a dangerous, ignorant child who had to be kept tied to a tree to keep it from hurting itself.

One of the Madrid high officials said, "The folk of New Spain are born to be silent and obey. And not to meddle in affairs."

You can't find a better formula for revolution. The only trouble was, in this case the ones who made the revolutions either didn't have enough power to bring one off or else didn't have the vaguest notion of what to do with a revolution once they had one. Or both.

Even a man like Diego Pujanza, who was politically pretty sophisticated, couldn't keep up with revolution. A few parish priests and some mestizo farmers would start a revolt, and Mexico City would send troops and a general. The rebels would be beaten, and the royalist general would take a large group of people from the opposition and line them up and have them shot.

Now and again a new general would proclaim himself dictator, and another revolt, or several, would break out and the whole process would be repeated.

These were all rebels-against-royalists types of revolts. Rebels supposedly represented local interests; royalists represented the interest of Spain.

The players were always the same. The rebels were the village priests and the peons armed mostly with hoes and pitchforks and machetes. The royalists were people from the high castes, including members of the army fortified with infantry, cavalry, and artillery.

After a while, when a revolution came, the royalists changed their role. They now wanted independence from Spain. So the head of government would not be Madrid but Mexico City.

At this time, there was a serious revolution in Spain itself, which the royalists well knew. It was not possible for Madrid to handle two revolts simultaneously, so when the high-caste folks of New Spain told Madrid they no longer wanted to be New Spain, Madrid let them go. Hence, independence for Mexico. It wasn't that simple, but the results were the same. In fact, for the Pujanzas in Goliad, it was that simple.

A republic was declared and a constitution written. There were fireworks and fiestas. The hated red-and-gold banner of Spain came down, and a tricolor for Mexico went up all the flagstaffs, in Texas, too, and the people were in a frenzy of happiness.

Except for a few who were skeptical, like the Pujanzas and Paco Salazar, who had had kin taken out at some time during the revolutions and shot down for no apparent reason.

Such a thing, though, had happened to just about every Mexican family in Texas, so you've got to suspect that the independence-from-Spain theme wasn't much more for them than an excuse to get drunk and eat like hogs and dance all night.

"They say all the words," Diego said. "Liberty and freedom and trade and no more Inquisition and no more Spanish police. But they have no idea what it all means."

Everybody waited for the wonderful changes. They had a president, but it was hard to find anybody who had voted. They waited for somebody to tell them about when there would be a real election and something other than a temporary president.

They had a republic now. But nobody could see any of this new liberty and freedom and trade with the Gringos the bureaucrats were always talking about.

"Damnation!" shouted Diego Pujanza. "The same people are running the government now that were running it before. I thought these were the shits we were trying to get rid of."

And to Paco he would say, "You can't go back and claim your inheritance in Bexar yet. We don't know who's in power there now, and maybe it's some of the same people who thought your father was a traitor and will think the same of you and take you out and shoot you."

"In a republic, they will shoot me?" Paco asked.

"Let's just wait a little while to see what this republic really is."

Sure enough, within weeks the republic was abolished, the constitution voided, and General Augustine de Iturbide, a royalist general who had been putting down revolts for years and had probably ordered over five thousand of his own people dragged out and shot, proclaimed himself emperor!

"Does it make you proud?" asked Diego Pujanza sarcastically, "The United States has only *el presidente*. But us? We have *el emperador!*"

But Emperador Iturbide didn't last long. In a matter of days, he was taken from office and marched outside. He stood before an adobe wall, as he had ordered so many others to do, and was shot. This time the man who claimed the dictatorship was a shrewd politician and an excellent army commander.

He was Antonio Lopez de Santa Anna. This time, when those little revolts broke out south of the Rio Bravo, they were put down with spectacular speed and savagery.

Lena Pujanza was proud of her young men, and would rather talk of them than of all the foolishness of generals and revolutions and republics. They were growing strong and smart, and they were good with horses, not just the riding of them, but the gentling and nurturing and careful selection for breeding. All talents, she pointed out to her husband, that they had from their *indio* blood.

"Let us not forget that they have Spanish blood, too," said Diego. "And the Spaniards knew husbandry and riding a long time before your people ever *saw* a horse!"

In that last summer they would be together and go to the shore and catch green turtles and cook them at the beach and eat the tender white meat and drink cool lemonade, the turmoil of Mexico seemed far away.

Paco Salazar saw a yellow goldfinch on that trip, very unusual because they flew in flocks, and this was too late for their migration, but there it was. He wanted to catch it, but stopped in time. It would have been a thing for Juan to tease about, his catching a bird for Rosalinda.

Since childhood, the little Molar girl had trapped finches and put them in the cages of twigs she made. On feast days or Saturdays, she would sell the little birds to people who came to Market Square in Goliad.

Legend had it that if one made a wish and released a bird back to the wilds, the wish would be fulfilled. You had to keep the wish a secret, of course.

In that same week that he saw the finch, there was a short haul to Victoria that Paco Salazar remembered all the rest of his life.

There was nothing unusual about it. They'd taken some cast-iron stoves there and returned empty. In a night camp just short of Goliad, half-a-dozen coastal *indios* tried to slip in and steal some mules.

The dogs barked furiously, and there were a few shots fired into shadows, as warnings more than anything else. But come daylight they found the dogs sniffing a bloody body lying half in the water of the creek where they were camped, a few yards downstream.

One leg had been chewed considerably. But the main reason the body was lying there was that a large-caliber bullet had gone into his chest.

"Your shot, Juan," said Diego, because everybody else had been using buckshot. "Probably from one of these miserable coastal bands."

They buried the man, and Juan looked gloomy the rest of the day. Paco tried to cheer him, with small success.

"You were doing your job," said Paco.

"*Sí,*" Juan said. "It could have been one of mother's relatives."

And Paco let the memory of a lot of things come over him at that moment, something he always tried later to control. But he thought of his father and mother and that dead man lying half in the creek back there before they'd buried him.

"I wish it had been a Mexican soldier," he said softly so no one heard but himself. It was like a benchmark. It was the beginning of a long time of dying.

Soon after Jaun had killed the *indio* thief, they had a visitor from Bengal.

In India, growing in water contaminated by human and animal feces, was a tiny bacterium, *Vibrio comma.* Luckily, human gastric juices are so ruthlessly powerful that usually when *Vibrio comma* came into the human body, it was killed by the juices and that was the end of it. But when the gastric juices were not enough, the sickness that came was devastating.

There was fever, diarrhea, vomiting. There was dehydration so severe the victims shriveled right before your eyes, the skin turned black, the smell was of death. The victims seemed to be rotting already, a horrifying reminder to anyone seeing them that this was what awaited all.

And what emphasized the horror was the speed. A person healthy at dawn on Sunday might be dead by midnight Monday.

This was cholera, and in 1826 there was an outbreak of it in Bengal. Not the first by any means, but the first that concerned Paco Salazar. At the time, there were a lot of British and Russian troops going here and there, and learned professors who study such things said eventually this strain of *Vibrio comma,* carried by solders, arrived on the shores of the Baltic and soon was in Great Britain.

By 1830, Ireland. The next year, Canada. Then the United States. And finally, the cholera arrived in Texas.

Chapter Three

Paco Salazar stood at graveside and wept as he had never wept when a boy and as he would never weep again. No one near him thought it unusual that a full-grown man should publicly display such childlike grief.

Beside him stood all that was left of the Pujanza line. His Uncle Diego and his cousin Juan. The others had all been laid low, the family's grim contribution to the great cholera epidemic that swept south Texas in 1833.

For some years now, Paco had been a part of this family, and those in the plain wooden coffins at the bottom of the pit had become truly his mother and siblings.

And maybe his agony was more profound and deeply felt because this was a time to grieve for his real father and mother, too, in some unknown grave at Bexar, if indeed in any grave at all.

At last, Juan Pujanza placed a hand on Paco Salazar's shoulder to help him turn away.

"Come, *mi hermano*." *Hermano* means either cousin or brother, and although these two were truly cousins, both knew that Juan was saying the word now to mean brother. It was like putting the stamp on Paco's place in this family.

"I will never have this done again," Paco Salazar whispered. "I will never marry and have a family that can be treated in this way by a cruel God!"

Juan gasped and pulled his hand back, as he might if he'd touched something very, very hot. His face showed his dismay and maybe more than a little anger.

"No, Paco, do not utter such monstrous things," Juan said.

All of this was quiet talk between the two young men that had not reached the ears of Diego Pujanza, still with his head bowed beside the grave of his wife.

Paco Salazar looked at his cousin and slowly, with tears still wet on his cheeks, smiled the most terrible smile Juan had ever seen, so he later said. Because the mouth looked like a smiling mouth is supposed to look, but the rest of the face did not. Most especially the strange gray eyes did not.

"It's not a worry for you," Paco Salazar said. "Maybe it's the blood of my father speaking. He was an enemy of His Holiness in Rome. At least the Inquisition thought so. But only a very small enemy. And you are not of his blood, my father, so you have nothing to be afraid about."

Maybe from that moment, Paco Salazar was consciously intent on pointing out their true relationship, that they were not really blood brothers no matter how they used the language to seem so. A thing he would never have done so long as Lena Pujanza lived.

It was not a point lost on Juan Pujanza, and from then onward, things were somehow not quite the same between them. And they would indeed be separated at times in the future, a truly unusual thing to those who had observed them for the past few years. *Los hermano gemelos*, twin brothers, as Lena had said. But maybe no more.

Paco Salazar's graveside sorrow was deeper than Juan Pujanza suspected. For only two days before, in that same cemetery, the same Dominican priest had said the same service of internment over the body of a girl come only recently into her womanhood.

The coming had been a lovely thing to watch, thought Paco, who believed that he and he alone had seen the butterfly emerge from the cocoon. And believed that he and he alone could have such silly, sentimental, downright idiotic poetry floating about in his head like a coastal fog, damp and cloying and featureless and impossible to penetrate.

He had no idea whether he should be joyous that he had not deflowered this lovely young girl, and hence saved her innocence, or if he should be dejected that he had not gone farther in giving her that earthly delight which now she could never know.

He wondered about himself. He wondered if the rather tame, gentle fire he had held in his heart for Rosalinda was all he could ever expect with a woman he really loved, really respected, really wanted to be mother to his children.

He knew that in the wild-horse hunting adventure in an unknown lady's bed, there had been some bungling and sweating and lack of dignity, but there was certainly plenty of passionate physical flame. Couldn't that happen with a woman he loved? Or was it just a rut? Like a wild javelina or even a stallion standing to stud? Hell, plenty of fire and flame there.

It troubled him that after the affair on the coast with Cisco's lady, that was how he'd felt—like a stallion just led out of the breeding stall after successfully being up on the mare. No more. No look back. Rosalinda wasn't in that same world. Was she?

Everybody in Goliad had known her and called her Rosa, of course. She had always been a lovely thing, black eyes big as sunflower buttons, they said, and cheerful as the little finches she trapped in her father's livery stable barn loft.

Señor Molar and Diego Pujanza, because of their closely related businesses, saw much of one another, lived in the same barrio, and often had their families together for *chili con carne* suppers in winter and watermelon feasts in summer.

Paco Salazar had been attracted to Rosalinda. His was not the panting, mad, sweaty lusting that sometimes marks emerging manhood, but a rather hesitant, embarrassed advance, which was greeted by Rosa with a great deal more aggressiveness than Paco himself either displayed or expected.

The first real touch of fingers had been at her initiative while they were with others from both families, gathering wild blackberries in the thickets along gullies that emptied spring runoff into the San Antonio River south of Goliad.

Rosalinda Molar was author of the first kiss, a quick and somewhat passionless brush of lips while Paco was harnessing an ox team in a Pujanza wagon lot.

Over time, it had grown considerably more serious, with a culminating clutching and fumbling on a high meadow above the river during the season of blooming bluebonnets.

Under the stress of Rosalinda's somewhat frantic if not urgent encouragements, Paco Salazar for the first time had that sudden thought, Is this what I am supposed to be doing to someone I think I may love?

Of course he did not think of such details at the moment he stepped back, so to speak. But later, he imagined he'd thought of it all clearly and had thus decided on a sudden cooling. He rose and helped her up, and she showed surprise and maybe disappointment. But she talked of other things and laughed as they walked back into town, and all the way she held his hand.

It had been a time of uncertainty, confusion, and all the unanswered questions in his head making things unbearable, which is how he'd heard being in love usually made things.

And that was all. It was the year of the cholera. The last time he saw her before her first nausea was on the street in front of the confectioner's shop. She was coming out as he passed on a horse, and she tossed up a tissue-wrapped piece of salt-water taffy, laughed, and without a word, turned and ran along the street to home.

In two days, she was gone.

So when he stood beside the grave of his own family, he had to recall, too, that a young woman he wanted to believe he loved had been snatched away. It had been a passion, if that's what it was, that lasted for three years.

Paco Salazar was very nearly as innocent as the young girl lying in her grave. Surprising as it might seem for a young man well into his maturity, had it not been for Cisco Pujanza's lady of the wild horses, Paco Salazar would have been a virgin, too.

And maybe, whether he knew it or not, some of Paco Salazar's resentment of an unjust god was about his having saved himself for three years for this girl, and then her being taken before either of them could know the full joy of passion together.

He never mentioned such a thing to Juan or anybody else. Maybe he didn't have any conscious thought of it. But surely when you consider what he did say at graveside, there had to be a kernel of resentment about Rosalinda's death somewhere inside.

Diego Pujanza worked through his sorrow furiously, pushing himself and his boys and his drivers and horsemen and peons hard. It was a good time to do such a thing, for business was good. Very, very good, even in those troubled times.

"The bastards in Mexico told Señor Estaban Austin and other Gringo *empresarios* to come to Texas and bring their colonists," Diego said with a vicious laugh. "Now, they are here, and they are running things, they have their own governor, they have their own state, they recruit their own militia. The powers that be in the past allowed them these things to make Texas attractive to them.

"Well, Gringos don't care who trades here. Ships from everywhere can come. We can carry anything to anybody, without all those damned rules. It's the thing I like about the Gringos.

"But now, the latest ass on the seat of the almighty in Mexico City, this Napoleon of the West, Santa Anna, wants to turn back the clock, and he has Austin arrested and put in jail without trial. Now this ass Santa Anna says he will make Tejanos follow his rules or punish those who do not as traitors!

"He will punish me, too, as a traitor, because I am not following his foolish rules but rather the rules of the Gringos, because in that way I am my own *jefe*. And I not only am my own boss, but can make *mucho dinero* with these *yanqui* rules.

"Well, my sons, to hell with Santa Anna, and his army, too!"

"And father," said Juan, "that militia the authorities allowed us to recruit in our own state to protect us against Comanches will now be a thorn in the side of this Napoleon of the West."

"The longer one thinks on it, the better it gets," said Diego. "Because one of the reasons the shits in power allowed the *yanquis* to come in such numbers was so the government would not have to worry about hostile tribes north of the Rio Bravo. The Gringos would take care of that, you see? But now they know they have hatched a bird that will eat more than one lizard!"

The man who assumed the mantle of dictator in 1834, Antonio Lopez de Santa Anna, had made a lot of friends in Texas during earlier revolts. Now he lost most of those. And made new enemies besides.

His first duty, after beating down any number of little brush-fire revolutions in Mexico south of the Bravo, where he had made a lot of enemies, too, was to attend to the pesky problem in the north.

He sent his brother-in-law, General Martin Perfecto de Cos, who did a good job of chasing rebels and jailing them and shooting a great many of them. At Bexar, a militia almost wholly made up of Gringos tried to make the Alamo into a fort they could defend. They couldn't. General Cos and his artillery took it easily.

Then Cos, who had never studied the American Revolution and what had happened to the British at Boston after they came back from Concord, made the mistake of settling down for a calm rest and period of gloating about having destroyed the Gringos' little revolution.

He should have moved around a little. Texans came from all directions, it must have seemed to General Cos, each of them armed and angry. And not all of them were Gringos. In short order, Cos had to surrender his Mexican army, which had never been much good at holding fixed positions like old besieged missions anyway.

Understandably, Santa Anna was not happy and swore to make Texans pay, especially Anglos. In his next pronouncement, he would promise to make Texans pay, especially Mexican Texans.

By now, obviously Texas had a war if desired. And Texas did desire, at least enough to make it happen. And the Pujanzas and Paco Salazar were bloodied, if only slightly, at Bexar in that rout of General Cos.

They had been there delivering a pair of cartloads of such things as cast-iron cook stoves and Dutch-oven pots and were ready for the return trip, their vehicles and animals in a park just south of Military Plaza, loaded with rawhides, when the Mexican army arrived.

Nobody in the Cos army bothered them. Maybe it isn't hard to understand. They were obviously Mexicans, and they just as obviously were not a part of any rebel garrison. And besides, Cos's army didn't have much use for a bunch of hard-as-a-plank hides that hadn't been cured.

So they were given the opportunity to watch. Which they did, from the west side of the river, among some of the adobe buildings of Barrio del Norte, the northern section of the growing town of San Antonio.

They watched through all of it. After the colorful blue-and-red-clad soldiers of General Cos took the mission and seemed to indicate a desire to take a long siesta, Diego Pujanza and his group took a siesta, too.

"Let's stay around to see what happens next," said Diego.

"I don't like being around so many Mexican soldiers," said Paco. "Or that pig Cos."

"We won't wait long," said his uncle. "And don't worry. I don't think they're going to be taking civilians now and shooting them."

"I am going to sleep with my pistols primed just the same," said Paco.

"Good." Diego laughed. "I have mine here, too, you know."

"I'm here with crazy men," said Juan. "Two men with pistols will hold off the Mexican army if they come to take civilian prisoners."

"No, no, Juan, not hold them off," Paco said. "Just kill a few as we slip away from them."

And although they were all chuckling about it, the other two heard the ominous ring in Paco's voice when he spoke of killing Mexican soldiers and could hardly help but recall that right here, in Bexar, was where the Mexican army had made Paco Salazar an orphan.

The nights were cool but not unpleasant for December. They slept in the wagon park in one corner of old Military Plaza. Most of the Mexican soldiers were across the river, camping in a scatter in and near Alamo Plaza.

They bought tamales from vendors who appeared in Military Plaza each evening before sundown, carrying baskets of the steaming corn-husk rolls fresh from the kitchen of some local housewife.

They could smell the zesty ground chilies and *cumino*, which was almost as good as tasting. They sat with their backs against the walls of San Fernando Cathedral and ate. It was hard to believe a war was happening less than a kilometer east of where they were sitting.

They were kept awake most of the night by militia and farmers and ranchers and everybody else coming in to take a few shots at the Mexicans. It was a mob militia, mostly Gringo, but with a considerable sprinkling of Mexicans.

The next day, as they watched the Texans battering the Alamo with cannons and rifles, a Mexican cannonball struck a wall close enough to shower them with chunks of adobe mortar. That was only moments before General Cos raised the white flag of surrender.

They stood by and watched the dispirited Mexican army march off along the Laredo Road toward Mexico, and they watched the Texas besieging army melt away. Because it wasn't a real army, it was just a bunch of men who had assembled for one job and then gone back to their real work, which had nothing to do with being an army.

On the way back to Goliad, with their load of hides, Diego Pujanza voiced the thought heavy in their minds.

"That army we saw surrender, it was the same army that murdered your father and mother, only it had a different general."

Maybe watching what happened at Bexar set their minds. None of them ever said. But certainly it had some effect. Because within a few days of their returning to Goliad, they all three began to think about the Texas militia.

William Barret Travis was an Anglo lawyer and land speculator who had now been given an appointment in what was called the Texas regular army. He was recruiting in Goliad because he knew the barrios there and he was interested in recruiting some Texas Mexicans. So far, his efforts had proved disappointing. He hoped his letter to Diego Pujanza, inviting him to city hall, would bring more pleasing results.

Travis understood this was pretty much a Gringo fight, as most Texas Mexicans figured, and they did little except stand on the sidelines and watch. After all, Anglos now far outnumbered Mexicans in Texas, and east of the Colorado River all the way to the Sabine, it was Gringo country.

But there were some Mexicans who hated the Mexico City crowd and Santa Anna enough to break out of a rigid ethnic pattern that was taken for granted in Texas and structured as much by Latinos as by Gringos. It was a pattern that was unavoidable, no matter how destructive. Their cultures were just too widely disparate to allow a cozy bedfellow relationship, yet.

More simply, Mexicans didn't much like Gringos and *norteamericanos* didn't much like the Mex.

But William Travis knew the Pujanza family and he knew Paco, and he wasn't surprised when they all came before him, in a group.

"I am glad you've come, Señor Pujanza," said Travis. "I wish more of your people would do the same. We fight for the Constitution of 1823 and a republic where all of us in Texas will be free to make a good life for our families."

"Perhaps later some will come, Captain Travis," said Juan Pujanza. "Perhaps they will see that our people are as abused by the aristocrats and generals in Mexico as are your own."

Diego looked a little startled at his son's words, but quickly recovered and nodded his assent, rather proudly, Travis thought.

"Good," he said. "I could not have put it any better. You would make a fine recruiting sergeant, Señor Pujanza. I believe I shall place you on my staff so you will be with me as I happen to see other young Mexican men, when your words will be valuable. How would that suit?"

Diego was beaming and Juan was standing with chest puffed up proudly, and Paco thought they were both acting like ten-year-olds. Juan was nodding his head vigorously.

There was a desk, of course, in this room where the walls had portraits of various Spanish kings, which Paco Salazar thought rather absurd, and there were stacks of papers and two sergeants of the Texas army shuffling the papers, and when Juan bent to sign his name to a piece of paper, the quill made a loud, harsh, scratching sound.

Then Diego and finally Paco Salazar each made their own scratches, and it seemed the noise alone was as important as the signatures in India ink on the parchment.

"If you serve on my staff, you will need to sign on with the Texas army," Captain Travis said.

Juan's chest deflated somewhat. "I thought I just did."

"No, you have joined the militia."

"What's the difference?"

"The difference is the militia takes its instructions from the county and other local leaders. The Texas regular army takes its orders and gets pay from Texas officials."

"We'll be paid?" Juan asked.

"Perhaps." Travis laughed abruptly and as abruptly was sour-faced again. Paco Salazar thought him one of those perpetually sour-faced Gringos. "Later. Now, would you join me, and assume the responsibilities of a non-commissioned officer?"

So Juan Pujanza became a corporal in the Texas army and on the personal staff of William Travis while his father Diego and Paco Salazar were recruits in the Goliad militia.

"I shall soon be taking orders from my non-commissioned officer son," said Diego, and they all laughed.

"I never knew it was so easy to become a non-commissioned officer," said Paco. "What does a non-commissioned officer do?"

They were walking back along the street to the cart yard, and with Paco's question, they looked at one another and all shrugged elaborately and laughed.

They knew Santa Anna was roaring in Mexico and would come, but they figured it would be spring, probably late spring. And Paco Salazar and the Pujanzas were committed to fighting him. But there was plenty of time. So now they just waited to see what would happen.

The Anglos were confused. Although it had nothing to do with the situation, even their name was confusing. White people who had come to Texas from the United States and now constituted a large majority of the population were called Anglos. This was shorthand for Anglo-Saxon, or English.

The majority of these were not ethnically Anglo-Saxons. They were Celtic. They came from a culture primarily designed on the English model, but they were largely Scots, Scots-Irish, Irish, Cornish, and Welsh by blood. All nationalities, in the old country, that didn't much care for Englishmen.

Like the Indians of the New World, who obviously did not come from India, this large portion of United States citizens in Texas was not correctly named either. And everybody who thought about it knew this. But it didn't bother them much.

So these misnomers did not confuse anybody. Other things did.

"They have *el gobernador y la junta*," Diego Pujanza said to his sons. For he had long since come to regard Paco as his son. "A governor and a council."

"*Sí.* The governor, a Mr. Smith they say, gives orders," said Paco. "And nobody pays any attention to him." They laughed.

"*Sí*," said Juan. "And the council gives orders, and nobody pays any attention to them." They laughed again.

"The governor and the council are having a war between themselves," said Paco. "The Gringos are running around, like *las gallinas* with the heads chopped off."

They laughed again, and Diego Pujanza wiped his eyes with a handkerchief and shook his head.

"Boys, this is serious business," he said, trying to keep from laughing again. "All of those Gringos east of the Colorado pay no attention. The meeting of Tejanos decides they will declare independence from Mexico, and they cheer and make some more instructions, but the Gringos over there just go on with other business, getting ready to put in next spring's crops, seeing to their cows that will calve in the spring."

"I heard Captain Travis say those Gringos feel safe, the ones along the Brazos and the Trinity, because Goliad and San Antonio de Bexar stand between them and Santa Anna," Juan said. "Do they expect us to stop the Mexican army?"

It had become serious enough now.

"I don't like it," said Diego. "That meeting of Gringos at San Felipe was supposed to recommend ways we could persuade Santa Anna to abide by the old constitution we were supposed to have when we were expecting to be a republic. Now, they say we are going to become a republic all our own. *Dios mio!* Most of our people don't even know what a republic is, much less how you make one work!"

Even so, they still laughed a lot at the Gringos, running around like chickens with their heads chopped off, with governor and council squabbling and nobody doing much of anything.

Then William Travis was sent to San Felipe himself, to recruit, and he asked Juan Pujanza to come with him because he said that maybe Juan could help get a few more Mexicans to join the Texan army. A few more good Mexicans, he said. Whatever that meant.

Confusion continued. Even the *yanqui* Texans were laughing at their governor and the council. But everybody figured they had plenty of time because the Mexican army would move more slowly than molasses in winter.

"The Gringo council finally did something," Diego Pujanza said. "They've made Sam Houston a general."

"I've heard of him, from some of the *indio* people at Bexar," said Paco. "The Cherokees call him Big Drunk."

"I wish Juan would come home," Diego said. "Maybe he will be back before anything happens."

But suddenly, in the first days of February, Santa Anna was at Laredo with an army.

Houston had no army, unless you counted the scatter of militiamen and what were called Texas regular army men. But nobody was sure where any such Texas regular army would come from or who had money to arm it. So at first, when Houston sent anybody anywhere, it meant that the person he sent rounded up anybody they could find and called that their "command" in the Texas army. Houston sent James Bowie, a Gringo who was a citizen of Mexico, to San Antonio.

"I've seen the man often, here in Goliad," said Diego.

"They say before he became a citizen of Mexico, he traded in slaves," said Paco. "And that he was a business partner with Lafite, the pirate."

"It may be," Diego said. "These are strange times. He married a Mexican woman, and they had two children. He lost them all to cholera. Wife! Children! May God reach out to him. I know his agony!"

Chapter Four

The council was in an uproar, as well they should have been. The governor was issuing orders. Something needed to be done to gain time, so much having already been wasted. The governor vilified the council, and the council impeached the governor.

It didn't matter. Governor and council continued to function. There was hardly any force a serious observer would call an army, but it had four duly appointed commanding generals at the same time.

Luckily, one of these was Sam Houston, who managed to finally emerge as the leader as the other three fell on hard times of one kind or another.

But with Santa Anna at the door, as the politicians put it, something had to be done. Certainly there was no army to defeat the Mexicans. So Santa Anna had to be slowed somehow so that all the Texas patriots and all the outside friends would have time to congregate and organize to fight. But how?

A certain Doctor Grant, who had once had property interests south of the Rio Bravo, suggested an invasion of Mexico. Well, maybe a raid on Matamoros, the largest Mexican town on the Texas border. The Council made Doctor Grant one of those Supreme Commanders aforementioned and dispatched him to Refugio, a place near Goliad, to prepare for the raid.

And James Fannin went to Goliad, collecting fighting men on the way. He, too, was named Supreme Commander of Texas forces. Before long, a certain General Johnson showed up alongside Doctor Grant with a few troops and a commission as Supreme Commander, the third such in the Goliad area. Each with his own force. Each refusing to take any orders from the others.

"This is unbelievable," said Diego Pujanza, who along with Paco Salazar was a part of Fannin's force now, in Goliad.

General Sam Houston thought so, too. He arrived in Goliad and for the first time became aware of the other Supreme Commander appointees. They all declined to follow Houston's orders.

So Houston gave himself leave from the Texas army and went north to talk to some Cherokees about fighting the Mexicans and eventually came back to loiter about when yet another convention was called at Washington-on-Brazos. Which took over running the war and ignored Governor Smith and the council.

But that was down the road apiece, as they say. At the moment, there was the terrible responsibility of slowing Santa Anna's march across Texas. The raid on Matamoros, of course! But the closer they came to it, the more all three Supreme Commanders realized they had precious few troops for such a venture.

Some of the troops they did have wanted to get to all that loot and the fair *señoritas* in Matamoros. They were restless. Especially a company from Mississippi and another from New Orleans, volunteers who came to fight for freedom, they said, to put down tyranny, they said, and have some fun, they demonstrated.

"I hear they's some a these wild Texas mustang ponies in these sand dunes," one of them said. "I'd like to catch some a them little paint ponies."

So while they waited for the war to begin, the chase was on for the famous little mustangs. The visiting gallants dashed about through the yellow clusters of straw grass in the folds of the dunes, looking for ponies. And sometimes, when they wandered as far south as the Gulf waters allowed, they caught the big, green sea turtles, the best tasting turtles in the world, so the coast-dwelling people said.

"What's the matter with me?" gasped Diego Pujanza, slapping his forehead with the heel of his hand when Paco told him about the mustang chasers. "Thinking of sea turtles at a time like this."

"I was thinking of them, too," said Paco, "because I remember when we went there and caught one, and Aunt Lena made soup."

"Yes. You were thinking about a better time when you saw the Mexican cavalry. Now I think of better times, too."

"Yes, of course," said Paco. "Mexican cavalry where we caught the sea turtle."

So the horse chasers were caught among the tyrant squadrons.

All the horse chasers, it seemed, were members of either the command of Doctor Grant or General Johnson, two of the Supreme Commanders. There is some indication that one or both of the Supreme Commanders enjoyed a little wild-horse chasing themselves.

In fact, Grant was captured by Mexican horsemen and treated very badly before they killed him.

"My God," said General Fannin, in Goliad. "What is Mexican cavalry doing *there?*"

Mexican cavalry continued to pop up among the wild horses, so it seemed. Then was gone. Then appeared again.

Fannin called together about twenty of his best riders, and Paco Salazar was one of these.

"We need to know what we have down here in the south," he said. "Feel out these cavalry units. Find out where they are coming from. I'm assigning you to scout all the approaches to Goliad."

Everybody had heard what was happening farther north. Santa Anna was driving up the Laredo Road toward San Antonio de Bexar, which the Texans would like to evacuate because they didn't have enough troops to defend it. But such a move would leave a wide-open road to the east for the Mexicans.

Diego Pujanza had a personal interest in San Antonio. Newly promoted Colonel William Travis had been sent to the Alamo and he was there now, and Juan Pujanza was with him, so everyone assumed.

But now, the immediate problem was feeling out their own front, which was Santa Anna's right flank. And what they were scouting turned out to be the advance of a Mexican army under General Jose Urrea, who had a reputation of being the best field commander in the Mexican army, especially with cavalry.

"Where the hell did *he* come from?" Fannin fumed.

Fannin's first scout, Paco Salazar, said, "Don't worry, Uncle Diego. There's not a cavalryman in the Mexican army who can get close to me when I'm up on one of those red horses of yours."

"Keep a pistol loaded, in case there is one," his uncle had said.

Paco did, but the pistol didn't help on the day he had to watch helplessly from a far knoll as a Mexican cavalry detachment caught some of the carefree horse hunters of Mississippi and New Orleans, rode them down, and killed them all with lances.

That night, after telling Fannin everything he'd seen, Paco Salazar found his Uncle Deigo standing on a sentry post at the presidio forge shed, even though the smith was still there working on mule shoes. The sharp note of his hammer on steel and the heaving red glow of the fire provided a somewhat appropriate background for the grim story of Refugio and San Patricio.

"Those Mexican lancers are the best horsemen I've ever seen, Uncle Diego," Paco said. "And they ride four or six together, like a team. It isn't just speed, but the way they turn, stop, change gait together. And their control. The points of those lances, all of them close together. Like the tongues of snakes. You've got to see it to believe it."

"I don't want to see it," his uncle said. "And I don't want you to see it again."

"I go out toward Refugio again at dawn," said Paco. "Don't worry."

"Yes, I will worry," said Diego. "Today, the Mexican cavalry got this Doctor Grant. Did you know? They treated him pretty badly. He was not well liked by them. But soon enough, it was the lance."

"Well, that's one less Supreme Commander we've got to listen to," said Paco, who realized even as he said this that it was as he had heard; when men fight wars, they find humor in some pretty grim places.

A few days later, Paco watched the vanguard of Urrea's army going into Refugio, where they cut off a detachment of Texas militia that was in town to evacuate some Gringo civilians who'd asked for help in trying to flee the Mexicans. People had been running east for the past week, going through Goliad and Victoria with all types of vehicles and draft animals and some pushing wheelbarrows full of possessions. These were mostly old people, women, and children.

There was good cause to be running. Santa Anna's policy for Texans had been published and was well known. Anybody in arms or giving aid to those in arms against Santa Anna's government would be summarily treated as a pirate and executed.

That day in Refugio, only a couple of the Fannin men escaped the Mexican lancers.

On this operation, Paco Salazar got closer than a scout was supposed to be, and a trio of the Mexican horsemen was suddenly there, cutting him off at the edge of the small settlement.

Paco Salazar crashed his horse through a stick-and-slat chicken coop, and one of the Mexicans pursuing hung the point of his lance in the tangle of sticks and slats and cotton rope. Paco gave a shrill whistle, the command to his roan to go full speed, and the sound confused the cavalry horse already tangled in what was left of the coop, and Paco seemed to break away around one side of the wreckage.

But the two following cavalrymen saw the move and swerved to ride to the far side of the coop and cut Paco off in all the flying feathers and splinters of hens' nests that had been shattered. Anticipating the move, Paco spun his roan and dug in the spurs, and the horse jumped back through the coop, head-on toward the cavalryman still yanking at his lance, trying to free it. But seeing Paco almost on top of him, the cavalryman clawed at his sash, trying to clear a saber, and Paco shot him square in the face as the roan slammed past the big cavalry horse and free into the pasture beyond.

Then he got away neatly, simply driving the tough little Spanish pony straight ahead across pasture and meadow into the plains as the pursuers came around the coop, and with horses squealing, tried to avoid trampling their comrade sprawled in the chicken mess, his face mostly gone with the passage of Paco's .60-caliber pistol slug.

Paco heard one of the Mexicans shouting curses after him. He didn't slow much until he was approaching Goliad's presidio.

Fannin listened, his face pale, and when it was finished, bent to a small field table and wrote on a piece of paper. To one of his aides standing in the room, he spoke.

"You said Houston's back at Washington-on-Brazos?"

"Yes sir."

"I have to tell him. Major force here in the south. I'll demonstrate toward Matamoros." He was still bent over, writing. "Yes, then march on to Bexar and reinforce Travis at the Alamo. He's been asking for that. I may not be able to. We'll get to Houston, perhaps, best of all."

Finally, he straightened, passed the message to Paco.

"Find Houston. By now, he's likely moved to Gonzales."

"Yes sir."

He ran to the stable lines, and Diego Pujanza was waiting with the last of the red roan horses.

"But that's Rojo, Uncle Diego," said Paco, taking this moment to reload the pistol. "That's your horse."

"It's your horse today," Diego said.

Paco said nothing. He finished with the pistol, shoved it into the belt hidden under a black sash he always wore.

"Be careful, son," Diego said, squeezing Paco's thigh as he settled in the saddle. Paco bent down and put his arm around Diego's shoulder. "Go with God."

"It'll be all right," Paco said. "I don't know what the General's going to do here. Couldn't tell from what he said. But it'll be all right. Come on, red horse, move!"

It wasn't until later that Paco learned Fannin had received orders from Houston to blow up everything in Goliad that would detonate or burn and head northeast.

After a quick dash from the presidio where his Uncle Diego stood immobile, watching him go, he tried not to think of what was behind him. Except for one moment, one only, he thought of the Mexican lancer, and thought that he, Paco Salazar had killed a man. And thought, No, not a man. A Mexican soldier!

Paco Salazar did not spare the roan. He lashed the little gelding through scatters of farm settlements and across the fields to avoid the straggling refugees on the roads, frantic groups of women and children and old men trying to get away from the Mexicans of Santa Anna.

He paused in a small town that was nothing much except a church and half-a-dozen buildings around a plaza with a water-trough fountain in the center. It seemed deserted as Paco skidded the horse against the fountain and leaped off the horse and plunged his face into the water.

He was loosening his saddle cinches as Red finished drinking, and he saw three men running out of one building and into another. They carried canvas bags full of something. He knew what was happening then.

These men were looters and had probably come into town on horses, screaming that the Mexicans were close behind. The people had scrambled away; the looters helped themselves. He'd heard of such things happening. It infuriated him, and he saw one of them again, running in and out like a Goddamned ferret. But he had to ride this horse on to General Houston at Gonzales, so he leaped on and shouted.

"Run, red horse! Run!"

By the time he reached Gonzales, he was ready to fall from the saddle. Men he took to be Houston's shouted directions, and he found the storefront with men and horses and an odd assortment of flags in the street. Assuming this was Houston's headquarters, he yanked in the horse, gravel and dust and bystanders scattering.

"Whoa, hoss! You tryin to run folks down?"

It wasn't easy stopping the gelding, but finally, his legs buckling, the gelding stood trembling and Paco Salazar slid off and stumbled into the store and saw Houston among many others. But even though he'd never seen the general, he knew him at once.

Paco was covered with horse sweat and slobber lather, his own sweat, and caked dust. He was breathing hard, but he told the story straight and clear as Houston listened, frowning furiously, and in the street behind him, the gelding Red, Uncle Diego's horse, gave a last rumbling gasp and coughed, blood spraying from distended nostrils, and fell dead.

After Paco Salazar made his report, General Houston had an aide give him a drink of Gringo whiskey, which he almost choked on, but got down nonetheless as General Houston slapped his back.

"Son, you're a damned fine scout! I expect I ought to team you up with another fine scout," General Houston said, and then shouted. "Mr. Smith! Deaf Smith! Come in here, please."

The man who appeared was almost as tall as Houston, but rail thin and with shaggy whiskers and a filthy slouch hat and buckskin jerkin and pants and fringed moccasins.

Paco Salazar figured him to be one of these North American frontiersmen or mountain men, the kind who seemed attracted to trouble, no matter where. He carried a Hawkin percussion rifle, and there were two pistols and a huge hatchet in his belt.

"Yer callin me, Gen'l?" he asked, and pale green eyes quickly swept Paco Salazar, head to foot.

General Houston assigned the young man to the older one, maybe not in exactly those terms, but there was no question in the mind of any of them as to who between these two was boss and who was being led. Or maybe watched.

Outside, Smith stopped and took a closer look at his youthful charge. He was chewing tobacco, and other than the brown stains from that, his beard was dingy gray.

"Yer a Mex, ain't yer, son?"

"Yes." Paco Salazar returned the older man's stare directly, and without really wanting to, he made his excuse for being in Houston's army. "My family was massacred by the Mexican army in the revolution of '24."

"Before my time in Texas, son. No matter." And he spat and grinned, showing surprisingly strong, young teeth. "You sho ain't no Mex-appearin man in some ways. Them gray eyes. Jus a regler white man. Whas your name, son?"

"Salazar. Paco Salazar."

"All to the good. Stay close to Ole Deef Smith. But I tell yer I ain't deef. I see you got a pistol. You know how to use it?"

"I do."

"All to the good. You come on, I'll get you a second one from my duffel. Two pistols. Gotta have two pistols you stay up with Ole Deef Smith. An a long rifle. Hafta have another pony, too, maybe a roan like that one you busted in here on. Need to get yer a nice hatchet, too. You like them roan ponies, son?"

"Sí, Señor," Paco Salazar said, with a thick Mexican accent.

Deaf Smith laughed.

"You bet, son. We be all right, all right."

It was March 11, 1836. It was a date Paco Salazar would never forget.

For on that day there were rumors of disaster from the west, and General Houston sent scouts toward Bexar from Gonzales, where he was trying to raise an army.

Paco Salazar stayed in Gonzales. He needed a little time to get his gear and the new red horse Deaf Smith had found for him into marching order.

But Deaf Smith went. What the scouts found struggling along the Bexar road not far from Gonzales was a group of refugees, half-a-dozen women, a freedman African, and a few children. The women were Mexican, except for one whose name, it turned out, was Mrs. Dickinson.

The women were strangely mute. They moved like sleepwalkers. One carried a baby, and the baby was crying. They were all filthy dirty, and a few had bloodstained clothing, but in each case it turned out to be somebody else's blood.

The first words were spoken by Mrs. Dickinson, as soon as she looked up and realized the horsemen surrounding them and coming in close were Texans.

"We're all that's left."

She spoke calmly, and then nothing more was said by any of them until they reached General Houston. They stumbled along a little farther until a hack the scouts had sent for came out and they climbed into it, still silent, still with heads lowered. The baby had stopped crying, and everybody wondered if it had died.

"It was like escortin a bunch of corpses," Deaf Smith said. "Them women was all played out, son."

Once they had clean blankets around their shoulders and hot soup and bread in their bellies, the women were more garrulous. Mrs. Dickinson's husband had been an officer in Colonel William Travis's Alamo army. If you want to style 188 men as an "army."

The story was given in bits and pieces, interrupted often by wails of anguish and sobbing. But details came. Not all the details. Some would need to wait until later, when they could listen to the Mexican side. But the women gave them what they needed to know.

After many days of raids and bombardment by both sides, with the heavy artillery advantage to the army of Santa Anna, the Mexican assault against the Alamo on the past Sunday, March 6, had come from all four sides.

But the rifle fire of the defenders, mostly frontiersmen, not farmers, was so withering that the attack had to be concentrated on the north wall, where the scaling ladders finally stayed up and the Mexicans went inside.

The fighting then was savage beyond imagining. A lot of firing in the first moments, then bayonets and clubs and knives and hatchets.

Travis had died cleanly, a head shot at the wall. Bowie was deathly sick in bed when they killed him, and Mrs. Dickinson had seen the soldiers toss his body into the air many times and catch it on bayonets. Nobody knew how Crockett died.

Paco Salazar had no intention of asking anyone for information on Juan Pujanza. He could hardly stand listening to what he heard. He had no intention of torturing himself just to have someone tell him what he already knew.

Many Mexicans had died. None of the women or the African had any notion how many. But the black, who got a better look around than the others when Santa Anna set them free, gave them a notion.

"Gen'l Houston, sah, dey was stacks of dead sojurs again the walls and all over de courtyard where dey had ta drag em outa the way to walk throo.

"In de edge of town across the river mainly dey was wimmin with shawls over dey heads, we kin heah em wailin, and we know soons we lef an de sojurs let em, dem people be over in dat fort going through dem bodies, tryin to fin they own kin.

"Or some of em gone rob bodies what got a watch or a gold tooth-pick or somethin nice, an they musta been two hundret buzzards in de sky, Gen'l Houston, wantin get down to da feast, but we saw people from de town dat sojurs made work already commencin to drag bodies over to a big fire they started over by the river, and I figure dey gettin ready start burnin up dead men, Gen'l."

"At the first, we could look across the river and see they were flying a blood-red flag from the bell tower of San Fernando Cathedral," Mrs. Dickinson said. "At the end, we could hear their band playing 'El Deguello.'"

"El Deguello" was a brassy tune that in the pantheon of Mexican army bugle calls means "No Quarter." Literally, *deguello* means massacre, slaughter, cut throats.

A little later, maybe thinking it might ease her grief, someone told Mrs. Dickinson that the convention meeting at Washington-on-Brazos had declared Texas's independence. She looked startled and after a moment asked when it happened, and they told her. Slowly, she bowed her head.

"That was four days before the Mexicans made their final assault," she murmured. "We hadn't heard about it yet. Independence, I mean. So at the last, the flag flying over the walls where they died was the old flag of the Mexican Republic of 1823."

"We were barely started on our march here when we heard the bells of San Fernando Cathedral in San Antonio begin to toll," one of the Mexican women said. "We could hear them for a long time in the night, as we came in this direction."

Paco Salazar tried to avoid hearing the bits and pieces of it. Already he had more pictures in his head than he felt he could handle. But it was impossible to stay clear of the damned thing. Everybody was talking about nothing else.

After dark, with the people of Gonzales wailing and weeping in the streets for their men lost at Bexar, and the men Houston had gathered and was calling an army preparing to retreat farther east beyond the Colorado and even the Brazo, Paco stalked out into the dark and sat on the earth and pounded the earth with his fist and spat on the earth and cursed the earth.

But he did not cry. And once more he thought of the Mexican lancer in the chicken coop with a savage satisfaction.

Paco Salazar had never imagined what it was like, an army. And this thing of which he was a member, this thing of Houston's, could hardly be called an army, at least not an army recognizable as such. It was more like an armed mob.

There were a few of the men and officers who had served at various times in various armies, and they stood out like naked maidens at the annual spring ball.

Most of the army was made up of people willing to be told what to do and sometimes how to do it, but they had no notion of concerted action, or mutual support, or fire discipline and movement. They were individuals with only one thing to give them any cohesiveness. They wanted to kill Mexicans. And they would do it starting at long range with rifles and deadly marksmanship and in close quarters with knife, hatchet, and club and with such vicious fury it was terrifying to anybody who ever saw it and survived.

Painfully aware of that, because he'd seen those men of Fannin's fight before they were cut down by lancers, Paco Salazar, maybe for the first time in his life, was thankful for his fair skin and gray eyes. Because in the confusion of a hand-to-hand fight, he didn't want to be mistaken for an enemy simply because he looked typically Mexican.

He and Deaf Smith had acquired another scouting partner, pretty much a replica of Deaf Smith himself, except that instead of a slouch hat, this Gringo frontiersman wore a New Orleans plug with a turkey feather in it. His name was Leander Reed. And like most of his kind, he was a philosopher.

As the army retreated toward San Felipe, these three saw a lot of action as rear guards for Houston's army. The Mexican cavalry wasn't far behind, which provided some excitement. But they didn't get too close. It wasn't their job now to engage Santa Anna's horsemen.

They still had time each day to exchange views, and views were something Reed and Smith had plenty of.

"Yes sir, son, you lucky you got that Gringo look," said Leander Reed. "If you was short and coffee colored, first real melee you got into one a these wild men would slice your liver out just from sight of you. But, hell, you don look no more Mex than I do."

"Well, they gettin mad enough to cut somebody's liver out. Complain how come we's retreatin!" said Deaf Smith. "All this belly-achin about not fightin Santy Anny. Hell, Houston ain't got enough people to fight my Aunt Polly, yet. That's what them boys at Alamo give Gen'l Sam, time to collect some sojurs."

"Doesn't look to me like the fight in Bexar gave us much time," said Paco. "Their army's right behind us now. What's that we been looking at all day, those riders with blue coats and shiny hats and long lances?"

"That's just their cavalry," said Leander Reed. "Nosin around. The main army's likely still back yonder at San Antonio lickin its wounds. From what I heard, that army got a little shelackin and they gone haft catch their breath a mite fore they come on."

"Hell, son, them boys at Alamo at least kept ole Santy Anny busy whiles our folks was doin all that foolishness about who was boss, and not gettin nothin done," said Smith. "If they'd been able to come right on, they'd caught us before that convention at Washington-on-Brazos, and wasn't nothin to keep him from goin all the way to the Sabine."

"Tell you somethin else, son," said Reed. "This here Houston knows now we ain't out here gettin our ass wet fightin for no republic no more."

"Oh? Then what are we out here fighting for?" Paco said, and there was enough heat in it to make Deaf Smith snicker.

"This Mex, he'll snap at you, Leander," Smith said.

"All right," said Reed. "You know what Santa Anna says and what he's done and is gonna be doin. All these Texicans you see on the road runnin for Louisiana knows. He says he's gone wipe out the Gringos in Texas. You hear, son? Wipe em out. Not just whip their army. Why you think he let that pitiful white woman and them others come out of the Alamo. Human kindness? Bullshit. He let em come out so Texicans would see how Goddamn final a bayonet can be, son, and to let em know he's got more'n enough bayonets for all! Man, woman, and little chile!"

Leander Reed took a deep breath. He was panting a little.

"No sir, son, you ain't fightin no more for something as fancy as the kind of government you gonna have here in Texas," Reed said. "What you fightin fer now is pure, plain, and simple. What yer fightin for is survival!"

They crossed the Colorado and kept going east. Along this line of march, or rather line of retreat, they got word from the south and Goliad. Mostly from friendly Texas Mexicans and a couple of Texas militiamen who had escaped what happened there.

While Houston was listening to some of this, Deaf Smith was in the General's tent, and afterward he found Paco Salazar, sitting cross-legged under his pony's head, reins in hand.

Smith went to him, his face dark and his lips drawn tight. As he watched Smith approach, Paco knew it was bad news again.

"Didn't I hear yer say yer had some kin at Goliad?" he asked. Paco rose slowly, bracing himself inside but holding a calm face toward the older man.

"Houston's gettin it now," said Deaf Smith. "An it ain't good."

Colonel Fannin had not burned Goliad and come north to join Houston, as he'd been instructed to do. Mostly he sat and tried to make a decision of some kind. He had some real problems, each one obviously beyond his competence.

The southern wing of the Mexican army closed fast. Fannin started to Bexar, but a wagon broke down and he went back into Goliad. He tried breaking out to the north as the whole Mexican army closed on him. There was a brief fight, but it was useless and Fannin surrendered, being assured he would be accorded the honors of war.

They marched Fannin's people back to Goliad, put them in confinement in the old army barracks. The next morning, the prisoners were marched out, expecting to be paroled to go home. Instead, as they marched out on the road, they were halted and shot by a Mexican regiment aligned for that duty.

In town, Texans wounded in various fights over the past week were dragged into the streets and shot there, lying in the dirt. The captive officers, including Fannin, were allowed to watch all this. Finally, the officers were shot.

Altogether, there were about 390 men of the Goliad garrison executed. About thirty Texans got away, mostly through the efforts of Mexican army officers who were shocked and disgusted with the executions.

As the survivors of the Goliad horror straggled in one by one, Paco didn't bother to ask about Uncle Diego Pujanza. If he's alive, Paco figured, he'll find me, he'll let me know.

But one of the Texas Mexicans among those who got away did come to him, saying he'd known Diego and that he was a lucky one. He'd died in the first fight when Fannin had tried to get to the Alamo. But Paco learned it was only a story told him in kindness, for Diego Pujanza was a prisoner shot down in the road. Like a dog. On Palm Sunday.

It left Paco Salazar calm. As though he'd already done his grieving. As though he'd paid all the tears required for the sum of it, for Juan and Diego Pujanza combined.

It was raining. They'd crossed the Brazos at San Felipe and paused to rest and watch the people rushing to escape the Mexicans.

This eastern Texas green country was heavily populated with Anglos. Now their men were almost all gone to serve with the Texas army somewhere, and the women, old men, and children were left in the path of Mexican armies burning everything, executing all *norte-americanos*. So they fled, their black slaves with them.

They were streaming toward the Sabine and the border of the United States. There were no vehicles except an occasional baby buggy or handcart. No animals except a few milk cows, and these were usually left behind quickly to bawl beside the sodden roads until butchered and eaten.

It was April, the month of rains. Everywhere the refugees were trying to move, the army had already gone before. So the roads were like rivers of sticky, clinging black mud. The smell of it reminded people of frogs.

Some of the oldest were dropping out. Some dying. Children were crying, mothers trying to keep them dry without any hope of it. You could hear the coughing a long way off. You could see little clumps of people—dark, huddled clumps at the roadsides, burying somebody.

As he stood under a dripping willow near the crossing, watching the retreat, Paco heard someone crying. He saw a man, hat off, sobbing as he watched the line of refugees, black and white, struggling along the road. Paco recognized the Gringo captain, Mosely Baker, sobbing. He commanded a group of riflemen who were considered to be the deadliest single unit Houston had in his army.

Paco felt a touch on his arm. It was Deaf Smith. He held his dripping beard close to Paco's face and whispered.

"Come on, son," he said. "Gen'l wants us. We gone go fine Ole Santy Anny."

It was a scout Paco Salazar remembered for a long time. Not least because of the education Deaf Smith and Leander Reed gave him, men not so ignorant as one might suspect from their appearance.

They were waiting with three other scouts in the dripping gloom of a thick growth of post oak and mulberry trees, where one of the faint roads meandered among the many coastal plain bayous. Leander Reed had picked this spot because he figured it was being used by couriers of Santa Anna's army along his southern wing.

They would wait in ambush, hoping to catch a messenger with some kind of dispatch that might give General Houston a handle on where the Mexican army was going next. Waiting meant talking, although under these circumstances the talking would necessarily have to be at whisper volume.

"Ole Gen'l Sam, he got the whole fight to do his ownself," Smith said. "Andy Jackson and the New Nighted States of America ain't gone come to hep fer two reasons. Too many of them Congress folks don't want no new slave state. An Gen'l Jackson ain't anxious to show off that he's gonna bully Mexico so's he can get Texas away from em."

"Well, most of the people fighting the Mexican army right now are *norteamericanos*," said Paco. "It's them who started this independent republic business."

"What I'm sayin," said Leander Reed, "is any help we gonna get from outside ain't gonna be part of no American army. The men who come to help come on they own."

"Or maybe when somebody like Steven Austin ast em to come," said Deaf Smith. "But Ole Jackson ain't sent no sojurs of his. An he won't. He'll make this a state, but he ain't gonna let Mexico or the British or French say he pulled Texas outa Mexico, then took er in."

"All this palaver of yours means," said Paco Salazar, "is that if we want independence, we have to get it ourselves."

Deaf Smith grunted and looked at Leander Reed.

"Didn't I tell you this here's the smartest Mexican you ever seen?"

"Hush up," Reed hissed. "I just heard something."

All Paco Salazar could hear was the rain in the canopy of hardwood leaves overhead and some far rumbles of thunder along the coast to the south. Reed motioned them to use their loops.

It was an old Comanche method to keep horses quiet while you were still up. A rawhide loop on the end of a stout stick. When a time approached that the horse might try some conversation with another horse passing, you twisted the loop on the horse's muzzle, pinching the nostrils as you would if you were standing on the ground beside the horse's head and doing it with your hand.

Paco just had his loop in position when he heard a bit chain rattle. Then there was the definite thud of shod hooves, a great many of them, on the wet ground.

They were very close before he could see them in the dark, and it was good they rode along the road, where there was no cover overhead, whereas Paco and the others were in the inky black shadows under the low limbs of the oaks.

The Mexican column was so silent it was like a dream riding past. Only the thump of hooves and the tiny click of bit chains. All the leather was too wet to squeak. The ghostly appearance was enhanced by the smoky vapors of breath going before each horse.

They were carrying their lances point down and to the rear to keep from fouling them in grass or sod as they moved along. It took only a moment for them to pass, but it seemed a lot longer to those hidden beside the trace.

"How many you tally?" whispered Reed.

"About twenty-four," Paco whispered. "I may have missed a couple up front."

"We need to find a better spot," said Reed. "If they're usin this trace for bunches that big, we got to have something else."

Leander Reed seemed to know where he was going as they moved slowly through the wet, lightning-illuminated night. Within an hour, they were situated once again beside a trail that looked to Paco exactly like the first one. And once in place, Deaf Smith was ready to talk once more.

"You seed some of these folks come to help us, son," he said softly. "The New Orleans Whippets. Georgia Mex Killers. Them firecracker companies from back east somewheres."

"I saw a couple of those units get butchered by Mexican cavalry at Refugio and San Patricio," Paco Salazar said.

"They were well intentioned," said Leander Reed. "But when they saw it was a tooth-and-claw to the death, some of em lost interest. We've seen some on the road, goin the other way now. Back to Louisiana."

"That's right, son," said Smith. "So now we comin down to see whose dog can hunt, it's gonna be mostly just them as has a stack in Texas."

"What I hate to see," said Leander Reed, "is all the folks been here for years, cut a farm or ranch outa the prairie or woods. Now that's who we're seeing on these roads, running to the Sabine for fear the Mexicans gonna get em."

"Can't blame em," said Deaf Smith. "Everybody knows what ole Santy Anny said. He gone do more than whup us. He gone wipe out all Gringos from Texas. He said it, he's doin it. He catch you, you gone be dead in the road with one a them pig stickers his cavalry is so good with. Man, woman, child."

"Yes, they know," said Paco. "And so do the few men Houston's been able to collect to fight."

"That's right," said Reed. "They know. Anglo Texicans and you Mexicans don't like Santa Anna either, they know."

"Damn, this rain's gettin to be a pain," said Deaf Smith. "You know, boys, bein a soldier ain't no particular disgrace. But it sho can be an inconvenience."

Again, Leander Reed decided this was the wrong place, so they moved. There was considerable lightning now. Some of it cracked close. They didn't move far before Reed found what he wanted, and they took position in heavy woods beside another trace. The dripping-wet night was miserable. The best serapes or ponchos couldn't keep them dry.

"Yes sir, Ole Gen'l Sam's outnumbered unless he can catch Santy Anny splittin up his army, then corner it a piece at a time," Deaf Smith said, settling into his sodden saddle at this new spot, ready to make more conversation.

"He ain't got many soldiers," said Leander Reed, "but they're all Texican, so they gonna be hard to whip if Houston can get em turned loose in the right direction against somethin doesn't outnumber em too bad."

You might think Deaf Smith and Leander Reed prophetic. Because it happened exactly as they'd told Paco Salazar it might.

But then these two knew a great deal more about war than Paco did. Both had been with Jackson in all those operations against the British and their Creek allies in Georgia and Florida and were with him still at New Orleans in 1815, when a couple of Scots regiments of the British army found out about Pennsylvania long rifles.

Their ambush was certainly successful. Just before dawn, after the rain had stopped, three Mexican cavalrymen appeared on the trace they were watching, a courier and two escorting lancers.

Before the Mexicans could get their long, unwieldy lances into play, Deaf Smith and another of the frontiersmen scouts rode down the startled cavalrymen and killed them with tomahawk hatchets.

The courier, startled and quickly surrounded, offered no resistance.

They took him to Houston, had him there by the time the sun was breaking through the wind-driven gray clouds.

As soon as the courier saw the temper of the Texans in Houston's camp, and maybe with the threat that he was going to be thrown to them like a hunk of meat, he was more than willing to tell them everything he knew.

Sure enough, Santa Anna was ranging along both banks of the Brazos, looking for the Texas government or the Texas army, he didn't care which, and burning towns as he passed through.

And Santa Anna had a schedule, which the courier unhappily related, of going from this town to that town to the other town. The courier named each specific town in turn, so Houston got a pretty clear picture of where Santa Anna was and where he was headed.

This has always been a very happy kind of information to have about one's enemy when one is contemplating battle.

So General Houston moved his army into a corner formed by Buffalo Bayou and the San Jacinto River, sort of in the direct path of what he knew to be Santa Anna's planned advance, and allowed himself to be caught by the Mexicans.

"And," said Deaf Smith later, "Ole Santy Anny made the biggest bonehead mistake of his life, an son, he'd been a pretty fair military man and politician, too. But Goliad and the Alamo give him the deadly thang Ole British General Pakenham had before New Orleens. Overconfidence, son, plain ole pure-d overconfidence!"

With the Texas army trapped, and no escape across the two rain-swollen rivers possible, Santa Anna decided to give his boys a well-deserved siesta before moving in to finish off the rebels at leisure. The Texans were trapped, so why not?

The sun had come out. The rain-wet prairie in this flat bayou country had exploded in a multi-colored display of wildflowers. From the blue sky came the sharp whistle of the little sparrow hawk and from some of the live oaks to the south the sad call of mourning doves. There was nothing of war about it.

To enjoy his rest completely, Santa Anna took off his medal-festooned uniform and placed his saber and pistols carefully aside, then lay napping in white underwear.

Attentive cavalrymen unsaddled their horses and were rubbing down the horses and the horses were muzzle-down, eating the fresh blossoms. Nearby were stacks of arms, bayonets still fixed, and beside them rows of infantrymen, sleeping, many with their blue coats off and hung on rifle stacks or bushes to dry out after the night's rain.

Without warning, a howling, swirling, hatchet- and club-swinging mass of riflemen plunged savagely into the drowsy Mexican camp. Blue-clad Mexican soldiers were scrambling madly about, knocking over stacks of arms, being butchered.

The Texans were coming from two directions into the Mexican camp. Troops that had been sleeping were leaping up only to be run over by scrambling comrades trying to escape the screeching Gringos from another direction.

There were a few sharp, crashing rifle volleys fired by the lines of Texans, and then these men came on swinging still-smoking rifles like clubs. Cavalry horses, frightened, yanked free of their holders and bolted through the camp, knocking down Mexican soldiers.

A Mexican non-commissioned officer was waving a saber, trying to shout orders, and three Texans crashed into him with knives and hatchets and left him writhing and leaped on to the next line of blue-uniformed soldiers struggling to find a way free. But each way the soldiers turned seemed swarming with rushing, leaping, screaming Texans.

This was a well-trained, highly disciplined army, but they only fought in tight formations, marching forward under the orders of officers, bayonets thrust forward. This was not their kind of fight. It was a barroom brawl. It was a Texas kind of fight, every man for himself, kill as many as you can, devil take the hindmost.

Some broke toward the open prairie, where Houston's cavalry cut them down. Mexican officers rushing about shouting orders made themselves targets. A large group of soldiers, trying to escape, drowned in the river.

The Texas army had two small brass cannons. They yanked them by hand to the edge of the Mexican camp and started cutting swaths through the milling, stumbling, staggering soldiers with grapeshot.

A large group of Mexicans, most without weapons, was corralled against a bend in Buffalo Bayou, and the Texans stood off with rifles and calmly shot and reloaded, shot and reloaded, cutting them down like tenpins.

Paco Salazar heard the cry at first as a faint bellowing above the rattle of rifle fire. Then it swelled and swept back and forth across the field from flank to flank.

"Remember the Alamo!"

"Remember Goliad!"

Like the wind blowing across the ocean of wildflowers, the shout for revenge surged and faded, surged again.

Hearing it and the screams and the crash of gunfire, smelling the stink of burnt gunpowder, looking at the wild panorama, Paco found it all impossibly incongruous. The canvas of blue and pink and purple and yellow blossoms splattered with slaughterhouse red.

"Get yousef a Mex er two, didn't yer son?" Deaf Smith would ask.

And Paco Salazar would nod. But he never told Deaf Smith that when the group of terrified Mexican soldiers ran, trying to escape, and had been trapped by the flooded bayou, and the Anglo men lined up as though for target practice and began shooting them, Paco, with the long rifle Deaf Smith had given him, dismounted and joined them.

He could not remember how many times he fired. But with each shot, he had muttered aloud, "Did she make a tortilla for *you?*"

They found Santa Anna with a mob of common soldiers they had taken prisoner. He'd put on a pair of enlisted-soldier trousers, and he'd managed to get his own white shirt before having to beat an inglorious retreat from his siesta.

"Yer know how we picked him out of all that bunch of scared Mex sojurs?" Deaf Smith would say. "Why, good land, them other sojurs was just bowin and scrapin and actin like he was God Almighty or some such, so you knowed this here wasn't no private sojur like he was takin on to be."

Paco Salazar hadn't tried to see the Mexican general because he wasn't sure what he might do, remembering the Pujanzas. And remembering how it felt to stand off and execute those Mexican soldiers at the bayou.

"Yes sir," Deaf Smith would laugh. "Ole Santy Anny seen how all them Texicans was lookin at his neck and kindly measurin it for a rope, and he figured he'd better agree to anything Gen'l Sam said, and he done.

"Then they had to hustle Gen'l Sam off to New Orleans, take care of that foot. Bad wound, that foot," Deaf Smith said, shaking his head and frowning. "They shot Gen'l Sam's *caballo*, Ole Saracen. One hell of a fine horse, Ole Saracen. Damned Mexicans are horse-shootin swine."

Deaf Smith looked at Paco Salazar and grinned, showing his beautiful teeth in his ugly face.

"Present company exceptioned, a course!" And then, going to his waiting duffel, "Son, I think it's a good time fer me to ride to Bexar. I know a little Spanish lady there. Yer like to trail along? I promise to get yer in plenty trouble!"

Chapter Five

Old Spanish land-grants seemed capable sometimes of jumping around like cactus spiders, particularly after a revolution or two.

Young Hernando Salazar had been given a patent for land at San Antonio de Bexar when Carlos IV had been king of Spain. Most of that he sold off as the land became more and more engulfed by the growing town, but there was still some left to him when the nasty little revolutions of the early nineteenth century occurred.

When Hernando showed his sympathy for the revolution and it was savagely put down by the royalist army, he was executed. In keeping with the usual practice, his property was confiscated by the state.

Under such circumstances, the land was usually parceled out to common soldiers who had sweated and sometimes bled for whichever cause it was that had triumphed—and hence whichever leaders were in a position to determine who owned the land.

So common soldiers were the beneficiaries.

Well, except for really choice property. Such as acreage with a mill on it or a private toll bridge or *una grande hacienda*. These kinds of property were usually taken by the official whose responsibility it was to parcel out confiscated land.

The land still owned by Hernando Salazar at the time of his demise was a semi-choice plot with a two-room adobe house having one window in front and a goat pen in back and a privy. These were good things, but location is what made the plot semi-choice.

Just to the west of it, two houses away in fact, was the Camino de Laredo, the Laredo Road, the main highway to Mexico. At a slightly greater distance north was the presidio of San Antonio and Military Plaza, which was not only troop barracks but the wide square where farmers came each day with their produce for sale.

In that direction, too, were Main Plaza and San Fernando Cathedral, the church that had been built by Canary Island Spaniards almost a century before Santa Anna's blood-red flag flew from its tower.

The neighborhood was still called Barrio del Sur, the northern-most fringe of the *labore abajo,* which was the lower, in this case southern, farm lot of 172 acres, as shown on the chart of the original town authorized by Viceroy de Valera.

But this was not a melon field or any such thing. It was a part of the town, cluttered with the houses of most of the town's Mexican population, except for the rich ones who lived in other sectors beside the Gringos.

In short, because most of the building in Bexar had been on the west side of the river thus far, centering around Main Plaza and in the ox-bow loop of the river there and around the presidio and Military Plaza, *el mercado* was an extension on the north side of this plaza with great bur oak and walnut and chinaberry trees, called a marketplace because that's what it became each day. For other reasons, what was left of the old Salazar grant was pretty near smack at the center of things.

It may still have been called Barrio del Sur, but it really wasn't a neighborhood in the south of town, it was closer to the middle of town and maybe should have been called Barrio del Centro.

But it wasn't.

So about 1814, the Spanish viceroy gave the Salazar plot to one Capitan Lopez de Felipe, who had been a faithful fighter for the Crown in the recent unpleasantness.

Obviously, nothing in King Carlos IV's original prize mentioned anything about passing the land down to nice people. Because Capitan Lopez de Felipe had the reputation in the Mexican army, and the Spanish army before that, of being a brutish, sadistic monster, and he had earned every bloody sobriquet proudly.

Capitan Felipe soon impressed his neighbors in Bexar with an apparently limitless appetite for French brandy, black cigarillos and recreation with ladies of the evening that lasted all night.

There were most generally cries, or perhaps they would be better described as screams, from the former house of Hernando Salazar during the course of Capitan Felipe's parties. And next day, it was not surprising to see one or more ladies of the evening with swollen lips and black eyes and various cuts and bruises.

Officers and men of Lopez's regiment were unanimous in their opinions. The Capitan was *un monstruo,* as has already been noted.

To have received such accolades from soldiers and officers of the Mexican army at this time meant that Lopez de Felipe was a harsh man, indeed.

Some said he got his comeuppance when the next revolution came round, this one the first pulsation of Mexican independence from Spain. Lopez de Felipe had the bad judgement to support the rebels, so when the royalists won, naturally, he saw a vision of himself standing against a wall with twelve soldiers aiming rifles at his heart, so he escaped with one of the best horses in Bexar.

For many years, they discussed the ride to freedom Felipe had made.

"Well, he had no choice," said one Gringo. "Any direction he turned, there was an enemy ready to tie his ass to a firing-squad post. So he had to ride west."

"For a Mexican army officer to ride alone to western country is insane," said a Mexican. "And the last seen of him, he was still wearing his uniform, very bad clothing in which to hide on the High Plains."

"By Gawd," said the Anglo Texan, "If it was me, I druther let ten *hombres* shoot at me all at onest than just go gallavantin off west of here without no considerable size armament and hell, maybe no canteen. He left in such a hurry."

"*Sí,*" said the Texas Mexican. "The high wilderness can be cruel to a man. It was to Coronado, *comprende?*"

"You called that, hoss," the first said, and they all laughed.

They didn't laugh at anything said. They laughed because they all knew that over a year after Capitan Felipe rode lickety-split out of town, as the Gringos said, it was reported to them that a Comanche buck showed up at the annual trade fair in Santa Fe trying to swap a Mexican army officer's saber for a bottle of whiskey.

A Bent brother, one of whom was governor of New Mexico Territory or some such thing or another, who was married to a Cheyenne and had a fort on the Arkansas and who was a big trader in that area, bought the thing from the Comanche.

Well, they said, if it wasn't a Bent it was somebody who knew them, or maybe it was kinfolk or maybe friends or a business partner. Anyway, somebody with credibility. It doesn't matter who bought the saber from the Comanche. The thing had been seen by a lot of people, and there wasn't any doubt about it, they said.

The blade was engraved.

"To Capitan Gonzales del Mores de Lopez de Felipe for gallantry at the action of Rio de la Babia."

Everybody knew there had been no battle anywhere along that small river in Coahuila during any of the recent revolutions. Only the execution of fifty-five rebels back in 1812 at Sabrina. The saber had been presented by General Iturbide, which was just fine and seemed to fit perfectly. As has been related, General Iturbide did not escape the firing squad himself.

It was all good for considerable bitter laughter. A great irony, all the way around. Nobody was ever really able to tie it up neatly. But it just had to be some kind of great irony, you just had to understand, they said.

"*Comprende?*" they said.

It was this kind of thing which caused early comers from Norte América to shake their heads in wonder at the twists and turns of Mexican politics.

When Felipe vacated, the old Salazar land-grant property was held by the new Mexican government and for a while was used as a residence for one of the married officers assigned to the Mexican army of Texas stationed at San Antonio.

For a long time then, it was empty, collecting the trash inside and out that all empty houses collect.

When the war for Texan independence came, and first one army then another was in Bexar, the house became a welcome camp for soldiers just passing through, so to speak, and it suffered the usual depredations of casual vandalism.

The last squads of fighting men who stayed there were part of Santa Anna's army. They were medical troops. From the house, they could hear all the cannons and the rifle fire across the river. They could hear the wounded brought to Military Plaza crying out for water, too.

This group didn't sleep much. They were on duty at Military Plaza, and by the time the battle was finished, the plaza was carpeted with bloody, lacerated bodies lying in the sun. They tried to recruit local

Mexican women just to carry water for the wounded and to drag away the dead.

Even then, the crying of men begging for water was a sound that did not stop for many days. And you could hear the cries from the house, but by then the medical corpsmen were so tired that when they had the chance to go there, they slept quickly and soundly.

Then the last of Santa Anna's army was gone. There wasn't much movement on the streets of Bexar immediately after the battle. Many people had escaped down the road to Goliad. The ones who stayed remained indoors for a long time after the army departed.

It smelled very bad in San Antonio. There were many dead missed by burial details. Probably wild animals dug up some who had been buried. When he marched away, Santa Anna charged the San Antonio *alcalde* with cleaning up the battlefield.

It was beyond the town's capability. Bodies were burned and buried in mass graves, and a great many were simply thrown in the river. Later, Alcalde Francisco Ruis said he had to dispose of 182 Gringo bodies and about sixteen hundred Mexicans.

It was only with the news of San Jacinto that the people of Bexar came out again and started putting everything, including their lives, back together. Then veterans, Gringo and Mexican, began to return. And Paco Salazar, too. Who had no problem finding his father's house.

Inside, there was a scatter of paper and tamale cornhusks and half-burned sticks and some of the original furniture. Most of this was broken in one way or another. All the good things had been stolen because there was no lock on either door and no glass or even frame in the front window.

On the street side, there was a shallow ditch between the front wall and the rutted and pocked path of cart and horse and donkey and boot and shoe and moccasin. Some bare feet, too. Because it was a busy little narrow street, even in rainy weather, when each passer left a signature in the mud.

Here there were weeds, some three years old, brown and gray green and stiff and snug against the adobe wall as though they belonged there. And some prickly-pear cactus.

Sometimes, there was water in the ditch. Sometimes enough to flow off to one of the irrigation ditches only a short distance away. In Bexar, irrigation ditches were only a short distance away from everything.

In the rear, in the goat pen, where the fences were gone, the wood slats long since taken by someone for firewood, there was a thick, two-foot-deep tangle of weeds and wildflowers and some tequila agave cactus, tall-stemmed, and the old, dried-blossom panicles that rattled in the breeze.

In a corner where adjoining buildings made a cul-de-sac, there were Spanish bayonet and yucca, the bayonet deep green, the yucca dead pale yellow with last year's blossoms still clinging. On the ground was a jungle of fallen leaves and sprouting weeds. It looked like a peccary might charge out at any time, or maybe a howler monkey. The privy door had gone the way of the fence palings. Into somebody's fireplace or stove.

The first night, it was raining. Paco Salazar put the horse in the front room. In back, the shelf where he could remember sitting and watching his mother make tortillas seemed much smaller. But he managed to sit there, a blanket tight around his shoulders.

The adobe oven was still there. It was black, unused for a long time. The pole shingles had come apart mostly, and a few had fallen down. Rain, coming through the gaps, made rippling puddles on the flagstones where he had watched his mother's bare feet, toes splayed wide apart, as she squatted before her oven, rolling his beans in hot, brown corn cakes.

He tried to convince himself that he was not hungry, and finally he fell asleep.

At Military Plaza, with the rain past the next morning, there was a lot of activity, but it was too early in the year for the farmers to be there with melons and yams and corn and tomatoes.

But the vendor stands were there, with the little canvas awnings over the charcoal stoves where the tamales and *chili con carne* were made and served to customers sitting on plank benches at wooden tables.

Some of the venders made green chili this time of year. They used sweet green chilies and bell peppers instead of tomatoes. Or they made black chili without tomatoes or green peppers but with molasses and browned suet, and a lot of ground chilies and red peppers. This was a brave chili indeed, everybody said.

All of them ground their various peppers there at the plaza, and cut, chopped, or shaved their meat there, too. Some used a straight razor to shave meat so thin you could see through it, and it liquefied as soon as it hit an almost red-hot iron skillet.

So Military Plaza was like a deep, thick pool of odor, all of it spicy and throat squeezing and good.

The wagon park was still on the south edge of Military Plaza, and there were a number of tents there and strings of mules and some oxen and a few horses.

"Ho, Paco," someone shouted as he came near the wagon park. He saw that he knew a number of these men who were freighters like his Uncle Diego had been. This one was Alex Mesero, of Bexar. "Ho, I see you still got one of those red horses. "*Que pasó?* How did that happen?"

"No, those died in the war," said Paco. "But I got one as near like them as I could find. I call him Rojo, the same name as the roan you remember, who belonged to my uncle."

That had been one of Uncle Diego's best horses, one that was a little rangy and with a color the Gringos called strawberry roan and maybe a touch of Arabian in the shape of his head. Uncle Diego said Red had the blood of Andalusia running in him, whereupon Aunt Lena had asked, "Then why did you geld him?"

"To gentle him, woman, to gentle him," Uncle Diego would shout. "We stood him at stud twice, and I needed him in the trade and he was too wild to trail with ox carts, so I did what I had to do. I gentled him."

Now Alex Mesero said, "I heard about your uncle."

He was standing at Red's stirrup, looking up and shading his face with his hand though he wore the wide Mexican hat.

"If I'd seen any of his livestock, I would tell you. I thought this was one."

Maybe Alex Mesero was quick to say this because he knew that in the past, he'd had the reputation of not paying too close attention to proper ownership of various horses.

"It's a thing I appreciate," said Paco.

There was a hunter's camp in the cart and wagon yard. A group of maybe half-a-dozen men just in from the plains with skinned buffalo meat hanging from ropes rigged between A-frame lodge poles. Hanging like red wet wash.

This is where the tamale and *chili con carne* people got their meat, but townspeople could buy it, too, and they were there now. There were a few Anglos, and a surprising number of these were women wearing large, floppy hats.

"Where are all the Anglos?" Paco asked. "I thought there would be more here."

"No new ones coming in now, since the Alamo," said Alex Mesero. "Plenty of Mexican soldiers around then. Times too uneasy now. Who knows where they are? *Quien sabe?*"

"Where are all the Texas soldiers? The barracks look empty."

"Only a few here. They say they're soldiers. They don't look much like soldiers to me. But whatever they are, they're across the river. They have a wagon park on Alamo Plaza. I don't think they got more than fifty soldiers here."

"What are they doing?"

"Hoping Santa Anna doesn't come back," said Alex Mesero, and they both laughed.

"General Houston's got him in jail," said Paco.

"Before he gets out and starts everything all over again, why don't you step off that *caballo* and we can get some tamales? And maybe something to sooth our thirst."

"*Bueno!* You have money?"

Alex Mesero shrugged. "Don't you?"

"*Sí*, a little," said Paco and laughed. "*Bueno!* Tamales and *cerveza*, then. A feast of welcome for my return to Bexar."

"I thought maybe mescal," said Alex Mesero. "A better fortification in case Santa Anna comes while we're feasting."

Paco Salazar laughed again and dismounted. Half-a-dozen small brown boys ran up to take his horse.

Officially, Texas and Mexico were still at war, but nobody on either side knew what to do about it, and even if they had any ideas, they had no money to effect them.

The new Republic of Texas was only partly evident with the appearance of a couple of men from Washington-on-Brazos to make official some of the people who had already been serving in some municipal posts and to prepare things for the election temporary president David G. Burnet had called for September.

One of the people already serving claimed to be a judge, which was fine. Nobody checked his credentials.

As everyone expected, Sam Houston would run for president. And one of the initiatives on the ballot would be to decide if Texas wanted to become a part of the United States of America.

"State of the Union?" asked one Mexican Texan. "I only want to have back the Constitution of 1823, the Constitution of the Mexican Republic."

"What the hell was the Constitution of 1823?" asked an Anglo Texan, who had been in Texas only since coming to join the fight after the Texas War for Independence started. "Why else was we fightin? To get this place into the Union! *That's* why, fer Christ sake!"

"You saw what Santa Anna thought of the Constitution of 1823," said a second Anglo. "You support it here in Texas, and he declares you a pirate and shoots you."

But as Paco Salazar said, Santa Anna was still in a Texas jail along with some of the officers and the soldiers closest to him. Rumor had it that they were not being treated too well. The Mexican general, leader of his nation, was seen sometimes being moved from one place to another in leg irons.

Those with good conscience who heard such things and saw such things hoped the elections would come quickly so that Santa Anna and his captive *compañeros* could be returned to Mexico.

Some who had lost friends and lovers and kin at Goliad and in various ranch and farm burnings, Anglos and Mexicans alike, had no such tender notions about how to handle the Napoleon of the West.

The capital of the new republic would be Columbia, where a temporary president, so to speak, was already in office and over which would soon fly the flag of the state, called the Lone Star—red, white, and blue, with a single white star. Five points, of course, like the stars in the flag of the United States.

Everybody expected to enter the Union, and soon. After all,

Anglos said, Old Hickory Jackson had sent General Ed Gaines with an army of United States troops to the east bank of the Sabine supposedly to prevent either belligerent in the Texas War for Independence from coming into Louisiana.

Now the war was over, but General Gaines was still there. But nobody could accuse Old Hickory of highjacking Texas from Mexico, because Texans had won the war by themselves.

What most of the Texas Gringos didn't take into account was what Leander Reed and Deaf Smith had pointed out to Paco Salazar back in the bayou country, that resistance to Texas statehood by northeastern anti-slavery senators like John Quincy Adams was a high and constant barrier.

But these were issues that didn't particularly bother Paco Salazar. In fact, it is doubtful he gave any of the political tug of war about to take place any thought at all.

Life in Bexar began to show an increasing heartbeat. A few Anglos were arriving, even though things were unsettled. Mexicans who had fled the armies of Santa Anna and hidden in the countryside were returning. There were already a few frame houses being built north of Military Plaza, and now there were signs that the town was going to spread to the east side of the San Antonio River.

Everyone interested in freighting was keyed up and getting ready for business because now there would be wide-open trade with the United States and everybody else, like France and Great Britain and all the sugar islands of the Caribbean.

There was almost nothing manufactured in Texas, which meant that everything from thimbles to ten-penny nails, plowshares to kitchen cutlery, had to be brought in from someplace else. This was as it had always been. But never before had Texas been expecting to grow so fast or have so many markets, once a few problems were ironed out. Like money.

Nobody knew where the money was coming from because there was very little of it around. One of the big problems of the new republic was finding a way to float a loan from somebody, probably the United States, and get some hard cash circulating.

Meanwhile, the Mexican government still did not recognize the terms of surrender Santa Anna had signed. His army was still straggling back across the Bravo into Mexico. Maybe. Or maybe the bulk of it was still in that no man's land just south of the Nueces. From that area, there were all kinds of panic reports of bandit raids. Only these bandits wore blue Mexican cavalry uniforms!

With this unsettled atmosphere, nobody was sure what would happen, even day by day. Under such circumstances, you can imagine the wild circus scene in any land office.

Well, no matter how bad you imagine it could be, it was worse.

Chapter Six

The harried Anglo behind the desk was mostly bald. He wore an old-fashioned broadcloth black coat with a high collar. The sleeves were too long. He was scratching with a quill pen on a paper before him, the topmost of a great scatter and pile and jumble of papers.

A handwritten placard was folded to stand up on the desk, and it proclaimed that this was "Judge Carville Wier—Justice of the Peace." He had been sent from Columbia in the president's confidence, he was heard to have said, to clear up land claims in Bexar.

This was the guard room of the first troop barracks on the west end of Military Plaza, and it had seen a lot of use. It was plastered, or had been a long time ago, and the plaster had fallen off the ceiling in a number of places, and off the walls as well, and the underlying slats looked like the bones of a carcass left on the desert and picked clean by buzzards.

A pair of gray-green whip-tail lizards ran in short rushes along one of the windowsills and up the walls and down again, at each pause staying stock still and blending so well into the color of the adobe that unless you saw them move, you likely wouldn't see them at all.

The lizards were more than casual observers. Their staple of diet, the common housefly, was in great abundance in this room, flies buzzing about and crawling with sticky feet on everything not moving.

Too fast to see, the lizards caught flies with a darting flick of their rapier-like tongues. But no matter how often and accurately they attacked the buzzing swarms, there was no noticeable decrease in the number of crawlers that caused all in the room to wave hands frantically at ears and in front of faces in the always futile effort to discourage the thirsty insects from seeking sweaty spots for a nice, warm drink.

The place smelled like old chalk and chewing tobacco. Of which there appeared to be a large cud beneath the left cheek of Justice of the Peace Wier. Proof of its presence was a dark and still-wet brown stain running through a stubble of black whiskers from the left corner of his mouth diagonally to about the center of his chin.

Standing behind Justice of the Peace Wier was a Texas volunteer army soldier from the garrison across the river, or maybe he had accompanied the official from the capital. He was in what was supposed to be an infantry uniform, and he was leaning on a long double-barrel shotgun. He also had a mouthful of chewing tobacco, but he went about the chewing of it with considerably more gusto and enthusiasm than did Justice of the Peace Wier.

From the glaze of his eyes and the odor of his breathing, the soldier seemed to be moderately drunk.

The room was full of men, and maybe two women in black, all of them Anglos and all of them, it seemed, talking at the top of their lungs and some of them rattling papers. A few seemed angry. One of the women held up a black parasol, not opened, somewhat like a drum major leading a silver cornet band or some such thing. Everybody seemed a little sweaty.

Paco Salazar, when he entered, removed his sombrero and slapped the wide brim against his leg as he swept it down, as though he made a salute of some sort. Everyone stopped talking and stared at him a moment, then returned their attention to Justice of the Peace Wier.

Paco Salazar waited for some time, and there was a number of Anglos who went before Justice of the Peace Wier, and there were words spoken and papers exchanged and signatures and other such things you might expect, and Paco Salazar was growing impatient.

What's more, he was growing bold as well, for before walking into this place, he had accompanied two of his former acquaintances in the freighting business to one of the *cantinas* near Military Plaza, where they had talked about the old days and Paco's Uncle Diego and what a terrible thing it was that he'd been taken out and shot by General Urrea's army at Goliad.

This was followed by tributes to the valor of Paco's cousin Juan, who had died just across the river in the last assault of Santa Anna's infantry against the men holding the Mission of San Antonio De Valera. At least, as they lifted their tankards, this is how they reconstructed it, although they actually had no idea how Juan had died.

On that day, with friends, and having had a number of tankards of heavy Mexican beer, Paco was capable for the first time of speaking calmly about his terrible loss.

What was best, after another tankard of beer, was Paco telling them of San Jacinto and how the Mexicans of Santa Anna were pinned against Buffalo Bayou and slaughtered like pigs.

By the time he appeared before Justice of the Peace Wier in the old army barracks, he was in a state that his Uncle Diego and Aunt Lena would never have allowed. Even at the last, when he was a man over thirty. It was a state that he had seen and of which he had heard and about which he had joked but had never experience.

He was, in a word, drunk. Not unpleasantly so. In about the same condition as the Texas volunteer soldier standing and chewing behind Justice of the Peace Wier.

And now he had waited long enough.

When Paco Salazar moved to the front of the desk and dropped his sombrero among Justice of the Peace Wier's papers, all talking among the Gringos in the room ceased once more, and perhaps one of the women even gasped in astonishment that a Mexican could act so uppity here among his betters.

For a long moment, Justice of the Peace Wier's eyes bulged and his chest heaved, and he finally looked up into Paco Salazar's face.

"You Mexicans better learn you wait your turn round here now, you hear me?" he said.

When Paco Salazar replied, he spoke in impeccable English, as only a man slightly drunk can, and maybe because English was not even his mother tongue, the edges of his words were strangely sharp and lacerating.

"Señor Comisario." Well, at least everything after the first two words was in English. "Do not be embarrassed that I am a Mexican. I am proud to be a Mexican. My father died for the Mexican Republic. My uncle died at Goliad and my cousin at the Alamo for the Republic of Texas. I was born here, in Texas, and it has been my home all my life, while you have probably been God only knows where.

"Now, I come to inform you that I am living on a lot of land which was given to my father in honor of my grandfather, given by the old

King Charles IV. I am not asking if I can live there. I am here to inform you that I am living there. It is mine, and I am living there. Here is the patent."

And Paco Salazar tossed the old patent down so it floated for a second and then lighted on the top of Justice of the Peace Wier's most important documents.

For an instant it was as though all breathing in the room was suspended. Then Wier drew himself up and took a deep breath preparatory to delivering himself of something or other, when he was interrupted by a loud rattle and thump from the rear of the room.

"Hold up, yer honor," a rasping voice shouted, and as the Anglos moved to make a pathway from the door to the desk, a man—clearly a frontiersman—using a Pennsylvania long rifle as a cane stomped forward. It was Deaf Smith.

Paco Salazar was more astonished than anyone else, because he'd never expected a friendly face here. Before he could greet his scouting *compañero*, Deaf Smith was leaning over the desk, shouting at Justice of the Peace Wier.

"Yer honor, Cap'n, yer jest go on now and give this young man what he wants," Smith shouted. "He's lost kin at Goliad and acrost the river at Alamo."

"I told him that," said Paco.

"Yer Honor, Cap'n, this here lad's lost his Mama and his Papa fer the old Mexican Republic!"

"I told him that," Paco said.

"This good hoss has fit Santy Anny at San Jacinto. He was a scout for Sam Houston."

"I told him that," said Paco.

For the first time, Deaf Smith turned and looked at Paco Salazar.

"You never done it," he said. Then back to Wier. "Sam Houston figures this young man hung the moon, and I'd shore hate to see a nice man like you, who as Paco says, prob'ly ain't been in Texas long like me and him has, get all twisted up with our new president, or gonna be next September, jes because nobody told him who this man was here in Bexar, an wouldn't write down on them books you got all about his Spanish land-grant and that it's still good as gold. You listenin to me, yer Honor?"

In the entire exchange, Anglos who witnessed it said, the official of the Republic of Texas said not a single word after his opening comments and finally signed the old Spanish document, entered it in a great ledger book of his own, and closed his office for the day as the old frontiersman led the Mexican out.

"Sergeant," Justice of the Peace Wier was heard to say to the Texas soldier, "leave us find a cool *cantina* and go there for a cool glass of mescal."

"Your honor," the soldier said, shouldering his shotgun, "them's the proper reward for hard duty!"

It didn't take long to get the house in order. Enough furniture to sleep on and sit on and set a plate of food on, but little more. There wasn't much time spent there anyway. Because trailing freight began again for Paco Salazar. Or just looking around, as the *yanqui* always said.

He had a lot of good experience; he had made a rather favorable impression on the town's Anglos with his performance in Justice of the Peace Wier's court when Deaf Smith came to the rescue, so to speak. And he found that his family name—both of his family names, in fact—was respected and well thought of, so there was no problem finding a freight outfit that would take him on as major-domo.

At least, not so long as there were any freight outfits doing business. It wasn't going as fast as a lot of people had thought it would.

Alex Mesero was a help, too. He'd freighted out of Bexar before the war, while Paco had been operating with the Pujanzas. So he knew the outfits in San Antonio.

But it was slow. Lack of cash and hostile countryside were monumental hurdles. And nobody knew what the Mexicans might do next. So ventures were few and modest.

One of the old familiar routes was closed now, for the time being. Mexico still considered Texas to be a part of its territory. So now, after a few weeks of uncertainty following San Jacinto, Mexican troops and bandits roamed pretty much at will between the Nueces and the Rio Grande.

Laredo, on the north bank of the Rio Grande, was in effect a Mexican town. If the Mexicans wanted to mount a sizable raid on San Antonio de Bexar, they could do it without much opposition. And they did.

But Mexico didn't have any more money than Texas did, so their military adventures were limited. But you could almost always find Mexican cavalry operating in the no man's land between the two southern rivers, the Nueces and the Bravo, or the Rio Grande, if you prefer.

And there were the Comanches.

"What yer got out here at Ole Bexar is two hostile frontiers," said Deaf Smith on one of his visits to the house of Paco Salazar, where he brought a bottle of tequila which they drank in the classic manner of the Spanish *caballero:* lick of salt, sip of liquor, bite of sliced lemon.

"And the Republic of Texas hasn't the money for an army," said Alex Mesero. "Militia is no good because you got to have people who do not always have to go home to plow or milk the cow. So all we have are these volunteer ranging companies."

By this time, Alex Mesero had moved in with Paco, being foot-loose since losing his wife to the cholera back in the epidemic of '33. So now the house just off Camino de Laredo had four permanent residents. The owner, the owner's amigo Alex Mesero, the owner's *caballo* Rojo, and the owner's amigo's *caballo*, a mare named Bluebell.

The horses had the rear room and back yard. The men had the front room. They shared the patio, where Alex Mesero had fixed the roof so they could all stay dry on muggy days when it rained and they wanted to sit outside and eat hot tamales. Both horses enjoyed the tamales, but only after they'd cooled.

"What did yer vaqueros do to make them hosses eat them tamales?" Deaf Smith asked the first time he observed this strange horse deportment.

"Just feed them the tamale with the husk still on," said Paco, he and Alex Mesero laughing already. "They think it's a new kind of corn, and before they realize it, they are addicted to tamales, meat and all!"

There were a great many such days when they sat and spoke of politics and business and family memories before the war and the cholera. For there was little for them to do now. Freighting business was almost choked off completely.

"We're going to need some kind of work soon," said Paco Salazar. "My gold coins have lasted a long time, but now the time is over."

"No money around, no business, hostile *indios*, rumors of Mexican armies coming," Alex Mesero said. "You can't do any freighting for somebody when they figure in every direction you take a string, you may lose the goods."

"We need to be running trains back along the Trinity or the Brazos."

"Plenty of business in the East?"

"More people," said Paco. "But no more money than here, I think."

"As soon as we get to be a state in the Gringo country, things will be fine," Alex said. "Only from what we heard the last time we were in Linnville, it's a dismal prospect."

"The drunk Portuguese sailor off that Baltimore ship?"

"Sí. He said those up-north Yankees aren't going to let Texas into their Union because of the slavery."

"You believe him?" asked Paco. "There's no way we can become a state?"

"You sound like you're ready to be a full-to-the-bite *yanqui*."

"If we were a state," said Paco, "we'd have a big government looking out for our interests. Business would be good. It makes sense. Since we got away from Santa Anna, it makes sense to be a state. But you think the *yanqui* won't have us now?"

"Sí. Unless our Gringos will give up their slaves."

They laughed.

"Then who picks all that cotton they've started growing in east Texas?" said Paco, and they laughed again.

"Well, I'm glad most of the cotton and most of the Africans are on the Trinity and the Brazos and the coast, where they've got the cotton," said Alex. "This slave business makes me uneasy."

"It'll be here, too, before long," said Paco.

"Not so long as we've got Comanches and Mexican army patrols roving around," said Alex and they laughed some more, although if you had questioned them, they'd have been hard pressed to explain what was funny.

"Well, at least all of them don't own slaves," said Paco.

"Yes, can you imagine Deaf Smith owning slaves?"

It was all right to laugh, even without there being anything funny.

There were things to be learned from Alex Mesero that Paco Salazar knew he didn't have any business learning. He began to realize how much Diego and Lena Pujanza had cloistered him, even well into his manhood when he might have been out roving around seeing what life was about in the other barrios.

Alex knew a great deal about stealing horses. He only stole horses from the Mexican army, he would always say, his eyes wide with innocence. But there had been times when the closest Mexican army unit was across the Rio Grande at Piedras Negras and Alex had money in his money belt from the sale of some horses.

At least Alex never asked Paco to come with him on any of these little forays that sometimes saw him gone from Bexar for two weeks or more. And he always shared his profits, if that's what they should be called, in the way of buying food and *cerveza*.

Sometimes he brought home a thing more powerful than beer. Sometimes it was pulque, sometimes mescal or tequila. He knew a great deal about these things, too.

"Ascención Caravajal, who has that *cantina*, he makes his pulque with maguey cactus," Alex said, screwing his face into a sour mask. "This is why it is like drinking horse piss.

"But Indelecio Madero, who was once a deputy *alcalde* somewhere in east Tejas, he makes his with tequila agave, like that stuff you have growing in your back yard, and he makes his mescal and tequila from the same plant."

"I can taste the difference," said Paco. "Even with the limited experience I have at such things. But none of that explosive stuff you drink is kind to my belly."

"You must take more salt and lemon with it, amigo. The salt and lemon make mescal or tequila *muy bueno*."

"*Quiza*," said Paco. "Maybe."

"Something was good for you that day you went into the land commissioner's office," said Alex Mesero and laughed. "From what I heard, you were walking like *el malo hombre!*"

"I was bad enough, all right," said Paco. "I was full of your Señor Indelecio Madero's damned mescal!"

So they spent more time than they wanted to lying about Bexar drinking and dancing at the fandangos and listening to rumors and to Anglos talking statehood.

"Goddamnit," one Texan recently transplanted from Georgia said. "Ole Hickory practically promised Sam Houston statehood, didn't he? What the hell's holdin thangs up?"

"Word now is they's lookin fer a non-slave state to come in at the same time we does," said another. "To balance the senators, fifty-fifty. Half from slave states, half not."

"Slaves has always been trouble," said another. "And they be trouble now."

"What the hell do you know?" shouted the first. "You blockhead peckerwood. You ain't never been able to afford a slave, so you gotta wool around them as has."

Alex Mesero, in their cavorting about San Antonio's social milieu, what there was of it, found himself sufficiently close to passion to think of marriage twice in those times. Paco Salazar never did, although his contact with *señoritas* was as you would expect from a bachelor of about thirty years.

Nobody cared to guess what Deaf Smith did, other than enjoy his reputation as one of General Houston's best scouts in the War for Independence. From time to time, between Mexican army raids on Bexar, Deaf Smith appeared in town, and he always visited his Mexican friends in the house in the Barrio del Sur.

Usually, when he came, he carried in his hands a bag of lemons and a bottle of tequila. Then one day he came with something of an entirely different nature.

It was evening, and they sat under the light of a single candle that rested on a beautiful single pedestal oak table, which, like all the furniture in the room, had come from the former home of a loyal Mexican in Barrio del Norte whose property had been confiscated.

On the day city officials came to collect the furniture to be auctioned, it was gone. Alex Mesero had been away from their *casa* throughout most of the evening before, and when Paco asked, Alex said he'd gone to help a lady move her furnishings from an old house to a new one she had just bought.

"With both horses and that small cart you brought here last month?" Paco asked.

"Sí. Sí," said Alex, blinking his eyes rapidly and looking extremely innocent. "Both horses and the cart. The horses were very cranky about being put to harness."

"I would expect as much," Paco said. "And what is all that furniture stacked in the cart in the back yard?"

"Furniture?" Alex asked, blinking rapidly. "Oh. Sí. Furniture. That was furniture she had left over. No place to put it. I told her we'd be glad to store it."

"I suppose we could make room," said Paco. "I also suppose we should move the furniture off the cart and into the house where it can't be so easily seen by some passing official of the Texas land office."

"I believe that the quicker we do that," Alex had said, still looking wide-eyed, "the better."

It was elegant furniture. At least for Bexar in that time.

So on this table Deaf Smith laid a large object under an oily cloth, which he removed with a flourish. Gleaming in the candle shine was a pistol, the like of which the two younger men had never seen. But had heard about.

"My God, one of those Gringo revolving pistols," said Alex Mesero. It seemed an elaborate thing, blue steel except for walnut grips. A trigger snapped down when it was cocked. It was a .36-caliber weapon.

"A six-shooter!" said Deaf Smith, patting the ugly weapon. "Now then, yer listen, my children, cause I'm gonna tell you a thang not to be missed by healthy young men in west Texas. Who has heerd of John Coffee Hays?"

Deaf Smith got only blank stares from both men.

"Well then, he is a fine young Anglo, from Tennessee like Sam Houston and Ole Andy Jackson and yes, by Gawd, Congressman David Crockett, who died just acrost the river there, was burned and throwed in a common grave with all the other heroes who was at the Alamo."

He had yet to say anything that would change their expressions, which were quizzical. As though they were too polite to ask Smith what the hell John Coffee Hays had to do with the pistol on the table or anything else.

"Well then," Deaf Smith said, a little louder, like he might be disturbed about their hearing correctly. "Jack Hays has started a ranging company here in San Antonio de Bexar, and this is the weapon he'll arm his men with to fight the Comanch' and the Gawddamned Mexicans. Present company exceptioned!"

"*Mi* amigo." Alex Mesero reached across the table and put his hand on Deaf Smith's shoulder. "What does any of this have to do with us, two peace-loving *hombres* who want only to run a little freight back and forth across this new republic?"

"Freight, hell!" Deaf Smith exploded. "Out here on the west edge of Gawddamned civilization, you got to worry about all these enemies you got first, *then* you can haul your Gawddamned freight."

Paco Salazar lifted the pistol and grunted.

"Heavy, but it has a good balance."

"Hell, yes. Ole Sam Colt drawed up the design on er and this one's a .36-caliber percussion. See, here's the nipples where you put on the caps after yer load each cylinder. Load er up Sunday, shoot all week."

Deaf Smith laughed and slapped the table, well satisfied with his own joke.

"Jesus Christ, men, who'd wanta fart around with haulin freight anyway," he said, "when you could be out there dustin Comanches er Mex sojurs?"

"Are you saying we might join this Coffee man?" asked Paco. He was cocking the pistol, releasing the hammer but holding with a thumb to allow it to go down easy on the cap nipples.

"Hays, Hays. Jack Hays," said Deaf Smith. "You bet your breeches I'm sayin join him. I tried my ownself, but he wouldn't have me because he says I'm too old and own property, and he wants young men who don't own farms."

"You own a farm?" asked Alex Mesero.

"On the Trinity," Deaf Smith said, waving his hand about impatiently. "Never mind that."

"Perhaps this Hays man wouldn't want two Mexicans. Present company *not* exceptioned!" Paco laughed.

"That's the best part," said Deaf Smith, ignoring Paco's ridicule of his English usage. "You ever heerd of Antonio Perez?"

"Why, hell yes," said Alex Mesero. "Everybody's heard of him in the barrios. He's an old Indian fighter."

"The same, by Gawd," Deaf Smith shouted, banging the table. "Well, he's gettin together some of you boys who is of the Mexican persuasion to fight alongside them Anglo boys Jack Hays is gettin. All armed with Sam Colt's six-shooter. They call em the Texas Rangers! By Gawd!"

So Paco Salazar's life turned toward ranging with Jack Hays. He was at the fight on the Pedernales, where the Rangers with Colt revolvers, outnumbered five to one, defeated a large group of Comanches, routing the *indios*, killing thirty of them. And they fought Mexican cavalry near Laredo many times, and in one skirmish Paco Salazar saw his friend Alex Mesero run through with a Mexican cavalry lance.

And he had the opportunity to avenge his friend in the same fierce moment, with Mr. Sam Colt's six-shooter. And saw both, amigo and Mexican soldier, die under the same Joshua tree.

And the fighting swept Paco along so fast, he hardly realized what had happened until that evening when they were seeing to their horses and wounded. And burying their dead.

He ranged with Jack Hays during that time when Santa Anna returned to power and his army twice moved on San Antonio and took it, mostly without any bloodshed, and once kidnapped every Anglo man in Bexar, fifty-seven in all, taking them back to Mexico. As prisoners.

In those two instances, Antonio Perez and his men, including Paco Salazar, were far up the Colorado, punishing Kiowas.

The years went on, and the violence never ceased in Texas.

Salazar was wounded in a fight with Comanches along the Nueces, and the *indios* were all around him after he fell, and they cut him and released him so he could run and they could lance him like they would a hunted buffalo, but Antonio Perez and two other Rangers were there in time to save his life but not soon enough to prevent his being scalped.

He was wounded seriously in that fight, and Perez cut him loose and told him, "*Dios mio*, Paco. You're almost forty, too old for this, so go chase some of these little *señoritas* and the younger *caballeros* will chase the Comanche."

So Paco left the Rangers and started doing what seemed to fit him just as well. Not freighting but guiding others along the frontier, this at about the time Texas was finally admitted to the Union as a state.

And he noted that a great many people had been wrong about that. At the end, slavery was no issue.

"Yes sir," said Deaf Smith. "The redcoat British been nosin round east Texas like foxes round the chicken coop."

"Here, too," said Paco Salazar. "I've heard of at least two businessmen loaned money and given promise of protection from Indians by Englishmen."

"Yes sir," said Deaf Smith. "Them British wants in here in the worst way, son, and lotsa folks now start rememberin the Revolution and the War of 1812, and they got a picture in their heads of the British pinchin the U.S. of A. north and south. In Canada and in Texas."

"The *yanqui* government doesn't like that much. English money. Then English soldiers to protect the investment."

"By Gawd, it's so, just like they done in India," Deaf Smith said and snapped his fingers. "You are the smartest Mexican I have *ever* seen. And you can stop gouging the U.S. of A. as the *yanquis*, because right quick, it's gonna be *your* gov'mint, too!"

They were in the usual place. Around that fancy table Alex Mesero had stolen for Paco Salazar's house, drinking tequila with salt and lemon wedges and eating tamales and green chilies and pickled jalapeños.

Before they had drunk and eaten their fill and gone to sleep, throughout the evening at various intervals, Deaf Smith would rise and hold up a glass and make a toast. To Alex. To the heroes of the Alamo. To the martyrs of Goliad.

There were plenty of things for that kind of toasting. The next morning Deaf Smith shook Paco Salazar's hand for a long time, looking into the Mexican's face and grinning.

"Time to say adios, my Mex friend," he said. "Ole Deef gonna go to that little farm on a branch that runs into the Trinity and just snooze a little and sip cactus juice a little and hear them nuts thump the ground when they fall in my pecan grove and smell the black locust next spring and listen one last time to the ole hooty owl in my mulberry tree."

"One last time?" Paco Salazar asked. "What does that mean, amigo?"

"I been old a long, long time, Paco," Smith said, and released Paco Salazar's hand and turned to the door and walked out onto the patio, where his horse waited beside the strawberry roan, and both horses looked up expectantly. Deaf Smith's horse was already saddled, and Paco knew the old man had risen before dawn to get himself and his horse ready.

"I ain't ever seen a horse like that roan," Deaf Smith said. "Eatin them tamales like he does."

"What was it you meant? One last time."

Deaf Smith mounted, grunting elaborately. He grinned down at Paco Salazar and shook his head.

"Hell, son, I hurt in every crease and crevice I got," he said. "And none of it's gonna get any better. I've seed the tiger more'n my share of times, and got no complaint. And now it's time to just set back and let Ole Big Man come get me."

Salazar started to say something, but Deaf Smith held up his hands and shook his head.

"No need to take on about it," he said. "I'll be fine. My place is close to a little settlement called Mexia. Nice little saloon there, family of freedmen niggers can cook a hog better than anybody I ever saw. I'll be fine.

"So adios, amigo. You're a nice man, Paco Salazar, fer a Mexican." And Deaf Smith laughed and wheeled the horse out and through the opening to the street and was gone.

Well, the British scare was real enough. Within days of Deaf Smith's leaving to go home to die, Texas was taken in, and not just from an English scare. There'd been a national election, and the popular sentiment nationwide was for Texas statehood. A convention of prominent Texans convened to write a state constitution acceptable to the Congress of the United States. It was done quickly, and Texas became the twenty-eighth state in December, 1845.

That convention was a gathering of outstanding men. They came originally from many states, mostly southern. But the name of one of them would be carried in Paco Salazar's mind to the grave.

He was Jose Antonio Navarro. As Deaf Smith would have said, a man of the Mexican persuasion. Of all the men at that convention who were on the committee to define the new Lone Star State with a Constitution, he was the only one who had been born in Texas!

Paco Salazar liked that.

Part Two

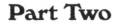

The Germans

Chapter Seven

When somebody tried to assassinate King Frederick William IV of Prussia in 1844, you might suppose they'd have asked Prince Carl of Solms-Braunfels all kinds of embarrassing questions.

Prince Carl possibly had reason to dislike the king. It was Frederick William IV, after all, who had bullheadedly kept to a policy of the divine right of kings, where all power comes down from the ruler, not up from the people. There is considerable evidence that Prince Carl was inclined toward some of the more republican ideas circulating in Europe since the French revolution.

At the time of the assassination attempt, there was plenty to be distressed about in Germany. Not just political things, but economic, as well. Some Junker aristocrats were pretty threadbare and were convinced that a few Frederick the Great–type wars would make things good again.

But everyone knew that Prince Carl was not exactly a bellicose, fierce, and competitive Teutonic knight who thought constantly in terms of how best to go stomp hell out of the French. Or the Russians. Or the Swedes. Or somebody.

He had been heard to say that he disliked war. You might suspect this was not aversion to combat but rather to a fashion of the Prussian officer corps of that time to boast of being men of *Eisen und Blut*. Men of iron and blood slept on the ground like the soldiers, and like the soldiers, they ate nothing but boiled beans and sausage.

So even though everyone might suspect Prince Carl of being unhappy with his lot, nobody supposed he had any more stomach for king killing than he did for boiled beans and sausage.

Besides, when the attempt was made on Frederick's life, Prince Carl was in Texas.

Unlike the rest of Western Europe, German states like Prussia did not use a law of primogeniture to control property inheritance from generation to generation. This meant that the eldest son did not receive the entire inheritance when his father died.

Hence, great aristocratic estates were constantly being divided among all direct heirs of old deceased princes, so holdings by single individuals became smaller and smaller with each passing generation.

This in a time when income was determined by the abundance of a man's acres. These old princely families did not dirty their hands with such things as commerce or the new emerging industries.

There were a lot of German aristocrats who were rather poor in the early nineteenth century. They were still aristocrats, of course, but a lot of them were poor as a *Kirchenmaus,* as the saying goes. Prince Carl of Solms-Braunfels may have been one of these, even though he still had the family castle on the Lahn River.

These Germans were sometimes energetic men, however, as was Prince Carl, and they began casting about for some idealistic objective that would occupy their thinking. For a sort of safe haven from all the revolutionary turmoil in Europe. What better way to find this haven than to encourage and assist their countrymen in planting German culture on New World shores?

A group of them formed a society for German overseas colonization. They had heard of the open spaces and wonderful climate and rich soil and ease of acquiring land cheaply, or even free, in what until recently had been the northern province of Mexico.

In a place now called the Republic of Texas.

They heard that under the old regimes, foreign immigrants had been welcome because the politicians in Mexico City, as in Madrid before, had not been successful in any plan to establish a solid culture throughout the vast land, even though they'd been trying for two hundred years!

Now, the Texans were welcoming newcomers. There was already a considerable population, Mexican and Anglo-Celtic, along the Gulf Coast and east of the Colorado River. But west of there and certainly beyond the Cross Timbers, at about ninety-eight degrees longitude, the land was mostly empty.

There is no record that the Germans understood the main reason Spain and Mexico had been unable to develop a viable society north of the Rio Grande and west of Fort Worth.

To wit: not very many Spanish men of substance were eager to expose their families to life in a country so broad and empty that normal government protection was pretty much nonexistent, except maybe in towns.

Beyond the towns, in the open, it wasn't only sandstorms and hail and tornadoes and white or Mexican *banditos* and rattlesnakes and scorpions.

It was Apaches. Well, it had once been Apaches. By the time the Germans became interested in Texas, the Apaches had been chased out of Texas. Except for the Lipans, who were scattered along the Rio Grande River. Now, the problem was the bunch that had chased the Apaches out. The Comanches.

Nor is it likely that the Germans knew that beyond the Cross Timbers, where the largest empty lands lay, it was typical High Plains country. Rock-hard soil, harsh winters, no trees, and scarce water.

Nor is there any hint that at the time of the decision to colonize beyond San Antonio the German aristocrats were aware that when Texas became a part of the United States of America, which would be soon, a war between Mexico and the Americans was inevitable — to determine, among other things, if their border was at the Rio Grande or the Nueces.

Maybe it didn't matter. The Prussians figured Texas suited their purpose of pan-Germanism for the benefit of the hard-working farmers who wanted to take advantage of cheap, wide-open spaces.

Maybe the Teutonic style of land speculation, unlike frontier speculation by most others, did not have as its major object making a lot of money for those who stayed behind.

So a group of nobles and aristocrats got together for this venture. They knew there would be plenty of common folk ready to go pioneering. There were all kinds of obvious reasons and just as many not so obvious.

Germany was getting crowded, for one thing. Even for yeomen farmers who had for centuries lived in the same house with their livestock, *die Menschen* upstairs, the cows below. Even people accustomed to this were complaining of population pinch.

And for everybody, there was an electric tension in the air. It was the time of Metternich's tightrope diplomacy and student riots and little revolutions popping up everywhere, frantic republicanism and rabble at the barricades. It was enough to turn the stomach of any traditional, conservative burgher or farmer or merchant. Not to mention of any aristocrat.

And just look at the New World, the Germans thought. Better get involved, because it wasn't going to stay new much longer.

Beautiful vistas. Rich soil. Balmy climate. Plenty of space. Each man his own king. Why, Hoffman Von Fallersleben had written a song about it: "On to Texas—Makes every heart burn with joy." A lot of credibility there. After all, he'd written "Deutschland, Deutschland Uber Alles," the German national anthem.

Everybody had read James Fenimore Cooper's books, "The Leather-Stocking Tales" and "The Last of the Mohicans." German youngsters at play with toy bows and toy arrows called one another Hawkeye and Deerslayer.

In the weekly magazines there were illustrations of the Noble Savage of America, his body discreetly covered yet with enough well-developed muscle showing to provoke gasps from the young ladies.

He was paying court to *das indianische Mädchen*, she always shown sitting beside the placid stream, eyes downcast with proper Victorian modesty, her smock exquisitely tailored, the fringes from her sleeves like Spanish lace. Perhaps there was a feather in her hair. A peacock feather.

In the background, some of the artists liked to place thick trees and lush ferns, a waterfall, and of course a peacock. And in the distance, faintly, as if in moonlight, what appeared to be a Greek temple or maybe a castle on the Rhine.

So Germany was full of people, common cobbler or turnip farmer, government bureaucrat or lord of the manor, who were anxious to get on toward Texas. There was so much talk of it, so much written about it, so many illustrations, that every literate German felt they knew all about Texas. Why, they'd even seen a map of it in *die Zeitung von Sonntag*. There would be no trouble filling the lists of recruits for a German colony in Texas.

So those aristocrats and noble gentlemen produced a document identifying their group as *Adelsverein*. Which meant the Society to Protect German Colonists in Texas, or some such thing.

They drank a toast with good Moselle wine, you would suppose. They bestowed the honor and responsibility of being advance skirmisher on Prince Carl of Solms-Braunfels and dispatched him in the direction of North America and the large plot of land already bought by two of their agents previously sent to Texas and since returned with glowing tales of Texas grandness. This from men who had actually seen Texas. Not a picture of it on paper, but the glorious land itself!

These men had also brought what was purported to be a deed for a very large piece of real estate.

They called it the Tract.

Prince Carl had not departed Bremenhaven when he suddenly realized that in the New World his land dealings would not be with Texas, as they had planned. His dealings would be with the United States, where there were high tariffs and good, black farming soil that was much more expensive and probably sought after by more people.

But the American consulate, where Prince Carl appeared wild eyed and visibly near nervous collapse, informed him that anyone desiring Texas land would be dealing with the state of Texas. One of the provisions of Texas joining the United States had been that Texas would retain all its public lands to administer itself.

You can bet Prince Carl said a silent *Gott sei Dank*. Anywhere else in the North American union, if you wanted public land, you dealt with the United States. Where Prince Carl was headed, you only had to deal with *die Bauer*, the local rustics. Thank God for Texas. Thank God, indeed!

It was wonderfully good news, and before he took ship for the eight-week trip to the western hemisphere, Prince Carl wrote his *Adelsverein* colleagues, congratulating himself on the good luck he'd always had due to the fact, he claimed, that he was a cousin of Queen Victoria.

There is no record of what Queen Victoria had to do with any of this, but apparently Prince Carl thought well enough of the idea to commit it to paper.

It was a nice touch, because at this time most Germans had a high and reverent regard for Great Britain and the little Queen there who, they were always quick to point out, was a Hanover and spoke German when she was alone with Albert in her private quarters.

Of course, what Prince Carl did not say was that half the aristocrats in Germany claimed to be Queen Victoria's cousins. And in fact, most of them probably were!

Prince Carl arrived on the Gulf Coast of Texas as advance man for *Adelsverein* with a retinue worthy of a British field marshal. There was a cook and a saddler and a surveyor and a man named Gottlieb Waldenburg, who wore lederhosen and was called the official hunter for Prince Carl.

This man, whose name meant hill in the forest, was the last of the Waldenburgs, who had served as *Jägers* for the Braunfels family in their timbered lands, back when the Braunfels still had timbered lands. All the male ancestors Gottlieb Waldenburg knew about had been in service to the Lords of Solms-Braunfels Manor as *Jägers*.

Jägers were German forest rangers and game managers. In the old country, they belonged to a respected group whose major function was to prevent common peasants from killing any of the roebuck and hares or cutting any of the trees in the lord of the manors' forests.

This particular trusted retainer was a short man, sour of face and pale blue of eyes. He had a great, flaring Moses beard. He understood his importance, even though you might wonder what a German *Jäger* was doing in frontier Texas, where every man and some of the women went about armed and might shoot anything that was edible and within range.

Herr Waldenburg carried himself with dignity and a show of contempt for the locals, even though it was very soon apparent that he surely enjoyed the locals' beverages, like *cerveza negra*, the Mexican dark beer.

Wherever the Prince went, Herr Waldenburg was not far behind, carrying one or the other of two fine double barrel English hunting guns, which although muzzle loading, were percussion-lock rifles that fired conical bullets, not balls.

One Anglo Texan, who like all Texicans thought himself an expert on firearms, asked, "I wonder if one of them pretty little popguns would put down a rutting bull buffler?"

"No matter," said another Texan. "If it didn't, the little pumpernickel could scowl him to death."

Most of the local Mexicans came to identify the hunter as that angry little Gringo who wore a little *pluma verde* on his little *sombrero azul*, A green feather on his blue hat. Or they called him *la cara de maleza*. Thicket face!

Waldenburg inquired of a Mexican man helping with the purchase of mules for the trip if he would guide the *Jäger* and Prince Carl into the forest primeval, where they might observe one of these buffalos and perhaps shoot it.

Showing the usual Mexican friendliness, tact, and native grace, the man did not laugh. Later he told some of his friends of the German's request.

"What did you tell him?"

"I told him that buffalo are not far away but that they do not live in *el bosque*. They live on the prairie. And if he went to see them, he should take with him many armed men."

"Did he ask why? *Por que?*"

"*Sí.* And I said, 'Because, Señor, sometimes the Comanches like to come see the buffalo, too.'"

Now everybody laughed.

"These *alem* . . . *!* These Germans! Funny! The next time he talks to you, ask him if he would show us one of these primeval *bosques*. Never have I seen such a forest!"

They all laughed again.

Maybe Waldenburg would have looked angrier still had he known the fun the Mexicans were having with him behind his back. Now they spoke of him as the angry little man with the little feather in *el sombrero pristino*, the primeval hat.

Unlike his Prince, Waldenburg had a family following with the main body of colonists. His wife, Gretel, and their youngest child, a daughter named Sophia, who was fifteen.

He was enjoying his freedom from these two as much as possible, having spent most of his life being nagged by one and scorned by the other. All his earlier love and passion for Gretel had long since burned to a blackened cinder, and as for the girl, she frightened him a little.

Prince Carl promptly made a fool of himself in the eyes of the Texans, who recently had fought a tough little war, when he began going about in a gaudy military uniform that would have made Santa Anna blush.

It wasn't a thing that sat too well with the people who had only recently been terrified at the approach of people in uniforms.

Galveston was the major port of entry for immigrants arriving in Texas by sea, many of whom transshipped from New Orleans. Naturally there was a state land office in Galveston.

When Prince Carl, with his hunter, went to call at the state land office and asked to see a map of the holdings his society had purchased, they stared at him for a long time, silently.

Rather reluctantly, they unrolled a chart of Texas and laid it out and explained that the Tract was far to the northwest, on hard, rocky ground with no water and no trees, in the middle of a major Comanche range, and many miles beyond any other Mexican or Anglo-American settlement.

Needless to say, the men who had sold this land to the earlier advance agents of the *Adelsverein* had long since departed Texas.

Prince Carl was flabbergasted. But undeterred. He would go out himself, in the general direction of the Tract, and buy land, land that he could see with his own eyes before opening his purse of silver and gold.

Good, said the Texans. There was a land office in Bexar.

So the Prince spent a week collecting transport and hiring Mexicans as guides and general workers. It wasn't difficult, hiring Mexicans. Those European coins were very desirable. In fact, any coins were desirable to a people who hadn't seen hard money for such a long time.

Before his cavalcade arrived in San Antonio de Bexar, Prince Carl had begun to appreciate the size of Texas and the variety of landforms there. His Mexican employees named the different kinds of trees and grasses and birds they saw and gave helpful advice on how to find water between major streams.

Also, they pointed out gullies, rock outcrops, streambeds, and other terrain features affording protection for a few men against chance encounters with roving gangs of drunk *indios*.

Prince Carl paused once, sitting his mule like a Black Forest knight, back straight, eyes squinting against the Texas prairie's glare, and asked if they might see *ein Heideindianer*. It took a while for the Mexicans to translate that.

On another mule, the official hunter Waldenburg gripped one of his double-barrel rifles expectantly.

"No, Señor," said Paco Salazar, the major-domo of the Mexican work party Prince Carl had employed. "No heathen Indians here, unless we see a party on the way to the coast to get salt or fish."

"Oh," said Prince Carl, disappointment in his voice. "I'd hoped to see one of these war parties I've heard mentioned."

"No, Señor," said Salazar. "If there are any like that here now, I have not heard of it. And if there were, we would only see those who wanted to be seen."

"Ah," said Prince Carl, as though he understood. "But could they watch us in passing? Could they see us?"

Paco Salazar and the other Mexicans looked at Prince Carl's scarlet hat streaming feathers, his sashes, brass buttons, medallions, ivory saber hilt, all shimmering brightly in the Texas sun.

"Sí, Señor," Salazar said as the other men tried to cover wide grins. "They would see you. From far off."

On this march from the Gulf of Mexico to San Antonio de Bexar, it became clear that though he had been a fool in other ways, Prince Carl had selected a good man for the boss, *el jefe*, of his workers.

Credit for this must be given an old German named Buche, who had lived on and off the coast of Texas since before the American-British War of 1812.

It was said he had been one of Jean Lafitte's pirates and had fought at the Battle of New Orleans. All anyone knew for sure was that he'd lived with a woman in a small Mexican fishing village on Matagordo Bay for some years and made a nuisance of himself with anybody who would talk to him.

Prince Carl had wanted to talk, all right, because he needed help and Buche might give it without their having to wallow around in English translations.

"*Un jefe* for a trip to Bexar?" asked Buche. "Of course. He's in town, too, just brought down a cart train of hides. Name's Salazar. Best man around for your purpose."

"And he's Spanish?"

"Hell no. He's Mexican," said Buche. "But he don't look it. Got skin color very near white as your own. Gray eyes. Modest mustache, not one of these outrageous cow-horn types so many Mexican men seem to admire. Does look very Indian, though. Matter of fact, you might say he's not Mexican but Texan, although Anglo Texans wouldn't call him that. But he fought at San Jacinto. You've heard of San Jacinto?"

"*Ja.* Since I've been here, I've heard of it so often I'm getting sick to my stomach at the name."

"Prince, don't say that to any of these Texans, even if it does make you puke."

"*Ja, ja, ja,* all right. This man, what, Salazar. Might he hire people I need?"

"Most assuredly," Buche said. "He has great experience on the plains. He was scalped once by Comanches, I've heard it said. I would guess Comanches. *Ja.*"

"Scalped?" Prince Carl was aghast. "But how could that be?"

"Oh, they took a little piece, back here." And Buche removed his hat and lay his hand flat on the back of his head. "You'd never know. He wears his hair in a queue at the back, like many men here. He was with the Texas Rangers off and on for a time. Served against hostile tribes and Mexican bandits and Mexican army troops."

"I've heard of these Texas state police," said Prince Carl. "I had supposed they were all white men."

"No, they've had a few Mexicans. Salazar was with John Coffee Hays when Hays led a body of Rangers against Comanches the first time they used Mr. Samuel Colt's six-shooter pistol. And they do not consider themselves state police as they would in Prussia."

"Incredible. But then why isn't this man in the war that's going on now?"

"That's the incredible thing here. Some ignorant United States Army officer refused to sign Salazar on as a scout because he's a Mexican, even after somebody explained that there are a lot of Texans who are Mexicans. American citizens. But Salazar was miffed and said he'd had enough war anyway, so Texas doesn't get his service this time. You do!"

"Then this man might assist me in my efforts?" Prince Carl asked.

"Prince," said Buche, who had been in the New World so long all that old German reverence for royalty had worn off, "this man is mule driver, man driver, vaquero, shootist, scout, old soldier, and for all I know can tell your fortune. Hire him. If anybody in Texas can help you, this is the man. Best of all, he's not married. They tell me he took a vow never to marry back when his family was wiped out during all the revolutions of past years. I don't know why he'd do such a thing. But you can't tell about these Mexicans. And don't be inquisitive about it; he might shoot off your top knot."

So Prince Carl had found Salazar, expecting to be disappointed after Herr Buche's elaborate compliments. It didn't work that way.

Paco. That's the given name Prince Carl knew. He was taller than most Mexican men Prince Carl had been near, but he had that same characteristic flowing movement of all the necessary muscles.

The Mexican workers liked him because although he worked them hard, he enjoyed a little fun now and then. As on the day he spoke quietly to Gottlieb Waldenburg, out of Prince Carl's hearing.

"Señor, don't make the mistake many of the Gringos do," said Salazar. "They have heard that *indio* fighting is done in daylight, under bright sun. Remember, Comanches like to attack you late at night, too. To cut your throat and steal your mules. They like the time when the stars are growing weak in the hour before the sun.

"When sleep has almost come and you hear in the darkness close on either side of your camp the call of two mockingbirds, rise up and look to your weapons, Señor. Those may not be mockingbirds."

And he clucked and ran a finger across his throat ominously.

That night, the party stopped in a grove of pecan trees. Four times, Prince Carl's official hunter leaped from his bedroll, clutching a double-barrel musket. Pecan groves are a favorite place for night-singing Texas mockingbirds.

Of course, on that night the calls came from night singing Paco Salazar and one of his men.

Well, the warning was not just a joke. To Prince Carl later, at a campfire, one of the best places to speak seriously, and after Waldenburg was in his bedroll, Salazar explained the night-raiding proclivities of Comanches. And while he was about it, of the Kiowas, too.

It wasn't all jokes with the *Jäger* either. Maybe after the mockingbirds, Paco Salazar felt sorry for Waldenburg. So he told Waldenburg he would teach him the Comanche language because in the future it would undoubtedly be useful in dealings with any of the local tribesmen who might be passing through, and with whom the Germans would have to do business.

"Why Comanche, and not one of these other tribal lingoes?" asked Waldenburg, because by then Waldenburg had been observant enough to see that there were a great many kinds of Indians in Texas.

"*El indio* here speaks Comanche, Señor," Salazar said. "On the Southern Plains, it is the language of *el negocio*. Of trade."

Astonishingly, Gottlieb Waldenburg was very good with languages, and Comanche is a speech of few complexities, so he learned quickly.

You might find it remarkable that teacher and pupil in this were not only teaching and being taught a language not native to either of them, but they communicated with one another in English, which was not native to them either.

Salazar tried to explain as much history as he could to Prince Carl as they moved toward the dream of *Adelsverein*. The Mexican didn't know all of it, but he had a good handle on the prime factors, and there was enough to make the hair on the back of Prince Carl's aristocratic neck stand up now and then.

Comanchera was the name given to a vast, ill-defined area of west Texas running from the Staked Plains southwest across the headwaters country of the Nueces, Colorado, Guadalupe, Brazos, and Trinity Rivers, and to within a few miles of San Antonio de Bexar along the Balcones Escarpment.

It had been the range of many bands of Comanches for over a hundred years, since they had ridden down into the Southern Plains and driven everybody else out and claimed the land for their own.

Well, they hadn't driven out a few of the other tribes, the ones they felt were no threat.

And this was Texas ground now, the public domain. Yet there had been no rush of settlers into most of this area, no matter if a good deal was offered by the state, because to settle on ground contested by Comanches took a tough and resolute pioneer, Salazar said.

When Prince Carl arrived in the Land of Promise, the butcher's bill of west Texas settlers dead or taken captive in Comanche and

Kiowa raids was about two hundred a year, according to the best estimates of Texas officials.

It didn't take too long for the German to realize that settling some parts of the Lone Star State might appear inexpensive but that bills of sale never mentioned how awkward it got when your neighbors were bad tempered, heavily armed, and had what they figured were some pretty serious grievances against you and all your tribe.

Much of the choice land on the near side of Comanchera had already been bought up by *empresarios*. These were men who would have been called land speculators on any other border. With money or the promise of it, they procured land from the state at rock-bottom prices, then sold it to immigrants who had the anticipation of land shining on their faces.

Some of these *empresarios* were honest, trustworthy men. The first two of them with whom Prince Carl of Solms-Braunfels did business in San Antonio de Bexar were not.

Prince Carl bought a large tract of land from the first one, then another tract from the second. And despite what he'd said, he bought these without seeing the land. Salazar saw the chart-map location of these plots and swore and threw his sombrero on the ground.

"We'll not go with you to those places, Señor," he shouted. "I know there will be no pay for me and the others if we stop now, but we won't go there!"

"Why not, in God's name?"

"*Sí! En el nombre de Dios!* That place is fifty leagues north of Bexar, on the Colorado River."

Prince Carl shook the chart-map. Fifty leagues? One hundred fifty miles! He shook the chart-map again.

"I'm going to find somebody and see about this," he said. "I'm going to see the *alcalde*, or whatever it is, the mayor or the governor."

"Come, Señor," said Salazar, yanking his hat back down on his head. "I'll show you the land man from Bexar. Why didn't you ask me first, Señor? You have to pick only a few men to trust in these places. Then trust no one else. *Comprende?*"

They found that in addition to selling him bad land, the Texas gentlemen who had taken Prince Carl's German gold and English sterling did not own a single acre of either tract. In a roaring fury, Prince Carl wanted to know where he could find these scoundrels, and he gripped the hilt of his saber so tightly his knuckles turned white.

Gottlieb Waldenburg was ready, with a double-barrel rifle held at high port, like a Prussian infantryman ready to assail the Russians.

"Bet your best dog you'll find em in Veracruz," said a Texan lounging in the land office. "Or maybe New Orleans."

There was a great deal of laughter. By evening, when it seemed everyone in San Antonio had heard of the German's problem, he swallowed his rancor and bought rounds of Mexican beer in one of the Anglo saloons. Everyone assured him they would find a trustworthy land agent for him in the morning.

Prince Carl perhaps drank too many tankards of the beer and began to wax eloquent about Texas hospitality, but he ended on a bad note, of course.

"There is this one thing I find disagreeable," he said. "I do not stand with slavery. I note that some men here do indeed own Africans. When we establish our settlement, there will be none of that, I can assure you."

The room grew quiet, and people began to drift out. They didn't make a headlong dash. But they were all going, many leaving half-full tankards.

"Some of the slave owners were Germans, too," Prince Carl mumbled as he found his way to his camp near the old Franciscan mission, where Waldenburg had long since staggered to his bedroll but where Paco Salazar was awake, waiting.

"Herr Salazar," Prince Carl said as he drew his bedroll over his face, "I am not so sure now that Texas is a place of beauty and light as we were told in the old country. I think it is a place of sand and wind and spiders and thieves."

"We will find your land for you tomorrow," the Mexican said. "One of the churches here we will go to in the morning for a small Mass and confession, and maybe ask the Virgin of Guadalupe to guide us."

"Of course." From under his bedding, Prince Carl's voice was muffled. "I have overlooked my Christian duty. We will go, we will find everything."

Maybe Prince Carl's change of luck was the result of his prayers. There is no doubt that he bought land for which he could claim true title along the Guadalupe River.

Of course, his Guadalupe was a long way from the old Tepeyac causeway into Mexico City where the vision of the Virgin was said to have appeared to a newly baptized *indio* named Juan Diego back in 1531, a vision revered ever since as the Lady of Guadalupe.

If Prince Carl thought he had divine assistance from a vision accepted by the Catholic Church as a true miracle over three hundred years earlier, he never mentioned it to anybody. Which was understandable when you consider that most of the colonists coming on behind him were Lutherans.

The land was less than fifty miles north and a little east of San Antonio de Bexar, near the Balcones Escarpment. It was beautiful land, with pecan trees, a few post oaks, and what a lot of people called a live oak but which was really an ancient red oak, on the crest of the only distinct ridge in the area.

Most unusual were a few cypress trees along the stream line, close to the Balcones, which you'd think was too far north and too dry to accommodate cypress.

But there they were. Prince Carl saw them and said to Paco Salazar, "*Danke die Jungfrau aus* Guadalupe!"

Here the water of the Gaudalupe and its tributary branches ran clear over shallow gravel beds. The soil was limestone, and very rocky. Close by was good, deep, black soil, excellent for grains and potatoes and pasture, but not much of this land was in Prince Carl's plot.

Salazar noticed this and hoped Prince Carl would not, because he might think it proper to retract his prayer of thanks to the Virgin of Guadalupe, and Salazar wasn't sure how such a thing might turn out.

Not that he was afraid. He'd never been too concerned with the wrath of saints. Maybe he just didn't want to embarrass the German.

By this time, Salazar had decided the Prince was crazy as a tumble-bug, but rather a harmless, nice fellow. For whatever reason, he agreed that the land Prince Carl had bought was delightful

Prince Carl knew the colonists were arriving on the coast, more than two hundred miles to the southeast. He must go there to lead them back. There was no time to lose, and he started his men to work, charging his loyal *Jäger*, Gottlieb Waldenburg, with the responsibility for the entire project during his own absence.

But before Prince Carl departed, he personally saw to the construction of a long, low, log building with a rough shake-shingle roof.

He named the place New Braunfels, waiting until the last moment to announce his plan for taking Paco Salazar with him to the coast. He left behind a stunned and somewhat anguished Waldenburg, who had no desire or ambition for such a vast responsibility.

No longer just the Official Hunter, but now the Chief, Gottlieb took more and more solace from the earthen jugs, beginning almost before his Prince and the Mexican major-domo, whom Waldenburg had supposed would be left to supervise the work, had ridden out of sight down the Guadalupe.

He found that he had learned more of the Comanche tongue from Salazar than he had Spanish, so his most usual means of communicating with his Mexican workers was in Comanche.

But in the construction of wooden houses with roofs and in the laying out of vineyards, there were a great many things for which words were not provided in Comanche. The Mexicans, once more with their native polite demeanor, made it as easy as possible for *el jefe nuevo.*

Which meant the Mexicans mostly nodded and grinned when Waldenburg shouted orders, ignored what he said, and built what was required.

History does not instruct us as to when Prince Carl came to the decision concerning his next move. Nor is there any record of why he opted to return to Germany. Maybe he was homesick. Or perhaps the trials of his endeavors at land acquisition in Texas were too much for his pride and self-esteem.

But now, Prince Carl simply dropped out of the story. The colonists, who were by this time landed, were at Indianola, a settlement on Lavaca Bay, a part of Matagordo Bay, at the mouth of the Guadalupe River. They had moved there from Galveston, their port of entry, according to instructions sent previously by Prince Carl.

Perhaps Prince Carl actually saw and passed on the mission to the man *Adelsverein* had designated commander of this group. More likely, from his appearance of haste to get home, he went directly to

Galveston. The colonists waiting on the miserable salt flats at Lavaca Bay came to know of his leaving only when one of Paco Salazar's men came to them and told them.

In fact, there was a time when the whereabouts of Paco Salazar were uncertain. Uncertain, too, was what part he played in any of this.

There is still considerable confusion about Prince Carl's movements. A slave in Victoria said he had seen the Prince there, with his red sash and plumed hat. A Mexican vaquero near Goliad reported the Prince passing there. A tavern keeper in Galveston claimed he stayed there for two nights.

One chronicler wrote that Solms-Braunfels led a large group back to the Balcones. Another assured his readers that he had taken a large group there on his first trip.

Listening to the people who knew him best was equally confusing. When Prince Carl was mentioned, what little of Gottlieb Waldenburg's face was visible above his beard would turn purple.

"*Lügner! Das Versprechen* he made with me broken!" he would snap. And maybe Prince Carl did lie and break a promise to his trusted *Jäger*. Maybe Prince Carl promised Waldenburg silver and gold. Nobody knows.

Prince Carl's cook, an invalid army pensioner named Haig, would shake his head and perhaps even shed a tear and say, "Ach, *der kleine* Carl. *Einsamkeit, Einsamkeit!* Little Carl, I'm so sorry for him, so lonely he was."

All Paco Salazar would say was, "*Mi* amigo," and nobody tried to push it any farther. It might have made Prince Carl happy to know the Mexican whom he admired had called him a friend.

Maybe the best and most accurate of all was the remark made by a mestizo lady of the evening in Galveston, whose name is lost to history and who could not have known Prince Carl for more than an hour or so.

"Señor Carlo *es un hombre muy confuso!*" And so he was. A very confused man.

It didn't really matter. What mattered was that now the story of German colonization north of Bexar took on a completely new character. And Prince Carl of Solms-Braunfels would never again play any part in it.

Now the man would be Heinrich Klaus von Meullerbach.

Chapter Eight

The people of *Adelsverein* squatted on the tidewater flats of Lavaca Bay and cursed the gnats and flies, the intense heat of day, and the bone-chilling cold of night, but most of all the clinging air heavy with moisture.

The humidity was a double concern because they were of a generation that still believed that most serious illness was caused by night vapors. So added to discomfort was the prospect of lethal malady, from which there was no escape because they were in the open, their only shelter the makeshift tents they threw up made of clothing and anything else they might find along the beach to hang over their heads.

"I feel like *der Uferwanderer*, a what-you-call-it."

"Beachcomber."

"*Ja!* And in the English always we are supposed to be talking. How you say, *ist aufreizend?*"

"Irritating?"

"*Ja!* And before long, we are going to have *Tod* some more with these peoples."

"More deaths."

"*Ja!* That word I know in the English."

They'd lost four of their number during the horrid eight-week sea voyage. Some said it was vapors, but it was typhus. Few among them knew this was a disease carried by mites and fleas whose hosts were the ship's infected rats. In fact, only a few even recognized typhus.

Everybody had suffered from seasickness. The sailors said it was the worst spring they'd ever seen on the Atlantic. The ship, an old Dutch brig, pitched and rolled wildly.

So nobody much noticed when the first one of their number grew sicker than usual, then became listless, then developed chills, fever. But they noticed when he became delirious, screaming hideously and writhing like a cut snake on the deck. Then the sudden quiet of coma, which was short. Death after the onset of fever at sundown came at sunup.

An old Prussian soldier, a drummer boy in the last campaign against Napoleon, helped wrap the body and slide it over the side after the ship's captain read his short burial at sea service from the little black book all ship captains have.

"*Schnell*," the old soldier said. "*Schnell*. As fast as the cholera. And on the cholera we put the name. *Ja! Der alte rasche Mörder!* Old Quick Killer!"

They had hoped that leaving the ship they'd left the sickness. But it had hardly begun. The rats on the boat that had transshipped them from Galveston were infected, too. And the incubation period for typhus is about two weeks.

The second day ashore, another man died. He was Wilhelm Hans Schiller, an armor artificer from Essen. As a youth, he had trained under the tutelage of old Friedrich Krupp in the great iron works on the banks of the Ruhr in Westphalia.

He was almost forty, a Lutheran, a widower with no children accompanying him. He had left a successful career in the Ruhr works for the chance of starting a new life away from the smoke and the hot steel.

He had paid his two-hundred-forty-dollar fee to become a part of *Adelsverein* with a light and happy heart, and with great expectations for an autumn of life spent puttering about in his own turnip patch, with perhaps a few hops as well. In a German settlement there would certainly be plenty of demand for good hops!

On shipboard he had met Sophia Waldenburg, whose mother was quick to point out that here was the fine daughter of a man who had gone ahead with Prince Carl of Solms-Braunfels, a very important man indeed, official hunter to the Prince.

Almost immediately, Wilhelm Hans Schiller had seen the many advantages of having a strong young wife to make his bratwurst and brew his sauerkraut as he stroked his turnips and hops in the fields all day under the tender Texas sun.

Besides, it wouldn't hurt to be married into the family of Prince Carl's *Jäger*, even though they were Catholic. No worry about religion was part of *der amerikanische Traum*. The American Dream everybody was always talking about.

As for Gretel Waldenburg, the hope of finding a husband for a headstrong young woman who grew less manageable by the hour was so appealing it took her breath away. And this Herr Schiller was a solid, respectable man in an honored profession who would provide security for her Sophia even if the turnips and hops didn't work out.

Sophia was ready to marry anybody. She was sick of being treated like a child in the society of the other women in this endeavor, and she wanted to be Frau Anything rather than continue as Fräulein Sophia.

Their long sea voyage was not a romantic interlude of panting and sighing lovers locked in one another's arms, whispering endearing lies and kissing passionately. Marriages among these people at this time seldom had such preludes, even in normal circumstances on dry land. People married for convenience or business or other practical reasons.

So romantic clutching and pawing and pressing of lips was out of the question, especially with both parties to the contract seasick most of the time.

But married they were, on a terrible day. The sky was lead gray, the cold rain came in squalls, the ship pitched and rolled. The sails of their square-rigger were half reefed, but still they snapped and popped.

The old Prussian soldier, standing as the groom's best man, later said the noise of the damned sails recalled the sound of cannon at Jena. The result of that Prussian defeat was Napoleon naming his brother Jerome King of Westphalia.

The old soldier had a peculiarly Prussian and distinctively military obscenity, which he used with considerable imagination in describing King Jerome's backside. In other words, the memories roused by the slapping sails were decidedly unpleasant.

One of the Lutheran ministers in the party said the service, since the only Catholic priest on board was too deathly sick to preside. The minister shouted it, actually, in order to be heard above the howl of wind in the sheets and braces. It was a ceremony bathed in salt spray.

Faces of bride and groom were pale green. The preacher's complexion was about the same. A small group of colonists had gathered on deck at the mainmast for the service. Among them all, the only face showing any signs of the delight usually associated with such happy occasions was Gretel Waldenburg's.

For the rest of the voyage, Sophia bundled her bedroll against Herr Schiller's bedroll at his place on the deck, but one or the other or both were always too ill to get on with the business of being husband and wife. As far as Gretel Waldenburg could tell, anyway.

So ashore, when Herr Schiller succumbed to the bites of ship's rats' fleas, leaving Sophia wailing and wiping tears, at least for what she considered an appropriate interval, it was natural for the good Lutheran Pastor Bauer to inquire if the marriage had been consummated.

"It was such a short time," he said. "And if it was never indeed a marriage, my child, we may consider it annulled rather than have you suffer widowhood so young and innocently."

"Oh, *Ja! Ja!*" cried Frau Waldenburg, who was unstrung at the idea that anyone might suspect that her son-in-law, being a man, could resist the charms of her daughter, even if the bridal chamber was a damp bedroll on a slick ship's deck. With everybody seasick besides. "It has been a marriage, pastor, *Ja, ja!*"

Sophia agreed. No matter to her, really, that there had been not the hint of consummation. She had no intention of giving up her new status in the group, that of a married Frau. And now maybe even better, of *die Witwe* Schiller. Sophia rather liked the sound of it.

So now it was to be the Widow Schiller. Such a young widow. Frau Wilmeth Meullerbach, wife of the new *Adelsverein* commander, began to take Sophia under her own considerably influential wing, which left Sophia's mother beaming with pride.

And why not? Her husband, official hunter and close associate of the former commander, would undoubtedly have a similar position with the new man. And now her daughter. How would you put it? Lady in waiting? *Ja!* Lady in waiting to the wife of the new commandant.

Frau Gretel Waldenburg was, without knowing it, the perfect example of so many of the *Adelsverein* folk. She was going to the land, according to all they'd been told, of soft sunrises, the land of growing green things, the land where the skies would shine Prussian blue over their contentment during four gentle seasons.

A new and peaceful life was opening to her, and now already her position in the group was to be powerfully enhanced by her daughter's marriage, and to a good man, of solid German industry. She had the prospect of many grandchildren around her cottage, where she and her respected husband, the *Jäger*, the official hunter, could sit in the evening and play with the puppies and sip dark beer and eat the cheeses her daughter had made in her own kitchen.

Well, part of that had been cruelly interrupted, almost aborning. But it would all be regained soon, in this wonderful Texas. All around were young men, unmarried men, going to the land of cherries and cows' cream, who soon would see Sophia's beauty. Everything was good, everything would happen wonderfully.

It was not an unusual dream. It was much like other dreams among those pioneers to Texas, of coming at last to a heaven on earth, or as near as anything ever comes to that, already the horizon brightening with promise.

They had just begun the trek north when Frau Gretel Waldenburg died of typhus. It was raining. She lay in her bedroll in the mud in the open because there was no shelter. The ministers of the gospel and a few of the women tried to shield her. But the rain still fell in her face as she gripped her daughter's hands.

At the end, she rose from her typhus delirium long enough to speak, looking into Sophia's weeping face, the girl bending over, trying to shield her mother from the rain.

"Don't let them leave me out on the prairie. Please, bury me. Bury me. Don't let the birds peck out my eyes."

That was all. They buried her, and Sophia lay on the grave in the mud, shaking, until Frau Meullerbach gently helped her away, Sophia still sobbing, "*Mutti, Mutti.*"

After that, Sophia became truly a part of the Meullerbach household. You see, as Frau Meullerbach explained, Sophia was still only a young girl, and in addition to being a sad widow, she was now an orphan as well. At least until they arrived at wherever it was the Prince had left her *Vater*, Gottlieb Waldenburg.

The immigrant leader, and with Prince Carl's exit the leader of the whole shebang, was Heinrich Klaus von Meullerbach. He was just as aristocratic as Prince Carl, although he didn't claim to be Queen Victoria's cousin.

There were other differences between them that Texans could not help but notice. Meullerbach was a Lutheran. This set well with Texas

Anglos, most of whom were Protestants. The fact that his group had many members who were Catholic seemed to indicate his tolerance, which set well with Texas Mexicans.

He didn't go around in outlandish uniforms, a relief to everybody, and he was sensitive enough to take United States citizenship in Galveston, signing "Henry Meuller" on all appropriate documents.

And he quickly showed his willingness to recognize that local Anglos and Mexicans knew infinitely more about this place than he did. The fact that he was cleanshaven, which made him appear younger than his contemporary Germans, helped him to ask questions without seeming to patronize people whose advice he needed.

In their first meeting, he and Paco Salazar began to take stock of one another.

"Never have I seen Heinrich so quickly enjoy a strange man's company," said Frau Meuller to the other leading ladies of the colony. "Like the brother, he treats this Herr Salazar.

"Have ever you seen hats so huge as they wear, these men? Sombreros. That's what they call hats. You see? I'm doing as Heinrich says. I'm learning their language. And the English, too."

Paco Salazar was learning, too. That this Henry Meuller wasn't likely to leave himself open to behind-the-back jokes, as Prince Carl did. He was no idealistic fool, but he might be too ambitious. Not for himself, but for *Adelsverein*.

As for himself, Paco Salazar made no mention of his past decade of violent action with the Texas Army of Independence and then with the Texas Rangers. That was behind him now, and Paco Salazar was the picture of peace.

But always beneath his sash or serape there was a large-bore Colt percussion revolver, and there was always a second one in his saddlebag. Almost everybody in Texas knew Paco Salazar had ridden with Antonio Perez and Jack Hays. They knew about the pistols, too. But the Germans didn't.

As for Meuller, he agreed with one of Prince Carl's decisions anyway. Selecting Paco Salazar as major-domo had been a stroke of good fortune. He was ready to face difficulties head-on, and he seemed to possess one trait of character a Prussian leader expected in a subordinate: unquestioning loyalty.

Their first decision together proved to each man that he could work easily with the other. It had been on the beach.

"Herr Salazar," Meuller said. "You will know our route, of course."

"Yes, Señor," said Salazar. "Direction is easy. We will follow generally the Guadalupe. But it will be slow. Women and children always make a journey slower."

"But it is not far," said Meuller. "Not according to the chart I have."

"Señor," Salazar had said and laughed. "In Texas, there is no such thing as a short journey."

The first problem was transportation. The belongings of the people were piling up along the beaches. There was more and more sickness, especially among the children. Not the dreaded typhus in every case, but respiratory congestion.

"We've got to get these people off this damned coast," Henry Meuller said. "We've got to get *out!*"

They were getting ready for war in south Texas. War with Mexico. That meant that anyone who had livestock and vehicles to sell was under pleasant siege by a horde of army procurement officers. Pleasant because those procurement officers had a lot of federal money.

"We can't compete with the United States for transport," Meuller said. "We've got thousands of people who have paid for their place in *Adelsverein*. And we're nearly bankrupt. We have to save what we can for those people coming behind. Herr Paco, can we walk?"

Salazar thought about it a long time. Finally, reluctantly, he nodded.

"It will be hard, Señor," he had said. "Very hard."

And so it was. These were mostly sturdy farm people from Hesse and Brunswick and Hanover, accustomed to hard work in the open. But the two-hundred-mile trek north out of the coastal flats, through the belt of oak and rolling terrain and then the prairie, was brutal. It was here, at the very first, that Sophia's mother had died.

It rained almost every day. When clouds rolled away to the east for a few hours, the sun blistered them. Some of the younger men began to grumble and damn this Texas and double damn those fraudulent stories in German newspapers about this Eden called Texas.

Most of them struggled on.

There were only half-a-dozen horses, including Salazar's, and these were loaded with critical medical supplies, weapons, water, money, and records.

Meuller and his wife walked. As did Salazar. As did everyone. The sick who could not walk were carried on stretchers or dragged on small travoises Salazar showed them how to make with poles and blankets.

Frau Waldenburg died two days off the coast. Her passing was a warning of bad things to come. There were some days so many died it was doubtful all got put in the ground properly as the marchers trudged past, heads down, feet dragging, shoulders bowed under belongings or sick children or old men or women clinging piggyback to some stronger friend or family member.

The old Prussian soldier, carrying a child on his back and a duffel under each arm, sang without any tune, a monotonous, dull chant over and over.

"'This is where my heart longs to be. On to Texas, on to Texas.' That's how they sang it to us when we came onto the boat," he said. "Oh where, oh where is *der Dummkopf* who sat by his warm fire in Berlin and wrote those words? Why is he not here, where his heart longs to be, drowning in this cold, slimy muck?"

A flight of buzzards began to follow the cavalcade, their frayed-end wings motionless as they circled in the gray sky behind the last of the struggling colonists. Many watched the great black birds by day and dreamed of them at night, thrashing out of wet blankets with nightmares.

In the rainstorms or sweltering heat of central Texas, they died. Their graves, had there been any headstones, would have marked a trail from the coast to the Balcones Escarpment. But Henry Meuller was a tough leader, and he kept them going. A few dropped off along the way, to try it on their own. But mostly they ploughed on to New Braunfels, through a country where they must have imagined no human foot had ever trod, it was so desolate and empty. When they finally arrived, it was a time of quiet and exhausted celebration.

By then the typhus had burned itself out.

They were on their ground at last. After grief and fear and dying, they could lie down almost reverently on the land they would culti-vate and upon which they would also grow their towns and churches and children. And where their hopes might take root and grow, too, God willing, with whatever sweat it might take, or tears or blood.

When the Spaniards came to the New World, they dreamed of streets paved with gold. For the Germans who came, gold was only a color. The color of wheat ripe in the sunshine.

Gottlieb Waldenburg was delighted they came because he knew he was not up to the job of supervising the settlement, even though a good deal of work had been done since Prince Carl departed.

The big community building had been completed, a number of rock walls built, a couple of vineyards laid out, and a big log house begun for Prince Carl's residence. And now this house was ready for occupancy by Herr Meuller and family if the rain would stop long enough to get the rest of the shake shingles cut for the roof.

Maybe the half-dozen Mexicans had done it all on their own initiative, but Waldenburg got the credit.

And there was a considerable stack of lumber, obtained before the war fever sucked all such things out of San Antonio de Bexar. The Mexican workers had been making adobe bricks and felling a few suitable trees along the bottoms for logs.

Henry Meuller was satisfied. He had something to start with, anyway, and people willing to work, although everybody was very tired indeed. Except the Mexicans.

Frau Meuller made a point of observing closely the performance of grief that Gottlieb Waldenburg gave for the loss of his wife and his joy at the reunion with his daughter. She told her husband that his grief looked to be sincere, if short. The *Adelsverein* official hunter had appeared not to be excessively *betrunken*, she reported.

But Waldenburg not being too drunk didn't change Frau Meuller's decision about Sophia. She set Sophia's course that first day, telling her husband it was only Christian kindness to *das unglückliche Mädchen*.

To which he replied that Sophia didn't appear to be all that unhappy, particularly after she learned she wouldn't be living with her father.

"*Das macht nichts!* No matter! With us this girl will live, and be *die Hausangestellte*, a maid for all things in my house, to cook and clean," she said.

So the Mexican workers built a nice pantry room behind the big house's kitchen where Sophia could sleep. They found that Frau Meuller could bark commands as well as or better than her husband, the only difference being that he could already speak a passable Spanish and all the good Frau's commands came in parade-ground German.

Which came from her standing beside parade fields in some Brandenburg *Kasernen* as a child and watching the soldiers of her father drill, he having been an officer in one of the famous Potsdam regiments, and her grandfather before that having been an officer on the great General Staff of Frederick II.

On Sophia's first night at New Braunfels, she was secure in the bosom of Commandant Meuller's family, as she liked to think of it. Subsequently, she never shared a home with her father. Nor did they ever sit at the same table.

Which, as it turned out, delighted them both.

Paco Salazar took the only three horses they had left and went to San Antonio de Bexar, taking some of Meuller's dwindling stock of coins, and within a week was back at New Braunfels with bags of dry beans, cornmeal, chilies, goat cheese, some tomatoes and garlic, and a very old steer. Lashed to the steer's back was a twenty-gallon oaken keg of dark beer.

The Anglos and Germans in Bexar were selling to the army all right, but in the Mexican quarter, Salazar had found these things that were so badly needed.

The Mexican major-domo brought news of the war, but at New Braunfels nobody was much interested, what with facing serious problems of their own.

But some of the young *Adelsvereins* went to join a unit being formed by a German immigrant from east Texas. They would be with General Zack Taylor to fight the Mexicans, all with the knowledge and consent of Henry Meuller.

"It's our country now," he said. "We came here to make our home. So it's our flag, too. Why shouldn't our young men march under it?"

"But your own Salazar, *der Chef* of New Braunfels. You send our men to fight his people!" Frau Meuller said. "How can you do that?"

"Yes, *Liebchen*, he is a boss here," said Henry Meuller. "And he is a Texan and had a cousin who fought these same Mexicans our young men have gone to fight, and the cousin was named Juan Pujanza, and he was killed at the Alamo."

"How do you know these things?"

"One of the other Mexicans told me."

"So?"

"So, *Liebchen!* Salazar became a citizen of the Republic of Texas because this is where he has always lived, as have many Mexicans. So, likewise, they are all Americans!"

"*Unbegreiflich diese Amerika!*"

"Not so incomprehensible as the old country in many ways," he said. But he didn't say it with much assurance. "Please, *Liebchen*, remember to speak in the English."

"Yes. I am still not happy our young men go to join with this company of soldiers," she said. "You know this man who forms this company of soldiers? August Buchel! That's who."

"He was a good soldier in German army, French army, Turkish army. He is a great soldier. Now he's a citizen of Texas also, as I've been told."

"*Ja!* And had to leave Germany because he killed somebody in a duel! And it wasn't the first," she said. "So!"

As for that steer Salazar had wheedled from somebody in Bexar, one steer wouldn't go very far among so many. But one of Salazar's men butchered the tired old beast and in a huge cast-iron pot, hung on poles over a hot pit fire in the yard before the council house, brewed a meat stew completely unknown to the Germans.

But they would soon cook it frequently, finding that because of the intense seasoning, it was ideal for use with meats that had possibly been lying around too long in the Texas heat. Before long, they would be as proud of their recipes for this as they were of their brat and blood and knockwurst formulas.

This stew was made with ground, dried chili peppers and tomatoes, and the Mexicans called it *chili con carne*.

"It is best with *los* frijoles *y las tortillas*," Salazar said

The Mexicans showed them how to cook the thin corn cakes, and they knew all about cooking dry beans. That didn't vary much from the banks of the Ruhr to the banks of the Guadalupe.

"Not only with your beans and corn cakes," shouted Gottlieb Waldenburg. "With *la cerveza* most of all!"

"*Sí*, with beer most of all," Salazar said.

"Already drunk, *der Toricht*," Frau Meuller whispered. "Foolish, foolish! All right Heinrich? In English for you. A foolish old drunk, that Waldenburg!"

It was a feast that night. And many brought out the bottles of Rhine wine and steinhager and cognac that had somehow survived that long journey on the ship, and then the horrendous march from the steaming coast.

It was their real celebration of homecoming that evening as they assembled around the large fire. They sang the songs of the old country, and there were tears, glistening in the firelight.

It was not sad, an evening of nostalgia. For the Mexicans sang and played their guitars and flutes and danced a wild fandango and one of the Mexican women danced and played a tambourine. Everyone cheered and applauded.

Gottlieb Waldenburg did a dance of his own as the Mexicans cheered as though this were a bullfight. And in his enthusiasm, the *Adelsverein* Official Hunter fell into the fire.

A great column of red and gold sparks swirled into the night sky, and everyone cheered the display, and Paco Salazar, who appeared to be the only male member of the entire party who was completely sober, pulled Gottlieb Waldenburg from the flames.

The great flaring beard exploded into flame, and Waldenburg was nearly smothered as laughing Mexicans extinguished the burning whiskers with serapes. It was only a short burst of flame, but it left very little hair on his cheeks and chin or hanging down his front.

And the odor of singed hair was very strong.

The children danced and shouted and laughed.

"*Ja, ja!*" they shouted. "*Herr Gestank, der kleine Herr Gestank!*"

The Little Stink! Well, the good *Frauen* of New Braunfels would have no such rudeness from the children, so a few were given the necessary butt dustings to emphasize that even though all the grown-ups might be acting like fools, the little ones still had the responsibility of being seen and not heard.

The famous *Jäger* lederhosen were singed black. The short *Jäger* legs were slightly blistered, and a little ox tallow was applied to them. This seemed to work, and as soon as they'd dragged the head of the house of Waldenburg back into the shadows, he fell immediately into a noisy sleep.

Everyone had a wonderful time, and the next morning they went at their work surely, methodically, as only Germans can, and soon the place began to look like a neat settlement in the Rhine Valley, except maybe there weren't as many trees and the buildings were of log and adobe and the roads were not cobbled but dusty. Until it rained.

Over the next few weeks it became obvious that Gottlieb Waldenburg was happy with his arrangement. He was building a small log cottage on the far side of the community vineyard facing the backside of the Meuller house.

He enjoyed his evening solitude. No worry about being nagged by a wife who increasingly had found fault with his untidy table manners, his snoring, his flatulence. Do as you damn well please, that was best. America was wonderful!

Certainly Herr Commandant, which is how he always thought of Henry Meuller, had placed no heavy burden of work on him. His job was seeing that predators did not molest the cows and horses and sheep, which were going to be coming into the colony in large numbers once the war between Mexico and the United States was finished.

Not much labor there! He could go about with one of Prince Carl's guns and shoot at a distant prairie dog now and again. But he always reminded the settlers that when they saw packs of wolves or grizzly bears or mountain lions, they should tell him at once so he could kill them.

For the hard-working German immigrants, who pretty much knew how to protect themselves against such things as four-footed marauders, Waldenburg provided some comic relief from their day-to-day sweat and toil.

And on the far side of the bare vineyard plot, what of Sophia, cook and lady's maid and who knows what all? Well, nobody doubted that she was delighted with her arrangement. There were those who said that because she was in the household of the commandant, she'd gotten pretty snotty. Maybe so. But Gottlieb Waldenburg didn't give a damn one way or the other.

It was perfectly clear to Henry Meuller that there wasn't enough suitable farmland for all the people. Prince Carl had bought too much scenery and limestone cliffs and not enough black soil good for crops. And successful crops were what would spell victory or defeat for the New Braunfels colony.

Meuller knew that the German community was stretching the border of Anglo settlement, protruding into Comanche country like a salient into enemy lines on a battlefield. He needed to enlarge the bulge to increase German acreage, no matter the danger or cost.

Being an aristocrat, Henry Meuller had never walked behind a plow in his life. But he was educated in the best methods of farming for his day, and he looked at the land and figured the runoff of surface water. And he sifted the dirt between his fingers, and smelled it.

He asked Paco Salazar a thousand questions about rainfall and temperature and what the Mexicans had learned they could and could not grow. Not that he planned to limit himself according to somebody else's failures. It was simply part of learning all he could about this land.

In the evenings, under candlelight, he made notes of what he thought would be needed. How many acres for *die Rübe, Kartoffel, Zuckerrübe, Hafer, und Mais.*

Meuller always seemed to start the list that way, then he would swear, scratch over what he'd written, and start again, in English.

Turnips, potatoes, sugar beets, oats, and corn. How much acreage for each? How much for pasturing animals once they'd begun their herds? All along black-earth bottom land. Nobody there now, close over the rolling hill, but it was Comanche country. The *Adelsverein* members were pressing their luck where they presently stood.

How long would it take grapes to mature enough for a harvest? Five years? And fruit trees, where could he get them, how long would they have to grow to be productive? What about planting more pecan trees? Were pecans marketable in a place like Bexar? Were walnuts?

Damn! Fruit took a long time, he knew, and things like walnuts even longer.

But they had to have land. They had to push that salient, somehow.

When he mentioned such things, Salazar and the other Mexicans wouldn't look him in the eye or say anything. He'd wait a few days and mention it again. Still, they were silent, as though such comments embarrassed them.

Finally, in July, after a hot, dusty day of work, Henry Meuller walked to the place where the Mexicans had their little tent camp on the banks of the Guadalupe. Most of them knew that soon their work would be done here, and they would be returning south, some to as far away as Galveston. So their living accommodations were strictly temporary.

Paco Salazar was different. Henry Meuller intended to hire him permanently and was already building Salazar an adobe house near Council House Square, which is what they were calling the plaza in front of the first building Prince Carl had built in the settlement.

Meuller intended to use the Mexican *jefe* as an emissary in San Antonio, too. Salazar had already shown that having a close contact with the old community there was a great advantage. There were a lot of Germans in Bexar, but they were like the Anglos, relative newcomers to west Texas and rather clannish, so if you wanted something from the Mexican community, you'd best have a Mexican trying to get it.

On this evening, when Henry Meuller went to the workers' camp, the major-domo was sitting on an empty keg before a small fire. There were three other Mexican men and one of their wives there as well.

When Salazar saw Meuller approaching, he spoke softly, and the others quickly rose and slipped back into the darkness around the tents.

Paco Salazar took off his hat, but he did not rise. The two men nodded, and neither of them spoke. Meuller took pipe and tobacco from his vest pockets and packed the bowl. It took a long time.

Henry Meuller squatted, not Texas style on his toes, but flat-footed, on his heels. Paco Salazar was surprised. This was how an Indian squatted, not a Gringo. It was how his mother had squatted when she made him *tortillas* y frijoles.

"Do you know why I've come, Herr Salazar?" Meuller finally said, puffing the pipe and watching Paco Salazar's face.

Salazar said nothing for a moment and then sighed and dropped his hat on the ground between his feet.

"I believe so. *Sí*," he said.

"I need more land. Can we do that? Why is there this tension here? I can feel it when I speak with an Anglo visitor or when I'm in Bexar, as though they are waiting to see what happens to us here."

Salazar shrugged. "Sí, they watch to see what happens."

"Well, the state of Texas doesn't seem to mind our taking up more land, but this Indian business sounds dangerous. Tell me all you can about it."

"I'll tell it, what I can," the Mexican said. "It is not a pretty story, Señor."

As he began to speak, he stared down at the peak of his sombrero and from time to time flicked at it with his fingertips.

"A few years ago, when Texas was a republic and Mirabeau Buonaparte Lamar was its president," he said, choosing words carefully, "the Penateka Comanches came to Bexar. They wanted to talk peace. There had been fighting for a long time. Raids. Small fights.

"This band came here from the north many years ago and took this country, driving out other bands. Some people call them *las comelas de la miel*. How do you say it? Yes, the Honey Eaters. Others call them Wasps.

"Comanches understand conquest, Señor. They didn't learn it from white men. They came here because they wanted to come. They were not being run out of someplace else. They took this land. They've held it. They'll hold it until somebody takes it from them.

"And they don't like people wandering around in their hunting area. Anglos, Mexicans, other tribesmen. On the other hand, they will go a long way to steal horses or children. Through any land they please. They take plunder to trade or to boost their own tribal population. They raid anybody they please. Even the few friends they have.

"All of this causes bad feeling. Shooting, casualties. They've lost some people, and they always worry about *la población*. How do you say?"

"Population."

"Sí. Population. They have many babies die. Their women do not have many babies to start with. They steal children from other peoples, raise them as Nerm. That's their own word for themselves. Nermernuh. The People. So they wanted to talk peace because they were being hurt with the fighting."

"I can understand all that."

"Señor, there's more than local Comanches. What we call the wild tribes, Nakoni, Yamarika, Kwahadie. All Comanches. All pass through Penateka country to raid south and east. Anybody—Spaniard,

Mexican, Anglo—who goes out to punish one of these northern raiding tribes has to ride through Penateka land. And there's trouble."

"Well, I can see where these, what is it, Wasps, might be upset to be taking punishment for somebody else's crimes."

"Oh Señor, they had enough on their own score to bring retribution. They have never been innocent virgins of the prairie doing nothing but smelling blue flowers every day."

There was the lash of a bitter edge in his voice, not so much anger as perhaps exasperation at being unable to explain it more perfectly, Henry Meuller thought.

There was a strange light in the Mexican's eyes, as from some deep, burning passion he wasn't sure how to control, and Meuller began to understand how a lifetime spent trying to deal with such things might be like reaching into the darkness for something and never finding anything, but knowing something's there.

"Excuse me, Señor," Salazar said. "I have many strange memories of these people. Now, let me go on."

So, Salazar continued, some chiefs came in to Bexar to see about a better arrangement for peace. Maybe three of their peace chiefs came. Maybe three of their war chiefs. They went into the city hall at Main Plaza with many of the white men, some of them Texas Rangers.

Over sixty members of the band came into Bexar that day. They stood and sat outside. The women squatted against the walls. The half-naked children played in the streets, throwing sticks for the local dogs to chase. Around the plaza, young boys held the Indian ponies.

The Comanches were in their best dress. Feathers and ribbons and porcupine quills. Their faces were painted, but there was no black for death. Or war.

"So they had not danced and sung to their gods for war," Salazar said. "They did not expect to fight. But they were very arrogant. There are many stories about what happened. I was not in the council house. I was not in Bexar that day. So I can only tell you what I believe happened from what I have heard. *Comprende*, Señor?"

"Yes, I understand."

"The proposition of the Tejanos was that Penatekas would live only in selected places. They would not do harm to white settlers or travelers. They would stay clear of all white settlement. In return, the

Tejanos would give them presents. The usual things. No weapons. Except maybe some hunting knives."

"They weren't being offered much for all that, were they?" asked Meuller.

"The Gringos were not feeling too kind to Comanches," said Paco Salazar. He took a cornhusk paper from a vest pocket, and Meuller tossed him his sack of tobacco and Paco Salazar rolled a long, lumpy cigarette and lit it with a stick from the fire. "*Gracias,*" he said.

He went on to explain that before any of this could take place, the Penatekas would have been required to give up all the white captive women and children they were holding. This condition was the clear signal for serious trouble.

"It is a thing I could never understand about these people," Salazar said. "They knew when they came in that white captive prisoners would come up. That was the most important thing on the Tejanos' minds. And they knew how the white man hated the way they treated captives. Yet, they came in anyway, not even prepared to fight."

The Comanches said they had only two captives. The whites said there were more. The Comanches said maybe other bands had some. They'd see about it. And meanwhile, one of the white captive girls the Penatekas had brought with them, apparently to trade, had been seen by some Texans.

She had been seriously mistreated, they said. The Comanches said they treated captives better than anybody. The Texans said this was a lie. Somebody inside city hall started shooting.

"From inside, the Gringos killed Comanches very quickly, and the firing started in the street as soon as the first man ran out of the council house. Everybody was shooting. The Penateka women and children old enough to hold weapons were shooting, too. Or rushing to get close enough to a Gringo or Bexar Mexican to use a knife. Bullets and arrows were impartial, killing red and white, man, woman and child.

"It was a madhouse, Señor, until a few surviving Penatekas managed to mount their ponies and ride out of town. Some of the Comanches were frightened and tried to hide in the alleys. They were all sought out and killed."

The Texans had taken a few Comanche captives, mostly wounded women and children. They sent one of the women to find the band and tell them that if all white captives they held were not released immediately, the Penateka captives would be put to death.

"It infuriated the Comanches," Salazar said. "They thought the Tejanos had broken a trust, violated a flag of truce, that the white flag of peace had been held out to the People and they had been massacred under it.

"So they tortured and killed all their white captives except a boy and one girl who had already been adopted into the tribe. Later, they sold the boy back to the whites, and the boy told what had happened in that Penateka camp."

Salazar shook his head in dismay.

"You see, Señor? Again, they do this thing that seems stupid. They release a white boy that they surely know will tell what they've done, and they know the fury this will cause in the white man's heart. Yet they sell him back to his family. As though they do not care if the white man knows things that will make him hot with rage. Can you understand that, Señor?"

"You've lived here all your life, Herr Salazar," Henry Meuller said. "Certainly if you find this incomprehensible, you can't expect me to understand it. Those white captives in their camp. How many were killed?"

"*Quien sabe?* Even the boy who was released did not always say the same when asked. All it took was one to set a fire of fury, Señor. Many Gringos and Mexicans, too, needed only a slight excuse to kill Comanches.

"In Bexar, many were killed. They counted thirty-two dead *indios.* Bexar's sheriff was killed in the city hall. A visiting judge was killed in the street, with an arrow shot by a Comanche child, they say. A dozen whites or Mexicans killed in all."

"You mentioned Comanche captives, wounded, taken after the fight?" Meuller said.

"Yes. About forty, they tell me."

"What happened to them?"

Paco Salazar looked into Henry Meuller's face, but he said nothing for a long moment. Then a small smile touched the corners of his mouth for an instant.

"No, Señor. They were not killed. They were women and children. How can I tell you? *Ellos escaparon de los* Tejanos."

"My Spanish is good enough to know you accuse the Anglos of letting them escape," said Henry Meuller. "Perhaps as though you would not have done so. Would you have killed them, *jefe?*"

The German got no answer except an elaborate shrug as Salazar gazed off into the night, where they could hear the whisper of water against the river's bank. And far beyond that an entire chorus of coyotes.

Henry Meuller knocked out his pipe against a log lying like a bench near the fire. He rose from his squat and stretched, but not finished yet, he sat now on the log and loaded a second smoke in the pipe bowl.

And waited. But realized Salazar was going no farther.

"And that was all?"

"No," said Salazar after a deep breath. "Some days later, they came back. With a chief named Buffalo Hump. He was the only great war chief they had left after the city hall massacre in Bexar. He rode into Bexar and challenged somebody to come out and fight. He had maybe three hundred warriors outside town. Nobody came out, for one reason or another. *Quien sabe?*

"Buffalo Hump took his war party south, all the way to the coast. He burned many places and killed many people. Some African slaves, he killed two of these. At Linnville, where you and your people arrived from Galveston, people got in boats and rowed out to get away from the Comanches. They sacked the town. Also the town of Victoria. But we caught them on the way back."

"We?"

"I was there this time," said Salazar. "There were many soldiers and Tejano Rangers. And Tonkawa *indios*. We caught them as they came back north. Drunk. Showing off the loot. They were trying to herd a lot of mules and horses back to Comanche country. They thought because no one had tried to stop them on the way south, no one would try to stop them on the way home.

"We made an ambush. There was a running fight. We killed many. The Tonkawas captured the pony herd. Some of the Anglos took scalps. Some of my people did as well. This was at the place called Plum Creek.

"It was so successful, Governor Lamar said go kill some more. They took a large company west and north, all the way to the forks of the Colorado. They found a Penateka village and destroyed it. They killed more than a hundred."

"How many of those were women and children?"

"Señor, fighting Comanches, it doesn't matter. Women and children can kill you as fast as the men do. We do not usually kill infant children, or women who are not using weapons against us. But sometimes these get killed accidentally anyway."

"I have heard otherwise," said Henry Meuller.

"Señor, there are always men, Gringo, Mexican, Comanche, German, who get the blood lust raging, and at those times, such men will kill anything. You surely know that. Such men need to be watched in a fight, or else they might even kill each other."

Henry Meuller thought about it, remembering stories just like this from soldiers in the old homeland, soldiers telling the horror of unbridled ruthlessness. He knocked out his pipe against the log and this time did not reload it, clamping it between his teeth cold.

"While we speak of things you might hear, Señor, you will be familiar with the story that after the Plum Creek fight, the Tonkawas cut a few legs from Comanche corpses, roasted them, and ate them."

Meuller's unlit pipe hung in his open mouth. He stared.

"Did you say ate them?"

"*Sí*, Señor."

"Do you believe that?"

Salazar made his elaborate shrug, eyebrows raised, head cocked.

"Who knows what the truth is? *Quien sabe?*"

Salazar swept up his hat and stood. The firelight showed yellow in his eyes.

"Since the council house massacre, Señor, the hatred in Penateka hearts for the Texas Gringo burns like hell fire. The hatred for my people has been there a long time. We have been fighting them since we first met on these plains more than a hundred years ago. Coming up from Mexico then, my people got as far north as Bexar and Santa Fe. But no farther."

And he moved back into the shadows and toward his bedroll somewhere among the scatter of Mexican tents. Meuller sat in the dying light of the fire, staring at the low, licking flames. He sat there until a few deep-red, glowing coals were all that was left.

Maybe in this long, lonely pause, with Paco Salazar's terrible story still in his ears, hardly hearing the mockingbirds of the Guadalupe, the coyotes of the Balcones Escarpment, maybe Henry Meuller came to understand why Prince Carl found a threadbare existence in Prussia preferable to the uncertainties of an outpost on the American frontier.

The brutality had to come as a shock to anyone who had read the enthusiastic letters of German immigrants who had come to places in the East and the North after the Revolution. If his *Adelsvereiners* learned what they'd let themselves in for, would there be a great exodus?

Henry Meuller figured that maybe life on the Rhine, even with occasional flare-ups of French Revolutionary radicalism, might be better than living on the Texas frontier.

Yet he knew, even as he thought this, that he was in for the long haul, and his colonists were as well. They'd stay.

But he also knew it was going to be necessary to deal with these Comanches. Somehow.

Chapter Nine

Three days after he'd explained the genesis of bad blood between Texans and Penatekas, Paco Salazar was waiting at the wet sink on the back patio of the big house at sunup when Herr Meuller came out to wash his face before breakfast.

"I am going now for a meeting with the Comanches," Salazar said.

"How can you expect a council with them after Plum Creek and all the rest? You're joking with me."

"I have a plan," the Mexican said. "We will count on Comanche hospitality."

"Hospitality?" Meuller was astonished at such a word being used in connection with a people he reckoned more savage than the Turks. He stood in the sun's early light, water dripping from his face, where now he had begun cultivation of a neat mustache. "Comanches? Are we talking about the same people you described the other evening?"

"*Sí*, they are famous for their hospitality. Not many Texas Gringos or Mexicans will admit to it, but it's true. *Es verdad*," Salazar said. "I don't know where they are now. So it will take a while for me to find them. Have presents ready. Gifts. Many gifts. You will need these gifts when you palaver."

Henry Meuller was stunned. He'd been pacing the floor trying to figure some way to get more ground for the people still coming. They'd already started a second town, a few miles to the northeast. They were calling it Fredericksburg.

"My God, Paco!" He blurted the first name, too shaken to be aware of this show of familiarity. "After the things you've told me, I'm fearful for you. Those savages will butcher you."

"I think maybe not," Salazar said, and he was smiling, not at anything funny being said but because he, like the German, belonged to a people with rather strict rules about the familiar form of address, including given names.

The major-domo was aware of Henry Meuller's embarrassment

now, as the German realized what he'd said and his face grew red. Which Paco Salazar marked as very unusual indeed, Henry Meuller blushing like a maiden. A good omen? He didn't mention it, because the *jefe* might not take it as a good omen at all.

"They are very proud of this hospitality of theirs. I go alone and unarmed, Señor. And they are always the inquisitive ones, these *curiosos* Comanches, like little children. They are out there now wondering who you and all these people are and what you are doing here. So they'll listen to me. I think. *Espero que sí!*"

"You'll need more than hope! Alone? Unarmed?"

"Yes. But I should have one glittering gift. To show them good faith."

"A gift. Yes." As he thought about it, Meuller dried his face with a small towel, even though the wind had already done the job. He tossed the towel aside and began to roll down his shirt-sleeves and button them. "We brought so little from Germany. Well now, wait. I've got an old Masonic sword. A ceremonial sword. It's not good for anything, except ceremony."

"I've seen it. It's good."

"An ivory handle, and a brass-bound scabbard."

"And a silk rope and tassel. That's good. And a small bottle of your brandy."

"You want to get these savages drunk?"

"No." And Salazar laughed. "I tease them with the brandy. They'll know that to get it before we have an agreement will mean killing me. So we'll have some conclusion, I'll give them the bottle of *aguardiente*, and leave them."

"Yes, and if they decide they will kill you for the brandy and to hell with the talk?"

"No, Señor. Comanches *son negociantes muy buenos*. Good traders. They will say, 'There's much more than one bottle of whiskey in this for me if I am patient.' They can be very patient if it means they will not sacrifice many gifts tomorrow for a quick drink of whiskey today. Especially when they know they are going to get the whiskey anyway. And it needs to be your German brandy. It will be different, not like spirits they've had from Mexicans or Gringos. It's important that it be different."

Meuller paced and fumed, slapping his sides, back and forth before Paco Salazar, who stood immobile. Then he stopped and bent his face close to the Mexican's.

"It is too dangerous," he said.

"These are not particular friends of mine," Salazar said with a shrug. "But Comanches do not make treaties for friendship. They make treaties like everybody else. For something they want."

"*Der liebe Gott!* This is terrible. What do we do, just pray and hope? We just start by praying, is that it? How will you find them? Do we just pray for that?"

Paco Salazar turned and looked across the rolling ground where the early-morning shadows of the building and the trees around it stretched out toward the west. He took off the big sombrero and brushed his graying hair back from his forehead.

"Out there," he said. "I will ride out there, into their country, and they will come to me. That part we do not need to pray for. What we need to pray for is that when they come, their blood lances are not thirsty."

On the morning Paco Salazar rode away, Henry Meuller watched, and his chest was tight and he was panting a little and muttering to himself about what a fool he had been to have thought he would come to America and spend his time in the study of nature, the growing of flowers and trees. And he shook himself like a dog.

He watched the Mexican grow smaller and smaller as he rode. The sun was on Salazar's back, and Meuller could easily follow his progress for a long way along the ridge line.

The rider was on the lip of a post oak ravine, a long way from the limestone outcrop that defined the Balcones Escarpment. He paused here, looked back toward the settlement where Henry Meuller watched, and waved his sombrero. He looked very small and alone out there, and a chill went up Henry Meuller's back.

Then for one instant, Meuller's gaze shifted to a pair of Mexican chickens starting a fight in his yard, and when he looked back along the escarpment, Paco Salazar was gone.

For two days, Meuller paced the floors in the council house and paced in his home at night. Frau Meuller cried and wailed at her husband as he continued to pace and mutter and look toward the west.

"You cannot expect him back so soon," she said. "*Liebchen*, drink some cool beer and think of other things."

"You know what I'm thinking of? That he carried a little five-shot Colt pistol, one of these new percussion-cap models. A Patterson, I think it was. Five shots. But do you think he plans to use it defend himself? Five shots against a whole band of Comanches?

"No. If the meeting goes badly, if he sees they will ignore his flag of truce, if there is anything terrible, he will not be taken by them to be burned and tortured. I know. If he'd intended to fight, he would have taken a larger weapon. No. That little pistol. If they try to take him as a prisoner, he will shoot himself."

"For shame!" Frau Meuller shouted. "That man shoot himself? You have gone too long in *die Sonne*, this miserable hot sun! That man would never shoot himself."

"You haven't come to grips with this place," he said. "But I hope you are right."

"Stop twisting your soul, *Liebchen*. He asked to go. You do not orders give here like those stupid corporals of the guard at the Potsdam *Kasernen*."

"I wish I did," said Henry Meuller. "I'd have ordered him to stay here, where he belongs."

His angst affected the whole colony, and he was smart enough to realize that no matter what he was thinking, he should steer around any talk of Salazar or where he was or what might be happening to him.

It didn't work too well. Finally, to get it off the minds of everyone, he said the mission had obviously failed. Poor Salazar. Gone in service to *Adelsverein*.

So the colony went about its work, trying to forget the failed mission. They said it had been foolhardy. But Henry Meuller kept looking to the hills and pecan groves and along the limestone outcrops to the west.

Actually, everybody else was cutting a look in that direction from time to time, too. A lot of candles burned in the Catholic chapel for Paco Salazar, and the three Lutheran pastors did a load of work in quiet, private prayer with individuals who came for support in their anguish.

You would expect that were the truth known, the colonists' concern was really with getting that Comanche land out beyond where the Germans presently were, but actually, a lot of the colonists had come to have something more than impersonal regard for the Mexicans in their community.

After all, they said, this is America. But when they said this, a few frowned and wondered why they'd said such a thing with all the hardships they'd already tasted, and a good bet they would taste plenty more. Like the wheat that might not come in this first full growing year.

And a few said, Well, don't worry about the Comanches now. That's Meuller's worry. Besides, you can't worry about wheat and Comanches all at once.

How much was a man expected to have on his mind at the same time in this America anyway?

As the waiting extended into the second week, they really did give up on Salazar, and nobody wanted to think of what might have happened to him.

A domestic drama had begun to play itself out. At least Frau Meuller thought it was dramatic. It concerned their house girl and cook, Sophia Schiller.

She whispered her concerns to her husband in bed at night, saying it was becoming scandalous, Sophia going so often to the pecan grove beside the river to meet men.

"And she goes on Sunday out on the prairie for picnics," she said. "Well, no. She stopped going on picnics. Why, I don't know. But all the rest. Swimming. Who knows? In the nude, I wouldn't be surprised."

Henry Meuller reminded her that in their younger days, they'd enjoyed a few swims in the buff along the banks of the Haver River in old Brandenburg. She contended that this was not the same. Sophia was playing the field, and some of her young men were surely of peasant stock and some were from old aristocratic families of Hesse and Hanover.

"This is the thing about America," said Henry Meuller. "We have no class distinctions here."

"*Stachelbeere!*" This was Frau Meuller's most disdainful exclamation and meant "gooseberries!"

"You tell me you are the same as these Mexicans?" she said. "You tell me von Kruger is the same as one of these Indian mule drivers? You tell me Count Munchsinger, who is first cousin to the elector of Wurthenburg, is the same as one of these free *schwarze* men who were slaves? And what about the ones still slaves. Are they the same as Frau Kunselmayer of Feiderburg? And what about. . . . "

"All right, all right, go to sleep, *Liebchen*. Stop pestering me about *das Hausmädchen* wiggling her butt for all the bachelors."

"And her *Vater*, that drunken Waldenburg, he doesn't take inter-est but lets her run around with no scolds from him."

"Well, you took her in like a big fat *Mutti*, didn't you? So he likely thinks he's not supposed to take any interest. It's your job now."

"Pastor Mayer. He should talk with her after his sermon next Sunday, if maybe I asked him."

"Best you don't make any effort to get those two together. She's Catholic, you recall. Besides, Pastor Mayer is young and handsome and single. You put them together, next thing you know, Sophia will have *him* in the pecan grove."

"Wicked, wicked, wicked, this Texas has made you wicked!"

Nonetheless, whether Henry Meuller admitted it or not, the young Widow Schiller was having a hell of a good time. Like Frau Meuller, she remembered the caste system in Germany, and gambol-ing about under the Texas moon with some young man until recently thought of as upper crust was exciting.

And in her position, she had ample opportunity to meet such young men. There was a constant stream of them in and out of the Meuller household both for social occasions orchestrated by Frau Meuller and for *Adelsverein* business requiring Henry's attention.

As New Braunfels grew, so did Sophia's happiness. The mocking-birds sang more sweetly for her. The south wind, even now in sum-mer, blew cool for her. The river flowed more gently for her, and the little blue-silver minnows nibbled her ankles with fish kisses while she waded with her evening beaus.

These beaus were a varied group. Some she had known before, perhaps on shipboard coming to America. Some she had heard of but never met. All of the young men who were aristocrats, or who at least had been in the old country, fell into this category.

She laughed at them and teased them because they were usually rather timid at first. Due to their background, they were completely unaccustomed to being alone in the darkness with a young woman and no chaperone in sight. It was as though they suddenly became aware that there was no need for the usual restraints and became clumsily aggressive.

Or else they were the kind of aristocratic young men who in the old country had specialized in chambermaids or milkmaids or tenant farmers' daughters or any others from a long list of young girls from what they considered to be the common breeding herd who could be cajoled or persuaded or maybe even threatened into clandestine meetings in the stables or the corncrib. These young men lost little time, knowing how to treat women of a lower class, so they thought, and the quicker the lay, the better, with no fancy words and of course, no wine.

But this was America, Sophia figured. So she was not so easy, and she rebuffed the arrogant ones by informing them she was as good as they were. So in some strange way she became for many of the young gentlemen a challenge which brought out fancy language, maybe even a little poetry reading.

The ones who had no "von" before their names, and who had never before owned land, simply plodded along, knowing what they wanted and going directly to it. These Sophia found easy to turn aside without hurting their feelings too much, although her suitors' feelings were of small concern to her.

Well, Sophia did like them all. The variety was as wonderful as all the rest of this business. Maybe there were even a few of her young men who grew drunk on the shine of a Texas moon and the scent of new blooming prairie bluebells, a few young men who whispered words of love.

But the common *Volk* of this generation of Germans—and Sophia was one of these—didn't spend much time on moonlight swooning or sniffing romantic odors, and certainly not on poetry, except for maybe a little quiet reading aloud under the shine of a winter-evening whale-oil lamp, a little Heinrich Heine or Ludwig Borne or even Goethe.

And though she enjoyed the aristocratic gentlemen, her favorites were the ones who, like her, still ate *Wurst* with their fingers.

Maybe if her mother was not lying in that muddy grave beside the *Adelsverein* road to the Balcones Escarpment, she could have explained to her daughter that such joys have to be paid for, sometimes in unexpected currency. Even when most of the joys are only hearsay. For, as is the case with individuals, what a community believes is the truth to that community, whether or not it bears any relationship to fact.

"Heinrich, I tell you, that girl is growing so bad," said Frau Meuller. "*Schlecht*. Bad!"

"Woman, I have seventy problems that are in front of that girl's badness," Henry said. "Besides, what kind of proof do you have for all this wickedness? Just gossip!"

There was no response to that. Frau Meuller knew that often a young lady who was high-spirited and thought of by more prudish observers as an obvious whore was indeed pure beyond belief but condemned by the less vibrant among her peers. Maybe from jealousy. Certainly from ignorance of the simple joys of life and laughter and exuberance.

And she had known those who were prim and cool and detached and never had a glance for the passing gentleman, yet who might be, beneath that calm exterior, *die feurige Dirne*. Yes, a passionate strumpet! Lying unseen, serpent among the rocks.

My God, she thought. I hope Sophia isn't one of those. Better she be innocent and suffer bad stories.

"It is still with *ein schweres Herz* I watch her," Frau Meuller said. "A heavy, heavy heart!"

"Please, my dear! *Bitte, bitte*," Henry Meuller said. "Go to sleep now. Go to sleep now."

It may be that Frau Wilmeth Meuller and most of the other ladies of New Braunfels were aware of the Widow Schiller's condition before she was. She apparently had nothing remotely resembling morning sickness. She was nineteen and strong and maybe so enthralled with her situation that she simply ignored any of the usual early warning signals.

"*Traurig, traurig*," Frau Meuller said. "Sad, sad. The poor, poor girl."

But soon, it could no longer be concealed, either from Henry Meuller and the other men or from Sophia herself. The time had come for letting out waistbands.

In the early afternoon, on one of the hottest days of that hot summer, Sophia had just finished cleaning the kitchen after the noon meal when she gasped, called Frau Meuller's name, and fell on the floor holding her belly in both hands.

Frau Meuller and three Mexican women served as midwives, and the delivery room was the room behind the kitchen of the big house, where Sophia had made her home since coming to this place.

So far as anyone knew, Gottlieb Waldenburg was unaware of this activity that would make him a grandfather. Because as chance would have it, he was enjoying an intense purple and red hallucinogenic nightmare brought on by sipping German steinhager and munching the little green button mushrooms the Mexicans called peyote.

When the baby issued, Frau Meuller understood why Sophia's belly had not swollen much. The baby weighed only a little over four pounds. Nobody expected it to live.

"It." That's how they referred to the baby in those first moments, even though they could see it was a boy. When the thing died, which they were sure it would, and soon, if they had not called it "he," maybe they could avoid that helpless feeling of grief and loss that would be certain if they came to think of it as a little baby boy. If they came to wonder why God had wanted to call him home so soon.

Maybe this baby would be going early to its grave in payment for its mother's sins, some of them surely thought. Maybe Frau Meuller thought so, too, but the idea of a young girl giving birth brought such a flood of compassion she never once gave anyone a hint of her disapproval of all this business. Except, of course, her husband, whom she regaled each night in their bedroom.

But there was toughness in the tiny, shriveled form, and he confounded everyone and lived. And without much complaining about it, either. He cried only when he was hungry, only a few sharp, harsh little barks, and then shut up, as though he expected that enough had been said to get what was required.

When the smoky baby color left his eyes, they were a blue so pale you could hardly tell there was an iris at all. They were remarkable eyes for another reason as well.

Frau Meuller exclaimed, "*Diesen kleine Knabe,* he does not make *mit den Augen* a blink!"

And it was true. It seemed this baby had no need for the usual eye-batting, and when he was awake, the colorless orbs fixed intently on any moving object near his face.

None of the community's young men showed any interest in stepping up as father for Sophia's baby. She didn't give any hints. Everybody from Henry Meuller down to the Mexican workers was guessing. They wondered if maybe Sophia was guessing, too.

One thing she didn't have to guess about. People were still civil to her, but now there was a coolness, even from Frau Meuller. This had become a staunch Lutheran and Catholic community, and having a little bastard pop up right in the big house gave a lot of people indigestion.

And once the child had grown a little, his playmates would be teasing and poking fun and calling names. Sophia didn't much care about the rough time the child would have, but she sure didn't like suddenly being treated like she supposed a reformed Hamburg whore would be, so she began to think about moving on. To where, she had no notion.

But that and everything else suddenly was put aside. Paco Salazar had come back.

Chapter Ten

It had been a long journey. Salazar was sure, as he told Henry Meuller, that the Comanches knew he was in their country before he got to the San Saba River. But they watched and let him come on, and he suspected it took some strong speeches by the older chiefs to keep the young men from riding out and practicing their lance work on him.

But they could see he carried no rifle and no lance, which Mexican vaqueros often carried. And on his bridle was a long white cloth, rippling in the wind beneath the horse's head, a flag of truce that sometimes a Comanche would honor. Sometimes not.

Skirting the Edwards Plateau, he finally veered north, away from the Colorado River. He was almost to the Clear Fork of the Brazos when he wakened from an apprehensive sleep one morning and they were all around him, about twenty warriors, some with black paint on their faces.

But they didn't kill him. They pushed him around a little, swinging their ponies' rumps against him. They waved the warheads of their lances in his face, and on some of the lances were decorative scalps.

Then two of them dismounted and went through all his duffel. But he finally realized that they had intended all along not to kill him. His lack of weapons and the flag of truce had done it. So they took nothing from him, finally allowed him to mount, and led him to their chief.

Salazar was extremely unhappy when he saw that the chief was a man whose name meant something that the Mexicans interpreted as Via Lobo and who the Gringos called Wolf's Road. He was a well-known fighter, a war chief who had made his name since Plum Creek by displays of cunning, courage, and utter ruthlessness against the enemies of the People.

Salazar had the satisfaction of knowing he'd made enough of an impression to be getting an audience with the top dog. And this man likely knew or had heard of Salazar and his record in south Texas, which included a lot of fights with Comanches.

But maybe, the Mexican told Meuller, the Comanche love of jokes saved his life. Via Lobo knew about Salazar's scarred topknot, and now, in a circle of Penatekas, he told the Mexican to doff his sombrero and turn about bent forward so that all the assembled could enjoy looking at his wound.

It was a wonderful joke. Everyone laughed. Two of the older braves bent over, too, pulling aside their flowing thick hair to expose scalping scars of their own. One pointed to his scar proudly and shouted, "Ute!" The other, showing his badge, shouted, "Lipan!"

Salazar knew they expected him to tell them whose knife had mutilated his head, and he bent and showed his scar again, trying to act proud as the Comanches had done, and touching it, he shouted in their tongue, "Nermernuh, a warrior of the People, a fighter of the True Humans."

With that, they pressed close to him, shouting, laughing, and pounding his back with the flats of their hands to show how much they appreciated the joke. It was a thoroughly painful moment because Comanches were always very vigorous in such things, so Salazar knew he'd end up with bruises across his back.

Which was better than being staked to the ground and having a fire built on his belly.

One of them even hugged him, smearing the Mexican's face with paint from his own cheeks.

After that they sat in a tipi with the sides rolled up, but it still smelled like buffalo suet and leather and sweat. Comanche women brought food, some dried meat in long, tough strips, and they smoked, first a pipe that Via Lobo produced and then long, awkward cigarettes rolled in white cornhusks Salazar had brought.

Via Lobo was delighted with the Masonic ceremonial sword, especially the silken tassel, but said it didn't look like it would be much good for killing buffalos. Everybody thought that hilarious, and there was another round of backslapping.

The idea behind this furious back pounding was to get somebody to draw back with pain, to admit they'd had enough. Salazar was determined to take anything they had to give without flinching. He knew how Comanche joking worked. Via Lobo said he would speak to the new white *jefe* who was now on the Balcones Escarpment. The reason he agreed to such a thing was that Salazar convinced him this was not a Mexican or a Texas group but a new tribe called *los alemáns*, meaning "the Germans" in Salazar's language. Most of this council was conducted in the language of the Comanches, which Salazar knew well, but there were many Spanish words scattered here and there in the conversation by the Comanche chief. Although the Comanches were disdainful of learning anybody else's language, after nearly two centuries of confrontation, they'd learned a lot of Spanish despite themselves.

The upshot of it was that Via Lobo would speak with the chief of this new tribe on the edge of Penateka country. And with enthusiasm. At least enough enthusiasm for them to give Salazar a fresh horse to ride back to New Braunfels.

Henry Meuller was exhilarated. There was fear and apprehension, too, and his wife and most of the others in the colony acted as though he was packing to ride off to his own hanging.

And he thought, Maybe I am!

The gifts had been brought up from Bexar and left lying in a lean-to shed behind the council house. Now they were loaded on two geldings because the Germans intended to leave these horses as part of their package of presents; they were reluctant to give the wild tribes any more breeding stock than they already had through theft.

Meuller had been hesitant about including anything that could be used in case of later hostilities, but Paco Salazar said some such truck was necessary or Via Lobo would know he wasn't trusted. Which would destroy any chance of an agreement.

So there were hatchets and packets of arrowheads and a small keg of gunpowder and two bars of lead. Salazar assured Meuller the Comanches would have a bullet mound of the right caliber for whatever firearms they already had on hand.

The rest was domestic stuff. To make the squaws' lives easier, Frau Wilmeth said. Iron pots and Dutch ovens, spoons, needles and thread, two bolts of heavy duck fabric, some woolen blankets, a basket full of glass beads and colored ribbons. And two rolls of heavy copper wire for making bracelets or earrings.

This was just the start. There would be more, a lot more, if the

New Braunfels community could get those additional acres Meuller figured they needed.

The Germans were ready to give shirts to every member of the tribe, enough bolt material to sew dresses for every woman and child, many trousers, metal tools, and woolen winter coats to ward off those annual northern gales of harsh wind that roared down off the Llano Estacado each winter.

Henry Meuller was ready to spend up to three thousand dollars on gifts, if it would mean additional land. A lot more than homesteading fees paid to the state of Texas would be.

"But my dear," he said to his wife, "from Texas we would be buying only real estate. From Comanches we would also be buying the hope of no German houses burning in the night, no German hair hanging in their lodges, no German babies raised to be heathens."

"Where to keep us safe from savages is the army? Are they so tired from fighting Salazar's people they do not protect us?"

"Salazar is a citizen of this country, not Mexico. Now hush, *du fettes Liebchen.*"

"Fat, indeed!"

Now that something was underway to solve his land problems, Henry Meuller could be a happy, playful lover in their bedroom once more. He did this as much for his wife as for himself because he thought perhaps it made her know that he still cherished her even though she had been unable to give him children.

On the night before his journey began, his wife held him so tightly for a time he could hardly breathe. But she did not cry, nor did she the next morning at first light as he and the Mexican rode off toward the high escarpment and she stood on the back stoop of their home, watching with a Mexican serape held tight around her shoulders against the cold.

"Goodbye, my dear," he called from the saddle.

"*Komm schnell nach Heim, mein Schatzchen.*"

"English, dear, remember. English."

"To hell *mit Englisch!*

When she turned back to her door, she saw that Sophia Schiller had been watching the men leave, too, and she put her arm around the girl, and they went back into the kitchen for a cup of coffee together.

Frau Meuller was touched that Sophia was there to see Henry Meuller depart on this dangerous mission. It surely proved the girl's affection for the man who had allowed her to live in his household.

They rode out in the early pearl-gray light of a Texas summer dawn. Each man held a pack gelding lead rope. Across the first low ground and onto a bare ridge a full two miles from New Braunfels, they went along the edge of a ruffed grouse dance ground.

It was the time of day for the prairie chicken cocks to be making guttural clucks and doing their stiff-legged dance with feathers flared, trying to impress a couple of the plain little hens and at the same time scare off competition.

It didn't take long to get beyond any country where Henry Meuller had ridden. This was rolling, short-grass prairie, the trees along the Guadalupe a long way to their right.

"We will be meeting with a chief the Tejanos call Via Lobo," the Mexican said as they rode. The wind was blowing hard, and he had to lean close to Henry Meuller to be heard. "Some call him Wolf's Road. That's what the Comanches call the stars across the sky's center. Wolf's Road. To my people, it's Via Lechoso."

"Of course. *Die* Milchstrasse. The Americans call it the Milky Way."

"While you haggle with him, look him square in the eye," Salazar said. "No matter what they do, act as though you expected it. Never show surprise. Never show fear."

They saw a sizable herd of buffalo grazing along the headwaters country of the Guadalupe and in the dusty distance to the west, toward the Edwards Plateau, a larger herd, long and winding like a dark river along the lower contours, where there was more moisture and thicker grass.

And there were pronghorn antelope. Usually in groups of four or five, plus maybe a couple of last spring's fawns, all still as marble statues, staring at the horsemen from far off, curious, but not curious enough to come any closer.

It was almost noon, and some ten miles from New Braunfels, when Meuller saw riders on their flanks, about a half dozen on both sides, seeming to materialize out of the sun's haze. Meuller saw their lances, and sometimes the sun glinted a bright reflection from their painted faces.

They kept their distance, riding parallel to the New Braunfels men. Meuller knew Salazar had seen them, but neither man said anything. Meuller felt the first chill rising along the back of his neck.

Then they were on a long ridge, bare of trees, wind blowing dust in their faces. The wind smelled strongly of sage, and there was a hint of the odor of wood smoke.

Meuller saw tipis along a creek line behind the ridge, conical lodges the color of old meerschaum pipes like the ones Henry Meuller had brought from Germany. At top, where the lodge poles protruded, the hide was black with the smoke of many fires. Children played around the tipis among a few tethered horses and soapberry bushes and half-a-dozen black willows.

"Temporary camp," Salazar said softly. "No large pony herd, no dogs. They've come out here and set up this place just for your talk."

The second little chill went up Henry Meuller's back.

On the ridge they moved along there was a brush arbor. Salazar had said the Comanches usually built these flimsy little structures wherever they paused for even a short while, if there was brush at hand. The only purpose of the arbor was to provide shade where the men could escape the fierce sun and sleep, smoke, talk, eat, play gambling games with sticks or stones, and sometimes copulate.

Once the bands moved on, the arbors were left to the elements, the constant winds and hail and rain. They could be seen, fragile and lonely, dotting the landscape and finally collapsing, coming apart, blowing across the plain in bits and pieces, disappearing completely before the wind.

One figure, sitting dark in the shade, was under the arbor. Behind him was a rough semicircle of about fifteen horsemen, most with lances, rawhide fringes on leggings blowing in the wind, along with loose hair.

The riders had shields, but the shields were inside rawhide covers, hanging at their thighs, which was a good sign. Uncovered war shields held at the shoulder could have meant serious trouble. In the glaring sun, Meuller could not discern the color of their paint except for a few patches of white along cheekbones.

As they approached the arbor and prepared to dismount, two Comanche boys ran out from somewhere—Meuller had no notion where—to hold their horses. After that, his whole attention was on the man sitting cross-legged in the arbor.

Wolf's Road was wearing his hair loose. It hung about his shoulders with only a single plaited scalp lock falling down the back of his neck and three pipe-stem fine braids that fell across his forehead and along the right side of his face. Huge brass earrings, a scarlet bandanna about his neck, a necklace of wolf teeth, a single daub of vermilion paint across his mouth, naked from the waist, heavily fringed leggings and moccasins.

His face had a strong Mongolian cast, the color of a freshly hulled walnut, with a hint of yellow. It was a flat face, high cheeked, lips delicately curved, with an Asian slant to eyes which were red rimmed, the whites laced with dark veins, the iris obsidian black like the pupils.

The whole of the face was rather like a pale cheese moon, Meuller thought, his impression reinforced by the lack of facial hair. All whiskers, all eyebrows, even eyelashes, had been plucked. Once more, the hard chill went along Henry Meuller's neck.

"*Saludo, jefe,*" Paco Salazar said. "Greetings, chief."

Wolf's Road's eyes never left Henry Meuller's face. He had a fierce and intense stare. He spoke a few words in his own tongue, and Salazar turned to Meuller.

"We talk a little first about the weather and horses and anything else he wants to talk about. That's how they come to serious talk. Soon, we'll get to the business at hand. After he's sized you up."

Salazar was speaking so softly, Meuller had difficulty hearing what he said. Then he realized Salazar was speaking low intentionally so Wolf's Road could not hear. Wolf's Road seemed to know what was happening but showed no signs of irritation.

This was the first Comanche Meuller had ever been near. So he did some sizing up of his own. At once, he was aware of a strong odor. Wood smoke and meat fat, maybe, with sage and cured leather and some quality he couldn't identify. The odor was not offensive and seemed to Meuller completely in keeping with this dry, sunlit, dusty, primitive setting.

He saw that Wolf's Road was as he'd heard Comanches would be.

Although he sat on a reed pallet, it was obvious that if standing, he wouldn't be very tall. He was short, squat, heavy.

Meuller supposed that when Wolf's Road walked, he would waddle like a duck, bowlegged and awkward. But mounted on a favorite war pony, he would become what everyone knew Comanches were: swift, agile, master horsemen. Lords of the Southern Plains.

Soon, there was some movement among the mounted warriors nearby, and a dozen old men and a young one walked through their line and came to the arbor and squatted in a semicircle facing Meuller and Salazar. The young man squatted directly behind Wolf's Road.

This young man was attired much as was his chief, and Henry Meuller saw such a resemblance between the two he figured this was either a son or younger brother of Wolf's Road.

Now one of the older men prepared a pipe, and they smoked, first Wolf's Road, then Henry Meuller, then the others in turn.

Wolf's Road lifted one hand as a signal, and the two boys who had run out to hold the New Braunfels horses pulled the duffel off the two pack horses and dragged it under the brush arbor, where Salazar began to show off the booty.

Meuller knew a few of the Spanish words but none of the Comanche that passed back and forth. But Salazar knew what Meuller wanted and what he would give for it. He also knew the German trusted him to bargain with the Indian. Now and again, to give the appearance that Meuller was actually taking part in the discussion, Salazar turned and spoke to him, translating what had been said.

Actually, after the old men and the young chief arrived—and Meuller figured that's what the young man was—Wolf's Road did most of the talking. Meuller supposed he was putting up reasons that the German's gifts fell short. Salazar interpreted part of what he said.

There was a lot of talk about this new tribe, *los alemáns*, with whom the Comanches had no quarrel. They were not barbarians, like the Anglo Texans and the Mexicans. And Wolf's Road directed a fierce glare at Paco Salazar.

It was at that point that Henry Meuller realized the cold sweat had stopped coursing down his back. And for the rest of the session, he looked at this short, squat, powerful man before him and wondered how such a man could be capable of the horrible cruelties ascribed to him and his people.

Maybe it was then that the German for the first time came near to understanding that he was face to face with a people not only different in place but in time. Millennia separated them one from the other. The Iron Age had come face to face with the Age of Stone.

This was why they traded with the white man, Henry Meuller thought. They couldn't make the metal themselves, and now they couldn't live without it; they were helpless before enemies who had it. He was profoundly moved, and in many ways even more frightened than before.

Because, as he later told Frau Meuller, he knew how to deal with an Englishman, an Austrian, a Russian, a Frenchman. He might not like them, but at least they were all taking their trouser material off the same spindle.

But these Comanches! Well, you were dealing with a strange and unknown breed living in a landscape as foreign as the moon.

"Now, now, *Liebchen*," his wife consoled. "You yourself said so. We will get accustomed to this land."

"No, no, not the land, that's not what I mean. It's bigger," Meuller said. "Listen, Paco Salazar told me this about them. I asked him about their religion and their God, and he said they have many many gods, and he said that when you ask them how the earth and stars and man were made, they shrug and say, 'Who cares about trying to know such things? It's here! We're here! Why do you want to worry about such a thing?'"

Frau Meuller thought it all entirely blasphemous. But lying in bed, listening to a pair of coyotes on the limestone ridge lifting their howls to the dark sky, Henry Meuller felt that cold tickle of hair rising on the back of his neck. Because now he could put a face on those people out there beyond the coyotes.

When their discussion was finished, just before they rose to go to their horses, Wolf's Road took the Masonic sword from under a blanket and held it up.

"Very fine," Wolf's Road said in perfect English. "Now my gift to the great *jefe* of *el alemán* tribe."

The young man behind him reached out, past a warrior named Buffalo Hump, and Meuller took from him a necklace of finely woven rawhide strands with a short, waxy pendant that Meuller knew at once was a dried human finger. Wolf's Road spoke in Comanche now, looking into Meuller's face with an expression of complete calm.

"The Cheyenne take trophies like this from their dead enemies, he says," Salazar translated. "The People do not take such trophies. This is the finger of my father's father, killed by the Kiowas a long time ago when the People and the Kiowas were not friends. My son Rides the Rain Storm makes this gift to you in honor of my father's father, and so long as you prize it, we will both keep this peace."

To oblige, Henry Meuller removed his hat and slipped the rawhide loop over his head. As the finger fell to settle against his chest, he had the horrible feeling that the fingernail was trying to scratch him.

If the finger pendant gave Meuller goose bumps when he first put it on, it was nothing compared to his feelings once they were home and he took it off and Salazar started talking about it.

"Why would he give me his grandfather's finger?" the German asked.

"Señor, it is not his grandfather's finger," said Salazar.

"Then whose finger is it?"

"*Quien sabe?*" Salazar said and shrugged. "Some old enemy. It is *una inocentada*. A practical joke."

"A practical joke? How in God's name would you know that? Did he tell you that?"

"No, no, Señor. That would destroy the joke, if you knew it was just a trophy taken from an old enemy," Salazar said. "These Comanches, they will defy death to recover their dead from the field of a fight," he continued. "*Por que?* Because they believe that if a body is mutilated, with a scalp taken or a finger or a hand, the spirit of that warrior will not go to the place beyond the sun, where one goes only if one has all his parts. It is a reason for them to mutilate dead enemies, to keep them out of that place in the beyond. So they don't have to fight them there."

"All right, all right. They don't want to bury a dead body if it's missing something. All right. But I thought Indians put their dead in trees."

"Not Comanches. They bury their dead. And if this was the grandfather, they would never, never have buried him without a finger.

Because such a thing would keep him from the place they go to beyond the sun."

"Heaven."

"Not exactly. Not like a Christian heaven. They don't go because they are good. Everybody goes. Things are as they are here on earth, from what I understand. Except there are no white men and plenty of buffalo. And it doesn't rain much or get cold."

"Then the finger really means nothing to them."

"Oh yes, it does," Salazar said. "It's a way for Wolf's Road to show the band that you are trusted enough to play a practical joke with, a very big practical joke, for part of it is your taking the spirit of the grandfather as a bond. As a kind of oath you will keep the treaty. Yet, he has outsmarted you because you do not really have the grandfather's spirit at all. He has made you think you have, but it is still safe in the place beyond the sun."

"So they're laughing at us."

"Sure. It's good to have Comanches laugh at you. They play jokes and laugh at their friends." Salazar shrugged again and smiled. "Señor, it's better to have them laughing at you than planning on which night they will come and burn your houses and steal your children."

"Incredible," Henry Meuller said and bounced the finger necklace in his hand. "Well, this thing never goes on my neck again."

"That's fine," said Salazar. "But keep it handy in case you ever have the opportunity to speak with Wolf's Road or his son sometime. If that time comes, be wearing it."

"Yes," said Meuller. "Yes. I can see the sense in that."

"You must not try to understand them too much," said Salazar. "With them *el espiritu fantasmo,* how to say, their soul, their spirit, their religion, something like this is in everything they do. Even in jokes. Nothing they do is outside their religious consideration."

"So it's important. Even if *ein Scherz?* Even if a joke."

"*Hace muy importante,* Señor. I can't tell you too much how important it is."

It was astonishing, all the Anglos said, that anybody was crazy enough to think you could make treaties with the Comanches.

All the Texans laughed. All the Mexicans shook their heads. Everybody waited for the first Comanche raid against German cattle or horses as the New Braunfels herds grew. Everybody waited for the first *Adelsverein* drover or farmer to be found gutted and scalped on the sun-soaked prairie.

In Bexar, there were bets laid on it. Pots grew large, and whoever came closest to predicting when the peace would be Comanche-ized, as they called it, would win all the money.

It was discussed at the bar in the saloons around Military Plaza.

"You ain't gonna get no Comanch' tied to a peace treaty," one Anglo was heard to say. "Dirty dogs, they gotta be out rapin and butcherin. Like they done my two nieces up on the Trinity."

"'Hell's pure fire, man. When they got peace, they ain't nothin fer the bucks to do," said another. "Savage bastards! They hunt a little, that's all."

"You're sure right, by George," said yet a third. "They don't plow. They don't saw timber. They don't herd no cows. They don't do nothin but hunt and fight. It's all they teach their young-uns."

"Hell's pure fire, man, a Comanch' band bein peaceful don't have nothin fer the bucks to do, do it?" the second Anglo said. "Like I said. Take a Comanch' band bein peaceful, got no real purpose, do it? War is the only thang they do, ain't it?"

But the weeks passed, and nothing happened. The months passed, and nothing happened. It was in fact years before any of Meuller's people died at Comanche hands, and then only after white settlement had moved far deeper into Comanche country than *Adelsverein*.

And by then, it was a last dying gasp for the Comanches, and everyone had forgotten Henry Meuller's agreement with the Penatekas.

Not only was there a peace with the Comanches but the Mexican war was over, and the young men who went off to join General Taylor were home again.

So the Germans grew and prospered, and everyone thought Henry Meuller was a big hero, especially Frau Wilmeth Meuller. He said this was all due to his Mexican *jefe*, whom he now called Paco without embarrassment, and Paco Salazar was seen to smile.

But Henry Meuller was not serene in spirit. He told Salazar, to whom he had begun to confide all things, that the damned Comanche fingernail was scratching his very soul.

They were near the river, standing in good black-soil land close to the Guadalupe and within sight of the Council House. They were watching more than supervising a group of German farmers transplanting about a dozen wild plum trees carted in by Salazar's men from the Nueces River bottoms north of Corpus Christi Bay.

Henry Meuller had taken to carrying the Comanche finger necklace everywhere he went. He had it now, in one of the many pockets of his long duster-type coat. And he took it out and tossed it up and down in his hand.

"Paco, I'm going to burn this wretched thing," he said. "I've made up my mind."

"No, no, Señor," the Mexican said, and he reached out a hand and laid it on Meuller's shoulder as he might do to a fretful child. "Can't I persuade you it is *muy importante?*"

"*Muy importante* or not, I'm going to burn it."

Salazar caught the pendant in midair as Meuller tossed it, and held it out, shaking the thin leather thongs that were braided, the loop passing through a pierced end of the parchment-like dried finger.

"Look at this, Señor," he said. "Thongs dyed red and black and braided carefully. Beautifully."

"Yes, it is beautiful, but the thing hanging from it is ghastly."

"It's all of a piece, Señor," said Salazar. "And listen, this kind of work is unusual for the Comanches. They are drab people. They do not decorate their lodges or their ponies or their bodies as do their friends the Kiowas."

Meuller stared at the Mexican, waiting for the point as Salazar began to wave the necklace in front of Meuller's face emphatically.

"The Kiowas hang so much copper and silver and glass on themselves and their horses that you can see them coming from far off because they glitter so in the sun. But the Comanches don't do that. When they do make these, how do you say? *Muy adornado.*"

"Very fancy," said Meuller, whose Spanish was progressing more quickly than Salazar's German.

"*Sí! Sí!* Fancy. When they *do* do such a thing, it is because to them this thing is *muy importante!* And every Penateka in Texas would look at that loop on the finger and know from the design and color of the braid that it came as a gift from Wolf's Road."

Meuller snatched the necklace from his major-domo and stuffed it in his pocket. He was frowning, but looking at the plum tree workers and not at Salazar, so the Mexican knew the agitation was not directed at him. Therefore it was safe to go on.

"You have surely heard, Señor, that tribes can be identified by their arrows. By the way they are grooved and painted. But that is for a whole tribe. This, this necklace, it is for Wolf's Road. His family only. Any Comanche in Texas can read it."

"And he'd make a joke with it?" Meuller sounded as baffled as before.

"Of course. Which, because of the way they think, makes it even more important. Sacred. This gift is to the chief of *los alemáns*, and he is important enough for them to play a great joke on. The greater the joke, the greater the respect. Would you want one of them to catch you without that finger now? Would you want them to hear somehow that you'd burned it?"

"Damn!" Henry Meuller snorted, shoving the wretched necklace deeper into his duster pocket. "Red heathens. Why must they be so strange? Well, come on, let's see to a system of some kind for irrigating these plum trees."

On the stem of every rose of happiness there is a sharp thorn, as Frau Meuller always said, and the thorn here was Sophia Waldenburg Schiller and her bastard child growing in Frau Meuller's house.

The worst part of this was that Frau Meuller had become inordinately attached to the little non-blinking gnome-like child, who was the least troublesome baby Frau Meuller had ever heard of, crying almost not at all, and then only in short bursts.

Frau Meuller was not an ignorant woman. And she knew as well as anyone that her attachment, which she refused to call love, to this child was a natural reaction for a woman who had always wanted children but had been unsuccessful.

She knew that Henry understood this, too, and she was tenderly grateful to him for never mentioning it or even hinting that the baby was in any way a substitute for her own child that had never come.

Frau Meuller's feelings toward the Widow Schiller were much more complex and hard to explain. The widow was pitied, as anyone would be who had lost a husband and mother at a tender age and had been left with a besotted father who obviously didn't give a damn about her or what happened to her.

Yet she was everything Frau Meuller, in her straight-laced aristocratic Brandenburger military family, had been taught to loathe. Sly, shrewd, self-serving, promiscuous. These were qualities distasteful in a man and in a woman absolutely unacceptable!

No matter that she was a hard and efficient worker. She had, after all, used the Meuller's hospitable dining room like a spider uses a web, there undoubtedly ensnaring many of her lovers. One of whom had fathered her bastard child!

Although from a different old-country class and educational background, or lack thereof, Sophia was no *Dummkopf* either. She had a good sense of what Frau Meuller felt, and each day she became more painfully aware of it and sympathetic to this good woman's anguish.

There was no way of retracting all the hurts Sophia had done her benefactor, but she could at least remove the embarrassment. She could leave and take the baby with her, although she admitted to herself that she really didn't care if Comanches came and carried the child off.

When nobody else was around, as when she was in her behind-the-kitchen bedroom nursing the baby, she called him *der Zwerg*. The dwarf.

So she would go. To where, she had no notion. With some show of defiance, to hide her own melancholy, she announced her intention to Henry Meuller. Not to Frau Meuller. But to the commandant.

You would suspect that Sophia did this because she knew if she broached the subject to Frau Meuller's wife, so many insurmountable objections would be thrown up by Frau Meuller, due to her affection for the baby, that by the time the commandant heard of it, the whole thing would be an impossibility.

Well, it has been observed that Sophia may have been sly, shrewd, self serving, and promiscuous. But also that she was no *Dummkopf*

So before Frau Meuller ever heard of it, Sophia's departure from the colony became another of those day-to-day problems for Henry Meuller and his Mexican *jefe*, Paco Salazar.

An addendum to the rest of the problem: the Widow Sophia Schiller was losing her milk.

Frau Meuller knew something was afoot, since she was sensitive to her husband's moods and methods. He and that Mexican of his were going about it *unter grosser Geheimhaltung*. With great secrecy indeed! But she didn't press it. From her girlhood, she recalled quite vividly that the colonel's lady did not question the colonel on matters of the regiment.

And the Widow Schiller and child situation was more than a household problem. Many of the staunch Lutheran ladies of the settlement were becoming cooler and cooler to Frau Meuller's invitations. The elders of all the churches were watching to see how Henry Meuller would settle what everyone considered an embarrassment to the entire community.

So Frau Meuller was one day presented with an accomplished fact. Somehow, Sophia and the child would be taken care of, and their departure was imminent. They would go to the considerably larger town, even city, of San Antonio de Bexar.

"Into the Waldenburg house could they move?" Frau Meuller asked, her voice quavering and her eyes moist with tears as she watched Henry over a supper platter of *der Rindsbraten*. "Then *der kleine Knabe mit dem Grossvater* would be."

Henry stabbed viciously at his roast beef with a fork and seemed to growl. It was a little frightening for Frau Meuller.

"The damned sot grandfather isn't interested," he said. "We asked him. Besides, you don't want the baby or his mother living with that swine. And please, my love, speak English, will you?"

"As *Grossvater*, Waldenburg is a disgrace," she said, too angry now to cry.

"My love, Waldenburg is a disgrace in other ways," Henry Meuller said. "How could you expect him to be any different as *Grossvater*? Damn! English, English!"

It made her laugh a little. As Henry Meuller had planned it would.

So Henry Meuller gave Sophia twenty dollars in gold and a letter of introduction to a friend he had in San Antonio de Bexar. And he gave her something else, which he told her to get rid of in any way she chose or to keep as a memento of New Braunfels. Or whatever she wanted.

It was the Comanche finger necklace. Sophia was unmoved by it, knowing none of its history, and stuffed it in a flour sack along with loose clothing, baby shirts, and diapers.

Everything, including the baby crib one of the German cabinet-makers had provided, went into one of those high Mexican carts with two wheels, this one hitched to a pair of quality New Braunfels mules.

Paco Salazar would drive this cart into Bexar. His saddle horse would walk along behind, reins tied to the cart, because Salazar seldom went twenty feet in any direction without his horse, which was a gelding he called Red although the horse was not a bay or sorrel or red roan at all, but a black with white hocks and a blaze face.

To be prepared for anything in these uncertain times, Salazar placed two Colt revolvers under the seat. Two Mexican vaqueros had come up from Bexar to ride alongside the cart. This, as well as all other details of Sophia's move, had been arranged by Salazar at Henry Meuller's instruction.

Henry had asked Paco Salazar to carry out his plan once arrangements had been made with certain German citizens in Bexar. Salazar knew San Antonio better than did Henry Meuller, and part of the plan had been his anyway. He had suggested not only a place for Sophia to stay, but a woman to nurse the child and care for it while Sophia worked at the employment Henry Meuller had found for her at Mrs. Wolf's Hotel and Cafe.

It was impossible for Henry Meuller to know that sending Paco Salazar on this mission was significant for reasons beyond Salazar's being a trustworthy employee.

The good Frau Meuller would not allow the cart to leave her dooryard until it was heaped with food and blankets and things like soap and needles and thread. And many of her old clothes. Henry's as well, so Sophia could put the needles and thread to good use on alterations.

It was a cold December day when they left amid wind blowing off the Balcones. For a long time after the cart had pulled away, until it was only a speck on the far prairie, Wilmeth Meuller stood on her rear stoop, holding a shawl around her shoulders, and wiping the occasional tear from her eye.

"*Der winzige Knabe,*" she whispered. "So tiny the boy. So, sad, sad. So sad."

Some distance away from the settlement, well on the road to Bexar, Salazar turned to his passenger on the seat beside him, bundled in a serape and holding a blanket around the small bundle in her arms. Sophia's face was barely visible.

"I have never seen this child," Salazar said. "I would like to see him, *por favor*, Señora."

For a long time, Sophia looked at the Mexican with something like warmth in her eyes, and twice she appeared ready to speak. She said nothing, and maybe the warmth was hostility, but finally looking down at the bundle in her arms, she drew back the blanket.

As the cold wind hit the baby's face, he gave a startled jerk, and his eyes stared out at Salazar's face, but he made no sound.

"How do you call him?" Salazar asked.

"Gottlieb Heinrich Waldenburg Schiller."

"Ah," said Salazar, reaching across to touch the baby's face lightly, very briefly, with his fingertips. And then he pulled the blanket back over the child's face. "*Bueno!* But I will call him something else. *Sí*. A German name I will call him, but some other German name. Let me see. Do I know a German name? Ah. *Sí!* Oscar. That's what I will call him, Oscar. *El poco* Oscar. Little Oscar. It's almost like my name, is it not, Señora?"

Those were the only words Paco Salazar spoke until they reached San Antonio as it was growing dark. Nor did the Widow Schiller break the long silence.

Chapter Eleven

The Widow Sophia Waldenburg Schiller lay awake in San Antonio de Bexar thinking of the end of her first Texas dream, hoping that now this was not only a new bed but the beginning of a new dream as well.

She would bend her considerable efforts and talents to make it so, and she figured that the first step was to put everything at New Braunfels behind.

And the one thing she needed to put behind most definitely was the very thing that had convinced her that any future she might have in Texas could not be in the German community at New Braunfels.

There was one event that most surely had to be remembered one more time, with maybe one last sigh, and then forced away, pushed out, erased. Forever.

She knew part of this was known by a few, part was known to herself and one other, and part was known only to her. And she swore to herself, if not to God or to the Virgin or to any of her Catholic saints, that she would never reveal what she knew.

She knew the others would remain silent because each, for his own reasons, was either ashamed of what had happened or else was considerate of certain codes of silence in such circumstances.

In fact, Sophia was aware enough of her own recent shortcomings and how they had marked her among the *Adelsvereiners* that she wanted now to forget and forsake them all. Including her own child, for whom she had no emotion except apathy, and who, indeed, was the culmination of what she'd come to think of as the Braunfels calamity.

Yes, apathy as much for memories of her own life to this point as for the child himself, for the two were inseparable.

So she would stop thinking of her little life up until now, and that included the child. She knew he was probably better off for it. At least, she told herself so.

Sophia Schiller was blessed, or cursed, with an instinct for controlling beaus without seeming to try. It was a talent at which some young women were maddeningly expert although they were too immature to have learned such. They just knew.

She was particularly good at playing beaus off one against another, as she had at the summer Sunday afternoon picnics.

In this exercise, some young German swain with a hack or buggy and a horse or mule would suggest an after-church picnic, and Sophia would accept on condition of bringing along another pair of young men, explaining, her eyelashes fluttering, that the vast, wild prairie frightened her unless there were at least three brave young men at her side.

How many virile descendants of Teutonic knights could refuse such a challenge?

Of course, the vast prairie was of no concern, but her virtue was. And she knew nothing could protect her virtue more effectively than multiple suitors stumbling about with the same object in mind, each one watching the others.

Thus it was that at a momentous Sunday picnic, about ten months before Paco Salazar went out to find the Comanches so Herr Meuller could have his treaty, Sophia and three young *Adelsverein* beaus came to know that indeed there were very real reasons to be fearful of the wild prairie.

They had driven quite some distance from the settlement, along the escarpment, and found a small depression in the surrounding plain where there were a number of black jack oak and soapberry trees offering shade. There was a cool breeze out of the west, and from time to time fat little clouds passed before the sun so that they could look out and see a plain that was dappled with patches of blue shadow and glaring tan light.

As the young German man driving the mule drew rein under the black jack oak, they saw a horned lizard, which they mistakenly called a toad, scurry across the sand and scab rock and into hiding among the lower soapberries, where the branches came to the ground.

Naturally, seeing such a thing was good luck, they all said, laughing happily. But each of the young men was already alert to what the others were doing. As they dismounted and elbowed each other aside, each trying to be the one to help Sophia down, their mouths still laughed but their eyes didn't, each one aware of his competitors' every move.

Despite all the pushing and shoving to see who would be closest to Sophia as she spread the pallet, opened the basket, and began to unload it, they presented the appearance of good fellowship.

Sophia had brought Meuller silver and china, and she arranged it on the pallet with a German fudge cake, a bowl of potato salad, and a whole baked chicken. As she went about these labors, the three young men tried to outdo one another in praising her reputation as a cook.

Everyone around the picnic pallet was well aware that the young gentlemen were not in the least interested in the food or Sophia's ability to prepare it. But they made a fine show of trying to hide their real interest, which was the movement of Sophia's ample and well-distributed anatomy under her dress and petticoats as she arranged the picnic layout.

The mule was tethered to one of the soapberry bushes, and the pallet had been laid on the ground nearby. As the eating was about to commence, the mule gave a little snort and fiddled his hooves about, rattling some of the gravel underfoot. This was a message the four people around the roast chicken and fudge cake were too involved with one another to notice.

Hence, when the four Comanches appeared, the ponies quietly moving around the mule and coming almost to the picnic pallet before anyone was aware of them, the picnic party was so startled and terrified that at least one of them—you would assume it was Sophia—shrieked, and all four leaped up and scrambled back against the hack, making the mule fiddle his hooves even more until there was a small dust cloud rising beneath the mule's belly, whipped away quickly by the breeze.

The Comanches were young men, naked from the waist except for bandannas around their necks. Each wore his long hair loose, with a single, braided scalp lock down the back. Their faces were painted red and yellow.

"Do something," Sophia whispered frantically as the leading Comanche leered at her.

They were all grinning, gesturing, and talking with loud, raucous voices. They held lances, blade up except for the leader, and he used his to point at Sophia and the mule and the chicken. They had quivers and short, horn-reinforced bows and arrows, and each had a shield on his right shoulder. But the shields were in their rawhide coverings. They had no firearms. Not in sight, anyway.

"*Der liebe Gott,*" Sophia gasped softly. "Please! *Bitte!*"

There was a single hawk feather hanging down beside the face of the leader. That was the only feather they saw. There were extravagantly long fringes on their hide breechcloths and knee-length moccasins and waist belts. Partly hidden in all the dangling fringes were the handles of knives and the heads of tomahawk hatchets.

With a sudden movement of his arm, the leader thrust the point of the lance into the roast chicken and lifted it. The Comanches laughed.

"Oh, *mein Gott,*" Sophia whispered.

The leader swung the lance around, the chicken impaled on the end. One of the other Comanches snatched the chicken off the lance, looked at it as the others hooted. He took a great bite of the chicken, chewed a moment, made a sour face, and spit chicken bits out onto the picnic pallet. He threw the chicken down, and it bounced about in the gravel.

This delighted the Indians, and they laughed again and shouted, their loud voices jarring on the ear. If they were drunk, there was no odor of it.

Now the leader kneed his pony closer to them, its forehooves on the picnic pallet. The iron warhead tip of his lance was only a few feet in front of Sophia's face. The others were silent now, listening, watching the leader.

None of the Germans had the vaguest notion what the Comanche was saying. They stood in their huddled group beside the hack, wide-eyed, open mouthed, pale.

"Don't move, for God's sake, don't move," said one of the German gentlemen. This one was the oldest of the group, and his name was Helmuth. He was holding Sophia in his arms, but under the circumstances, there was no passion in his embrace, and he wasn't even aware that his body was pressed to hers, a circumstance he certainly would have enjoyed otherwise.

"*Um Gottes Willen,*" Sophia whispered. "Do something, for God's sake."

None of the young men moved. The Comanche leader had begun a dialogue with one of the others. They laughed a great deal. They jabbered. Confident. Arrogant.

Suddenly, the Comanches were no longer laughing. And their eyes were focused above the Germans standing beside the hack. And then giving the Germans a start as he rode around the soapberry bush and into their view was Paco Salazar.

The Comanches watched him intently, edging their ponies back. Salazar was very casual as he moved his horse close to the picnic pallet and then slowly, his face turned always toward the Indians, dismounted. The large rowels on his spurs jingled softly.

"Señora Schiller," he said, without looking away from the Comanches. "Come hold this horse. Now! Do it!"

As though coming out of a trance, Sophia jerked free of Helmuth's arms and stumbled to Paco Salazar's horse, and he handed her the reins, still not looking at her. She knew him, of course. He'd been in the Meuller house many times. But this was the first time he had ever spoken to her.

He very deliberately moved a step closer to the Comanches and swept his serape back across his shoulder, exposing his shirtfront. The Comanches' gaze seemed jerked to Salazar's middle. There, in the sash about his midsection, were the hard, polished butts of two Colt revolvers.

He spoke a few words in Comanche. The young leader grunted. Salazar spoke again, and after a while spoke to the German young men, but still with his eyes on the Indians.

"I've welcomed them," he said. "I've told them we are glad to see them. Have any of you got tobacco?"

Helmuth did. One of the others, too. The tobacco was in highly polished pouches from the old country.

"Good," said Salazar. "We are now going to give them a gift for their chief and allow them a way to back out of here without big shame attached to it. All right?"

"Yes, Herr Salazar," Helmuth said, and his voice squeaked.

"Walk over very slowly and give them the tobacco, pouches and all," said Paco Salazar. "Look at them square in the face and smile. Do it. Now, Señors."

Both young men struggled to smile. They looked very sick. But they got the tobacco to the leader nonetheless, and he quickly took the pouches and began to scowl. But he was still watching Paco Salazar, who spoke to him again.

After a moment of that, the Comanche leader seemed to hesitate. Salazar spoke a few words in English.

"I've told him we give a present for his greatest chief. A fine gift. He should take it to his chief with our greetings, and of course, they can smoke a little of it on the ride home."

Now, again, he spoke Comanche. In very warm tones, friendly tones. Finally, without any word, the young Comanche turned, as did his companions, and they went off, along the ridge. Almost as mysteriously as they had come, they were simply gone. Out of sight into a depression where no depression was apparent. But they were gone, their ponies sliding away silently, more like cats then horses.

Nobody said a word. But they all looked at Paco Salazar now, almost as intently as had the Comanches. He dropped the serape back across his front, concealing the guns, and walked over and picked up the chicken. He tore off a leg and took a bite, and turned then, chewing. And when he spoke, it seemed to be only to Sophia.

"Señora," he said, chewing and pointing at the area around them with the chicken leg, "*No es una junta merienda*. This is no picnic ground. You and these young men have come too far. Now go home before our friends decide to return and finish this chicken."

Nobody needed any encouragement. The men started to scramble into the hack, and Sophia dropped the rains of Paco Salazar's horse and ran over to the picnic basket.

"Señors, Señors," said Paco Salazar and waved his chicken at them, and they all scrambled back to help Sophia get everything that belonged in the Meuller kitchen back into the basket.

"Do you want the rest of this chicken?" asked Paco Salazar. Sophia didn't say anything. She shook her head violently and leaped up into the hack.

But the boldest of the young Germans, Helmuth, held the mule's reins, and for a moment he looked at Paco Salazar.

"What were they saying?" he asked.

Salazar tossed the well-chewed leg bone aside, tore off the second leg, and threw the carcass under one of the small soapberry trees, scaring out the horned lizard that made its second appearance, but only for long enough to find another hiding place in the sand.

"They wanted to buy Señora Schiller," he said. "They offered two horses."

They stared, shocked, and Paco Salazar suddenly laughed.

"It's not a bad price," he said. "I told them it was not enough because she was my wife."

Sophia Schiller gave an audible gasp of dismay. But by then, Salazar had grown more serious. He had begun to eat the second chicken leg, too.

"Something you can learn here. If you come on these people and they have no black on their faces, chances are they have not done any singing and dancing with their own personal god to prepare them for a fight."

"Their own personal god?" asked one of the Germans. "These savages have a personal god, each of them?"

"Most have more than one," said Salazar. "It's all a part of their medicine. Their power. But the most important god is always the one who deals with war. And unless they've made some medicine with this one beforehand, they are a little uncomfortable about fighting. They like to prepare themselves for fighting.

"And at the same time, they know we will jump into a fight flat-footed, as they say, without any preparation at all. They're uneasy with that; it's something they can't understand, going into something where they might die without doing a little singing about it with their god before it happens.

"So you can take advantage of this. Be bold, quick, and get out. Like playing a card game of chance. They are always dangerous. You've got to learn how far to push it. Six-shooters always help. They don't like six-shooters."

"This is why you let them see those pistols at once?"

"*Sí!* They saw twelve shots," said Paco, still chewing. "This is good chicken."

"Herr Salazar, what would have happened if they'd decided they wouldn't leave, but would fight, even if they hadn't prepared for it with their god?" asked Helmuth.

"Why of course," said Paco Salazar, and he shrugged slightly. "I would have killed them. Now go home."

The young Germans held on as Helmuth whipped his mule around and away, and Paco Salazar watched them, chewing on the last shreds of meat on the second drumstick. He looked across the plain toward the north and west. The Comanches were nowhere in sight.

He walked to his horse, eating the last of the chicken. He held the bone close to the horse's muzzle, and the horse sniffed, puffed, and turned his head aside in disgust.

Paco Salazar laughed and tossed the drumstick bone into the brush.

"All right," he said. "I thought you might like chicken. I had a horse once, a red horse, and he liked tamales. But you, you are a strange horse, aren't you? You are not a red horse; you are a black horse and you don't like tamales, do you? Or chicken. You are a very strange horse, do you know that, amigo?"

And he mounted and rode toward New Braunfels, following the faint smell of dust the mule and hack had raised. He didn't hurry. Now and then he glanced back along the escarpment, but of course, there was no longer any sign of Comanches.

It was pretty obvious why none of the young picnic Germans was saying anything about those four Comanches or anything else relative to Sunday afternoons on the Balcones Escarpment. It was embarrassing to admit a Mexican saved them from some kind of fate worse than death at the hands of wild aborigines.

It was even worse to be branded a fool over having sugarbutt so bad their judgment deserted them, allowing them to wander too far out onto dangerous ground.

They were horrified at the thought that Paco Salazar was bound to tell Herr Meuller the whole business. It never entered their minds that the Mexican had no intention of doing so because he'd attached no importance to the incident, passing it off as a bit of bad judgment by a group of horny young tenderfeet.

But Sophia thought about it from a different perspective. She didn't mention it to anyone, either. She was fearful that were she to talk about what had happened, her face would show how wonderful she had come to think Paco Salazar was, how beautiful he was, not just handsome, but beautiful.

She had seen him many times, often at very close range in the Meuller house, but she had never really looked at him, really *looked*, because after all, he was a Mexican.

She had seen his *casa*, a small one-room house behind the Meuller's main barn, built for the major-domo, used only when he was at New Braunfels. When she went onto the back patio in the evenings to throw out the dishwater or to toss corn to the chickens, she could see the orange light shining in the single window of that little house, so she always knew when he was near. And when there was no light, she knew he was probably in San Antonio.

But she'd never thought about it. Paco Salazar being near or being away had been of no concern, of even less than no concern.

Now it was of concern. She went to the back patio two-dozen unnecessary times on the Monday after that Sunday of the horned lizard and the four Comanches, just to look for him. And on a night just a week later, the light was there, and after she'd fed the chickens, she stayed in the dark shadows of the patio for a long time, watching it.

And the next morning she heard him talking with Herr Meuller just outside her kitchen while she was preparing the Meuller breakfast. The sound of his voice once more made strange stirrings inside her chest. That's when she decided on the chicken.

Lying awake in her pantry bedroom behind the kitchen, she thought about herself and about Paco Salazar. She knew that the Mexican *jefe* was respected in this community, not only for his efficiency in dealing with livestock and workers, but also for his character. Everyone saw him as clean and compassionate, reverent and righteous.

She compared that with what she knew most of the citizens of this community thought of her. And she had to laugh, recalling a little joke she had made for herself. That she would be rich if she could buy a hog for the sins of lust she had committed and sell it for the sins of lust all the people thought she had committed.

So she was well aware of the reputation she had built for herself in New Braunfels. It had never particularly bothered her. She liked men. She liked to have fun. Despite what so many people thought, these two things did not automatically result in some sort of sweaty coupling in the grape vineyard or hayloft.

If the truth be known—and Sophia knew it—the young men in this community knew what she was: a tease. And no young man anxious for respect from his peers would admit that after all his fawning and wiggling and gift giving and panting around, all he got were a few giggling hugs and pecking kisses.

The times she had actually succumbed to a man's advances could be counted on the fingers of one of her hands, not inclusive of the thumb. Three had been mistakes, each time after too much wine during one of the community celebrations, and always regretted the next morning, and never repeated with the young man in question.

And one had been in Germany when she was eleven years old and didn't really count, having been in the nature of exploration and without any emotional upheaval or aftershock or any of those other things girls were supposed to suffer when they were introduced to carnal knowledge too early.

In fact, as Sophia recalled the incident, she had been the aggressor and the fourteen-year-old boy the terrified partner. Maybe he'd had the aftershock; she didn't know.

Anyway, later, lying in New Braunfels thinking about it, Sophia was a little sorry about the bed she'd made for herself, because she'd have liked to be able to take Señor Salazar his baked chicken without all those blemishes her reputation had suffered at the hands, or rather mouths, of the community *Hausfrauen*.

Oh yes, she was going to take him a baked chicken. He'd said that was good chicken, hadn't he?

Then after she'd decided, there was a long spell when the orange light wasn't there. Salazar's house was dark, and there was no sign of the Mexican during the day.

But Sophia had patience, and it was rewarded finally when Salazar returned from Bexar with machinery for a sawmill on one of those outrageous Mexican carts. The light was there that night, shining in the purple gloaming, and Sophia was humming in her kitchen.

Next day, she saw him grooming the black horse in one of Meuller's lots near his adobe house, and she immediately killed a chicken and stoked the fire in the kitchen range. She was not concerned about being interrupted.

At this time of day, Frau Meuller never came into the back. And at any time, she never questioned what Sophia was doing, feeling apparently that a cook trusted enough to put food on her table should be trusted to run the kitchen without somebody else poking their nose into it.

Anyway, by full darkness, Sophia had a beautifully roasted chicken, golden brown and juicy and smelling as only a golden-brown, juicy roasted chicken can smell.

"*Ach, Du schöner Vogel, Du!*" she whispered softly. "You beautiful bird, you!"

"*Entre!*"

This was one of the few Spanish words she knew, so Sophia pushed open the door and moved into Salazar's one-room *casa*. He was in shirt-sleeves, and she realized she had never seen him before without a jacket of some kind.

There was a small table with two candles burning—rather extravagant, she thought—where he sat polishing a pair of silver spurs with cruel, gigantic rowels. There was a clutter of tinware on the table, some showing signs of recent food. There was a small earthen jug.

The candles were enough to illuminate the small room. There were a number of stools, a rather large bunk bed along one wall with rumpled blankets spilling over its sides, and a clothes closet, not much more than a box that could be moved around to wherever. It looked more like a box than a clothes closet.

"*Guten Abend!*" Sophia said and moved directly to the table with her platter, covered with a tea cloth, as he stared at her in frank astonishment. "I have here some food for you to eat. Some, how you say it, *das Brathuhn!*"

Suddenly he laughed, because it was apparently all rather comic to his mind, and he saw her smile now as he laughed and realized that her brazen entry had been a performance she had willed herself to do no matter the consequences. Like a rebellious pupil screwing up courage to talk back to the teacher.

"Roast chicken," he said. As she placed the platter on the table between the candles, he pulled off the tea-cloth cover and laughed again. "*Sí!* I've been smelling it for the past hour. I wondered who would have the pleasure of eating it."

"You could smell it here?" she gasped, like a schoolgirl again, giggling and sitting down at the table, placing her elbows on it, all boldness now, looking at him while he tore off a drumstick and started eating. Chewing, his mouth full, he indicated the chicken and looked at her, and she shook her head.

"*La gallina de oro!*" he said.

"This I don't know," Sophia said. "I don't know this language much."

"I said it was a golden chicken. That's how I'd say it in English. I don't know how you would say it in German."

Even in the soft glow of candlelight, she could see the streaks of gray in his mustache. She liked it because he had it trimmed neatly, not hanging down like old lace covering his lips, as so many of the Germans did.

He returned her gaze, and she laughed, a little embarrassed, and looked for something to say and quickly picked up one of the spurs. She touched the rowel, turning it slowly.

"It is a cruel thing for *das Pferd, ja?*" she said.

"The horse doesn't think so, if you don't kick his flank with them," said Paco Salazar.

"*Ach,* so you got these, what is it, *der Sporn?* But you do not put them on the foot?"

"They are spurs in English. They are *las espuelas* in my language. You can choose which you want to use," he said and laughed and continued to eat the chicken.

"This languages, is too many for me," she said.

"You are doing well in English," he said. "We've been speaking English all the while, and you have no trouble understanding do you? But about *la espuela.* . . ."

"The spur!" she interrupted, and they both laughed.

"You see? You can learn the English quickly," he said. "But now, the spur. I wear these only for being handsome, with a fine red serape, because they shine and jangle when I walk and dance."

And she knew he was teasing her. She lowered her eyes and placed the spur back down with the other. She was no longer laughing.

"I beg your pardon, Señorita. I had no intention of offending you. In truth, the spurs mean much to me. They were given to me by an Anglo named Hays when I left the service of the Texas Rangers. I have never worn them."

She looked at him then without smiling, and she was not thinking of spurs but that he had called her Señorita, not Señora.

"I wanted to come and thank you because of those bad men on the escarpment, and bring you something, *das Geschenk*, a gift from me."

She paused, but her eyes did not waver and continued to look squarely into his without any of that rash boldness he'd marked at first. Rather with some kind of urgency or what he suddenly thought of as a soft determination.

And it was then that he knew what this visit was all about.

"Sophia," he said, and he knew she recognized immediately that his addressing her in this familiar way signaled that he knew what her being there meant. He almost laughed, thinking that despite the confusion of three different spoken tongues here, there was no chance of error in the meaning of this unspoken language. "I am old enough to be your father."

Her eyes remain steadily fixed, and her lips seemed to set in a hard line of resolve.

"I knew that before I baked the chicken," she said.

"Your life is with those people there," and Paco Salazar nodded his head in the direction of the big house.

"I knew that, too," she said. "But not for this night. For this night, you are the young Black Forest knight. And you've already killed the dragon."

He started to say that he'd heard these Germans always pumped their children full of the fairy tales of witches and princes and toads and gingerbread houses deep in the dark woods, but he stopped himself in time. This was no child here, and she wasn't thinking of any fairy tale.

"Sophia," he said, reaching over and placing a hand over one of hers, "I see that now you have no trouble with these confusing languages."

And as he smiled, she did as well.

"*Vielleicht!* Maybe."

They could hear a whippoorwill on the far side of the grape vineyard, in some low persimmon trees. Somehow, the soft notes seemed to intrude on the dimly lit room as no other sound had since Sophia arrived.

"Sophia," he said. "Would you lie with me in my bed?"

She waited so long to respond that he thought perhaps she was preoccupied with the night bird's song. But finally, she had reached out to first one candle then the other, and with thumb and forefinger pinched out the light.

And so she lay awake now on the first night of the beginning of what she expected to be a new life. And she thought of New Braunfels, and she thought of what the people there thought of her.

And she thought of Paco Salazar, and she thought of the baby, *el poco* Oscar. And she thought of that night and how before dawn she had gone back to the big house and how she knew as she went that never again would she make that same walk, no matter where her kitchen might be, no matter where Paco Salazar's bed might be.

And it had happened as she expected. And afterward, Paco Salazar came to the big house only when necessary and then never came inside, where they might meet face to face. And all around the settlement, he was kind enough to stay clear of her, too.

And she knew he was doing this not because he was fearful of a renewal of what had been between them that night, but rather to allow her that prerogative of renewal.

And even during her last, she hoped, connection with New Braunfels, the ride to San Antonio de Bexar, he had volunteered to be the driver of her cart, allowing her the final opportunity to exercise that prerogative easily, with him sitting close beside her. And not pushing it, only being there if she wanted to make the decision.

And she could say she loved him in some strange way, and turn to him again and be accepted. She was sure he would take her, and on her terms.

But she didn't. She did not do it on all those nights when she could look from the Meuller's kitchen and see the orange light in the window of his *casa*. She did not do it during various nights of community celebration when everyone was feeling so festive and gay. And she didn't do it on the ride from New Braunfels to Bexar with him sitting right beside her.

Because he had been right. He was old enough to be her father, maybe her grandfather, and she was not prepared to start a household with a husband who would be ancient while she still had the juices of vibrant life running in her body.

For most German girls of twenty, it would have made no difference, and in fact many of them married older men. But Sophia was not most German girls. Salazar's being old now was no matter. But in twenty years, to Sophia, she knew it would matter.

So she had not turned back to him, and she knew he had not really expected her to but was simply giving her the opportunity. And she couldn't do it. He was too old.

And with that thought, she realized that whether she was of low birth or high, she had somewhere, somehow assumed the haughty caste consciousness of a Potsdam aristocrat, which Frau Meuller was and Sophia was not.

The sum total of it all was that she wanted another chance in another social climate, and no affection she had for the Meullers or the Mexican or the child was strong enough to hold her in the lifetime pattern she could see down the years if she stayed at New Braunfels.

Even if there was that soft, strange love for Paco Salazar, he was too old.

Besides, he was a Mexican!

She could hear the night sounds of San Antonio. There was a dog barking. Somewhere there was a cornet playing, far off, in another barrio. Someone nearby was cooking onions. It had begun to thunder. Soon she could smell the rain, before she heard it, coming down finally in a downpour on the pole shingles on the roof over the patio in back.

She could hear the raindrops like buckshot, rattling the dried blossoms of the tequila agave.

From the next room, where the woman and the child were sleeping, there was no sound. Nor were there any animal noises from the back, because all the animals and the cart had only paused here and then started back for New Braunfels, and she had a brief moment thinking of Paco Salazar driving the big Mexican cart out there in the dark, in the rain.

And then she slept soundly in the bed that Alex Mesero had stolen a long time ago.

Part Three

The Tonk

Chapter Twelve

When British General John Burgoyne brought an army down the Lake Champlain–Hudson River Corridor to split off New England from the rest of the colonies in 1777, he had a lot of German mercenaries with him. They didn't do him much good.

At a place called Bemis Heights, New York, the American colonial army met Burgoyne and gave him and his partly German force a sound thrashing. It was a two-day fight later called the Battle of Saratoga, and it may have been the single most decisive battle of the American Revolution.

All the credit for the victory was taken by Horatio Gates. Actually, Gates had almost nothing to do with it, except he wrote the report afterward, which included the aforesaid credit but did not mention Benedict Arnold's name.

The decision was won on both days when the army enthusiastically followed Arnold on the field despite Gates's ordering him to stay in his tent. The future traitor was a tactical genius and compelling leader.

Anyway, in all the shot and shell and confusion, a Hessian grenadier named Klaus Silesia was seriously wounded and left on the field for dead as the British retreated for a while and then surrendered.

It would be better at the outset to account for the name and have it done with. This man was of questionable character. A resume of all he had done in his homeland to require his running off to join the army would be a study far beyond the scope and interest of our story. Just suffice it to say he was in some very deep trouble and sought a hiding place in uniform.

His name was not really Silesia. That was the German state from which he came, most likely. His real name was never revealed by him or anyone who knew him. But he was not the kind of uneducated dolt you'd expect to find in one of those German regiments, which were famous only for being rented out to first one monarch and then another for various wars, like the American Revolution.

Of course, the American colonies couldn't afford to rent any German regiments, but the British could.

After Saratoga, Grenadier Silesia lay torn and bleeding when the combatants moved to other business. But as luck would have it, there were many German settlers in this area, and although they were patriots each and every one, they were also compassionate, and Lutheran, just like Grenadier Silesia.

A farmer's young children found the wounded man, and he was taken into the farmer's house, washed all over with soap and water by the farmer's sons, and fed hot soup by the farmer's wife and daughters.

The uniform, bloody and torn, was thrown in the fire. Among the other equipment, there were objects which armies always require a soldier to carry, like a canteen, but there were no weapons.

You can imagine the soldier's surprise when he recovered enough from his wounds to understand how his fortunes had changed. He was among people who spoke his mother tongue, they were kind and gentle to him, they fed him well, they gave him clothes to wear, and they even invited him to accompany them to church services when he was well enough to be up and around without assistance.

It strengthened his resolve to leave his German regiment by fair means or foul and become a citizen of this land. He was not the first, nor would he be the last, German mercenary who came to the English colonies to put down the colonists' rebellion and stayed on to help them make a country.

Eventually, Klaus Silesia ended in Schenectady, where there were plenty of Germans, married a woman originally from Hesse, managed a hostelry, and fathered seven children, the one of interest here being Roth, who wanted to follow his father's trade and did, but found Schenectady too small for his appetites and went to New York City, where there were plenty of Germans, too.

From this, you would suspect that German immigrants rather liked clustering together. It was true. Germans could fit into a wider environment, but they liked other Germans around, too. This is very important to remember with regard to the next episode of the Silesia saga. Because the next episode had to do with finding a place where there were plenty of Germans with whom one could cluster. Or perhaps hide is a better word, in the case of the Silesia involved.

This Silesia was Ulrich, grandson of that old Hessian mercenary, first offspring of Roth Silesia and his wife, who had been daughter to the publisher of a German-language newspaper in New York.

In 1837 there was a terrible panic in America, brought on by many things, but partly by speculation in what was called bank paper.

Bank paper was the currency issued by banks. That's where the "paper" part comes in. These pieces of paper were little more than IOUs, or promissory notes from the issuing institution, say First City Bank of Manhattan, telling everyone that these slips of paper could be used as money in the conducting of business and could be redeemed for gold at the bank on demand.

This was an effort to establish some kind of currency so business could be conducted without people having to haul around heavy metal coins all the time, and also to allow credit and to do all the things paper currency is supposed to do.

The problem was that people had to trust this stuff and couldn't go running to the bank to get their paper redeemed constantly, because the banks didn't have the metal to back up the notes they had out. Which was a kind of borrowing.

Anyway, this kind of money could create wild speculation. Which it did. And a man like Ulrich, whose mother was in a newspaper family, often saw opportunities.

Particularly because, as you might consider, newspaper folks might know things about banks before the general public, like when new issues of money would be made or outstanding notes devalued or certain issues voided. And newspapers were published once a week in that era, which meant a person might know such things a long time before the general public.

Hence, someone like Ulrich, knowing things ahead of time, had many occasions on which to make a small profit here and there, while maybe a lot of people were losing the farm. Soon after his speculations began, Ulrich's advantage became common knowledge, which was extremely embarrassing.

Now Ulrich was not a criminal. Well, not really. He was only taking advantage of a system. But there were a lot of people, like those who lost the farm, who didn't much give a damn whether you called Ulrich a criminal or not. They were ready to get out the tar and feathers or even a rope.

Sensing his peril early, Ulrich took passage on a coastal schooner. Having heard many stories of a German immigration of some force, which he might join without attracting too much attention, he vowed to make a new life in the business at which his father Roth and grandfather Klaus had been successful. A hostelry and cafe.

If he could only find a town where such things were needed. In Texas.

Maybe it was a good time for change. The country was surely changing. The whole world was changing.

For the first time in memory, the United States wasn't jawing with Great Britain over some problem like the Oregon Territory, which President Polk had solved with diplomacy. And there didn't appear to be much chance of a war breaking out with France or Spain.

Internationally, the tone was set somewhat by the feeling everyone had toward that eighteen-year-old girl who had become queen of Great Britain and empress of India. Everybody loved Victoria, even though when Ulrich Silesia left New York, she had been on the throne for more than a decade and was no longer a lovely little girl.

Now America had the Monroe Doctrine.

That'll sure keep them nosy Europeans out of our business, people said.

And "our business" included a real plateful. On the Pacific coast, California was now a state, the thirty-first star in the field of blue, the completion of Andrew Jackson's ambition and Thomas Jefferson's dream. And the crowning glory of Mr. Polk's Mexican War.

Things would happen out there when a man digging a millrace discovered the glimmer of hope in the rocks and set off the first great internal migration. It was followed by stampedes to various sites in the Rocky Mountains, Alaska, New Zealand, South Africa—an entire century of gold-rush fever. And the first rush was in California.

Slavery was still gurgling in the trouble pot, but for a time it had been pushed to the rear, maybe, by the Missouri Compromise, which was a Henry Clay piece of legislation passed in Congress allowing Missouri to enter the Union as a slave state but prohibiting slavery in all other territory north of Arkansas.

Or if you like, in all territory north of north latitude thirty-six degrees, thirty minutes.

People found ways to spell progress. In the northeast, somebody figured out how to pull teeth or cut out a bad appendix without pain. At about the same time, somebody else strung a metal wire along tall poles set in the ground from Washington City to Baltimore and sent a coded message along it. You had to know the code to read the message, but what the hell. It was progress.

And in at least three states they had passed legislation setting ten hours a day as the maximum time a child could be employed in a textile mill or coal mine or whatever. Now there's real progress for you.

There were already a few railroads being built in the East, the start of a one-hundred-year era of those monster machines called locomotives rumbling past, belching smoke and hot cinders and scaring hell out of good horses.

A steamboat had paddled to the end of navigable water on the Mississippi River, docking finally on a sandbar at Fort Snelling, in the northernmost part of the old Louisiana Purchase, the site of a future state called Minnesota and the future city of Saint Paul.

There were over seventeen million people in the United States, and about twenty-five hundred of those were in San Antonio, where everything seemed pretty much as it had been before statehood. Those Texan philosophers who ten years before had said Bexar would soon be inundated with cotton and black African slaves had been wrong.

Texas was already becoming a cotton kingdom, but it was all east of the Colorado. In the broad valley of the lower Brazos, all of the Trinity country, and the pine woods area of the Sabine, it was solid Anglo country, big-planter heaven, and home for most of the slaves in the state.

Bexar was still dead center on the hostile Comanche frontier. San Antonio was a trade town, becoming one of the biggest hide markets in the world.

You might call it a transportation center. It was the jumping-off place from the United States to Mexico, for anybody who wanted to go there. More important, it was the jumping-off place, too, for California, along the southern route. Stagecoach lines serviced the whole state, because there wasn't a single foot of railroad track anywhere.

Visitors from Europe and the East made jokes about what Texans called roads. Nonetheless, you could walk into a Butterfield office in San Antonio and buy a ticket for San Francisco or Saint Louis, with a reasonable expectation of reaching either destination in two or three weeks, unless the rivers flooded or the Comanches decided to ride out of their High Plains country and scald out a few stagecoach stations.

Of course, if you were going to California, once you got past El Paso the Comanche problem was pretty much behind you. From there to the Gila River crossing, all you had to worry about were Apaches. Except for Mexican bandits. They might show up anywhere from the outskirts of San Antonio to Yuma.

Taken all together, traveling in the time of Ulrich Silesia could be an adventure.

Most people weren't interested in that long-haul travel. They were still edging out west of San Antonio to set up a homestead or ranch or whatever you want to call it. There was plenty of empty land there for anybody who had guts enough to try holding a few acres of it. Amazingly, there were a lot of people hungry enough for home owner-ship to do just about anything.

The first senators the new state of Texas sent to Washington City complained to the secretary of war and to the president himself about the lack of army protection for Texas citizens. About 190 people had been killed or carried off by Comanche war parties over the past year, they said.

Well, all the appropriate officials were saddened and offered con-dolences, but nobody sent any troops that made much difference.

"They send us a couple of these damned infantry outfits that sit in a fort somewheres," said one Texican. "What is it they think is gonna happen? They think the Comanch' gonna ride up to this here fort and stand still long enough for somebody to draw a bead on em?"

"Them people in the United States don't know what Comanches is like down here," said another. "You got to have cavalry out there shootin hell out of em now and again, not lollygaggin around trying to make a peace treaty. You gotta treat em like Rangers treat em. Powder burn hell out of em now and again, with six guns!"

"It sticks in my craw the way they act," said yet another. "All that New Mexico business. That really sticks in my craw!"

The "New Mexico" business stuck in a lot of Texas craws.

Texas always claimed the land east of the Rio Grande as well as north. This meant half of New Mexico, including Santa Fe. So at the close of the Mexican War, the Texas governor sent Judge Spruce Baird to take charge of New Mexico county.

The nasty part of this was that President Polk had promised Texas that this land belonged to the Lone Star State. But before Texas got congressional approval to become a state, and to include that slice of New Mexico, Polk was out of office, and everybody else was adamantly opposed to a single square inch of New Mexico becoming a part of Texas. This was particularly true of New Mexicans, who figured they had their own history and didn't need to borrow any from Texas.

So Judge Baird, meanwhile, traveled to Laredo, across Coahuila to El Paso del Norte and hence up the Rio Grande and to Santa Fe, where the United States Army informed him that a convention of New Mexicans had already met to write a territorial constitution and that he, Judge Baird, and all of Texas could go jump up a rope.

Judge Baird was offended, of course, but had no recourse but to return to Columbia. So he traveled up the Santa Fe Trail and across Kansas into Missouri and south to Arkansas and still south to enter Texas from the northeast corner.

His route home was interesting for what it tells you about west Texas. And what it tells you is that at the time, it was not safe to travel across west Texas, hence the judge's wide swing-around to get home.

Anyway, when Judge Baird told his story to the pols in Columbia, there was much wailing and gnashing of teeth, you would suppose, and talk of sending Texas state troops to Santa Fe or at the least of secession from the Union which Texas had just joined.

The U.S. of A. finally paid Texas a lot of money and assumed some Texas war debts. But the whole episode left a bad taste. Particularly since Texas's defense against its constant enemy had such little support from the same federal government that had forced the New Mexico thing down its throat.

"By God," said Spruce Baird. "I thought when we joined their Union, it meant we were supposed to be defended by the regular United States Army, like all other citizens of the republic!"

"Well, they be recruitin good young lads fer the Ranger companies again," said one Texan. "John Coffee Hays gettin too long in the tooth I reckon fer field campaignin. But they'll be new ones to replace him."

"*Sí*," said a Texas Mexican. "And Antonio Perez. The hero of all *niños* who play in the barrios. But hard men to replace."

San Antonio was the center for all that, too. Unlike east Texas, where white man meant Anglo, in Bexar it likely meant Celtic. Scot, Welsh, Scots-Irish—that raw breed that always seemed to be at the cutting edge of any American frontier. And they made good Rangers.

But when Ulrich Silesia wrote to his father in New York, you would have thought that all of Texas had been designed especially for Silesia and his personal endeavors.

"It is impossible to describe," he wrote. "I tremble at the thought of being so blessed. Here I am, in Texas.

"In east Texas there are plantations, and much cotton is grown there. I am told there are counties where the black Africans very nearly outnumber the whites.

"The Cotton East, some of the locals call it. The whites there are almost all from the Old South of the United States. Georgia, Mississippi, Alabama.

"Here, you will be happy to know that most whites are from the North and East, such as myself, or from Europe, as we had heard, but not only from German states. There are Swiss and Austrians and Danes.

"But this will surprise you. I am told at present there are more Germans in San Antonio than all other whites and Mexicans combined. These Mexicans, by the way, father, are people who have been in Texas for three or four generations and are the true natives.

"Well, they are the true natives if you don't want to count the savages. I am unconcerned with them. It has been a long time since they rode into San Antonio with any mischief in mind."

Although in later years he grew less diligent in advising his father of his life in Texas, at first Ulrich Silesia was more dependable than the mail service itself.

"Dear Father: Sometimes your letters arrive via Galveston on the coast, but yesterday I received one only a month old that had come to Saint Louis and hence along the stagecoach route through Missouri and Arkansas.

"Can you imagine? Even when it entered this state, your letter was still over two hundred miles from its destination. Distances are formidable in Texas.

"Good news. I have bought a place in the very center of San Antonio de Bexar. It is constructed of logs and adobe brick and some local white limestone and is ideal for my purposes. It will be ready for business in the fall as a hotel, boardinghouse, and cafe. Or *die Gaststätte*. But I try to do everything in English here, as I did there. May Grandfather rest in peace!

"It is on the north side of Main Plaza, a great square directly in front of the biggest church here, the Mission of San Fernando, which the Catholics will call a cathedral as soon as they can get a bishop assigned here.

"That may take a long time. This place would impress you as being somewhat primitive still. You might watch two hogs rooting in the street at the center of town in the afternoon and the same evening attend a lovely ball given by an old Spanish family or one of the big Gringo hide merchants, with fine food and fine wines and a string quartet playing music by one of the German masters.

"By the way, I have no trouble buying material or hiring good people. My U.S. coins are a rarity here. Most money in circulation is Spanish or Mexican silver and a little gold. Some of it was minted in the days of the Bourbon kings of Spain. Business is conducted by promissory note. Some of our businesses issue notes like currency. There is no bank.

"Before I forget, let me tell you of my latest venture. I have purchased a small group of buildings in what you might characterize as an alley behind my hotel and I've begun a brewery there.

"There are plenty of people here who understand the art of brewing beer. Surprisingly, the Mexicans make a very passable beer themselves. But I will have a good *deutsche Braumeister*. In fact, I have found one already. His name is Heimel Uttegard.

"Lastly, I have decided on a name for my hotel and cafe. In view of your having told me when I was a child bouncing on your knee that my name meant Wolf—the bold and fearless, remember?—I am calling my place in San Antonio Mrs. Wolf's Hotel and Cafe.

"Using that 'Mrs.' presents the appearance of a lovely, fat, motherly lady in the kitchen making wonderful things to eat. The Wolf part will appear to be bold and fearless when I am asking guests to pay their bill.

"Please convey my most sincere affection to mother. I wish I could show her a field of blooming Texas bluebonnets. Or wild daisies. Perhaps next spring I can press some of our wildflowers and send them to her. She would be captivated.

"Your obdt. son, Ulrich"

And in another:

"My Dear Father and Mother: I have been remiss in explaining the religious atmosphere in San Antonio, and thanks to your questions about it, mother, I am now reminded.

"All the Mexicans are Catholic, and so are a considerable number of European whites. A few German whites are Catholic, but most of these are Lutheran. Among Anglos, there are various Calvinists, to include Presbyterians and Baptists, with the Celts among these leaning toward Methodism.

"You may recall a few years ago all the talk we heard of great revivals in the South and along the frontiers, among the Protestants. That seems to have died out now.

"The Catholic presence is most apparent because of the missions. These are everywhere and very old. It was a mission that started this settlement in the first place, and the Franciscans are still in evidence.

"In other news, we recently had what they call a twister storm. The wind blows and it rains and hails and thunders and lightnings and frightens everyone and then goes away quickly, and everything smells fresh and clean.

"I have served the first of my own beer in my own cafe. Competitors, both German and Mexican, surround me. Never fear."

After Ulrich Silesia's mother died, his letters began to contain material he might have considered indecorous earlier.

"In the rare chance you might hear I have taken a mistress, I can tell you it is not true. But I can explain how the gossipmongers of San Antonio could come to such a conclusion.

"During the first months of my residence here, I met and became friends with a man named Meullerbach, who now calls himself Meuller. He brought a large contingent of our people from Deutschland and settled north of San Antonio, establishing a town called New Braunfels. This is part of the German immigration we heard about in New York.

"Recently he asked that I do a good turn for him and find employment for a young woman of his community who had had the misfortune of giving birth to an illegitimate child and wanted to reestablish a residence in San Antonio.

"I agreed. Her name is Sophia Waldenburg Schiller, and her child, a son, is about two years old now, I understand. I have never seen it. She was widowed some years ago, so her husband was not father to the child.

"She was brought by Meuller's major-domo, a Mexican named Salazar who is quite famous around here as an old Indian fighter of the republic period. He established her in a small house he owns a short distance from Plaza de Armas, or Military Plaza, in a Mexican quarter of the town. It is south of Via Dolorosa and just off Camino de Laredo.

"(I use these Spanish names to acquaint you with the flavor of our fair San Antonio.)

"Señor Salazar deposited Sophia and her child here under the care of an Indian squaw he found at one of the missions, I assume.

"At first, the gossipmongers had Sophia as mistress to this Salazar. But that fell through quickly, disappointing a great many drooling busybodies, because Salazar doesn't stay in his own house when he comes to town, which is infrequently, but rather spends those nights with ox cart or Ranger friends.

"Soon, Frau Schiller came to me asking if she might make over one of my storerooms where she could stay, and I agreed, thinking she would spend a night there now and again.

"But no, she moved in to live, just downstairs from my own quarters here in Mrs. Wolf's Hotel and Cafe. She goes to visit her son perhaps once or twice a week, and then not for long. To take money to the squaw, I assume, to run the household. The squaw has a goat, I am told.

"It has been a wonderful situation. Sophia is a demon for work, and this puts her on the scene twenty-four hours a day. I trust her with more and more of the establishment.

"Sophia is not unattractive. So every billy-goat randypants in town, among the English- and German-speaking gentlemen, has mounted a campaign for occupancy of her bed. She has rebuffed them all soundly and sometimes in language loud enough to be heard out on Plaza de las Islas. (That's Main Plaza, where Mrs. Wolf's is, so named in honor of the Canary Islanders who came here a century ago and built the cathedral and the governor's palace.)

"So the lewd-mouths have me sleeping with Sophia each night. My close friends joke with me about it because they know it is absurd."

"Tonight it rains. Not often does it rain here. It is cold. If it rains enough, the river will flood and there will be water over the sidewalk in front of the hotel.

"At least it gives me some rest from this Texas Tower of Babel. There are no customers in my taproom or dining room, so I am not bombarded with the sounds of all those voices, all those varied tongues.

"Father, the sounds of voices here remind me of the cacophony of talk along Wall Street or at the Fish Market in Fulton Street. There is English, of course, then Spanish and German in equal doses, and often babbles of an Indian speech, I suppose Comanche, because they tell me it is the trade language of the Southern Plains.

"Yet when the sound of it is not there, I catch myself thinking something important is missing. Well, *das machts nichts!*

"It is a lonely night. My thoughts are much of New York and when you and mother and brother Willie and sister Bertha and I would sit before a nice fire on a late October evening and Bertha would read the poems of Schiller.

"What an irony! My most trusted employee now here in the wilds of a Texas frontier was married to a Schiller before he died. I doubt there was any connection. Although one never knows. Perhaps my cook and barroom matron was indeed once married into the family of our favorite poet.

"I saw her child today. The Indian woman who keeps him

appeared on the far side of Main Plaza with him, and simply stood there, a rather tall woman draped in a colorful Mexican serape, with the child beside her, seeming so tiny. And so inquisitive. Looking up and down and all about the square, and there was plenty of activity, this being before the clouds and the rain came.

"Then Sophia saw them. Or perhaps there was a prearranged meeting. She walked across to them, and she spoke for a moment with the Indian, returned to her quarters behind the kitchen, then walked back across the square and gave something to the Indian woman.

"Money, I suppose. Whatever it was, it appeared to be what the Indian woman came for because she led the child away.

"Throughout all this, I did not see mother and child touch once. When Sophia went to them the first time, I saw the child look at her approaching, then for a moment more watch as she spoke with the Indian, then seem to lose all interest and once more start looking first this way and then that across the square.

"For her part, I did not see Sophia once look down at her son. It rather disturbed me, in some strange way. Now this rain comes to dampen my spirits more.

"I sit here feeling the damp cold, listening to the rain, and wondering about that child, somewhere now in the south barrio, in some adobe hut. Alone with the Indian woman. It seems cruel. He has a mother under my very roof. He has a father in New Braunfels. I understand he has a grandfather there as well. Yet tonight when it is cold and raining, he is alone, with only a savage heathen woman to console him in his fitful slumber."

Just south of Via Dolorosa near Camino de Laredo, in a two-room adobe house on a short, narrow street that was little more than an alleyway, named Calle de Armador in honor of an early Spanish official of Bexar and property of famous Indian fighter Paco Salazar, there slept that night the child, with indeed no one to console him in his fitful slumber but the heathen savage.

It fact, this child seldom needed consoling in his fitful slumber because he never had that sort of trouble when it was time to sleep. When it was time to sleep, which under the present circumstance was indicated by the heathen savage, he lay down and slept.

At first on the floor, until finally the woman insisted in tones the child quickly learned indicated there would be no deviation, at which time he got into the bed Alex Mesero had stolen and went immediately to sleep, while she slept on the floor beside the bed.

On the next night, however, he insisted, without words, of course, that he would not sleep unless she get in the bed too and, with actions and facial expressions and huffings and puffings, indicated that he would brook no discussion about it. From then until some time in the future the both of them slept in the bed Alex Mesero had stolen, and so far as anyone could tell, the child showed no signs of damage to his personality due to loneliness.

At least, not for the time being.

Chapter Thirteen

The cuckoo bird lays her eggs in somebody else's nest. So when the cuckoo chick breaks out of the shell and looks up and sees a thrush or a blackbird or a finch, it probably figures this is mother. And all the other chicks in the nest are brothers and sisters.

Of course, the cuckoo chick does not look anything like the big bird or the other chicks, but the cuckoo doesn't know this, there being no mirrors in the nest.

The mother bird knows the difference, because she can see all her own chicks alongside the cuckoo. But she doesn't protest, and she brings the foundling worms and grubs and spiders and other good things to eat just like it was one of her own.

Nobody knows when the growing cuckoo realizes the big bird in the nest is not its mother, if indeed it ever does.

Nobody ever knew when Poco Oscar Schiller came to realize the Indian woman suddenly in his life was not his mother. Maybe, according to some who later came to know him, he knew from the start, even though he was only about two years old.

This was likely true. Nobody tried to deceive him about it. He saw the woman who was his true mother often enough to recognize her, and why not? She'd nursed him and cared for him, although rather haphazardly, for all of his life up to that point, and there weren't very many other people who had had anything to do with him. So his infantile memory wouldn't have been clouded with a lot of other images.

The Indian woman didn't cuddle and coddle and sooth and stroke the child, as you might expect a woman to do who was trying to gain a child's affection and confidence. But she was always there, and most people who later knew Poco Oscar said he'd likely have snorted and puffed and resisted any kind of softness and would have been downright antagonistic toward anyone who tried cuddling and coddling and soothing and stroking.

And maybe the Indian woman sensed this right away and treated him with a sort of cool detachment on purpose, knowing that was the key to his obedience.

"Them redskins can do that kind of thing sometimes," said a lot of Anglo Texans, speaking with the authority of those having gained insight to local aborigines primarily by shooting at a lot of them. "You can't ever tell what they might be thinkin. Specially a Tonk."

Well, whatever she was thinking, from almost the moment Paco Salazar deposited Sophia Schiller and Poco Oscar on her doorstep, she had the child's complete attention, which he seemed more than happy to give, and everybody knew it. Sophia and the boy and Salazar. And the Tonk knew it, too.

The woman was a Tonkawa. This was one of the Texas coastal tribes of the Atakapa-Karankawa language group, of which the Wacos were the best known.

All those tribes were cannibals, according to lot of observers, mostly other Indians. Tonkawas never denied it.

Tonkawas were a tall, handsome people. They liked tattoos. The men displayed this type of art on face and body. They parted their hair in the middle and wore it long. The women usually docked their hair at the shoulders.

"Tonks used to kill buffler like the plains tribes when they had enough bucks to organize a hunt," said a Ranger who knew them well. "They eat fish and oysters and crabs and anything else they take from the Gulf. Be a frosty day in Old Nick's pasture you ever catch a Comanch' or Kiowa eatin any of that water grub."

"When my grandfather came to Bexar from Mexico," said a Texas Mexican, "Tonkawas were as far north as the Salt Fork of the Brazos. They were hunting then around the Edwards Plateau. There were about twenty different bands. Then the Comanches came. Now, the bands are all gone. And there are not many Tonkawa *hombres* left."

They made good scouts, and Texans used them a great deal in campaigns against Comanches, which didn't help endear them to the Lords of the Southern Plains.

"The Comanch' don't forget such things," said the Ranger.

So the Tonkawas were on the road to extinction, like many other

Texas tribes, victims of white-man disease and Comanche war parties. For them, it was a very short road.

The Tonkawa woman in Paco Salazar's house on Calle de Armador had been one of the Cava band, *cava* likely being a word that meant eastern in the Tonk language. Their name for themselves meant "the most human people" and sounded something like Titska Watitch. There were a lot of "swish" sounds in Tonk talk.

Newcomers to the frontier like Ulrich Silesia found it remarkable that most Indian tribal names meant "the People" or "the Human Beings" or something like the idea that these were the main folk and everybody else was secondary. Which wasn't a new concept to anybody who'd ever read the Old Testament of the Christian Bible.

"But this holds true only if it is the name the tribe has given itself," Ulrich Silesia wrote his father. "When a tribe is known by a name some *other* tribe has given them, it almost always translates as 'Enemy.'

"So the name 'Comanche' is not Comanche. It is a Ute word that means 'Him who wants to fight me all the time.' A long and rather poetic way of saying 'enemy.'

"The old settlers around here tell me it is apt, because the Comanches play no favorites. Among the tribes of Texas, they are the enemies of practically everyone."

Anyway, somebody at the Dominican mission in Bexar gave the Tonkawa woman the name Titch, from that last word of her tribal name, so that's what she was called. Titch the Tonk.

Some time prior to the days of the Texas Republic, a group of Cava Titska Watitch was in a buffalo-hunt camp at the forks of the Concho and Colorado Rivers when they were struck by a Penateka war party. The Tonkawas were a small group, foolishly deep in Comanche territory, and even more foolishly, they'd brought along their women and children.

Although the outnumbered Tonk braves fought well, the fight didn't last long. Most of the Tonk women died fighting beside their menfolk, and the few who didn't die wished they had before their abuse finally resulted in painfully tortuous deaths as the raiders rode back across the High Plains to their own tribal encampment.

Comanche war parties didn't necessarily pause to torture or rape women taken prisoners. Sometimes they kept moving, fast. Anything done was done on the move.

"If they decided it was time to run, they could do it fast, and far," said the old Ranger. "You couldn't run em down. You had to wait until they stopped.

"Each buck would have three or four ponies and they'd switch four, five times a day. If you had a posse could do thirty-five miles a day, the bunch you were chasin would do sixty. The trick was to fig-ure out when they might slow down."

On the raid in question—or maybe instead of raid it should bet-ter be classified as a defense of home ground—among the captives to survive the ride to the Comanche camp was the beautiful child who would later become known in Bexar as Titch the Tonk.

It was by design that she was saved, along with three other girls. They would be raised as Comanche children if they could survive a rather rigorous few months of switchings and competing with the dogs for food and unpleasant harassment by the old squaws.

But once they were accepted, there would never be any discrimi-nation against them as outsiders by anyone in the tribe. They would be Comanche. Not by blood, but by association and training.

Titch weathered the initiation for six months. That was a long time, but she was slow being adopted into a Comanche family because some of the women were jealous of her handsome face, which obvi-ously appealed to a lot of the men. And there was a tough spirit that went along with the good looks.

But finally she was accepted into one of the more important war-riors' lodges, where there were three wives, which showed how rich in horses this man was, which in turn gave some indication of his prowess as a fighter, all of which was good for Titch because it meant that henceforth nobody was going to cause her a lot of trouble and pain.

So it started being a pretty good life for her. She could play in the pony herd all day and all night, too, if she wanted, so long as she did her assigned chores like carrying water or keeping the dogs away from drying meat.

Late spring and late fall were bad times for playing in the herd. Those were the big drying times, when the hunters brought in tons of buffalo meat to be cut in strips and hung on wooden scaffolds to dry. To keep dogs and crows away, the children guarded the meat racks, using long switches to protect what amounted to the Comanche larder.

But there was still plenty of time for a child to grow up in the herd, learning about horses and how to speak Comanche and how a boy was different from a girl.

This last activity extended far past the time when a person was considered a child, of course, and among Comanches, it was expected that by the time a girl was old enough to be a wife, she already knew everything there was to know about satisfying her husband.

"When they go to the wedding bed, most white men want a loaf that ain't been sliced," said the old Ranger. "But if a Comanch' buck found his new wife was a virgin, he'd figure he paid too many horses for her."

Titch came to the age of marriage and went beyond without a husband because the man who had taken her into his lodge and come to think of her as a prized daughter wanted so many horses for her that nobody could afford her.

To connect Titch with other things, this was in the early years of the Republic of Texas. She was almost fifteen, as near as anybody could figure later, when people got interested in the milestones of Paco Salazar's life.

While Penateka bucks were trying to collect enough horses for this bride's ransom, Titch's band was encamped in the breaks of the Neuces Rivers one winter day when it was struck by one of the Jack Coffee Hays Ranger patrols and a savage little fight ensued.

Within a few moments, those Comanches not victims of the Rangers' Colt pistols vanished like smoke, and there were a number of captives left behind. At some point in the fracas, Titch had been dumped from a horse and knocked unconscious, or else she would likely have been fighting like a cornered Yucatan tiger, as befitted a Comanche woman of fifteen.

So the Rangers had a close look at her while she couldn't resist, and the Captain of the force, Antonio Perez, saw the tattoo on her belly, a blue figure like a turtle, about the size of a ripe persimmon.

He wasn't familiar with this device, but his lieutenant Paco Salazar was, having grown up in Goliad and having had a lot of experience with coastal Indians.

"She's a Tonkawa," said Paco.

"I didn't think she looked like a Comanche squaw," Captain Perez said. "What is that? A religious totem?"

"I don't know, but a few Tonk bands tattoo the turtle on their babies in the first week of their lives," Paco Salazar said. "I suppose it means something. Maybe she'll tell us."

"She'll spit in your eye and try to gut you with a knife is what she'll do," said Perez. "You know about these people Comanches capture and bring up to be Nerm. They're always more barbaric than the Comanches."

But it didn't work that way. It seemed that Titch knew enough about captivity and getting along in that capacity that she was docile as a good burro, so Captain Antonio Perez said when he told Hays about her.

There was a Dominican mission school in Bexar, and Paco Salazar took her there, and she became something of a fixture, at first as a student and then as a mission secular general handywoman, doing everything from cooking to making beds to tending the goats to translating, because as time went on, she seemed to be one of the few people around who could handle a conversation in just about any language that might pop up.

And a lot of different languages popped up in a mission dedicated to teaching Christianity to Texas *indios* who had never heard of Jesus, much less things like the Trinity and Resurrection and the stone tablets Moses brought down from the mountain.

Among the coastal tribes alone, of which she was originally a part, there were at least a dozen different dialects, and then there were the Caddo peoples and Wichitas and splinters off the wild tribes, like Lipan, Apache, Kiowa, and Comanche.

This was all in addition to German; Czech, which was prominent in any one of a dozen places in that part of the state; Spanish, which was the mother tongue of the monks and priests; and English, which was the secular language of the town and the lingo of government in Texas.

At first, the monks watched Titch pretty closely because sometimes their charges who didn't quite fit in with all the others had a tendency to run away and take a few gold candlesticks with them. They never had that trouble with Titch. She seemed satisfied to stay and do whatever they wanted done. She was haughty as a princess around everybody, but she did what she was told and she learned what they were trying to teach.

Soon, she was trusted as one of the regular secular mission employees, and they had her going with the cook to Military Plaza each morning to buy the meat for the mission mess. It gave everybody a chance to get a good look at her.

Word was quick to get around town that they had a young woman at the mission school who had been a captive of the Comanches for some years, so she became an instant curiosity. And of course, a lot of these people came around wanting to do good work, so they said, but really trying to see a female who'd lived through wild-tribe captivity.

All such busybodies already had their own ideas about the dreadful things that had happened to her. And every scenario had her ravaged by a lusting horde of naked young warriors with blood-dripping scalps dangling from their belts.

"Can you imagine the unspeakable things they did to her?" said an Anglo matron. "But then perhaps it was what she was accustomed to. She is one of them, you know, although I understand not a Comanche. I suspect they're all the same, Satan's lust consuming them."

Years later, when an old Ranger talked about Titch, he always chuckled when he recalled the interest she aroused.

"I don't know what people expected to see," he said. "She was more than ordinary comely. I expect she'd been in the bushes with two-dozen or so Comanch' bucks by the time Perez and Salazar recaptured her.

"What the hell, that's how the Comanch' done thangs. Nobody was gonna see some mark on her tellin how often she done it. The thing that marked Comanch' women and others like em and made em look like the devil taken a bite out of em was havin babies. After a few years of that, the bloom for sure come off the rose.

"But that Tonk? Hell, she never did have no babies. I guess her innards may have been misadjusted like sometimes it happens. She looked pert near the same ten years later as she did the day Salazar brought her into that mission school."

Ulrich Silesia certainly noticed her.

"Dear Father, another episode in the developing saga of this woman who has come to practically take charge of my hotel, the Widow Sophia Schiller.

"I believe I mentioned in a previous communication to you that when Sophia came to San Antonio, her child was taken in charge by some Indian squaw. I had no idea who it was, of course, and there was no reason I should have known.

"Well before this occurred, I had noticed a striking Indian woman who came to market each morning with a monk from the Dominican school, and I was told she was a student there, or had been, and was now rather an assistant to the padres.

"Let me describe our market square. Each morning in Military Plaza, farmers come with their produce and hunters with their meat and small ranchers with beef and mutton. They set up stalls or sell from a cart or wagon.

"They have begun a system which I hope they will continue. At dawn, when it is still gray, and the dogs are just coming out and stretching and yawning, they sell to people who are in the food business like myself. Also to the men and women who have the chili and tamale stands in all the squares throughout the day.

"Once we have bought what we want, the farmers and meat people begin selling to the various churches, all of which have kitchens either for the padres or for the mission schools. When these customers are served, the general population of housewives comes.

"By noon, the whole thing is done, and the farmers and ranchers and hunters are gone, and Military Plaza is back as it was to begin with.

"This woman, the tall Indian woman, was with the second group of buyers, the church people. Among so many cowled monks and priests with shaved heads and whatnot, she stood out like a pine tree in the desert.

"By discreet inquiry I found that she was called Titch and was a Tonkawa, one of these terrible bands of natives who are supposed to be cannibals. I must say, I never imagined a cannibal who looked like this.

"Then after Sophia came to San Antonio, I no longer saw the Indian at market each morning. I thought nothing of it.

"Shortly after Sophia moved into my building, I saw the Indian woman again. But not at market. I think I told you. She was with Sophia's child!

"What a coincidence! This wild Indian woman they rescued from Comanches some years ago now cares for my best employee's child. *Das Kindermädchen*. Have you ever heard of somebody leaving their child in the care of a cannibal? It is hilarious.

"Don't despair that I have lost my senses. This woman is not going to eat anybody and probably never has had a taste of human flesh. It's just a story they tell. And the whole thing struck me as funny.

"As you know, nursemaids have always made me laugh since I was a child and we first moved to upper Manhattan and you and mother hired that Swedish girl to take care of me, which everyone thought was fine until you discovered her one day showing me her breasts and how to make the nipples hard by pinching them.

"Mother certainly failed to see any humor in the situation. I was brokenhearted, of course, that you fired the poor girl. I wonder whatever happened to her?

"Well, time to close and make my shopping list for market tomorrow. You know, I rather miss seeing that tall Indian woman each day moving majestically among the oxen and carts and wagons and green vegetables and hanging quarters of buffalo and geese and ducks and chickens parading around."

When Sophia Schiller had first seen the Tonk squaw, she was petrified with fright. Paco Salazar had made no move to ease the meeting. As soon as he'd pulled up in front of his *casa*, where the Tonk stood impassively waiting, he jumped from the cart, and he and one of his vaqueros began carrying Sophia's duffel into the house.

There was a moment when Sophia stared up at the face of the woman while the woman coolly measured her top to bottom with a quick glance. The woman said something completely beyond Sophia's comprehension, and Salazar called out a translation.

"She wants to know if the boy is weaned. You can Deutsch *sprechen*. She can *comprende* a little of that," he said, completely unaware of mixing three languages like they were brown, white, and red beans in a chili pot. "Her name's Titch."

Sophia didn't say anything. She nodded. Which was all the Indian woman needed, apparently, for now she stepped forward and took the child from Sophia's arms, and for anybody who might have been observing, it was the last time Sophia was ever seen to carry her son.

This was not so much a function of Sophia's neglect as it was of the Tonk's rather belligerent insistence that if Paco Salazar had hired her to take care of this child, then she was going to take care of it without any kind of interference from anybody.

She indicated this as soon as she was inside the house that first day. She took the tiny boy from his cocoon of blankets and held him up and looked at him closely.

"And his name is Poco Oscar," Salazar said, still unloading the cart. The Tonk grunted. "Talk English as much as you can. They both need that. They'll pick up Spanish on the street."

All this while, the boy's bright, colorless eyes were focused on the Tonk's face, and there was an intensity there much like you see in the eyes of a deaf-mute trying to read the lips of somebody talking.

"You are a little man, ain't you?" the Tonk said in English. "A little man, but a man, ain't you?"

Then she set Poco Oscar on the floor on his two spindly legs, and he immediately flopped onto his butt, and she bent and lifted him to his feet again.

Now, with his eyes still on her face, he blinked a few times and began, if small children do such things, working out some way he'd stay on his feet without any assistance.

That's how she left him as she went about her own chores making the *casa* ready for new occupants. So Poco Oscar would struggle upright, wobble, bounce his butt on the floor, and start over again. She didn't help him; she didn't encourage him.

It was surely obvious even to Sophia that Tonkawa ideas about childrearing were not exactly compatible with German methods. But under the circumstances, Sophia wasn't in any position to object too much, even had she wanted to, and there's not much evidence that she objected at all.

The Tonk woman did not pick up Poco Oscar until she had fed

him frijoles and tortillas, bathed him in a dishpan filled with water from the cistern on the patio, and tucked him into the bed Alex Mesero had stolen.

By then, Paco Salazar had returned Sophia from Mrs. Wolf's Hotel, where she would begin work on the morrow. The Tonk said nothing at all but indicated Sophia should lie on the bed where her son was already asleep.

As she lay down and the Tonk blew out the whale-oil lamp, Sophia heard the cartwheels on the rutted street as Paco Salazar drove away.

Sophia had suspected she would see little of Paco Salazar from that moment on, and then only when he needed to talk with the Tonk woman for one thing or another. And she had been right.

And maybe the first night lying there in Paco Salazar's house and hearing the breathing of that big Tonk woman in the same room, Sophia felt like a little girl who knew she'd best be good or she'd get spanked. And the scary thing was that Sophia didn't know what the Tonk woman figured was good.

So maybe that was one of the prime reasons she got out before long and went to make her home at Mrs. Wolf's, an environment she understood, leaving the *casa* on Armador alley to the child and the Tonk.

Which, as it so happened, pleased Sophia well. And the Tonk, too. And it certainly pleased Ulrich Silesia. And eventually, when he had the ability to say so, it pleased Poco Oscar best of all.

You can't help but appreciate the world of difference between being constantly looked over by a proper German *Hausfrau* and a full-blooded Texas Tonkawa Indian.

One was cuddling and wet kisses and subdued childish vocal chatter and hot chocolate to drink and overprotection from the possibility of bumps and bruises.

The other was generally being ignored, seldom spoken to, and touched never, except in absolutely necessary instances, a diet primarily of *pasteles de maiz* and frijoles *refritos*, and a no-nonsense checklist of what you could and could not do.

Maybe Poco Oscar liked corn pie and refried beans better than hot chocolate. Maybe even at a little past two he wanted to know his perimeters and what the rules were. Such things were not unheard of.

At any rate, Poco Oscar very quickly stopped being a baby and became an energetic child. Even so, his world was the *casa* and the yard behind, which he shared with the goat, for Titch the Tonk would not allow him into the street yet, not even in the alley in front of her door.

As his walking improved, which it did quickly because she wouldn't carry him, they often went out on the street together, as Ulrich Silesia had observed. She would hold his hand as they walked, going slowly to accommodate his short steps.

"It is a strange sight," said Silesia. "The runt of a boy, the towering savage. It's like an awkward duckling with the protection of a fierce, black-eyed eagle."

It was an apt description. The old Ranger enjoyed telling the story of the knife.

"The Tonk had been at the mission school a good while," he said. "One morning she was at the market on Military Plaza with one of the monks.

"There was a work crew of horse wranglers in town. Come up from down around Patricio and Regugio Counties where they'd caught some of them Gulf Coast wild ponies, and they was in Bexar to sell em.

"Half-a-dozen of em was just stumblin out of the south barrio where they'd made a night of it with a couple ladies who was in that business. Pretty fog-headed, they was.

"One of em seen the Tonk. She was standin over beside of the old troop barracks building close to the governor's house. So this yahoo went up to her and he never said nothin. He just reached for her up front, right here, see?" And the old Ranger grabbed his shirtfront.

"Well, the Tonk made a quick move, and her arm whipped around, and it was so fast nobody even noticed anything in her hand until all of a sudden this yahoo is standin there with his hands still out and this kindly pained expression on his face and the blood runnin down his front like you was pourin molasses out of a ten-gallon hat.

"One cheek and the end of his nose had been laid open. Then ever'body seen this blade, musta been fourteen inches long. She was holdin it down close to her side, but they say all you needed to do was take one look at that Tonk's face and you knew she was ready to use it again and you knew she coulda took that yahoo's head plumb off on the first swipe she took at him if she'd been so inclined.

"All the other horse wranglers seen it wasn't a good situation. They was standin not ten feet from where the Vigilance Committee had hanged an ole boy not ten days ago, on one of them chinaberry trees at Military Plaza, for doin some criminal work in Bexar that they didn't cotton to, so them wranglers figured it was good to get the hell off the square before this cut yahoo sobered up enough to start screamin about bloody redskins and women with knives and runnin around actin like a fool in somebody else's town.

"The Tonk faded away, and for about a month she stayed close inside the mission school until all the local yahoos stopped brayin about allowin such a wild woman loose on our streets and a redskin besides. But it blew over.

"And I can tell you this. From then on, whether she was by her ownself or if later on she was walkin with that runt kid, nobody ever bothered her."

"Dear Father: More on this Tonkawa Indian squaw and my Sophia's child Poco Oscar. Everyone in Bexar now knows that's the child's name.

"You might find it interesting, as I did, that the name is a combination of a Spanish word meaning tiny and what is essentially a German given name. It rather neatly sums up the boy's situation, I suppose.

"Sophia tells me the name was given the child by Paco Salazar, the famous Indian fighter I've mentioned before. I have the inexplicable feeling that Paco Salazar has more to do with Sophia and her son than we see on the surface.

"Anyway, now when the Tonkawa woman comes to see Sophia to get money to run the household, she no longer waits outside in the street but comes inside the kitchen. At close range, the Indian is even more striking than from afar.

"There is such a strong relationship between that woman and the boy. I have never heard her speak to him. Yet he watches her like a little hawk and does as she bids, but she bids him with her eyes only, no words.

"A look from her and he knows to go to his mother for a brief hug or pat on the head, he knows to sit or stand by the door, he knows when to take her hand and be prepared to walk out into the alley.

"Never does the child look to his mother for direction, you understand. But to this woman. Poco Oscar knows Sophia is his real mother, too. At least, the Tonkawa has taught him to call Sophia something that sounds like *pia*, which I am told is mother in Comanche!

"I asked Sophia why the Tonk would have the child learn that instead of the English or German or Spanish word for mother, and Sophia just shrugged and said it was of no importance.

"I have begun to keep candied lemon rind and sugar drops we buy from a New Orleans wholesaler so I can give him a sweet when he comes. He never approaches me, even when I've held the candy out to him, until he looks at the Tonkawa and she tells him to take the candy with some kind of command I cannot see.

"Sometimes it is *geisterhaft!* Yes, it may be silly, but still, it's rather spooky!"

In fact, Poco Oscar called the Tonka *pia*, too, of which very little can be made. Because like a lot of words in Comanche, this word could mean more than one thing. It could mean "aunt" as well as "mother."

She was teaching him all the time. She taught him how to count the number of times mice ran across the room at night by the trace of their tiny pugs in the morning dust.

She taught him how to make a cut stop bleeding with a mud compress. She taught him when to expect rain from the way the clouds blew in from the south, where, she explained, there was big water, water that covered everything as far as you could see.

She taught him how to catch grasshoppers, pinch off the hind legs, batter them with cornmeal, cook them in beef suet fat, and eat them. She took him to the San Antonio River to catch fish. And showed him how to scale and gut them and pin them to a flat piece of wood and prop this upright close to the fire to broil them, so they tasted even better than the grasshoppers.

She took him to San Pedro Creek close by, and to the irrigation ditches, and showed him how to find salamanders. They made a mud swimming pool for the salamanders on the patio, letting the mud dry in the sun until it would hold water.

They pushed sticks into the mud all around, making an enclosure, a palisade, like the corrals that were made for horses and cows, only this one was for salamanders and only a few inches high, only two feet across.

She taught him always to look in the bedding before lying down, look in shoes and sandals and pants and shirt before putting them on to be sure he'd shaken all the scorpions out.

She taught him a religion of self-reliance and to put his faith and trust in no one but himself and her and to always listen to his instinct and intuition and in strange surroundings never to stand long in one place.

Once, when Sophia visited for a few moments, she gave Oscar a little neck chain with a cross on it to play with and, whether by design or accident, left without it.

When he realized he had the necklace all to himself, he made a great ceremony of giving it to the Tonk, and she responded in kind, doing a little dance and making a little Comanche chant song.

She told him that when the brave warrior went out on a war party and returned with many scalps and captives and horses, he gave these things as gifts to the chiefs and to the older warriors who had helped him get his medicine and to his favorite wife.

"Yes, yes," Oscar said. "I will give all the ponies I take to you, my favorite wife."

"Sure, to me, your favorite wife." And she laughed and saw immediately the laugh was a mistake. His face turned furious in a certain way it had, and she immediately stopped laughing and with a serious nodding of her head tried to repair the damage.

"Sure, of course, all your fine ponies to me, your favorite wife!" And she added, "I will be so happy to have all those good horses."

It still wasn't enough.

"You'll be a fine husband one day," she said, very seriously.

Now his face softened, and soon he gave a little smile, looking at her face.

"Yes," he said. "I will be a fine husband for you."

It wasn't a request or a suggestion or even a question. It was simply a statement of fact.

"Yes. I will be a fine husband for you."

Neither of them ever spoke of it again.

By the time Poco Oscar was old enough to enter the Lutheran school the Germans had begun in San Antonio only the year before, Titch the Tonk figured he was as ready as anybody ever gets for white man schooling. She figured maybe she'd already given him enough Indian education to possibly prove embarrassing under certain circumstances.

Chapter Fourteen

A lot of his old freight-business friends said Paco Salazar went back to active Rangering because now there was a better firearm available to punish the Comanches.

The pistol that had revolutionized Indian fighting back in Texas Republic days had been the Patterson Colt, a fine revolver to replace single-shot pistols. But now there was the Walker and the Dragoon, better balanced, more reliable, easier to reload, and carrying a heavier punch.

These were cannons. Both .44-caliber six-shooters with eight-inch barrels, and they weighed almost four pounds. One of the local saloon wags said seeing a man strong enough to hold one of these Colts in each hand and still control a charging pony was enough to scare hell out of any Comanche.

"Them dumb Indians ought to know you can't hit nothin from the deck of a runnin horse," said a self-appointed expert. "So it don't matter what you might be shootin."

"You can hit em all right," said the first. "If you know the trick."

"Oh yeah? And what's the trick?"

"The trick is to get so close before you shoot that the muzzle blast sets their hair on fire."

Some of his friends said Paco returned to the chase because recently the northern wild tribes, like the Nakoni and the Kwahadie Comanches and their friends the Kiowas, were still trying to scald out all the western counties, and the United States Army was not much in evidence and when they were didn't know how to deal with the Nerm.

"Why hell, these generals they got is used to them Sioux and Cheyenne and Crows and other nice redskins," said a recent cavalryman of the state militia, who was therefore an authority. "They don't know nothin worth knowin about the Comanch' er the Kioway, neither."

But Paco Salazar's friends on the Balcones, like Henry Meuller, knew the real reason he went back to work for the latest San Antonio Ranger captain, whose name was Sam Walker. He didn't have enough to keep him busy working for *Adelsverein* anymore.

And maybe friend and employer Henry Meuller came closer to understanding this than any of the others.

"Señor Salazar always felt somewhat guilty, I believe, that he did not accompany his Texas Ranger comrades during their extensive campaigning for General Taylor in the war with Mexico," he said.

"At that time, you will recall, he was helping us. Perhaps he thought he had had enough of fighting his old country in the Texas War for Independence, although his hatred of the Mexican army never abated. Or perhaps he was simply bored, having had that earlier experience of warfare. He missed some kind of action. Old combatants do that, you know."

Whatever the reason, before riding west to join a company of Rangers operating out of El Paso along the Pecos River, where they hoped to lay ambushes on the old Comanche war trail to Mexico, he came to see Herr Ulrich Silesia.

It was late at night, and they talked in Silesia's upstairs bedroom, because Silesia sensed that Salazar did not want Sophia to know he was about. She was already in bed, but safety first had always been Ulrich Silesia's motto.

There was a window open onto Main Plaza below. There were white cheesecloth curtains on the window, and they blew lazily in the soft breeze from the south. They could hear someone playing a guitar in one of the south-side barrios as they smoked cigars in the darkness and quietly talked about a message Paco Salazar had been commissioned to bring from Titch the Tonk concerning Poco Oscar.

It was a message that should have been specifically directed to the boy's mother, but the Tonk had apparently been adamant about having it delivered to some white man whom she trusted. This was a position Ulrich Silesia obviously filled. And all Silesia could figure about such a method was that the Tonk suspected her ultimatum would fall on deaf ears if taken to Sophia alone.

Which, when he thought about it, Silesia figured was a pretty solid suspicion.

"She said now the white man must take his own child for the day-time," said Salazar. "She said her own medicine can only go so far because it is weak now, and he needs the white man's medicine."

"Señor Salazar, I have no notion of what that means."

"I'm not sure I do, either," said the Mexican. "But I'll try to explain."

He drew a great deal of smoke from the cigar, and the tip glowed red, and he inhaled the smoke and seemed to settle more deeply into the wicker armchair, in which he sat by the window.

"Her medicine. She's speaking of Tonkawa gods."

"Religion then?"

"Partly. What she's saying is that the Tonkawa medicine obviously isn't very good because it hasn't done much for the Tonks lately. But the white man's medicine is good. That's the medicine she wants Poco Oscar to have. She says she can't teach him anything about it. She says she's got a lot of gods, and she knows the white man's got only one. Poco Oscar needs that kind of medicine."

"She thinks a person's gods determine what he has, what he gets, how happy he is?"

"Of course. Medicine is everything. Medicine is why the whites can make things like guns and metal knives and her people can't. But there's another part to it, in addition to the sacred. White man's school."

"All right. But she went to that Catholic mission school and has been there for years. She still claims she doesn't know anything about the white man's god?"

"She didn't say she doesn't know. She said she knows plenty about Jesus. But she doesn't believe all of it. So it's not her truth. Her power. She wants Poco Oscar to be able to see if it's his truth, his power."

"Does that mean that despite all her time at the mission school, she's still not a Christian?"

"That's what it means," Paco Salazar said. "So she can't keep Oscar for this important thing. She thinks he needs teaching about white man's medicine by someone who has it."

"Well, all right again. Why doesn't she just get him into the same school she attended? The mission school? That takes care of the sacred and the secular at the same time. Bible and multiplication tables in one basket."

"She says it's not her decision to make," said Salazar. "Somebody in Poco Oscar's world needs to decide which white man's medicine he takes. Which is her way of saying Catholic or one of these others. Because which medicine he takes is about something besides religion."

"What then?"

"About tradition. It's about grandmothers. That's what she said. You follow your own people, not somebody else's."

"Don't you find that strange?" the German asked. "From what I hear, she lived with Comanches, and they are a people who believe you can become a Comanche no matter how you started. And they had indeed made her a Comanche in all but blood by the time you and the others recaptured her."

"All that is true," said Salazar. "But you're talking about what Comanches believe and I'm talking about this Tonkawa. And no matter how long they held her, she still remembers she is no Comanche. She still hears the singing of her own grandmothers."

"Then I suppose, with Sophia taking part in this decision whether she likes it or not, we've got to get Little Oscar into school."

"No. *You* have to get him into school. By daylight, I'll be a long way down Camino del Rio toward El Paso del Norte."

When he reached the bottom of the staircase in the waning light of a single wall-bracket lamp, Salazar saw Sophia standing against the wall, a blanket wrapped round her shoulders. Her eyes were wide and watched him, and he stopped before her for just a moment.

Then lifted one hand and laid his palm gently along her cheek. And then, without a word, was gone.

It was a good time for a boy to start school in Bexar. There were some choices. The mission schools had been there for a long time, and in the year Little Oscar Schiller was ready for the first forms, some of the leading German merchants and proprietors in San Antonio had started a Lutheran interim school that included an opening prayer each morning, as about the extent of religious teaching, and a heavy hand on reading, writing, and arithmetic.

It was an interim school because the men who started it knew a public school system would be in the works soon. The men most responsible for getting this school going were all on the city board.

Ulrich Silesia was one of them, and he wrote his father that it was

224

almost as though he'd had a presentiment of that visit from Paco Salazar and the requirement that some choice be made about the white man's schooling for Little Oscar. And, as he also wrote, because she was his employee and a trusted member by now of his entire operation, he felt a special responsibility toward Sophia and her child.

Even though she was pretty nonchalant about the whole thing.

In addition to Silesia there were Gunther Roth, a horse and cattle buyer and the Market Master of Military Plaza; Frederick Hausmann, the biggest general store owner in Bexar; and Jerome Falsworth, sawmill owner and the first man to start the operation of a gristmill for maybe a hundred miles in any direction.

They were all Lutherans except Falsworth, who was a Presbyterian. All except Silesia had children ready for school. The entire Protestant population of Bexar was ready to pitch in for a school other than one of the mission variety.

So for Little Oscar, there was a happy combination of factors that contributed to his education.

"Dear Father: So we now have Little Oscar in school, and each Sunday he attends church or Mass. His mother refuses to participate in any of this, if you can conceive of such a thing.

"I take the little *Kinder* to services in our church, and the Tonkawa takes him to the mission school Mass.

"It sounds like a competition, does it not? The Tonk and I seeing who will win the little soul, and he not really caring much one way or the other. He's rather bored by it all, it seems to me.

"We won't keep this up much longer. We'll allow Little Oscar to make up his own mind. Rather, he'll make up his own mind whether we allow it or not. Perhaps he already has. I must say that I've never seen such an independent little rascal. Only a small bundle but like gunpowder. You expect a big explosion at any moment."

Titch knew about the small package, the explosive content. She'd seen Poco Oscar become enraged over something, when his little face would go almost purple.

He never expressed any anger toward her, and it seemed that her quiet, steady gaze at these times did a lot to calm him. She made no other effort to interfere with his passions. You might say she controlled him with her silent eyes.

And he was brave. Nothing frightened him.

Well, two things did. Lightning. Which made the Tonk a little uneasy, too.

The other thing that terrified him was a regular, repeated, common occurrence that came about every three weeks, never changing and easy to explain, as she had tried to do with no success. It was the visit of what they called *el trapero de excusado*, the privy scavenger.

In one corner of the back yard, hidden behind an overgrowth of Spanish bayonet and yucca, was the small, wooden privy. Which, by the way, the Indian had taught Poco Oscar to use almost as soon as he was able to walk there and back.

For a few pennies, *el trapero* came round on a regular basis to empty *el excusado*. He had a cart and a donkey and a lot of pails and washtubs that rattled and clanked in the night. He carried a lantern with a smoke-encrusted globe. Hence, the only light it gave off was a dim orange glow.

No matter if he was in a deep sleep, Poco Oscar woke when *el trapero* came. He shivered as though with a great chill, and he sobbed silently. When Titch reached out in the darkness to touch him, he gasped and moved away from her hand.

This lasted until *el trapero* had finished and moved on to some other house in the barrio, and then the child would go limp and be asleep instantly, it seemed, and she would wipe the sweat from his body without waking him.

Titch told Ulrich Silesia she guessed Poco Oscar thought it was *el linterna del* Espiritu Santo, the lamp of the Holy Ghost, and she pointed out, to be sure he didn't miss it, that this fear had been there before they started taking the boy to church, where he first heard anything about a Holy Ghost from anybody in this world.

Implying, of course, that the tad had heard about such things from some supernatural source.

Silesia laughed about it. Until he told Sophia Schiller what the Tonkawa had said and Sophia went into what Silesia described to his father as a hysterical religious fit, babbling about her sins and her son possessed by Satan and keeping the child away from her so she might have some chance of redemption.

It disturbed Ulrich Silesia deeply, and he didn't tell anyone else what the Tonk had said. To the Indian, he knew such a thing as other world voices was a wonderful kind of medicine to have, even if it scared the hell out of you, but for Sophia and just about anyone else he knew, it was a mark of something close to witchcraft.

The upshot of this was that when Titch the Tonk needed money for her household, Silesia gave it to her now, deducting it from what he paid Sophia. This was because Sophia pleaded for him to do it so she wouldn't have those necessary times of coming face to face with her son.

As a matter of fact, he rather enjoyed it, because he was becoming fond of both the boy and the Indian woman. There were many things between those two that he found admirable, as he wrote his father.

And one thing leading to another, as it always does, it was this close association with the boy that led to Silesia's discovery that Poco Oscar had such myopia that at close range, he was nearly blind.

The Tonk had mentioned this, saying that he was clumsy and often reached for something and missed it. Which was very bad indeed if one were playing with a big sandstone scorpion, which Poco Oscar often did. For some miraculous reason, he was never stung.

At any rate, Silesia took the boy to the big general store of Frederick Hausmann, which stood on Main Plaza immediately east of Mrs. Wolf's Hotel, and there, in a marvelous box full of many kinds of eye spectacles, found three pairs that worked well.

Unlike most children, who despised the very thought of wearing eyeglasses, Little Oscar was delighted. They let him see so many things he had missed before, Silesia wrote to his father.

In response to that letter, the elder Silesia wrote back from New York expressing surprise that such a sophisticated article as eye spectacles could be found in the wilderness of Texas.

That city council, of which Ulrich Silesia was a part, took a census. Nobody was surprised when they came up with a big number. There were thirty-five hundred people in San Antonio de Bexar.

"They moved the state capital to Austin recently," said Gunther Roth, Market Master of Military Square. "And they have no more than a thousand people, counting the damned legislature, I expect."

227

"Be thankful they didn't decide to put the capital here," said Frederick Hausmann, the mercantile man. "We'd have to put up with those east Texas cotton-country aristocrats."

San Antonio was a strange town, Silesia wrote his father. There were many Mexicans in the streets, but the storefronts mostly advertised names like Heusinger or Schesburg or Koenig or Griesenbeck or Schmeltzer.

And when the outdoor markets became so crowded and confused they needed a traffic director, the town council chose Gunther Roth as Market Master, even though Mexican farmers and traders with something to sell usually far outnumbered Anglos at market time on both Main and Military Plazas.

There was no caste system, but the community was three-layered. The Anglos attended their Presbyterian or Methodist churches and took Sunday as a serious day of rest. The Germans went to their Lutheran services on Sunday morning, but Sunday afternoon was an activity time, for playing ballgames and going on picnics. The Mexicans took part in Mass and confession as the spirit moved them, but there was plenty of Sunday-afternoon fun with horse races and chicken fights after the wonderfully noisy fandangos on Saturday nights.

And all these Mexican diversions were attended by a considerable number of Gringos, and often by their ladies, too.

The Anglos had established what they called a casino club, and there they held all sorts of social functions. There was certainly no lack of activity around the two principal plazas, and now people were beginning to build houses on the east side of the river, near the old Alemada, and there was an Alamo Plaza now, so far just a dirty army wagon park.

Horse and vehicle traffic on Military and Main Plazas was so heavy that in the afternoons, the mission school north of San Fernando Cathedral lined up all its pupils who lived in Barrio del Sur and a priest or monk led them across Commerce Street and on across Dolorosa.

The little children looked like a long line of ants, winding among the wagons and stacks of hay or firewood or watermelons or penned geese and turkeys.

"And now," Ulrich Silesia wrote, "there are nuns leading the little Catholics.

"I believe I failed to write that recently a school for girls was estab-lished. Later one for boys. In September, a priest with seven sisters of the Ursuline order arrived by coach from Galveston. Within a few weeks, the Ursuline College for Young Ladies started classes.

"The Ursuline order is French, and that is what these nuns speak. One more language to contend with here. We are becoming a true international language center.

"The school, by the way, offers courses in French, English, Spanish, and German. I do declare, if there was such a thing as a Comanche dic-tionary, I think the sisters would teach that as well!

"I may not have told you also of the stagecoach line. The San Antonio section is under the supervision of a Mr. Raymond Burton, and they rent a corner of my first floor, actually a part of my cafe, as ticket office.

"This means that the stagecoaches coming or going from here to El Paso or Fort Worth or Galveston or Laredo or the Gulf Coast load and unload at my door on Main Plaza. One member of the curious crowd I can always count on to be there observing is Little Oscar, if school is out. Sometimes the woman is with him, sometimes she is not."

In the new Gringo school, there were no pupils other than Poco Oscar who lived south of Dolorosa. On the first day, the Tonk woman took him as far as the San Fernando Church, where Ulrich Silesia met them and escorted the child across Main Plaza and to the adobe school building that was some distance north of the square.

After that first trip, Oscar Schiller was on his own. That seemed to suit him just fine. In fact, sometimes he could be seen standing alongside a wall or against the trunk of a chinaberry tree, watching the Catholic children pass in their long file. And his expression clearly said, Listen, I'm sure glad I'm not with that bunch! Look at that old man in the long black gown yelling and waving that stick around!

That busy street Poco Oscar had to cross originally had been the Camino Real, the King's Highway between Louisiana and Mexico. East of the river it was called Street of the Powderhouse, or Camino del Casa de Polvara or Via Alameda, because of the cottonwood trees there.

But the whole thing was called Commerce Street, and that's what it was. It formed the northern side of both Main and Military Plazas.

Many of the major businesses of the town were along it: Ulrich Silesia's Mrs. Wolf's Hotel and Cafe; the Hausmann Mercantile; Gunther Roth's freight company and Market Master office; half-a-dozen saloons; and the long, one-story adobe building on Military Plaza called the Governor's Palace.

"I have always been fascinated by that unattractive building," Ulrich Silesia wrote his father. "Over the front door is a stone engraved with the Hapsburg Coat of Arms. The stone is dated 1749, at which time Ferdinand VI was King of Spain. Somehow, such a device here on the Comanche frontier seems badly out of place."

For the first time, there was a building to interrupt the space of Military Plaza. A two-story city hall and behind that a jail, complete with a surrounding stockade wall. The city hall had already become such a popular nesting place for bats that it was being called the Bat Cave.

On the nights when there was no fandango in the plaza below, and there was hence a relatively profound silence, you could hear the squeaking of the furry little beasts at dusk as they flew out to hunt.

In one of her bedtime talks with Poco Oscar, the Tonkawa said it was like the sound of the Great Cannibal Owl, sweeping through the night sky looking for people to eat. The Comanches called him Pe Ah Wen Pits.

This was supposed to frighten the child, as a ghost story would, or like the German story of Hansel and Gretel and the wicked witch. Or at least impress him. It did neither.

"What do the rest of the people call the big owl?" he asked, without showing too much interest in any answer she might give him. It was as though he knew the game she was playing, and he was willing to play if it made her happy.

"They don't call him anything," she said. "Nobody has ever heard of the Great Cannibal Owl except the Nerm and the Kiowas."

Poco Oscar thought about it for a minute, then said, "And me. Now I've heard about him, haven't I?"

"Yes," she said, and she was trying not to smile. "So be on the look-out for him."

Poco Oscar thought about that, then said, "I will."

In San Antonio de Bexar there had grown up an extra-legal system of law enforcement very much like that found in many communities of the Cotton South.

It was called the Vigilance Committee, or some such thing. It remained dormant until its members, usually including some of the community's leading citizens, decided it was time for action.

When this happened, the official or regular apparatus for law enforcement became dormant until the trouble was resolved, at which time the Vigilance Committee retired from the scene and the regular agencies of peace and dignity resumed their official roles as constable, sheriff, judge.

At a tender age, Poco Oscar Schiller observed this function of frontier self-government. Of course, he could hardly be expected to understand it. But then there were a lot of grown ups who didn't understand it, either.

At the end of each school day, walking to the south barrio, the boy passed across Main Plaza, walking past Mrs. Wolf's Hotel and Cafe and then San Fernando Church, the front of the hotel plainly in view all the time.

It was an impressive front—a two-story affair, with a porch running the entire length of the building on both floors, the lower porch acting also as a sidewalk along Commerce Street, the one above a covered balcony looking down on Main Plaza.

On the ground floor, and at the west end of the porch, there had been a number of fatal shootings when various citizens had become too enthusiastic about some kind of argument they were having and proceeded from words to pistols. It was called Death Corner.

Needless to say, Ulrich Silesia was dismayed and chagrined about that name, but there wasn't much he could do about it.

At any rate, on a particular Monday, as Poco Oscar was walking home, taking his time as he always did, looking at all there was to look at across busy Main Plaza, Death Corner became the scene of yet another violent debate.

For over a week, two men had been in town, sleeping in the wagon and stockyard that had developed in one corner of Military Plaza.

These men were of the rough sort, Ulrich Silesia explained to his father, having been drunk most of the time they'd been in town and bragging in the saloons and *cantinas* about the money they'd made in Durango selling Yaqui Indian scalps to the various agencies of the Mexican government who paid bounty on such things.

Some of their conquests of defenseless *indios* were loudly detailed with gory descriptions, and they said what made it so wonderful was that the Mexicans paid just as much for the hair of a defenseless three year old as they did for the hair of a full-grown man.

These gentlemen were named Kato Sprigs and Humbolt Something-or-Other.

On the Sunday previous to the date in question, these men had lost a considerable amount of money to a local laborer who worked on San Antonio's irrigation ditches and whose name was Jesus Montez. Jesus Montez was well known and respected in Bexar, because although he was only an illiterate worker of little affluence, he paid his debts and was a nice man.

Jesus Montez was walking along Commerce Street when he was accosted at Death Corner by Messrs Sprigs and Humbolt, who had been attending Goshen Steiner's bar in the billiard parlor close by. Shouting ensued, and the two gentlemen of the Yaqui scalps accused the Mexican laborer of cheating them on bets at the chicken fights.

During the course of this discussion, Sprigs moved behind Jesus Montez, and suddenly there was an explosion and a cloud of powder smoke, and Jesus Montez staggered forward and fell on his face in the street, the back of his shirt on fire from the muzzle blast of the pistol in Sprigs's hand.

Whereupon Humbolt drew a revolver from beneath his coat and, shouting obscenities, shot Jesus Montez three more times as the young Mexican lay in the street, his body jerking spasmodically as each slug struck him.

The two then marched off toward Military Plaza and left the body of the Mexican where it was, to be tended to by the crowd of people who rushed up once the two gunmen had gone. Among these people were Jesus Montez's wife and his two young children, who had been following him at some distance, each of them carrying a small bundle of kindling wood on their heads, since this was a commodity the family often sold at market.

From his place, tight against one wall of San Fernando Cathedral,

Poco Oscar Schiller observed all this, and with the sounds of the wailing wife and children still in his ears, he ran to the *casa* in Calle de Armador and told Titch the whole story.

The Tonkawa was amazed that the boy's recitation was not hurried, nor did it show any undue excitement or fear. It was a simple, straightforward account of a horrifying scene, told without fanfare by a tiny child.

She reached to him, to lay her hands on his shoulders, wanting to reassure him and explain that such things were not meant for the eyes of children. She saw at once she had made a serious mistake. He drew back, and his eyes glazed over with anger.

"Don't call me *poco* again," he said. "Don't ever call me little again."

For a moment she stared at him, and then she nodded.

"Yes. I will never call you *poco* again. You are no longer *poco*. Is that good?"

It took a while, as he glared out the window at the goat in the back yard, who stared back at him with its marble yellow eyes.

"Yes," he said. "That's good."

It was only the next day that Oscar Schiller saw the workings of that extra-legal apparatus. One of the big chinaberry trees in *el mercado* section of Military Plaza had been chopped down.

It seemed that shortly after the shooting in Main Plaza, the two gunmen had been observed in a Mexican *cantina* west of Laredo Street and were there confronted and taken into custody by the marshal of San Antonio, who had with him about a dozen men armed with large-bore shotguns.

Needless to say, against such a display of firepower, the two ruffians went peacefully to the new jail on Military Plaza, joking all the while that they expected to get fined no more than fifty dollars for killing a Mexican, and that it had certainly been fifty dollars worth of fun.

After the marshal and other members of the regular system of law and order had all gone home to bed, a large body of men on horseback arrived at the jail and requested the keys, which the jailer was more than happy to provide, obviously realizing that the extra-legal organism had come to life.

The Vigilance Committee took the prisoners only a short

distance, to the chinaberry trees on the north side of Military Plaza. On the way, the leaders of the committee were careful to explain to the two prisoners why they were being given this special attention.

The historical record does not reveal what, if anything, was said by Messrs Sprigs or Humbolt before they were hanged side by side from a large limb of one of the chinaberry trees.

The Vigilance Committee always cleaned up after their work, and they cleaned up this time. Waiting to be sure the two victims were dead, the committee cut them down, threw them across a mule, and carried them away for burial.

Then everybody went home to bed, and the official law enforcement apparatus was back in operation.

Next morning, everyone was talking about the chinaberry trees, and Oscar Schiller, carrying his school slate of course, detoured to the woodlot north of Military Plaza called *el mercado* and there, with a great many other citizens, viewed the hanging tree now lying ingloriously on the ground in a tangle of its own limbs, chopped down with what obviously had been a sharp hatchet.

Without asking, but by listening only, Oscar Schiller was able to learn that the deed had been done by one of the priests at the San Jose mission, in protest of the execution.

And that evening, Oscar Schiller told the Tonk the priest had been bad.

"But the priest was angry that the Vigilance Committee would kill two people."

"Maybe the priest would not be mad if he saw the two men shoot the little Tejano," Oscar said. "Señor Montez."

"Do you know these people?" the Tonk asked.

"Sure, his boys," said Oscar Schiller. "Ramon and little Jesus. We caught some salamanders in San Pedro Creek."

"Do you know where they live?"

"Sure. Just a little ways, across Calle de Laredo."

"All right," she said, turning to her kitchen table. "Eat a tamale and sit still and wait."

He sat and ate, watching her take more tamales from her oven and place them in a wicker basket with a stack of corn tortillas and some cinnamon buns. When he was finished eating, Oscar led her to the Montez *casa*, and as they approached along the alleyway, they could hear the soft wailing.

Along the wall of the house there were half-a-dozen Mexican women with black shawls over their heads, some of them rocking back and forth and keening. Oscar Schiller wasn't very comfortable with all this, but the Indian dragged him inside.

There it was the same. More of the older women squatting with their heads covered. The wife of the slain man sobbing as she was comforted by a priest Oscar Schiller recognized as the one who led the Catholic-school pupils across Main Plaza each day. He had heard them call the priest Father Paul.

He didn't see Ramon, but little Jesus came over to him, and his eyes were large and damp in the lamplight and very black.

"You like cinnamon buns?" Oscar Schiller asked. Little Jesus nodded. "We brought some. We brought some tamales, too."

They stood around for what seemed a long time. Oscar Schiller had the feeling that if they stayed much longer they'd get their feet wet, what with all the tears being shed. Except he noted with some pride that the Tonk was not shedding tears but just standing back in a corner, watching.

"You still got them salamanders?" Oscar asked.

"They died," Jesus said.

"Mine, too."

They only stayed about ten minutes. To Oscar Schiller, it seemed more like two hours.

Meanwhile, on Military Plaza, Market Master Gunther Roth was taking care of that tree the padre had cut down. It was his job to take care of anything having to do with the plaza, so he assumed this included getting rid of old hanging trees.

Using his considerable charm as the Market Master, who assigned places for traders to set up their wagons and for food venders to light their chili pots, it wasn't difficult for Roth to persuade a few regular users to take up crosscut saw and double-bit axe and turn the chinaberry tree into a great many loads of firewood, which were stacked in a most prominent spot before Roth's freight sheds to be sold.

Still other volunteers agreed to stand by the stack at market times and sell the wood, turning over all proceeds to Gunther Roth, who would give the money to the Widow Montez.

And that weekend, Oscar Schiller walked downstream from the town along San Pedro Creek, where there was a kind of potter's field, and saw the two wooden headboards, for as everyone knew, the Vigilance Committee did a thorough job of things, including setting up markers for the men they hanged.

Oscar Schiller had heard the stories about the burial and how they had dug the graves and threw in the bodies and covered them. And while some of the dark riders were on the ground doing the dirty work, so to speak, the others remained mounted and discussed the headboards.

Apparently there were a number of men on the Vigilance Committee with an appreciation for the need to be accurate at such times for the benefit of a curious posterity.

"We put their names, and their crimes, and the date."

"What crime?"

"Murder, of course."

"But the second one shot when Señor Montez was down and maybe already dead."

They had thought about that a while, and made their decision. And Oscar Schiller read the result on the headboards:

Kato Sprigs	Humbolt Something-or-Other
Hanged	Hanged
Murder	Disturbing the Peace
1850	1850

And the significant thing was not what the Vigilance Committee placed on the headboards but that Oscar Schiller, young as he was, could read it.

Chapter Fifteen

A boy like Oscar Schiller had more than the usual distractions at school that can be expected from the teasing and harassment of other students. For boys of this age seem always delighted to find in other boys what they perceive as an eccentricity to be picked at like a scab.

Anybody who wore glasses was always a target. The teasing he took for that only made Oscar Schiller defiant.

He was a runt, too, and maybe that saved him from a lot of knocks from boys who wouldn't start a shove-and-hit fuss because all of them were bigger and shied away from being called bullies. And although he was naturally belligerent, he had enough presence of mind to avoid fistfights.

He was the only boy in the school who lived in Barrio del Sur. That was Mexican country, the Gringo boys shouted, so Oscar Schiller was just a bleached-out tamale.

Worst of all, some of the German boys had heard enough of their parents bedroom talk to know Oscar Schiller was a bastard, so he got a lot of jibes about being the runt who didn't know who his father was and whose mother called him *der Zwerg* and was ashamed to sleep in the same house with him.

So Oscar was called the tamale bastard dwarf.

And that made him defiant, too, as though he were proud of every fault the other boys found to jeer about.

One boy who took particular delight in razzing Oscar Schiller was John David Jenkins, whose father was a land speculator and lumber-yard owner. And a lawyer besides. Also a Presbyterian.

Oscar despised John David, of course, and his dog as well, a black mastiff named Blacky with a bad temper. Because of the Jenkins family, Oscar had decided he'd never be a Presbyterian.

His religious options were narrowing. Because of Father Paul and the murder of that chinaberry tree, Oscar had ruled out the Catholic church, too. Although it hadn't been Father Paul who cut down the tree after the lynching at *el mercado*.

But back to the schoolyard.

John David Jenkins had his own pet name that infuriated Oscar more than all the other things he was called combined.

"Chili bean!"

The first time he came home after hearing it, he was in a fury until bedtime. It took the Tonk almost a year to get him to tell her what it was that so disturbed him. Her soothing him by pointing out that it was just a name and that besides, there wasn't any thing wrong with chili beans only made him madder.

It was to get his mind off John David and his black dog that the Tonk took out the Comanche finger necklace Henry Meuller had given Sophia when she left New Braunfels. The Tonk told Oscar what she knew of the finger pendant background, which wasn't much.

"It's like a prize, isn't it?" Oscar Schiller asked. At the moment he was wearing the thing around his neck, but Titch had warned he could never wear it outside their *casa*.

"Sure," she said. "Like the medal you won at that white man's school."

It was true. The boy had been honored above his classmates. A high point to hold up against all the harassment.

Mission schools gave out little medals for pupil excellence. They were small brass medallions hung on strips of colored ribbon. The profile of a saint was on each medallion.

The Lutheran school did the same thing, only it didn't have a saint's profile on its medallions. There was a letter "A" instead, indicating the top grade in the class. And a red, white, and blue ribbon, which was supposed to be patriotic. Texas patriotic, not U.S.A. patriotic.

Oscar Schiller won his medal because in about the fourth form, he scored higher marks in arithmetic than any of the other boys.

He was proud of it, too, running to Mrs. Wolf's to show Ulrich Silesia, who insisted the boy stand still long enough for him to bring Sophia in from the kitchen to see what a champion her son had become.

"It was the first time I have ever seen her with a shine of affection on her face, and she touched the medal and said it was wonderful, in German, of course," he wrote his father. "Then she withdrew with that strange look in her eye that always comes when she's near the boy. She is truly afraid of him, or at least what he stands for.

"It is sad that such a strong superstition and ignorance can keep a mother and her son apart. It makes them strangers, in fact."

"I must admit it doesn't seem to affect the boy much."

Some of the Mexican boys had a good enterprise trapping what they called wild pigeons. *Las palomas*, which the Anglos called mourning doves. Dove pie was a popular dish in such places as Mrs. Wolf's Cafe, and the birds were used in all kinds of delicious ways in many housewives' kitchens.

The boys used box traps made of sticks and set with any one of a number of colorful baits that made the curious doves come into the boxes for a look-see and then find it impossible to get out again.

The birds were placed in a heavy fishnet-type onion bag and sold live to one of the Military Plaza poultry traders, who retailed the birds live each day along with the usual chickens and geese and ducks and turkeys.

From these traders you also bought eggs and goose feathers and pickled chicken feet, pickled pig's feet, pickled goose eggs, and pickled anything else the vendor could think of to put in his briny brew and let soak for a couple of months.

The best among the dove catchers was Ramon Montez, son of the man who was shot outside of Ulrich Silesia's cafe and a friend of Oscar Schiller. As he grew, Oscar Schiller spent much time in Military Plaza, only a short distance from his home, and this was the scene of much of Ramon Montez's dove hunting, so he was often there, too.

They formed a natural friendship. And it was natural, too, that Oscar Schiller became interested and then involved with the pigeon business and formed a kind of partnership with Ramon Montez. This partnership included another of Oscar Schiller's friends from his school, Hermann Roth, whose father was Market Master and who hence spent a lot of spare time in Military Plaza, too.

You would think a business enterprise by three such young boys would be very haphazard and catch-as-catch-can. But such was not the case. The boys allowed that Ramon would be leader, because he was there first, so to speak, and the other two would be "Rangers."

Leader Ramon assigned sectors to each Ranger and took one himself. Oscar Schiller's sector was in the west side of town. The area was called *el madererio*, the lumberyard, because Jerome Falsworth had built a sawmill on San Pedro Creek there.

The boys soon shortened this to *el madero*.

Each day Oscar set one trap in *el madero* at a spot beside San Pedro Creek in the shadow of an old abandoned adobe house and close to where Jerome Falsworth had built the sawmill. There were a lot of hardwood trees there, good for nesting doves.

This was maybe the best dove-catching spot in all Bexar. Soon, Oscar Schiller was catching more birds than the other two combined. And this made them all happy because they were in a cooperative and profits were shared equally, no matter who brought in the birds.

"That little wart the Tonk woman keeps," said Fred Hausmann, who ran the big mercantile on Main Square and had a banking service which was very popular because there was no regular bank in Bexar. "You know he's started depositing money in my credit accounts? He's got $1.35 in there already. Catching doves. Hard to believe."

Oscar Schiller's favorite spot at *el madero* was a quiet place, away from the wind, with some low trees that doves liked for nesting, but all overhung with a canopy of sycamore and black oak trees.

In July, the first month of their partnership, Ramon Montez had brought the other two here so that they might see a thing he had mentioned but they didn't believe. Doves nursing their young.

They crept through the old abandoned shack to a vantage point Ramon had used for two years just to watch the birds. There was a nest in a small persimmon tree, not four feet from their faces, and they lay quietly and watched, as though they were scouting a hostile Comanche village.

Sure enough, the adult birds would fly in and sit on the edge of the nest, facing the three large chicks, and the chicks would pluck at the adults' breast feathers with their bills.

From that moment, the Mexican boy had the most credibility with the other two it was possible to have.

So *el madero* became a sort of special place for Oscar Schiller, because he'd learned something there. And maybe as his medal for excellence in school might suggest, he was already placing a high premium on learning.

Besides, *el madero* always produced. On all the days he'd trapped there, only once was a trap empty. And to make up for that, on three occasions there were two birds in the snare.

On a cloudy Friday afternoon, Oscar Schiller was in a hurry. He'd checked all his other traps and was going to *el madero*, running because it had started thundering and he knew he would get wet if he didn't hurry.

As he rushed down through the brush to the bottom of the ravine, he thought at first that the trap had been blown off the section of old adobe wall where he always set it. Then as he came closer, he saw it lying some distance away. It had been smashed, along with the two doves trapped inside it.

Oscar moved to the smashed trap gingerly, almost on tiptoe, almost holding his breath. He bent and touched the sharp end of broken sticks. There was a mass of gray down, feathers, bloody flesh, bird legs and beaks all askew, a horrible mush.

And as his mind accepted this and he started to think that somebody had stomped his birds, he smelled the dog.

When he rose and wheeled about, John David Jenkins was almost within an arm's length, and behind him was Blacky, his leash tied to a tree. Oscar Schiller was furious with himself for being so preoccupied with the smashed trap that he had allowed them to come this close undetected.

"Hello, chili bean. You little fart chili bean!" J. D. Jenkins snickered. And he reached out to shove the smaller boy. But he didn't shove.

This had been a special day at the school, a day called Presentation Day, when teachers gave honors to good students and all old winners were asked to wear their awards. So pinned to Oscar Schiller's shirt was his arithmetic "A" medal with the red, white, and blue patriotic ribbon.

It was this that J. D. Jenkins grabbed and yanked violently. The little cotton shirt ripped down the front, exposing Oscar Schiller's tiny ribcage, and as Oscar lifted the onion bag with four doves he'd taken from traps earlier and tried to swing it like a weapon, his glasses fell off.

"Hey, hey, what's the matter, you little dwarf chili bean?" John David yelled, laughing and jumping back, now shoving Oscar down and jumping back still more to release the dog. "Get him, Blacky. Get the little shit kicker, get em, get em, get em!"

Oscar Schiller's fury was not completely blind, because as the dog strained at his tether and then leaped forward, barking furiously, the boy spun and leaped up along the stones rolled down from the old wall. He almost made it completely, but not quite, and he felt a harsh pain at the back side of one thigh and heard the rip of his trousers.

But then he was high on the old wall, and the dog leaped at him fruitlessly. Oscar Schiller squatted there, feeling the blood running down his leg and into his shoe, and John David was laughing at him, encouraging the mastiff.

"You want another bite of that chili-ass?" J.D. shouted. "Wait a minute. Wait a minute. Look a here, dwarf head."

John David smashed the glasses with his shoe heel, then took the onion bag Oscar had dropped and began swinging it with all his force against the old wall. The birds were fluttering in the bag, making mewing cries. Feathers were flying, and the dog was going mad with excitement.

"Leave the birds alone," Oscar Schiller cried. "Leave the birds alone, you dumb son of a bitch!"

J.D. laughed and dropped the onion bag with the mangled and flopping birds. He was still holding the fragment of the cotton shirt, and he opened his hand and there was the arithmetic medal. He calmed the dog enough to get the medal tied to the heavy leather dog collar.

"Look at that, look at that, dove guts," he shouted.

The rain put an end to it then. It had begun to come down harder, with the promise of worse, and John David, pulling his dog along, left the ravine, but once he looked back and shouted.

"You tell on me, chili pot, my daddy'll have the sheriff put that Indian whore you live with in a jail and they'll beat her ever night." J.D. laughed, and the dog started another furious round of barking and straining to get back to the wall where Oscar Schiller still crouched. "You hear me, chili puke? You tell on me and my dog, my daddy'll get that dirty pig whore who changes your dirty diapers, you hear?"

The rain came harder, making big splatters on the dry adobe wall that Oscar squatted on, and he stayed for a while, the tears running along his cheeks and the cold rain running across his chest, and he watched the blood running from under his leg and down the side of the adobe wall with the rain. Blood and rainwater indistinguishable, running down the old wall together.

Even though it was later than usual and raining hard, Titch was not concerned that Oscar Schiller was late for his supper. Small and young as he was, she had come to trust his self-reliance.

She was under the patio roof cooking tortillas in the adobe oven when she heard him in the back room. By now, they had separate sleeping arrangements, he still in the large brass bed and she in a wood-frame bunk Ulrich Silesia had brought. She had her own corner in the front room.

She called to him, but he made no answer. So she rose and went in and saw at once the ripped shirt. He had no hat, nor did she see the dove bag. He was looking at her with hard, hooded eyes, and when she tried to touch him, he pushed her hand away.

"All right," she said. "Get out of the wet clothes and into something dry."

She had started back to her oven when she saw the blood on one shoe, and now when she came to him, there was a look on her face that told him resistance would not be tolerated.

When she saw the wound, she knew it was a bite, and as there were no wolves or coyotes roaming the streets of Bexar, she assumed it was a dog.

"Get on this table," she said and helped him onto the table, face down, and stripped off his pants and underwear. There was a clean slice up the back of his right thigh and a smaller tear on his back. His trousers and the belt had been opened up as though by a razor.

From a number of bottles and boxes along the wall shelf behind her bunk, she took leaves and dust and pollen and God only knows what all, put everything in a china cup, and mixed it with a small bit of Silesia's beer from a jug she always kept for him if he happened to stop by, which he had begun to do.

The paste she made from this mixture she rubbed into the cuts, and the one cut on the thigh she bound with strips of mattress cover canvas, very tight, and tied it with cotton string.

"Where is your school prize?" she asked. "For doing the numbers?"

There was no answer. She washed off the dried blood and gave him clean underwear and trousers. And went back to her oven. Oscar Schiller said nothing as they ate, and nothing as they went to bed. But after it was dark for a while, and the rain had stopped, Oscar called to her and she rose and went to his bed.

"There's no lightning with this rain," she said. "Besides, it's finished, I think."

But it wasn't his fear of lightning.

"Could John David Jenkins's father put you in the jail?" he asked.

She waited for a long time to answer, thinking about it. Maybe giving Oscar Schiller a chance to tell her more. But he said nothing, and she finally realized she had heard all she was likely to hear, at least for the present.

"Booth Jenkins is a rich man and he has a lot of friends and he is a lawyer," she said. "Why would he want to put me in jail?"

There was no answer, and in the dark each of them seemed to be tensely listening to the other breathing.

"If he wanted to put me in jail, or anybody else, he likely could do that," she said. "He has a lot of money and he's a lawyer and is supposed to be a friend to Judge Belcher, and they say Judge Belcher is getting very old and can't remember things much and so he has this Jenkins tell him what to do. But why would he want to put me in jail?"

She figured she would get no response, and she was right. So finally, she touched Oscar Schiller's chest very tenderly and then rose and went to her own bed.

But the boy had told her a lot with his question. She knew whose dog had put those wounds in the child's back. The minute Oscar Schiller mentioned the name Jenkins, she knew. That black mastiff was associated so strongly with the Jenkins household it was almost like another child of the family.

And she had not been unaware of the Jenkins boy's place in Oscar Schiller's affections, and she supposed the hatred was reciprocal. So there had been a fight perhaps, maybe over the medal, which was lost or taken by brute force, the dog pitching into the fray at some point.

She was not happy with this at all. What happened the next Monday morning made her less happy still. The boy had stayed indoors all day Saturday and Sunday, not even going to watch the dancing in Main Plaza on Saturday night or the chicken fights in Military Plaza on Sunday.

As he was getting ready for school, she caught him in her corner of the front room, taking her bone-handled knife from the wooden box under her bunk. The thing was almost as long as Oscar Schiller's arm.

She took it away from him quickly, but gently, and sat on the edge of the bunk and held her arm around him in a firm grip, the knife in her other hand.

"No, you can't do this," she said. "Your blood is too hot now, you would kill somebody. Then they would put us both in their jail. Sometimes the white man hopes we do a thing when our blood is hot. Then he can do whatever he wants with us, and even our friends cannot help us."

"He put it on his dog's collar," said Oscar Schiller, and his voice quavered.

"Leave it the way it is," she said. "Make your mind forget. Be strong and brave. We can't make any trouble with somebody like Booth Jenkins's son. Are those glasses good?"

"Yes," he said, touching the steel rims of one of the extra pairs of spectacles Ulrich Silesia had provided.

"Go to school," she said. "Don't talk to anybody about this. Someday you can tell me all of it. Now, let your blood cool. Let your medicine keep you calm. Patience is a warrior's best medicine. Not hot blood. So do nothing. Promise me."

"Yes," he said, and he rose and she went to the door with him and watched him walk all along Calle de Armador until he turned onto Camino de Laredo.

And Oscar Schiller didn't tell anyone except his two business partners, and he told them only part of it, but for the next month all three of them together went to the dove traps in *el madero*.

Children were always getting cuts and bruises, so Oscar Schiller's wounds attracted little attention. The Tonk kept the leg bandaged until it healed enough not to be noticed.

John David Jenkins did a lot of leering and snickering, but he stayed at a distance. And Oscar Schiller and his business partners ignored the bully.

Later, on the streets, J.D. had the mastiff on a leash, and the medallion dangled from the heavy leather collar. But John David gave no explanations, and neither did Oscar. Maybe Ulrich Silesia made as good a guess as any.

"Father, it turns my blood cold to think of that Jenkins boy taking the medal away from Little Oscar and hanging it on his damned dog! But apparently some sort of arrangement was made, because Oscar is showing no fuss about it and is making no effort to have it back, and I know how proud the lad was of that token.

"God only knows what treaties and compromises young boys may make with one another, or for what purpose.

"But I suppose the tragedies of youth are as nothing compared to what may come. Stunning news today."

Captain Sam Walker of the Texas Rangers had arrived late at night and was already in the hotel and sleeping before anybody except Ulrich Silesia knew about it. He always created a stir when he came back into town because he had replaced Coffee Hays as maybe the most popular Ranger.

·Well, along with Big Foot Wallace.

Walker was famous for more than fighting Mexicans and Comanches. It had been Walker who went back east to find Samuel Colt and tell him how he ought to improve his revolving pistol. The result was the first real combat sidearm, the Walker Colt, which quickly evolved into the Dragoon.

Captain Walker carried a package with him, a bundle wrapped in buckskin, and when he had the audience he'd requested with Ulrich Silesia the morning after he arrived in Bexar, he placed this bundle on Ulrich Silesia's desk.

First, Silesia had a pot of hot coffee sent up from the kitchen and then offered cigars he had bought from a drummer out of New Orleans and a platter of French cookies from the same place.

The German could not help but note and report to his father the incongruity of a rough, large, weather-beaten, heavily armed Texas Ranger sitting in a wicker chair by a cheesecloth curtain, sipping coffee from a hand-painted cup of Dresden china, and munching a dainty sweet cracker that had a lineage going back to some pastry shop in Paris.

"You know Paco Salazar?" Walker finally asked.

"Yes. Not well, I'm afraid. I see him so seldom. The last time we spoke was many years ago, when he returned to Ranger duty. It was here where we sit, in fact. When he returns to San Antonio, he stays to himself, with friends in the southern barrio, I suppose."

"He brought this woman here, didn't he?" Walker asked. "This Sophia Schiller?"

"He did. It's quite common knowledge, I expect."

"Good," Walker said. He leaned forward and placed his cup on the table and carefully unrolled the package he had brought.

Inside was a leather money belt, very old. Then two well-used but well-cared-for Colt Dragoon pistols in holsters, with all the usual accompanying items. Powder flask, cup full of percussion caps, grease cup with cloth patches, .44-caliber lead balls.

Very carefully, Captain Walker opened one of the money-belt pouches and pulled forth a piece of old paper and then even more carefully unfolded it. Brown and crinkled at the edges, the document was coming apart along the folds.

Laying it on the table, face up, and holding it down with both hands, Captain Walker asked Silesia if he knew what this was, and the German said it was an old Spanish land-grant like others he had seen.

"You know where this property's at?" Walker asked, and after only a moment of study, Silesia said he did.

"The woman Sophia you spoke of, she works for me, as I'm sure you know, and her son and a hired woman live in this property on Armador Street."

Walker turned the paper and pressed it down again. Here there was writing of more recent date.

"With sound mind and common good sense, I give as behest the property shown hereon to Frau Sophia Waldenburg Schiller in case of my decease."

It was signed by Paco Salazar, and below his signature were the signatures of Samuel Walker and two witnesses identifying themselves as Texas Rangers. And then a date, only two weeks previous.

"I don't understand," said Silesia.

"When he came back to the Rangers," Walker said, "Salazar came to me and made this will. A lot of men do it, if they're lucky enough to have property. Or anybody to leave it to." Captain Walker laughed shortly, but it wasn't much of a laugh for mirth. He puffed at his cigar before continuing.

"The stipulation is the same for all of em. In case of death, this will, already written and witnessed, is dated by me and gotten into the proper hands. At the time of his makin this will, Salazar said he wanted it given to you for proper disposition here in Bexar County."

It took a few seconds for Ulrich Silesia to frame his question, even though he knew at once what it was and what its answer would be, as well.

"Are you telling me Paco Salazar is dead?"

"I am," said Walker. "It was on the Salt Fork of the Brazos. I'm happy to report no Comanche killed him.

"We seen some wild ponies, or ponies that maybe escaped from a Comanche herd someplace in Palo Duro Canyon, and we was tryin to catch em all. Salazar and another Ranger was ridin along the top of this cutbank and it caved in, and Salazar's horse pinned him and the other horse come down on top. Got his head, bad crushed, but at least it knocked him senseless from the start.

"This here was a death blow, that horse fallin like it done. I heard Salazar's head pop. He never had no idea what hit him. You can take that as a comfort to anybody that cares.

"I'll tell you this, Mr. Silesia, they'll be some loud wailin and gnashin of teeth in the barrios tonight when they hear about this."

They sat for a while, with not much more to say, and it was obvious to the Ranger that the news of Salazar's death had affected the German deeply. Not as the death of a friend would, but rather like the passing of somebody who one just comes to expect will be around no matter what comes.

When Silesia asked Sophia Schiller upstairs and into his office to show her the grant, she bent over the table and stared at it as he held it flat for her. There were all the vectors, the latitudes and definitions and the signature of Alcalde Vicente Armador and of Hernando Salazar.

The document had been executed in brown ink, or perhaps, Silesia thought, the ink had turned brown with age.

Then there was the endorsement by a representative of the Republic of Texas and Paco Salazar's signature. Silesia turned the paper, and Sophia stared at the will written in Salazar's sweeping hand. That and all of this last in black ink.

"What is it?" she finally said, in German.

"The Spanish land-grant to that property your son is living on," he said. "It's like a deed, showing ownership. And this on the back is Paco Salazar's will, giving it to you."

It took a moment for her to realize what this meant. But when she straightened and looked at him, Ulrich Silesia knew she understood that Salazar was dead.

"The Texas Ranger captain who was with him when he died came," he said gently. "He said Paco Salazar died quickly when a horse fell on him, died without pain. I know he meant a lot to your community with all the help he was to you when you first arrived in Texas. I know Herr Meuller will be very sad."

For a long moment, Sophia turned her face toward the window and looked down into the bustle of activity on Main Plaza. Later, Silesia wrote his father that it was impossible to tell from the expression on her face what Sophia was feeling, but whatever it was, he said, it gripped her strongly, making her shudder repeatedly, as though she were being shaken by some powerful hand.

Then she turned, carefully folded the paper, carefully put it inside her bodice, and walked out without a word. Ulrich Silesia was left with an explanation still in his mouth about getting the document to the proper Bexar County authorities so that a record could be made of the transfer.

Well, later, he thought, and now to tell the Tonk and Little Oscar. It was early Saturday morning, so he hoped to find them both in their barrio *casa*. And walking across Military Plaza, he reminded himself that he had to stop thinking of the boy as Little Oscar, because although he was still small, he was old enough to resent such a nickname.

Their reaction was expected. The Tonk's face did not change when Ulrich Silesia told them, even though she knew Paco Salazar was the man who helped recapture her from Comanches and brought her in to the mission school.

Nor did Oscar Schiller show any more than a casual interest.

And walking back to Mrs. Wolf's, Ulrich Silesia knew there had been no show of emotion because for the one it was rock-hard self-control and for the other it was a matter of not really knowing the deceased, except as an occasional visitor who spent a few moments talking softly with the Tonk and then was gone in the night.

"It's worked out well, I suppose," Ulrich Silesia wrote. "Sophia no longer has to feel obligated to Salazar for the use of his house. She owns it now.

"There is some talk that a few people, Booth Jenkins among them, are interested in buying much of the old residential property on the edge of the south barrio because they want to build business property there. It makes sense. So close to Military Plaza.

"Jenkins isn't the nicest man I can think of to do business with. But we'll see.

"For now, I will inform Henry Meuller at New Braunfels about the Salazar tragedy, they having been close associates and friends. Someone from New Braunfels is in Bexar every day to do business at our post office it seems.

"Perhaps I failed to mention, we have finally been given a post office. It's in the Hausmann Mercantile next door because of the proximity to the stage station in my building. The coach line has a contract to carry the mail, which provides a large part of their income."

But Ulrich's father never read that letter. Little over a week after it was mailed, a letter came from New York, from Ulrich's sister Bertha.

The old man had been called to his reward, she wrote, and laid to rest in a nice predominantly Lutheran cemetery in a German community of east Manhattan Island some distance north of the town and away from the crowds and the carriages.

She said there was a nice view through the elm trees of the East River. And in winter, when the leaves were down, you could see the farms of Queens.

This news left him disconsolate. Repeatedly, he caught himself at his bedroom desk late at night, taking paper and opening his inkpot and sharpening a quill, all in preparation for a letter to his father.

After a while, he realized that the letters had been as much for himself as for his father, so he began writing again, addressing them to no one, and finally calling them his Journal of Life on the Texas Frontier.

Ulrich Silesia had no way of knowing that one day those journals would be found in an old steamer trunk in a musty basement and published by a well-known and respected university press. Had he known, he probably would have stopped writing.

Chapter Sixteen

The California gold rush had an early effect on Bexar that continued for a long time. So long, in fact, that for almost a decade, when a stranger came through town headed for California he was called a forty-niner.

A lot of strangers came through. At times, the locals were a little startled at the flood of land speculators, pimps, whores, gamblers, gunmen, lawyers, and even a few honest men and women. Death Corner earned its name many times over as people in Main Square had to run for their lives while some of the riffraff tried to settle arguments by spraying bullets all over the plaza.

The members of the Vigilance Committee hardly had time to rub down their horses before they had to ride out once more to introduce some miscreant to one of the chinaberry trees. One of Goshen Steiner's billiard parlor hangers-on said that San Antonio had doubled in population since the gold rush started.

The town council spent a lot of time wrangling about passing new ordinances to control the "foreigners" passing through. They hired a couple of new constables. They posted a law against discharging firearms inside the city. For good measure, they also passed a law against pigs running free in the streets, without explaining what that had to do with the forty-niner invasion.

"I don't see many men carrying pans for washing gold or picks and shovels," said Frederick Hausmann. "I suppose somebody in California is making a fortune selling them that truck."

"These people we're getting mostly aren't miners," said Ulrich Silesia, who had spent a lot of time talking with forty-niners in his taproom. "These are the ones who will live in towns and end up with all the money the workingmen grub out of the stream beds and the mountain sides."

"Well, I'm thinking about trailing a herd of cattle out there," said Gunther Roth, and he looked at the only Mexican on the council,

Señor Juan Estaban Pardo, a highly successful horse breeder and corn rancher. "Johnny, do you figure I could find two-dozen vaqueros who'd be willing to hire on for such a drive, for percentage share of profits?"

"Sí, you could find five dozen, if you desire," Pardo said. "But the only cows you can round up in our area will be very tough cows indeed, and I understand they have very fat cows in California."

"Yes, but all these people going there," said Roth, "I suspect they'll run out of home-grown cows quick, if they haven't already. And from what I hear of prices there, a man could make *mucho dinero* even on bony cows with lots of gristle."

Everybody laughed.

"It's not an easy route, along Camino del Rio to the pass, then along the border all the way to California," said Pardo. "With a well armed group of vaqueros, you'll have no Indian troubles. But what about water?"

"I heard that when General Stephen Kearny took his army from Santa Fe to California during the Mexican War, he used his Mormon battalion to dig wells all along the route," Roth said.

"Gunther," said Frederick Hausmann, "I think maybe you smell a chance for some business advantage here."

And they all laughed again.

A lot of people saw the chance for advantage. There were times when you couldn't buy an egg in San Antonio for less than fifty cents. Ulrich Silesia was selling floor space in the halls of his hotel on a night-by-night basis to people looking for a place to sleep. He charged a dollar. A blanket was another dollar.

The stagecoach that ran on an irregular basis along Camino del Rio to El Paso was always loaded, with people riding on top. The stage-coach company always provided a couple of well-armed riders to go along to protect against Comanches.

Everybody understood that if the Comanches really wanted to stop one of those stages going across the southern edge of their territory, it wouldn't be any problem for them. But for some reason, they seldom attacked the coaches.

"It's too far south of the good buffalo ranges for the Nerm to bother with em," said one of the Military Plaza hunters. "So long as you don't run into a war party out lookin fer Lipans down along the Rio Grande, you're likely all right."

Anyway, the company put on extra coaches. The California trade filled them, too.

The bathhouse business was booming. The river was used for everything in Bexar. Drinking water, cooking water, bathing, live-stock scrubdowns, vehicle washings, sewer. A few enterprising souls had put in bathhouses, canvas affairs that provided a little privacy for dressing alongside riverbanks that were kept clean and chili carts where you could rent towels and have a snack.

These were particularly popular with the forty-niners, most of whom had taken a ship from somewhere to Indianola at Matagordo Bay, then a coach or whatever transport they could find to Bexar, which was the jumping-off place, as they called it, for California. So it was a good bet they all needed a bath after such a trip.

It was because of the forty-niner trade that Oscar Schiller quit the dove trade. He told Titch he was getting too old for that sort of thing anyway, so he started hanging around the town's two hotels, catering to people passing through, people who needed help with baggage or wanted to know where to buy boots or where to get good chili or who had horses to sell.

There was more than one set of raised eyebrows at what all this child knew, and him at such a tender age, the strangers in town not realizing that Oscar Schiller was too old to be called a child anymore. So maybe it wasn't surprising that if you wanted to know where there might be one of those beautiful *señoritas* who knew about having a good time, he could direct you.

And it seemed that the first thing on every Gringo's mind when he first came to San Antonio was those beautiful *señoritas*.

A great many forty-niners left wagons parked in the streets and plazas while they fitted up for the long drive west. Of course, there had always been some of that, because of settlers going to local plots, but now it was hard to get a cargo cart along Commerce Street because of the congestion.

This led to a lot of jockeying back and forth of ox teams and mules, a lot of geeing and hawing, a lot of shuffling and repositioning of

255

wagons and carts, and a lot of confusion. Boys Oscar Schiller's age had all left school to earn a penny here and there helping with livestock, maybe helping to get the streets untangled. Or maybe sometimes getting underfoot.

There were a lot of arguments and uncounted fistfights and scuffles and pushing and shoving, which all the boys like Oscar quickly learned to avoid by scrambling up on a wagon and observing from a perch of safety, out of the range of thrown bottles or rocks.

Six times one of these fusses turned into a pistol fight, but most of the forty-niners were as unaccustomed to firearms as they were to handling half-wild oxen, so during that whole time, only one man was killed.

"These pilgrims are dangerous," one of the Steiner billiard hall regulars said. "That scramble last Friday night sounded like the battle of New Orleans, and there was enough smoke to choke you to death, but when it blowed away, there they was, not a scratch on any of em!"

The deadly arguments occurred when headstrong immigrants got involved with Texas gunfighters.

There were more serious encounters in the country out beyond the last scattered settlements of Bexar. Comanches had begun once more to make serious trouble, and a number of farms and ranches along the Edwards Plateau were burned out, the people lucky enough to escape staggering into San Antonio with horror stories of warriors with black paint on their faces.

Raiders were all coming now from the far reaches of Llanos Estacados, the Staked Plains, and they were taking almost no captives. So the incentive to mount punitive raids against them was not as strong as it had been in the past, when the need to free captives gave the Texans urgency.

"You've got to go a long way to hit em now," said Sam Walker, the Ranger captain. "All the way to the headwaters of the Brazos or the Red. These bunches we're seeing now are raiding parties, on the move, no base camp near by. They can pop up anywhere."

When Ulrich Silesia went to the Salazar house on Armador Street to take Titch the Tonk some money and a wheel of cheese he'd bought from a Galveston shipmaster, who said it came direct from Hertfordshire, England, he mentioned Indians for the first time ever.

"I think the Comanches have seen all these new immigrants going to California," he said. "I think it's upset them."

The Tonk looked at him for a long time. She was standing where she always did when he came, against the wall by the back door, on one foot, the other drawn up against the wall.

"The old men tell them that maybe the white man is finished coming, and he's got all he wants, and now he'll stop," she said. "The old men don't want war because they know how it will end."

She glanced at Oscar Schiller, who was leaning on both elbows at the table, watching her speak.

"So for a little while the young men say, all right, we'll see if no more of them are coming," the Tonk said. "Then these people come and go on toward the west. Doesn't matter where they go. What matters is they've come. So the young men in the wild tribes rise up singing and tell the old men they are fools and the young men ride out to fight."

"Don't the young men know the old men are right?" asked Silesia. "Don't the young men know they will lose?"

The Tonk lifted her head in a way she had that showed disdain and impatience and scorn, her eyes shining.

"Young men do not think about what will happen tomorrow, only what is good today," she said. "Besides, among Comanches, that's what they are born to do. To fight."

A few days later, Oscar Schiller ran home from Military Plaza, and he was breathing hard and obviously excited, which the Tonk found unusual.

"Somebody said you could see it," he panted. "So I ran into the church. . . ."

"What church?" she interrupted.

"San Fernando, on the plaza," he said. "We were running up the stairs in the bell tower. . . ."

"Who is we?" she interrupted again.

"Just some people, me and Jesus Montez and Hermann Roth and a lot of men from the plaza, and we went to the bell tower and looked out toward the plateau and we could see it."

"See what?"

"I'm trying to tell you," he shouted, red faced by now. "We could see the Camino de Chihuahua. Far out, there was something burning. There were two fires. Very bright fires. It was hay, in two wagons. We could see horses riding around and there were some of them on the ground. . . ."

"Some of who on the ground?"

"Comanches, Comanches! The Nerm! I'm trying to tell you! Some of them on the ground unhitching the oxen, but then they shot them and left them dead, and Mr. Silesia said the oxen were too slow so they couldn't take them, and there were some men riding out there from town and the men on horses at the wagons finally rode away. The wagons were still burning.

"And one man was running this way, and the men on horses came to him and some of them rode on and got off their horses, and there was another man there on the ground, and they lay him on a horse behind the saddle and came into town.

"He was dead and they'd scalped him. And somebody said it was two of Señor Juan Pardo's men who had been cutting hay down along the Nueces someplace and were bringing it in for market here in Bexar."

Titch drew a deep breath and went to her stove.

"All right. I'm glad you've seen Comanches making their fight," she said. He waited for more, but there was no more. He was still a little irritated with her, and his voice was strident.

"Why?"

"I wanted you to see them," she said. "Before it is too late."

"Too late?"

"Yes. I wanted you to see them before they are all gone."

John David Jenkins had not quit school. His daddy Booth was already installed as the Bexar prosecutor and acted as though he intended to make a life's work of it while using his position to snap up the good real-estate deals that came to the attention of county officials before they were known to the public.

Booth Jenkins made no bones about his mission—to get his son, J.D., back east to a fine school and then settled finally in San Antonio to help his daddy manage a good part of the growing town where the

Jenkins family would have a large interest, due to the elder Jenkins suck-ing up all that Barrio del Sur property he was already greedy for, where commercial enterprise could be developed adjacent to Military Plaza.

All this according to Ulrich Silesia, who, if you recall the reason for his rapid exit from the city of New York, was an expert on know-ing about the advantages of having prior knowledge in any deal where making a profit was involved.

Of course, Ulrich Silesia didn't say a lot about this to anyone he didn't trust because Booth Jenkins, in his position as prosecuting attor-ney, and in who knew *what* position on the Vigilance Committee, could do some pretty bad things to any citizen he saw as a threat. Jenkins had bragged about how he could use a grand jury as a deadly weapon.

Anyway, Oscar Schiller and his friends had no reason to look out for John David and his dog Blacky during school days. On Saturdays and Sundays, J.D., with his dog on leash, would pop up here and there and sic his dog on Oscar or Jesus Montez.

He'd never let go of the leash, but he'd work the dog into a lather, until it was frothing white slobbers like a sweating horse. J.D. would hold the leash and kneel beside the straining dog and say, "Sic em. Sic em. Go eat that chili pot and that tamale Montez. Get em Blacky, get em."

Then if some adult came past and glared at him, J.D. would go away, but not hangdog. He'd shout at the boys, who were usually perched on something high by then, like a Mexican cart or the rock wall around the jail yard in Military Plaza, to be out of the range of Blacky's teeth in case he slipped the choke collar off the leash.

"Hey you, chili pot, you a little birdie up there," J.D. would taunt and laugh. "Hey, you better go home and get your redskin mammy to help you. Ole Blacky here mount that Indian whore like she was a bitch in heat!"

That one almost brought Oscar Schiller down to fight, but he knew how a fight with John David Jenkins would end. So he kept his promise to Titch and let it ride.

And Oscar never mentioned any of these incidents to the Tonk because he didn't want her to know how J.D. ragged him mercilessly.

But then John David began loitering around Military Plaza and Laredo Street late in the day. To get home, Oscar Schiller usually passed this way, and from time to time, J.D. and his dog were waiting.

Oscar had to run for the head of Armador Street; then J.D. would squat, in full view of the Salazar *casa*, to yell a few more insults with the dog going crazy, trying to get free of the leash.

Titch watched this performance on many occasions, but by the time Oscar came into the house, she'd have moved away from the door. She said nothing to him. And maybe he knew she'd seen, maybe not. But if he'd looked at her eyes, he'd have known something was making her savagely furious!

Almost everybody in town thought John David was a little smart-aleck shit. But nobody had the nerve to slap him around. Daddy or the city marshal, Dubb Shirley, would have dealt roughly with anyone who did.

So they all put up with Blacky's terrorizing Oscar and his little Mexican friend. And they all put up with J.D.'s obscenities, which some of the German *Hausfrauen* thought were the most ghastly things they'd ever heard, made even worse by what their husbands said of the senior Jenkins: that he was actually proud his son was the uncontested champion bully of schoolchildren on San Antonio's streets.

"I wonder how long he'd be the big bully," said Frederick Hausmann, "if somebody took that black mastiff out and shot it?"

But other than the gleam in his eye about that barrio property, Booth Jenkins was a good prosecutor. Better than most would have been, many of them figured, because everybody knew how crooked that office could get with some lawyer picked by chance. At least Booth was a known quantity.

And John David never bothered the boys of more prosperous Mexicans or the Anglos. Silesia noticed that. He also noticed that something had happened to Oscar Schiller's arithmetic medal. It no longer dangled from Blacky's collar.

Probably nobody ever put the whole sequence together, but Ulrich Silesia came close. He didn't have much chance of getting the first part.

After the two ruffians had killed Jesus Montez, the Tonk had spent a lot of time at the Montez *casa* in the Barrio del Sur helping the widow with her children and cooking food she provided from her own larder.

So there wasn't much doubt about Señora Montez's gratitude to the Tonk, and any time a favor was asked, not much question but that it would be granted. Like borrowing the Montez dog, a sweet hound the boys called Coco. She was one of those large, lazy hounds not good for much, but sweet.

It had been a week when John David Jenkins was close on Oscar Schiller's heels half-a-dozen times, twice at the end of the street, where the Tonk could see him making that obscene observation about what his dog Blacky would do to the Indian woman if she'd come out in the street to play.

That night, before he was asleep, Oscar Schiller heard someone at the front of the house, talking through the window, and he recognized the voice of Ramon, the older of the two Montez boys.

He made out the name Coco. There was a moment of quiet whispering; then he heard the Tonk go to her room in the dark. She kept some of her things in a wooden box under her bed, and he heard her slide it out. She was back at the window then, and he was sure he heard Ramon say *el estro*.

He knew what that meant, having spent his life on Bexar's plazas where there were animals of all kinds and casual talk of their breeding. So the Montez hound was in heat. He wondered why the Tonk would now rummage around in her room in the dark, then leave the house. Maybe he'd misunderstood. Maybe the dog was having pups, and they needed help.

But help a dog with pups, an old hound? Since when? But he was sleepy and pulled the blanket over his shoulder. He woke when Titch came in, and his window showed gray light, so he knew it was near dawn.

Oscar Schiller hung about for a long time that morning, thinking maybe the Tonk might tell him where she'd gone during the night. She didn't, so he forgot about it and went out on his usual rounds.

It was a school day, so no worry about J.D. and Blacky until later in the afternoon.

It didn't take long for Dubb Shirley, the city marshal, to start asking around about the Jenkins's black dog. He spent a lot of time nosing through the barrios, but he stopped in to visit with all the German merchants, too. What he wanted to know was, had anybody seen the dog?

"They keep the dog in a pen in back of the house," he told Goshen

Steiner at the billiard parlor. "There's a gate, and somebody opened it night before last and the dog got out. They ain't seen him since."

"J.D. probably forgot to lock the gate," said Goshen. "That's probably what it was."

"He says no. He says he shut the gate and latched it like always. He says somebody has stole his dog."

"Stole that dog?" asked Goshen Steiner. "That dog? Hell, nobody except Booth Jenkins and his boy could get close to that son of a bitch without getting his leg tore off. Who'd have the guts to steal a mean-spirited dog like that anyway?"

The marshal stopped by Mrs. Wolf's Cafe, too.

"Mr. Jenkins is pretty upset," he said.

"I suppose you get attached to a dog after a while," said Ulrich Silesia. "Even one like that."

"The boy seems half crazy," said Marshal Shirley. "I never seen anybody carry on like that. He says he'll burn down all of Mex town, is like he puts it, if any of them people got his dog."

John David Jenkins wasn't on the street much now. Surely he wasn't afraid of somebody like Oscar Schiller or Jesus Montez, but maybe there were some older, bigger boys who had had a taste of J.D.'s bully-boy tactics, and without Blacky to escort him, John David might figure he was in peril of a bloody nose.

So the mystery stretched out for a week, Marshal Shirley still looking for the dog, but no trace was found. Then one evening when the Military Plaza seemed less crowded with immigrant wagons than usual, Ulrich Silesia took advantage of the lull to have a dish of *chili con carne* at one of the stands.

He was seated on a raw wooden bench, eating from a tin bowl on a square-shaped table with a hollow center, where three Mexican women stood and ladled out the food. Whale-oil lamps at each corner of the table cast a fuzzy orange glow. A number of young Mexicans were sitting along the wall of the jail compound, strumming guitars and singing.

When Goshen Steiner came and sat beside Silesia, he was smoking a long black cigar that smelled very bad. He looked about in all directions, furtively, as though he figured somebody might be spying on him.

"You know, I think I've stumbled onto something about that Jenkins dog," he said. "That oldest Montez boy, he does odd jobs for me. Good boy. He says the night that black dog got out of his pen, the Montez dog was in heat."

"So you think you've got a love affair between Blacky and that old Montez bitch?"

"No, listen, it's better," Steiner said. "You know that runt kid? Your cook's his mother. And his Tonk keeper?"

"Of course. I know them very well."

"On this night we're talkin about, that Tonk come by the Montez house and borrowed the bitch," Steiner said. "The Montez boy said she'd asked a long time ago to let her know when that dog came in heat. So when it happened, the boy went and told her and she come and took the bitch."

"Took the bitch where?"

Goshen Steiner sat there blinking in the lamplight, puffing his cigar.

"To that mastiff's pen behind the Jenkins house."

"Why the hell would she do that?"

"Can you think of a better way to take a mean dog's mind off chewing on your leg?"

Now it was Ulrich Silesia's time to sit and blink. Chewing his *chili con carne*.

"All right. So what then? Let's assume the Indian took the bitch over there to the Jenkins house so the mastiff would forget about being mean for a few minutes. Why? And where's the mastiff now?"

"Hell, I don't know," Goshen Steiner said, and he threw his cigar on the ground, where it made a little shower of red sparks. He leaped up and started across the square toward his pool hall. "It's about to drive me crazy, tryin to figure out what's goin on."

Two days later Ulrich Silesia was at the mercantile, looking at some ocelot pelts Frederick Hausmann had bought from a hunter from Mexico.

"He says he spends a year at a time in the high-plateau country of the Sierra Madres in Durango," said Hausmann, holding up a pair of the delicately fine furs, tawny yellow with black spots. "He has two freedman Africans, and they live on javelina and rattlesnake and hunt these little cats and cure the hides right there. I wish I could get a wagon-load of these to Hamburg. I'd make a fortune."

"How many would it take to make a lady's coat?" Ulrich Silesia asked.

"I suppose perhaps you could do it with twenty."

They had no more chance to discuss the imminent demise of ocelots, because Goshen Steiner appeared and tugged at Ulrich Silesia's sleeve and made a lot of faces and hissing sounds. Pulling away from everybody else in the store, Goshen positioned them behind a barrel full of axe handles and whispered with a quaver of excitement in his voice.

"I told you, I told you something was going on," he said. "This morning two Mexican boys found the black dog. The Jenkins dog, in the river south of town."

"Well, good. Now I assume they've told Booth Jenkins and that's the end of it. Too bad his dog drowned."

"Drowned? Drowned?" Steiner gasped, sputtering. "When's the last time you heard of a dog drowning? Hell, Ulrich, the dog's head was cut near off, that's what happened, and then the whole mess thrown in the river. Only it didn't float away. And nobody's going to tell Jenkins his dog's throat was cut. He'd go crazy running around having people arrested."

"I can see a problem, but arrested on what charge?"

"I'm not a lawyer. But Booth Jenkins is, and he can sure as sin find something to arrest somebody for if they cut his dog's throat! Or if he suspects they did!"

"Where's the dog now? The dog's body, I mean?"

"The kids who found it dragged it out on the prairie and buried it someplace. They're scared stiff Jenkins'll get them if he finds out they're the ones found it. But they're so damned happy the dog's dead, they couldn't keep completely quiet. They told me, knowing how I despised that vicious mutt. I'd wager your little bastard friend knows all about it by now."

Actually, the only thing Oscar Schiller knew was that the dog wasn't on the street anymore, trying to get at him with those long, angry teeth.

Some of the boys who lived in the same barrio as the Jenkins family did reported that the pen where Blacky was usually in residence was empty and lizards were seen crawling lazily across the grassless yard in front of the doghouse, a sure sign that there was no ill-tempered mastiff there.

Once, Ulrich Silesia saw Booth Jenkins and John David on Military Plaza, and the boy was pointing to Oscar Schiller, who was helping unload some charcoal at one of the chili stands. Some time later, Marshal Dubb Shirley confronted Oscar Schiller on the covered sidewalk in front of Mrs. Wolf's Cafe.

Oscar Schiller was still wiping meringue off his face from the lemon pie he'd just treated himself to with a penny of the money he'd earned helping the plaza chili vendors. And who knows, maybe taking some pride in the fact that his mother baked those pies and they were famous all over Bexar.

Ulrich Silesia saw this as well, and as Dubb Shirley led the boy along Commerce Street, past San Fernando Church and into Military Plaza and thence to the city hall and jail, Silesia followed. The German paused in the shadows of the cedar elm trees behind the church and watched.

The marshal and the boy didn't go into the city hall. Instead, they went into the jail stockade, and then Ulrich Silesia saw them mounting the stairs that ran outside city hall to the second floor and going through a door there.

Ulrich Silesia didn't like the looks of that. The prosecutor's office was there on the second floor. When they went through Jenkins's door, Oscar Schiller looked very small and frail.

As the shadows began to lengthen across the plaza, most of the vendors broke up their counters and went home, but there were still many people there among the wagons and along the sidewalks. Some of the musicians who usually played at night were gathering near the wall of the old governor's house, and there was the soft, silver sound of a flute. There were mockingbirds, too, in the chinaberry trees of *el mercado*, the park at the west end of the plaza.

Still, Ulrich Silesia waited. And at last when Oscar Schiller came down, Ulrich Silesia went to him and walked with him across the plaza toward Camino de Laredo.

"What was it?" he asked.

"John David's daddy. He was askin all about John David's dog."

They passed by one corner of a stock pen where a whale-oil lantern hung, and the German stopped and took the boy's shoulders and turned him toward the light and bent to look closely into his face.

"Your nose is bleeding," he said. "What happened up there, boy? Tell me!"

"Nothing," said Oscar Schiller. "He just smacked me because I couldn't tell him anything."

"Who? Who smacked you?"

"John David's daddy."

"Was John David there?"

"Sure. Him and that Shirley, with the badge. John David kept yellin I hated his dog and wanted to do something bad to it, and I called him a yellow-livered snot, and that's when his daddy smacked me. Just with his hand. Not his fist. Then they told me to get on home."

They stood there for a moment, Ulrich Silesia panting with fury.

"That son of a bitch!" he whispered. "We've got to do something about this. Grown man slapping a boy."

But the instant he said it, he started reconsidering. Mostly reconsidering who it was he was about to bring to account. The county prosecutor.

"Well, maybe not," he said, and he started hustling the boy on toward his home. "Did they hurt you?"

"No! I spit on John David, too," Oscar Schiller said.

"Oh, that's wonderful. Oil on troubled water. You've got some strange ideas about cooling things down," the German said. "Listen, don't say a word to Titch about this. She might go after somebody with that knife of hers."

"I know that," Oscar Schiller said. "You think I'm crazy?"

It was later that evening, back in his room, that Ulrich Silesia thought about what he'd said and how when he'd mentioned Titch and her knife, for the first time the Tonk's blade had entered his thinking about Goshen Steiner's mystery of the black dog.

And that was all of it.

Or at least, Ulrich Silesia thought that was all of it. After a month of dealing with forty-niners and the heat-up in Comanche and Kiowa raids and the usual town problems the council had to deal with, Blacky the mastiff was simply forgotten.

The Western Texan, San Antonio's newspaper, reported all the problems the town council had to deal with, like how to control what was dumped in the river upstream from where drinking water was taken; and how to discourage the immigrants from using city streets as campgrounds; and how to keep the bridge and the fords in good condition for the increased traffic back and forth, what with all the new building on the east bank and the dirt yard in front of the old mission at the Alameda now called Alamo Plaza and about to be cobblestoned and already as active as the plazas on the west side. The newspaper presented the general oversight of a town that now boasted fifty stores, twelve restaurants, two hotels, four churches, and twenty saloons.

Jesus Montez came early one morning to the *casa* of Oscar Schiller on Calle de Armador. He told Oscar Schiller he wanted to show him something before Señora Montez sent it away with her brother's hide cart on the next trip to Galveston because it might be dangerous to keep.

Oscar Schiller didn't ask any questions.

In a small, enclosed space behind the Montez *casa*, there was a number of old boxes. The goat was there, too. This was the Tonk's goat. She had given the goat to the Montez family to use after the tragedy of Señor Montez's demise.

Although they didn't have what you'd call a genial friendship, Oscar Schiller and the goat had been acquainted a long time. They reacted to each other as they always had in the Tonk's back yard. They kept their distance and a wary eye on one another.

But the goat was soon forgotten. In one of the boxes were the Montez hound and seven puppies. They were short-nosed, short-tailed, black puppies.

"Three weeks old," said Jesus Montez.

"God Almighty," Oscar Schiller gasped. "Them ain't hound pups. Who's the sire?"

"Ask the Tonk," Jesus said.

"What are you talkin about?" Oscar said.

"She come got our bitch one night when the bitch was in heat," said Jesus. "She ask mama long time ago could she borrow our dog when she come in heat. So she done it, and that dog of ours was gone the whole night."

Oscar Schiller stood there looking at those puppies, and his mind was whizzing around.

"Ramon went with her," said Jesus. "He was gone all night. He brang our dog home."

"Well, where's he at?" asked Oscar. "Get him. I wanta know about this."

"He won't tell," said Jesus. "He swore a big oath with that Tonk of yours. He won't tell. If he told, he say the Tonk promised to cut off his ears."

"Titch won't cut no boy's ears!" Oscar snorted.

"The hell you say!"

"Come on, now, get Ramon out here. Nobody gonna cut his ears off."

"The hell you say!"

There was no way under the sun Jesus Montez was going to get his brother, and no way under the sun his brother would say anything if he'd made some silly oath with the Tonk, and Oscar Schiller knew it.

So sputtering with disgust, he told Jesus Montez he sure had a box full of ugly half-mastiff pups and left, stomping up the street toward home.

But halfway there, he stopped and sat on the floodgate of an irrigation ditch and started working out the puzzle. By the time he was finished, he'd decided this business of solving mysteries was the best thing he'd ever done and hoped he'd get to do some more of it someday.

Oscar Schiller took off his sandals. Somewhere along the system, the Bexar irrigation engineer had opened a sluice, and water was tumbling through the ditches. It was dirty brown, but it felt clean and cool on his bare toes as he dangled them and thought about what he knew and what he didn't know.

He knew: that the Tonk had made arrangements to have a bitch dog in heat and when the time came led the dog somewhere. And Ramon Montez went with her.

He knew: that Ramon Montez had returned home with the bitch just before dawn and at about the same time the Tonk had returned to her *casa*.

He knew: that two days later, the Jenkins black mastiff dog was found dead in the river.

He knew: that two months later, give or take a day or two, the bitch gave down with a litter of black pups.

Oscar Schiller knew, had known since he was only old enough to talk, that the gestation period for a dog was sixty-three days. Give or take a day or two.

And of course, he knew about the big knife the Tonk always had close at hand. He'd grown up with that knife until it had become something he hardly thought about, like a favorite shawl the Tonk would wear a lot.

So with that, he pulled it together and said to himself that it had happened like this: the Tonk and Ramon got to the dog pen behind the Jenkins house. The details there, Oscar didn't try to figure. The important thing was the bitch in heat, which tended to make any male dog forget everything else.

So they got Blacky's attention. Maybe inside the pen, maybe just outside after opening the gate. Maybe the Tonk threw the dog into the pen first and then went in when Blacky was busy.

However it happened, the Tonk didn't step in at that moment. She let the male dog mount and even complete the whole business. And then, using the leash on the bitch, she and Ramon had dragged both dogs out into the street and along to wherever the Tonk cut the black dog's throat.

Oscar Schiller had heard from people on the plaza that dogs had to hang up or the pups wouldn't happen. So the Tonk let it go all the way—the pups arriving proved that—then killed the dog.

Then separated the bitch from the dead male, threw the male into the river, and came home. Ramon had led the bitch to her pen, where she had those black pups just two months later.

Oscar ran home without putting his sandals back on, and she was on the patio, squatted at the oven, making tortillas. She glanced at him as he stood there grinning at her, and she knew something was different.

And because he was sure he'd figured it all out, he was as brazen with his talk to her as he'd ever been.

"Why did you let that black dog go on and make those pups?"

He thought she might at least have showed a little surprise. But she didn't. Her expression didn't change as she watched her corn cakes browning.

"You see the pups?" she asked.

"Yes. How come you let him be papa to those pups? How come you waited to cut that mean devil?"

"Sure, he was mean," she said without looking up. "But stopping anything from breeding with his own kind is bad. That's what has happened to my people, you know that? We don't have any chance to go on with our children. We are soon gone. I don't like it much. So I let that dog go ahead and have his children."

He'd stopped grinning now because it wasn't fun anymore. It was the kind of serious thing that sometimes made a lump in your throat. And made you sad. Or sorry.

"Well, he was a mean dog," he said lamely.

"Listen," she said, and she rose and walked to him and put her hands on his shoulders. "That dog was dead as soon as he bit you. I just had to wait for the right time. He was a mean, no-good damned dog. So he was doomed, because I couldn't figure out how to do the same thing to the boy that let him loose on you. But I wasn't going to stop his pups. His pups are not him. Remember that."

He thought about it for a minute and gave a weak little shrug.

"That dog won't bite me again."

"That dog won't bite nobody again!"

She dropped her hands from his shoulders and turned back to her tortillas.

"Go wash your face. We'll eat some supper together."

Oscar Schiller would remember it as the time Herr Meuller came for a visit, from New Braunfels, and stood in the kitchen with Ulrich Silesia and talked with Sophia. Oscar didn't add anything much to the conversation. But he was interested in Herr Meuller.

Everybody in Bexar—in fact, everybody in most of Texas—knew what Herr Meuller had done with that Penateka treaty. It was still holding good, although the Comanche war parties were plenty active all along the Indian frontier.

He was a big man, and he had a beard now, a pretty bold beard in fact. But it didn't make him look fierce like a lot of German beards did. He was smoking one of those long-stem pipes, and it was the color of the piano keys on that piano they had in Gunther Steiner's billiard hall and saloon.

Sophia seemed glad to see him, but she didn't add any more to the conversation than Oscar did. The gist of it all seemed to be that Herr Meuller's wife had insisted he check to see how Sophia and her son were getting on.

Herr Meuller asked Silesia to refresh his memory about Oscar's age. "Ah, well, I thought so," he said. "I'd expected to see a bigger boy."

"He's small for his age all right," said Ulrich Silesia with a rather embarrassed laugh, knowing that Oscar, like any normal young man, hated to be standing around while people talked about him as though he were not there.

"When a babe, Poco Oscar *sehr kleine*," Sophia said.

Oscar Schiller held his head down so that his face was hidden by the brim of his Mexican hat. He hated that "Poco" business.

They talked for a moment about their mutual acquaintance, Paco Salazar, and how sad it was that he had died out on the High Plains chasing Comanches. Well, Herr Meuller and Silesia talked. When Salazar was mentioned, Sophia turned back to her stove in a flurry of activity, to keep something from burning, perhaps.

But Oscar Schiller noticed there was nothing on the stove but a large coffeepot.

After Herr Meuller was gone, Sophia spoke to her son in one of those rare moments when she acted like a mother.

"You always remember," she said. "Herr Meuller is a fine man, and we wouldn't be alive today of it hadn't been for him and his good wife and how they cared for us."

It was the kind of thing Oscar Schiller figured he'd soon forget. And maybe he did. But when the time came when he needed to remember, he'd bring it back all right. He was already an expert at filing information in his mind, ready to be pulled out like a letter from one of postmistress Elizabeth Burton's mailboxes.

Chapter Seventeen

Ulrich Silesia wrote in his journal that business competition was growing fierce in San Antonio de Bexar.

Across the river, Alamo Plaza was challenging both Main and Military Plazas as a center of commerce and community activity. Already there was a ladies' millinery shop, a bakery, and a restaurant that was serving beefsteak dinner with wine for forty cents. The surge of California immigrants had died down, and prices had plunged correspondingly.

The United States Army was using the old Alamo mission building for storage, but the rest of the military establishment had moved to what they were calling the Armory, south of Main Plaza on Flores Street and cheek-by-jowl with one of the big German flour mills that were making their appearance up and down the river.

The headquarters for all army operations in Texas was at the Armory. This was the butt of many bitter jokes. Headquarters for a lot of saber swingers, the Texans said, who plan the moves of infantry or dragoon troops from one fort to another along the frontier, where they can safely watch the Comanches raise hell in the surrounding neighborhoods because there are no horse soldiers to chase them away.

Well, a lot of San Antonio's businessmen saw the United States Army as a mixed blessing. The blue coats were doing little to slow Indian depredations, but on the other hand, the army spent a hell of a lot of money in San Antonio.

Besides, the United States Army had assigned a cavalry regiment to the Texas frontier at last, but little was seen of this regiment around San Antonio. It was fragmented out in small detachments on patrol where the hostiles were most active.

"Trouble is," said city marshal Dubb Shirley, "band of Antelope Comanch' scald out a family somewheres along Middle Fork of the Concho, and by the time you get a cavalry outfit there, the Comanch' has already forded the Prairie Dog Town Branch of the Red and gone into Palo Duro Canyon."

"Which is to say about how far away?" asked Ulrich Silesia.

"Which is to say how far away from where?"

"Well, from here, I suppose."

"Which is to say about two hunret miles more or less, so to speak."

"Well how far is that from the Middle Fork of the Concho, or whatever that was you mentioned?"

"You mean where the Antelopes or Kwahadies burned out this man and his place?"

"Well, yes, where we are supposing such a thing happened. How far is this Dog Fork from *there?*"

"Prairie Dog Branch."

"All right. Branch. How far from there?"

"Which is to say about two hunret fifty miles, more or less. So to speak."

Whereupon a group of citizens around Ulrich Silesia's beer-and-cheese table late in the evening would opine once more how glorious was the mental prowess of their city marshal.

"He'll tell you all about west Texas," said one, "and he has never been west of the escarpment you can see from the San Fernando bell tower."

"He's got it right about the hostile raids, though," said another. "The only chance you've got is to run them down and punish them. They make war by springing surprises on their enemies, so they're not usually going to hit you where you're waiting for them."

"I wonder if they turned Dubb's cavalry loose on them yet?" somebody asked, and they laughed.

Not long before this, the army had brought a few camels west to test their use in arid places, but they hadn't worked out. They eventually faded away somewhere in south Texas.

But the day they paraded through the streets of San Antonio, they had caused a sensation, with nobody more dramatically enthralled than Dubb Shirley. The city marshal had run up and down the sidewalks shouting, "Street, street, street," and pointing as the camels walked by, as though anybody needed the street pointed out to them.

Dubb got close enough to one of the mangy-looking beasts for it to spit on him, and his enthusiasm cooled.

Even so, Dubb was there at the camel pen each day on the front patio at the old Alamo, but keeping a respectful distance. When the army herded its dromedary squadron away toward Brownsville, Dubb had seemed downright distraught.

Thenceforth, those camels would always be known as Dubb's humpback cavalry.

Anyway, the growth of San Antonio around the old Alamo had nothing much to do with where the army was or what it was doing. The Alamo was becoming a commercial area simply because the town was growing and there wasn't any close-in space left on the west bank.

A man named Joe Menger had a brewery and taproom there and was building a hotel alongside Alamo Plaza. In his taproom, he was selling whiskey at the going price, a nickel a glass, but now and then he could offer it with ice for fifteen cents.

That ice was a pain, Ulrich Silesia wrote in his journal. You had to have it shipped by wagon or cart from Indianola on Matagordo Bay, packed in sawdust. Then you had to have an icehouse built as airtight as possible, and plenty of sawdust to help the ice keep as you chipped away at one end of it.

There were a couple of sawmills operating along the river and a couple more in the New Braunfels area, so sawdust was no worry. It was the ice itself that was a headache.

Having come from the northeast, Silesia was not unfamiliar with the old New England enterprise of cutting ice from ponds and lakes and rivers in winter and storing it to sell in summer. But a barge coming down the Hudson River with winter ice to sell in a sweltering New York City July was not the same as an oceangoing sailing ship transporting ice two thousand miles from its source.

So most of Bexar's precious ice was manufactured someplace closer than a New Hampshire frog pond.

At the time, there were likely not three ice-making enterprises in New Orleans that could supply local demand and have a surplus to ship to west Texas. So incredibly, Texans actually had some ice that had formed the winter before in someplace like Baskahegan, Maine.

Shipped in thousand-pound chunks, the ice went down the coast and around Florida and into Matagordo Bay, where it was cut into five-hundred-pound chunks and loaded on wagons, then trundled at the speed of mules or oxen walking for over one hundred miles, dripping all the way.

People could make ice cream, preserve meats and poultry, and enjoy cool drinks. But ice was expensive because of the elaborate icehouses required to store it and the cost of transport. It galled Ulrich Silesia that he paid for ice by weight when every mile it traveled and every moment it remained in the icehouse unsold it got smaller.

"We've got to build ourselves an ice plant," said Ulrich to his friend Gunther Roth. "I pay for five hundred pounds of ice, and if I'm lucky, I sell two hundred pounds before the rest melts and runs through the cracks!"

Silesia confided to his journal that ice was almost worth the effort and the loss just to see how Oscar Schiller loved it. When a load of ice consigned to Mrs. Wolf's Cafe on Main Plaza came, the boy was already on the cart by the time the ox teams drew it into the head of Commerce Street east of the river.

Which caused Silesia to pause in his writing and grind his teeth with irritation. Ice from the Gulf came via the Goliad Road and hence into town from the east, passing alongside the establishment of Silesia's competitor Menger at Alamo Plaza first, which meant Menger got his ice thirty minutes before Silesia did.

"Well, hell, Gunther," Silesia said. "I was here first, so I should get my ice first!"

It was so childish and absurd, they made a standing joke of it. Jerome Falsworth, the man who owned the biggest sawmill in Bexar and provided the sawdust for Mrs. Wolf's icehouse, made a carefully lettered sign that patrons hung over the taproom bar. It was there three days before Silesia saw it and liked it so much he kept it.

> Menger's ice gets to town first.
> But Silesia's ice is made from colder water!

Ulrich Silesia was watching Oscar Schiller closely. So far, he'd seen no signs of any serious reactions to what was happening. What was happening was that Oscar's friends were all outgrowing him, going their various ways because they were involved in things bigger boys did, while as yet, Oscar wasn't much bigger than he'd been at eleven.

None of that group was in school now, except for John David Jenkins, and he'd been sent to Baton Rouge to attend some fancy boys' prep school. The others were already beginning to ease into the community's work force.

Some of the boys Oscar Schiller's age were out on the prairie rounding up wild cattle and driving them in to the herds the vaqueros of Gunther Roth and Juan Pardo seemed constantly to be making up for a drive to California.

This was a good thing. There were plenty of wild cattle on the surrounding prairies, the descendants of bulls and cows left abandoned at farms and ranches after Indian raids. There wasn't much to slow their increase. Comanches didn't butcher the cattle so long as there were buffalos.

"Comanch', he'll take buffler ever time," said the old Ranger sitting in a rocking chair on the second-floor front porch of Mrs. Wolf's Hotel, whittling and chewing tobacco and watching the passing scene below. His name was Buster Lloyd, and he'd ranged with Paco Salazar. "If you had some experience eatin longhorn and then a time come where you had a selection, you'd take buffler, too."

"All right," said Oscar Schiller, leaning on one of the cast-iron railings that ran the length of the porch. "If the Comanches like buffalo so much, why haven't they ever put em in a pen so all they need to do when they get hungry is go out to the pen, like we do, and slaughter one?"

"Why, sprout, you askin a Yucatan *tigre* to turn his spots to stripes," Buster Lloyd said. "That stockyard business takes all the fun out of it. Young buck studies half his life on the chase. He loves it. He lives for it."

"What's he study the other half of his life?"

Buster Lloyd laughed and spit. "Hell, sprout, I expect you know the answer to that one. The other half he spends on studyin war."

But making some money chasing down wild cattle wouldn't do. Oscar Schiller was extremely uncomfortable around horses, and even small mustang ponies were too big from him to handle easily.

He'd tried the turkey business. The prairies outside town were swarming with wild turkeys. Nobody knew why. Of course, Comanches didn't eat turkey, either. But that didn't explain it.

Simple snares always worked on these birds, but it was hardly worth the effort. You couldn't get more than twenty cents for a bird. Cleaned, it might bring forty cents.

Oscar Schiller gave turkeys up on the evening he knocked at the door of a well-to-do north-side home and a German *Hausfrau* saw the turkey in his hand and snorted.

"Don't bring me any dose birds here," she yelled. "I vant one dose birds, I go out my back yard mit eine stick und knock one out of my pecan tree vhere Mr. Turkey und all his relatives come in from vilderness und roost every night und mess all on my nice vicker yard furniture! I tell you vhat, boy. You clean dat bird, I give you a dime if you get all pinfeathers out."

He was enterprising enough. He came to be called the Bag Boy around town because he was always on hand for stagecoach arrivals and departures. Ulrich Silesia had begun to pay him a little wage for all the things he did around Mrs. Wolf's Hotel and Cafe in addition to lugging guests' luggage. Silesia got a large brass handbell to keep at the registry desk, so when guests needed help he could ring it, hoping Oscar was nearby.

And Oscar usually was.

Soon, however, the bell took on a new purpose. Oscar Schiller began to signal the arrival and departure of coaches by standing beside Ranger Buster Lloyd's rocking chair on the balcony porch of the hotel and ringing the bell so you could hear it all over San Antonio, encouraged with each swing by the grinning, spitting Ranger Lloyd.

Oscar Schiller made a science of this, as he did with most things. He knew the general schedule of coaches because he made such a nuisance of himself with Mrs. Raymond Burton and her daughter. As we've seen, Burton owned many Texas lines, and the operation of the Bexar end of the business was left to the women.

The Burtons finally began to realize that Oscar Schiller could provide a good service for customers, so they started to cooperate with him by giving him advance notice of all runs and changes in schedule and anything else that might be useful in answering questions about the coaches or the mail service, which was a natural tie-in, considering that the Burtons had the mail contract for Bexar and Mrs. Burton was postmistress.

The Burtons paid Oscar Schiller a small salary, too. He earned it. He ran to the San Fernando Cathedral and up into the bell tower near the time for an incoming stagecoach, and once he saw its dust, he ran back down, across the square, and into Mrs. Wolf's, grabbed the brass bell, ran up to the second floor and out onto the porch, where Ranger Lloyd would be waiting in his chair, and began tolling the arrival, making all the pigeons fly up from the red-tile roofs along the north side of Military Plaza.

Then, just before the driver snapped his whip and released the brake and started the next leg of his trip, Oscar would run back up to the balcony, having finished his work helping passengers board, and ring the bell some more to signal the departure of a stagecoach from San Antonio.

Buster Lloyd told him a story about announcing stagecoach arrivals.

"They tried using a bugle on the stages," he said. "So when the coach come in towards the station out there on the plains somewheres, they could blow the horn and let the folks at the station know it was friends acomin and so no need to fort up. No need for nervous folks to take a few shots at em from a distance with a buffler rifle.

"But they had to quit. It didn't do no good cause pretty soon hostiles was endin up with bugles from various places, so the stage depot folks in them isolated stations never knowed when they heerd a bugle if it was a coach or a Comanch' war party tryin to get in close before they was discovered."

Father Paul, the Franciscan who had been a teacher but who now was an assistant to the new bishop assigned to Bexar, was aware of Oscar Schiller's stagecoach activity. The priest stopped Oscar on the street one day.

"My son," he said, "you make so much noise running up the steps in our bell tower, you disturb the penitents at confession."

They were on Military Plaza, and from here, the bell tower at the cathedral was the highest structure in sight. Oscar Schiller cast about for something he could look at, but his eye kept coming back to that tower. He pushed his hands deeper into his trouser pockets and shrugged.

"I can see the coaches coming from up there, Padre," he said.

"Oh, I know that," Father Paul said. "But I wonder if a bell tower in the house of God is the right place to do such business."

Oscar Schiller shifted his eyes and shuffled his feet, searching for something to say. He thought maybe his face would burst into flame. Then he saw, past the church and at the corner of Commerce Street and Main Plaza, Ulrich Silesia on the sidewalk, and the German seemed far away and very small but big enough for Oscar Schiller to see the bell shining in his hand.

The sound of the bell above the noises of the street was the most wonderful thing Oscar Schiller had ever heard, and he dashed around the priest without a word, but in the full knowledge that everybody in San Antonio knew that when the bell rang, it was a summons for the Bag Boy.

In Mrs. Wolf's taproom, Ulrich Silesia was still holding the bell when Oscar Schiller bounded in, his eyes glinting behind the thick glasses of his spectacles.

"Here I be," he said.

"I see you are," said Silesia. "Go milk the goat."

Oscar Schiller's mouth dropped open. He stood rigid, and then Ulrich Silesia and half-a-dozen drinkers in the taproom began to snicker. He realized then what had happened, and he ducked his head and grinned.

"Gotta watch out for them holy joes, boy. They'll roast you for breakfast," one of the taproom drinkers shouted.

Ulrich Silesia's grin widened, and he waved Oscar Schiller away. As Oscar turned, head down, he thought that these big Mexican hats were good because they could hide so much of your face when you were embarrassed.

Well, maybe a lot of friends would come to his rescue at times like that, but for the next couple of Sundays, Oscar Schiller went to the Mass that Father Paul said at the little chapel in the Franciscan mission school.

Everybody knew Oscar Schiller had never been baptized in the Catholic church. He didn't know when to kneel and he didn't cross himself at all, but he was there. Twice. And nobody ever said anything more to him about using the bell tower at the cathedral for a lookout post.

Well, he did try to make a little less noise on the stairs.

Buster Lloyd and the boy often went to a downriver cutbank, where they fired one of the old Ranger's Colt pistols. Lloyd had taught Oscar Schiller how to load and prime the weapon. It was a Dragoon model, so heavy the boy had to hold it with both hands.

It was there that Oscar told Buster Lloyd about the confrontation with the priest and all the rest of it, including his going to Mass. Buster Lloyd laughed.

"Sprout," he said, "one day, you're gonna make a helluva fine politician!"

Ulrich Silesia actually wrote the words in his journal: Now is the Romantic Period of my life.

When Raymond Burton started his stagecoach business and got a mail contract, he pretty much left his thirty-year-old daughter and his wife to run the San Antonio ticket and post office while he spent his time in the field, keeping stage stations straight and buying horses and figuring out routes that had the least chance for Comanche disruption and doing all the other things a stagecoach owner does.

At first, Burton set up his station and post office in one corner of Mrs. Wolf's hotel lobby. Then he built a post office and stage station flat against the east wall of Silesia's hotel. This was a small, square frame building with a second floor for living quarters.

In the natural course of events, Ulrich Silesia and Elizabeth Burton saw much of one another. At first, theirs was a business association. But slowly it became something else. They went together to have tamales at one of the Military Plaza vendors. They strolled near the river and watched a vaquero wash and groom one of the fine Arabian-blood stallions of Juan Pardo.

Silesia took out two books his father had sent him years before, still unread, and sometimes in the evenings they would sit on the second-floor porch and she would read by a whale-oil lamp and Buster Lloyd would sit nearby and listen and occasionally say, "Well, I declare!"

The books were Dickens's *Oliver Twist* and Washington Irving's *The Alhambra*, a collection of stories about Moors and Spaniards. The

Moors and Spaniards got more "I declares!" than Mr. Dickens by a long shot.

Often, the couple would attend a fandango.

It had been noted by many Anglos that when a Mexican woman danced in the old Spanish style, Ulrich Silesia tapped his foot in time with *las castañuelas*, the clicking castanets. Now, it was noted that Elizabeth Burton tapped her foot, too, an astonishing thing for an Anglo lady to do while sitting on a wooden bench in Military Plaza, watching a fandango, hearing the strumming guitars and the sharp notes of the cornets and the shouts of the dancers, smelling the pungent smoke of firecrackers, and sipping lemonade.

Then Ulrich Silesia escorted Elizabeth Burton to a casino club tea dance. Everybody figured that was it.

And it' was. The Texas frontier not being a place where people doted on long betrothals, they were married before the end of that same year, and San Antonio was the scene of a historic wedding that had everything from classic candles and a white veil in the Lutheran church to frontier whiskey and a dangerous shivaree in Main Plaza.

To everyone's relief, nobody was killed or wounded in the discharge of firearms during the shivaree. The only casualty was a brother of Jerome Falsworth, a state representative from east Texas who was in Bexar visiting from the capital at Austin. Victim of too much Mexican mescal, he mistook the courthouse for his hotel, and going up the outside staircase, he took a wrong turn at the top and fell into the jail yard, breaking his left arm in two places.

The couple took up residence in rooms at the rear of the second floor of Mrs. Wolf's Hotel. To anybody watching, it seemed they continued their relationship as before — which is to say, it seemed like it was strictly business. That impression was misleading.

Privately, they were not demonstrative people, yet they were kind and tender to one another. And maybe the measure of their mutual affection — a better word for their feeling than love — was that Ulrich continued to write his journal and he asked Elizabeth to read each entry. Not only that, he provided her with all those pages he had written before they were married.

She was a smart, well-read woman, and Ulrich Silesia was more than willing to take her not only as a companion in his chambers and a lover in his bed but as a partner in his business.

None of this had much effect on Oscar Schiller. He had been doing business with Elizabeth Burton for a long time in his capacity as stagecoach greeter. They had a mutual respect for one another, and she especially enjoyed listening to his searching questions when he was talking with Ulrich or Buster Lloyd.

Ulrich Silesia didn't want to become involved in Texas land squabbles. He wanted to just buy his property, clear and simple, work on it, cause no trouble, and stay free of entanglements. And now, care for his wife.

But good intentions didn't matter. As a kind of unofficial guardian for Oscar Schiller and mentor for Sophia, he found himself bound up in a part of the vicious fight Booth Jenkins was making to obtain all the buildings facing Military Plaza on the south and the property immediately behind that.

Property ownership was sometimes the mind and matter of wild confusion. Because all untitled Texas land belonged to the state and not the nation, the United States Land Ordinance of 1785—establishing the excellent system of standard townships of thirty-six square miles, divided into sections of 640 acres and determined on survey from a central baseline and principle meridian—did not apply.

From the beginning, in 1793, there had been surveys made around Bexar, but there was nothing standard about them or the way the land was distributed. There were Spanish grants, grants to old soldiers, and, once Texas broke free of Mexico, squatters' rights claims, property purchased from various kinds of speculators, and land sold by local officials because of foreclosure or because, for some other reason, the land had become state property.

There were a lot of titles not quieted under law, either in fact or because they were so specified by some official who had something to gain. It was not unusual for property to be taken, especially from Mexicans, and put on sale by the local government as public domain.

A land commission had been established to keep things straight, but there were no rules of engagement for its members, and their contribution was more than likely to add confusion and bitterness to an already hopelessly confused and bitter situation, especially for Mexicans.

Locally, one of the Bexar land commissioners was also the county clerk, who was responsible for registering claims and keeping record of them. Any time there was some question about ownership that this person, whose name was Ernest Kilpatton, could not solve, it was passed to the commission as a whole. The commission decided who owned the land.

The only recourse then was to present a case in court before the circuit judge, Hiram Belcher, who was notoriously friendly with Booth Jenkins and other lawyer-speculators.

From there, an appeal could be made to the Texas Supreme Court and from there to the federal system. But the state supreme court rubber-stamped local decisions on land disputes, and United States courts at this time had established as their primary function the validation of state court decisions.

All of which meant that if you had a problem with a land title, you'd best get it fixed short of the judicial system or you were in a losing cause.

And that was where Ulrich Silesia found himself. Well, that was where he found Sophia Schiller.

Since he'd given her that Spanish land-grant and the pistols and the bequest of Paco Salazar, and she had taken everything and gone back down to her pantry kitchen room, he'd heard nothing more or it, had thought nothing more of it.

Then, about the time that John David Jenkins came back from that Louisiana boys' school, strutting around with hard collars on his shirts, Ulrich Silesia began to hear rumors that Booth Jenkins was about to bring an action before the land commission to get the old Salazar *casa* on Armador Street declared public domain.

John David's return probably had nothing to do with this, Silesia figured, but he used that event to mark the moment.

At once, the German hurried to the Barrio del Sur, and his wife insisted on accompanying him. They found the Tonk grinding corn with a stone pestle in a wooden bowl, sitting cross-legged on the rear patio.

She didn't know anything about any paper, she said. But somebody else had come around asking about it, too, wanting to see it, telling her it was needed at the courthouse.

The visitor that day had been city marshal Dubb Shirley, and when they heard that, Elizabeth Silesia snorted and spoke loud enough for the Tonk to hear.

"Can you smell Booth Jenkins?"

"Yes," he said, and asked the Tonk what she'd told the marshal, and the Tonk said she'd told him to get out of her house and stay out.

"What did he say?"

"Say?" the Indian said, and she looked at Silesia as though he might be demented; then she looked at Elizabeth Silesia, and a small smile touched one corner of her face. "He didn't say much. He just left in a hurry because he didn't want to lose his ears."

"Lose his ears?"

She seemed to have lost all interest in the subject now and was looking down into the bowl as she ground the corn.

"Lose his ears?" he repeated. "What does that mean?"

"What I told him," Titch said without looking up. "I told him if he didn't leave I would cut off his ears. He walked right in, sneaking along like a spider, but I heard his feet. And when he came to where I was working like I am now, I had the knife out. He saw it. He walked out very fast."

"Well, I hope he doesn't return," said Silesia.

"He will not come back," she said, still pounding away at her corn. "If he does, I will do what I told him I will do. I will cut off *los cojones suyos.*"

The German knew enough Spanish to understand what that meant, and so did his wife. She giggled all the way back to Main Plaza, and when Ulrich told Buster Lloyd what the Tonk had said, he laughed, too. The former Ranger thought it was funny as hell, that the cannibal Tonk was ready to castrate the town's representative of law and order.

"I'd like to have seen Dubb's fat face when she said that," said Elizabeth Silesia. "Maybe I need to get a nice, big knife."

Ulrich Silesia didn't think it was so funny. It still left the problem of where that title stood, legally. So he called in Sophia Schiller, and when she came, the kitchen foreman, Heimel Uttegard, came with her.

Ulrich Silesia didn't have the time or inclination to ask any questions. Besides, probably anybody would know more about land-tenure problems than Sophia, so whatever reinforcements she had might be useful.

They went to see the county clerk, Ernest Kilpatton, who took a look at the old patent from the king of Spain and nodded and wrote a note in a large ledger book, using a feathered quill pen. And started to put the paper in his safe.

"Wait, sir," Ulrich Silesia said. "We want that grant paper back. We'll keep that, if you please."

"Oh, we keep land documents here," Kilpatton said. "They're safe and secure in our strongbox."

"Well, if you please, we've been keeping money in Mr. Hausmann's safe at his store for a long time, and that's where we want to keep this paper, in the very same money belt where it's always been."

"It will be secure here," Kilpatton said, getting a little red-faced.

"We'll have the paper," said Heimel Uttegard, and the county clerk surrendered it and they marched away, looking more confident than they felt. At least, Ulrich Silesia didn't feel very confident.

"This paper," he said, tapping the money belt Sophia held close to her breast, "is the key to everything. As long as you have that, your chances of keeping that property are good. Without it, you don't have much chance."

"We're on his book now," said Uttegard.

"Did you see how easily he wrote the entry?" asked Silesia. "He can take it out just as easily."

"Why would he do that?" Sophia asked.

"Because somebody very powerful wants your property!"

Later, in their room, Elizabeth suggested that perhaps they should volunteer to take the grant and place it in Hausmann's safe.

"No, no, no," Silesia whispered. "I don't want to get any more involved with it."

They lay listening to night-singing mockingbirds in the bur oaks along the front of San Fernando Cathedral, both awake and lying wide-eyed in the dark, smelling rain on the breeze that was coming in through the window facing toward the escarpment.

"I just feel sorry for that poor, ignorant girl and that little boy."

"Yes, but you should know, that boy may be little but he can take care of himself, I suspect," he whispered. "Sophia, she's another case."

"It appears to me that your kitchen *jefe* may be stepping up to take care of Sophia," she said and laughed softly.

"We'll see," he said, but he still felt uneasy about it.

Chapter Eighteen

For Ulrich Silesia, it was one of the worst days of his life. It started with Oscar Schiller shaking him, yelling that Mrs. Elizabeth was in the post office helping her mother make up the mail for the stagecoach run to El Paso, due to leave in a few minutes, and there was nobody in the kitchen downstairs at Mrs. Wolf's Cafe to fix breakfast for the hungry people waiting there.

The next two hours were a madhouse on the north side of Main Plaza.

Dressed mostly in the underwear in which he slept, Ulrich Silesia began to throw food into pans and skillets in the kitchen. At least a fire had been set. Recruiting anybody he could find along his sidewalk or around the corner near the billiard hall, he began to serve his customers.

Oscar Schiller suddenly found himself hauling hot platters of beef-steak and eggs from Silesia's noisy kitchen to the dining room. Sometimes he dropped a little in passage.

The other waiters who had been shanghaied were all as young or younger than Oscar. Luckily for Silesia, it was a Saturday and no school was in progress, so there was a good supply of boys on the sidewalks.

Or at least, there were boys on the sidewalks before Silesia and Oscar started hustling them into Mrs. Wolf's Cafe for service as waiters. After a few moments of terror, then a few more moments of soaking up quick, shouted instructions from Oscar, the boys took to this new game with gusto and some considerable talent for running with a plate of red beans in one hand and a dish of beef hash in the other and getting only a little on the floor or customers' laps.

Except for the few people who were trying to eat and get out to catch the westbound stage, everybody seemed to enjoy the spectacle of Ulrich Silesia sweating and swearing in German over his massive cast-iron stoves. As word passed around the square, people came in for breakfast who had never eaten there before, just to watch.

Not half the people had been served when Silesia fried his last egg. He shouted for Oscar Schiller to run up the street to Hausmann's store for reinforcements, but Oscar, by now having taken command of the dining room and the street urchin busboys and waiters there, sent Jesus Montez. It was the move of a natural executive delegating responsibility just in case something went wrong. If the eggs got dropped along the sidewalk, it would be Jesus Montez's ass, not Oscar's.

But the eggs weren't dropped. Oscar Schiller always said that he learned that day that in order to avoid disaster, you planned for it to happen, and then usually it didn't.

Anyway, by the time Mrs. Silesia finished her work at the post office and saw the El Paso stage off and came to the cafe, most of the breakfast customers were satisfied, and a few even stayed most of the morning to help clean the eggs and pan-fried potatoes off the floor and the tables and chairs and the walls, and some even scrubbed pots and pans at the kitchen sinks.

Oscar Schiller made $2.70 in tips.

It was almost noon before things had cooled down enough for Silesia and his wife to face their hired-help problem.

For two days they were busy training a new pair for the kitchen, both Mexicans and both old hands at one of the Military Plaza chili stands, and hence well familiar with producing food for hungry people. The only thing they really needed was to develop a sense of urgency. A lot of Mrs. Wolf's Cafe's patrons were in a hurry.

During that time, the Silesias had moments, upstairs in their private rooms, to think about what had happened. And to think about the letter found on Sophia's bed pillow.

"For Herr Silesia, *danke*, much you done for *mein Sohn und* me also as well. God flow down over you *und* Frau Silesia *und mach gut. Aufwiedersehen.* Sophia Waldenburg Schiller."

The parlor was on the back side of the building, so the windows did not open onto noisy Main Plaza but on to a vista of rooftops and the canopy of oak and sycamore trees near the river and the pecans on Soledad Street.

Beyond that, they could see the front of the old Alamo Mission, where the United States Army was refurbishing the building, plastering over the worst of the artillery damage from the fight in 1836. Also, they were raising the facade so that the building would look a little more like a mission.

This was a favorite place for them, and here, sitting at a long library table with Sophia's letter lying open between them, they watched the sparrows playing in the tile eaves at the back of Hausmann's store and munched gingersnaps and sipped limeade, concluding that in a burst of uncontrollable passion their two faithful employees had run away together.

This infuriated Ulrich, but his wife found a certain romantic fascination with the whole idea.

"What would have happened," she asked, "if you'd swept me up and run off to Veracruz with me?"

"Your father would have been after me with a posse and enough shotguns to threaten the sovereignty of Mexico," he said.

"Little fear of that with Sophia," Elizabeth said. "I understand her father is still the village sot at New Braunfels."

"Damn!" Ulrich said.

"What is it?"

"I wonder where that deed is," he said. "That deed may get to be a bone of contention around here. I hate the idea of getting into a property mess."

"Why would you?"

"We've got some responsibility, it seems to me, to her son," said Ulrich. "There's nobody else to defend his rights. He's still a minor, nobody but that Indian to see to him. We're all he's got."

They sat on either side of the table and stared at one another. Then he sighed and shook his head as she reached out and took one of his hands in hers and held it tight.

"We'll do what we have to do," she said. "I've rather been expecting this."

"Sophia and Uttegard? Running away together?"

"Yes. I think I knew it," she said. He stared at her, wide-eyed.

"You *knew* it?"

"Not in exact detail," she said, patting his hand. "I knew there was something going on between them."

"How did you know?"

"It's a feeling you have sometimes," she said. "Don't you ever just *know* something's about to happen, but you have no notion of how you know it?"

"No. I don't."

"Well, never mind, dear," she said. "All we need to do is just be patient and soon, everything will come clear."

"I doubt it will ever become clear," he said, "but I intend to find out a lot more than we know now."

The situation didn't take too long to untangle. Sophia and Uttegard hadn't done much to cover their tracks. During the night before that wild breakfast at Mrs. Wolf's Cafe, they'd driven a hired buggy to the ranch house of Hermann Steinmetz about seven miles out on the Camino del Rio and there flagged the coach next morning and paid for passage to California.

There was nothing unusual about somebody flagging the stage in mid-career. It was done all the time. But it was somewhat remarkable that Sophia and Uttegard had been able to save enough money for such a trip, which usually ran about four hundred dollars from San Antonio to the Gila Crossing.

"They've been planning this for a while," said Elizabeth Silesia. "It took time on the wages we pay for them to have saved this much money."

"Well," said Ulrich defensively, "they lived in this building and ate our food, so what did they have to spend their money on? Pair of shoes now and then maybe. Sophia went barefoot most of the time, too."

Then on the morning of the fifth day, waiting for them when they came down in the pre-dawn was the Watitch Tonkawa, and she was holding a large package, something bulky and wrapped in butcher paper tied with twine string.

The Indian didn't say anything. But she looked pretty grim.

"Take her up to the parlor," Ulrich said, and Elizabeth led Titch upstairs, and they spoke not a word on the stairs or in the parlor later. Elizabeth indicated a chair at the library table and the Indian shook her head, and Elizabeth sat at the table herself and they waited. Silently.

When Ulrich came into the room, the Tonk stepped forward and placed the package on the table and unwrapped it and pulled back the paper, then resumed her place against the wall.

Elizabeth Silesia would say it was like watching a stork in the old country, standing on one leg in a chimney nest, because that's how the Tonk stood, on one leg, the other leg drawn up and the foot flat against the wall at her back.

Now lying on the table were Paco Salazar's two pistols with all their accouterments and the old money belt. Seeing that, Ulrich Silesia knew what was in one of those pouches and swore under his breath.

"She brought it to me and said not to ever let it be taken away," the Indian said. "But she said to show you and you'd know what had to be done. Then I take it back with me, like she said to do, for the boy."

This time, Ulrich Silesia did not swear under his breath, but loud enough to be heard on Soledad Street below. He sat at the table and went to the money belt and the pouch that bulged and pulled forth the old patent he'd seen when Ranger Walker brought it after Paco Salazar's death.

Now there was new writing on it, in blue ink, in a very tentative script, partly in English, partly in German. Some of it was smudged.

"*Bitte*. To take this and give all of it the land and house and the guns to Gottlieb Heinrich Waldenburg Schiller. *So ein Erbe*. Herr Paco Salazar *und* Sophia Waldenburg Schiller. *Es gehört mir*."

"*Erbe*. It's a last will or bequest," he said.

"What's that last pronoun?" Elizabeth asked, pointing.

"Yes, yes, I see the damned thing," he said. "Why couldn't she have been a little more careful? All this time she's been in Texas, why hasn't she learned more English, for God's sake?"

The pronoun in the last phrase was almost illegible and badly written besides. It could have been *es*, which would mean "*it* is ours." Or it could have been *er*, which would mean "*he* is ours."

So Sophia could be saying that this was her quit claim to the Armador Street property that had belonged to Salazar and herself, giving her the legal right to bequeath to her son. A thing Ulrich Silesia already knew.

Or she could be saying that Oscar Schiller, the boy, was entitled to the property by natural inheritance because he was the son of Sophia and Paco Salazar, a thing Ulrich most certainly did not know! Oscar Schiller. *He is ours!*

"My God," he said and sat there and wondered what the hell to do next while Elizabeth continued a study of that enigmatic pronoun. And finally gave up.

"I think it's *er*. I think it's *he*," she said. "Why would Sophia write something as obvious as that Salazar owned the property and then she owned it? Everybody knows that."

"So she's telling us something we don't know, which reinforces Oscar Schiller's claim to this property," he said. "It was given to a Salazar by a king of Spain. That Salazar gave it to his son, Paco Salazar's father. So now it comes to Oscar."

"It's got the power of legality and of tradition as well. Old family Spanish land-grants around here hold up pretty well. I never would have imagined that little runt Oscar being in line for a Spanish family land patent. That's strange," Elizabeth said, and he wished she hadn't said this for fear of it upsetting the Indian, but the Tonk gave no indication that she had heard, although she certainly had. Ulrich Silesia turned in his chair and looked at her.

"What did Sophia say about all this?" he asked.

"She said keep it away from everybody, but you should see," the Tonk said. "That's all."

"Did you show it to Oscar?" he asked.

"No."

He thought about it for a long time. Apparently too long, because suddenly the Indian came to the table and quickly rewrapped everything and tied it.

"I go home," she said. "You tell me when to show Oscar he's got a house now."

For some time after the Indian had gone, they waited in the parlor, Ulrich still at the table, drumming on its polished surface with his fingers, Elizabeth going to the window and with elbows folded across her chest watching the soldiers across the river climbing on the scaffolding along the wall of the Alamo.

"It looks like a big cheese in the sun," she murmured "A big yellow Swiss cheese with all those holes in it. Cannonball holes."

"Well, we need to get on to the county clerk's office and get this newest twist recorded. And that damned clerk, the last time he wanted to keep the deed there. He'll do it again. You wait. They'll try again to get that paper."

"The Bat Cave bandits you're always talking about?"

"That's right, all that Bat Club gang, the lawyers, old Judge Belcher, District Attorney Booth Jenkins. A nest of land speculators. Real-estate robbers. That clerk's one of them. Two minutes after we file that new deed, the royal denizens of Batdom will know about it!"

"You've got to tell me about this Bat Club."

"Nobody knows anything about it except the members. One of these silly secret fraternities, special handshakes and strange passwords. Politicians."

"Well, Bat Club seems an appropriate name for it," she said, "seeing that these people work in the place everybody calls the Bat Cave because those beastly little animals roost there."

"That's the bunch we're up against. It's who everybody is up against if they've got any land these bastards want."

"But," Elizabeth said turning back to the table, "as I've said, old Spanish land patents are pretty solid."

"Yes, yes, if the patent is in hand. But you lose one, you're in trouble. Jenkins gets his hands on that deed we just saw, Oscar's land could be up for grabs. So they'll try to keep that paper again when it's taken to what's his name in the clerk's office."

"Kilpatton," she said. "But the notation will be made in the clerk's record book."

"My dear," he said, "watch what this Kilpatton uses to inscribe these truths in his book. A lead pencil. You can erase a lead pencil. But they don't even do that. Somebody just challenges a Spanish claim in court, and the court decides, no matter what's in the book. Without your patent at that point, it's over."

"All right," she said. "We've got to do this thing, I suppose. The Indian can't. So let's ask Buster Lloyd to strap on one of those big six-shooters he used when he was a Ranger and have him tag along with us."

"Sweet Jesus, Liz, are you suggesting we start a big shootout in the county clerk's office?"

"No," she said. "I'm just suggesting we let plenty of determination

293

show on our part. Buster with a big six-shooter showing would make us pretty determined, don't you think?"

"All right, all right," he said throwing up his hands. "But first, don't you think we owe it to the new owner down there on Armador Street to tell him about all this and invite him to come along?"

"Absolutely," said Elizabeth. "And his guardian, too. And speaking of that Indian, who pays her now?"

"Who do you think?" he asked, looking owlish.

"You know, I think she'd do the job without any pay," she said. "I think she thinks of her role more as mother than guardian. And I think she needs to go with us to the courthouse, too."

"I figured you'd think that," he said. "Well, with Buster and his pistols and the Tonk and her reputation for big knife work, we ought to be intimidating enough for anybody we meet."

"What bothers me is what Booth Jenkins is going to do once he hears that the only person standing between him and that piece of land is a young boy with no visible family to support him."

"Elizabeth, if you'll just look around here, you'll see that Oscar Schiller isn't standing completely alone."

"All right. Another thing that bothers me is that Oscar Schiller isn't old enough to understand he's sitting on a piece of valuable property in this town and he may not give a hoot one way or another."

It bothered Ulrich Silesia a bit that his wife sometimes had a closer finger on the pulse of Bexar than he did. What she'd said about Oscar Schiller and the ownership of the Armador Street property was exact.

Oscar went along with what Buster Lloyd called the *casa* posse. They convened upstairs at Mrs. Wolf's. The Tonk had somehow gotten Oscar into a clean white smock; a pair of calf-length canvas trousers; a bright red, green, and white serape; and a Mexican straw hat with a brim that Liz Silesia said was as wide as Oscar was tall.

Around his neck was a colorful leather cord suspending a parchment-like pendant about the size of a small breakfast sausage. Elizabeth Silesia lifted the pendant and examined it, Oscar Schiller looking up into her eyes innocently, much as a desert trapdoor spider might watch a dung beetle as it crawled into its hole.

"What's this?" she asked.

"A finger," he said.

She managed to keep from shrieking, but she leaped back as though she'd been stung by a yellow jacket and turned away from Oscar Schiller as her husband and Ranger Lloyd laughed. At least the Tonk paid no attention all, her expression as clear and cold as a slab of Ulrich's ice.

"Put the awful thing under your shirt," Elizabeth said. She started to say something about barbarians, but with the Indian there, she decided against it.

"It's my good luck," Oscar said, dropping the finger pendant down the front of his smock. "It came from the Comanches."

"Well, I wish they'd kept it," she said.

They marched over to Military Plaza and into the Bat Cave and into the clerk's office, and the circuit clerk, Ernest Kilpatton, was waiting because he knew they were coming.

Everybody in town knew it. A lot of people were on the sidewalks along Commerce Street and Via Dolorosa and in the San Fernando Cathedral garden watching. Mostly the Anglos were hoping the clerk would refuse the Spanish land-grant. And the Germans and Mexicans mostly were hoping Oscar would win.

Not many of them understood that today was not yet the time for winning or losing. This was just the beginning. And in fact, the whole thing was anticlimactic, because the clerk, giving Buster Lloyd and his two bolstered six-shooters a glance, and giving the Tonk, whose knife he knew all about, a glance, wrote down the information in his book and returned the patent, and the parade retraced its steps to Mrs. Wolf's.

Through the whole thing, Oscar Schiller had been as unconcerned as anyone could be, although he watched the entry of the plat description in the book.

Afterward, they had a discussion about where the deed should be kept, and finally the Tonk agreed it should be put in Mr. Hausmann's safe because they could trust him to keep quiet about it being there.

And because there wasn't much use for them on Armador Street, they decided to bring the pistols to Buster Lloyd and let him hold them for Oscar, because Lloyd knew how to keep them clean. And sometimes he and Oscar could walk along the river and shoot at various targets like turtles and spots on tree trunks with Oscar's very own weapons.

Then when they were alone in the parlor, Liz Silesia did the thing she was dreading but that everyone, including the Tonk, had said needed doing. She spoke with Oscar about the meaning of that extra writing on the patent.

She had figured that the best way was to attack the subject head-long and get it finished. So at the library table, with Oscar nibbling at her gingersnap cookies, she sat straight-backed, hands folded in her lap, and looked as serious as she could.

"My dear, we need to talk a moment," she said, "so that you know better what's happened here, with your property."

"That's fine," he said. "I wasn't plannin anything this afternoon anyway."

"Good, good," she said, resisting an urge to shout that this business should be taken seriously. "Oscar, do you know who your father was?"

"Sure. I don't remember him much," said Oscar, talking around a large mouthful of gingersnap cookie. As he talked, he swiped crumbs from the table with both hands. "He came a few times to talk with my Tonk mother. And I guess he came here to talk to my Braunfels mother, too. I was usually asleep. I was too young to remember him much. So he died before I was very old." As he talked, his spectacles magnified the intense, lifeless blue of his eyes. "I was a bastard, you see."

"Well, we don't need to talk about that," she said, fluttering her hands, brushing crumbs, too, where there were none to brush. His blunt statement seemed to throw everything out of kilter. "But you knew who he was?"

"Sure," he said. "He was a Texas Ranger and before that a soldier when Texas fought Mexico and he knew Sam Houston and he was at San Jacinto."

She sat for a moment, staring at him, astonished that he knew about Salazar, astonished at how he referred to the two women in his life as his Tonk and Braunfels "mothers."

"Is something the matter?"

"No, no. I just wondered who told you all that?"

"Well, some was told to me by my Tonk mother, before I knew he was my father, but he brought her out of a Comanche band a long time ago. He was a damned good Comanche fighter," Oscar said. "And some of it was told me by my Braunfels mother before I knew who he was. Then just before she went off to California, where she told me she was going, she told me who he was, that he was my father and all. Just before she went to California."

"She told you ahead of time she was going to California?"

"Sure. Didn't she tell you?"

"Did she tell you why she went to California?"

"Sure. She said Dubb Shirley was mean and sayin things like she was a whore and would end up dog meat in the river, and she knew he was doin it for Booth Jenkins so Booth Jenkins could get the house me and my Tonk mother lived in."

"The town marshal did that and she just left you behind to face it?"

"She was scared," Oscar Schiller said, still eating the snaps. "I wasn't scared. And she wanted to leave here anyway, go where nobody knew who she was or anything, with a new husband. Hell, I don't know, she was just scared is all."

"Oscar, you're too young to be talking like one of those stock-herder men," she said. He stopped chewing and stared at her.

"What stockherder men?"

"Never mind. Listen, Oscar, are you sure your mother didn't say anything else to you before she left for California?"

Oscar Schiller frowned and looked up at the ceiling and then at the window, still frowning, then at the dish of cookies. He took another one.

"Yes. She did," he said, biting into the cookie. He chewed, looking at her, his eyes unblinking behind the thick spectacle glass.

"Well," she said. "What did she say?" Her voice shook with a touch of impatience

"She said maybe someday I could come to California and see her."

Chapter Nineteen

At irregular intervals, the coach from Indianola brought a few periodicals and newspapers, all of which Ulrich Silesia cherished because they were his last link to what had become another world. Since his father's letters had ended with the old man's death, his only contact with former home and family was the *New York Herald* and *Harper's Weekly*, the illustrated newspaper.

He spent many evenings at the library table, a whale-oil lamp casting its fishy smell and orange glow across the room, bent over the spread pages of Mr. James Gordon Bennett's newspaper, wearing a pair of Hausmann's Mercantile's magnifying eyeglasses, making an occasional acid comment to Elizabeth, who always sat in a nearby rocking chair, working with an embroidery hoop and pillow linen and thread, fingers moving like a concert pianist's, the thimble making its dull pewter shine in the light from Ulrich's lamp.

If the breeze was from the south or west, as it usually was, the scent of fried sweet peppers and garlic and tomatoes came through the cheesecloth curtains from the Military and Main Plaza chili stands. And at this time of day, in the evening, there was always music. Sometimes nearby, sometimes far away, maybe from the Barrio del Sur, where *una guitarrista* strummed the chords to accompany his lament for an unfaithful lover.

Now, these sessions were especially good because they not only brought news of his old pasture but served to take his mind off Oscar Schiller's property problems.

In fact, these sessions had become a gathering place for others, as well. The Silesias had never intended to establish a San Antonio salon, but they did so despite themselves.

Former Texas Ranger Buster Lloyd often joined them. He was living as a permanent guest at the hotel. He had lost a young Mexican wife, as Jim Bowie had, during the great cholera outbreak before the War for Texas Independence.

Sometimes Frederick Hausmann and his wife, Bertie, came. Sometimes Juan Pardo, the Mexican cattleman, when he was in town overnight. He never stayed in a hotel room at Mrs. Wolf's, preferring a bedroll among his vaqueros in the Military Plaza wagon park. A lot of people who had stayed in one of Ulrich Silesia's hotel rooms said Juan Pardo made a wise choice.

This was a sore point with Ulrich. The Menger was advertised as a grand hotel, as good as anything in New Orleans, which it probably was, while Mrs. Wolf's was still one of those frontier establishments where if you bought a night's lodging you never knew how many other people would be sharing the bed with you.

To rub salt in that wound, when United States senator Sam Houston was in San Antonio, he usually visited the Silesia evening sessions round the library table. But he always slept in a bed across the river at the Menger. Which he most certainly did not share with anyone. Well, at least not with any uninvited strangers.

Anyway, it was a salon. Sometimes the Roths came, and the Falsworths, who were two of the few Anglos and Presbyterians, the Bexar participants being mostly German and Lutheran. Plus an occasional businessman from Laredo, Mexican and Catholic, sometimes came.

Ulrich Silesia was proud of this show of tolerance and the cross section of people his salon represented in a place and time when crows flocked only with crows, and owls only with owls, so to speak.

And sometimes in one corner, hunkered down on a footstool, was Oscar Schiller, listening, his eyes behind the thick glasses glinting in the pale orange light. When he was there, Oscar usually stayed the night, simply leaving his stool and lying on the bare floor beside it, where Elizabeth Silesia would come later, after he was asleep, and throw a serape over him.

One class of Texan was never represented. Cotton-country people. Not rich planters or Puritan-type Baptist and Methodist farmers who toiled on their own subsistence plots between the big sprawling Texas plantations worked by slaves. These people were mostly east of the Colorado.

But even if they had lived in any number around San Antonio, they would hardly have appeared at the Silesias' library table, because they were all sympathetic to slavery. Few of these farmers owned slaves, but they became violent when somebody mentioned the possibility of abolition.

As Sam Houston told Ulrich Silesia, to these people abolition meant equality. And a black man being equal to a white was intolerable. The only source of self-esteem many of them had was that they were white in a racially mixed society.

"You see," Houston said, sipping from his water glass of Madeira, "the east Texas planters are smart enough to know that nobody else except abolitionist radicals—not even Mr. Lincoln—has said they will do away with slavery in the states now in the Union. Only that there will be no more slavery in new states or territories.

"But east Texas small farmers are convinced that Yankees will abolish the institution. They've heard too much of that hysterical horseshit from John Calhoun and the rest of South Carolina, and the weeping and gnashing of teeth from all the sanctimonious New England poets who have about as much notion of the national constitution as they do the problems of living in a county where there are more blacks than whites."

Here Houston would usually pause and bang Elizabeth's library table with his fist, making the cookie dish and all the glasses jump.

"So slavery in Texas is safe under the federal constitution until Texas has figured out what to do about this blight of human bondage, which that fool Calhoun raves must be maintained in perpetuity. But the small farmer still thinks that a black Republican, as they say, elected to the presidency, will free all the slaves in Texas now!

"This is something they cannot abide, and the fear of it clouds their minds, so they ignore the fact that Mr. Lincoln has already stated without qualification that he'd not abolish slavery where it is already established. But they can hear only the wild rantings of Calhoun and the holier-than-thou ravings of Yankee fanatics who are ready to destroy this Union.

"Yankees will take any secession as rebellion and will come after us hammer and tongs, rightly so, and then all that we think is dear in the South will be gone. Because we cannot endure against them!"

It was this kind of talk that made Ulrich Silesia read his New York papers intently, and with a constant frown. It was this kind of talk that made Oscar Schiller in the corner blink his eyes rapidly. It was this kind of talk that prompted a comment from Elizabeth Silesia.

"I wish Sam Houston would take his harangues over to the Menger when he comes to town!"

For her, the best gatherings were those at which she and some of the ladies could talk about the latest book in San Antonio by Charles Dickens, *Oliver Twist*. Or better yet, Washington Irving's *The Alhambra*, which was of special interest in a place like Bexar, where the old Spanish influence was so apparent. The book detailed much about the lives of Moors and Spaniards during the seven centuries when the Islamic Berbers and Arabs occupied most of the Iberian peninsula.

But Elizabeth Silesia's best efforts couldn't shut out the reality. Her book salon would discuss the old favorites like Gogol's *Taras Bulba* or the Dumas classic *The Count of Monte Cristo,* and then Stowe's recent tear-jerker, *Uncle Tom's Cabin,* would have everyone dithering about slavery.

Even with their songs. At the casino club the men's glee club would sing "Rocked in the Cradle of the Deep" or the rousing "Buffalo Gals Won't You Come Out Tonight" or "The Two Grenadiers" in German, and then suddenly there would be slavery again with their rendition of Foster's "My Old Kentucky Home."

Elizabeth wished she could be like Oscar Schiller, carefree enough to stroll around Main Plaza as he did, singing the new tune everyone loved, "The Yellow Rose of Texas."

Instead, she was sentenced to share Ulrich's gloom.

"Do you know it is about the same distance from here to Galveston as it is from Albany to Buffalo?" Ulrich said one night, bending over a German-language atlas Elizabeth had brought with her bride's treasure. "About the same distance as from Berlin to Epinal, France. About two hundred fifty some miles."

"Translate that," she said. "I'm still unsure of these Saxon measurements. And what does it matter how far it is from Albany to Buffalo, except that this was once your family's stomping ground?"

"All right, just listen," he said. "That's a little over four hundred kilometers. Now take Albany to Buffalo. There is at least one turnpike, an all-weather road. There is the Erie Canal. There is a railroad. All of this to move things back and forth, cheap and in a hurry."

"Yes, I know what roads and canals and railroads do."

"Well, over that same distance, from where you sit to Galveston, there is no railroad, no single road worth the name, no trace that is passable when it rains for two days, and of course, no canal."

He waited for a reply, but she made none, her fingers working like plump little animated German sausages over the pillowcase in her hoop.

"What's more, there are no real long-distance stagecoach routes in Texas that are Texan. There are lines going from Saint Louis or New Orleans to California, and they happen to pass through Texas. But there are no regular scheduled runs of coaches between this state's largest towns. Galveston, San Antonio, Brownsville.

"Did you know there are more people in Syracuse, in my old home state once again, than in all three of our largest towns combined? In Chicago, Senator Houston told me there are more than a hundred thousand people. In Saint Louis, more than one hundred fifty thousand. We have in Bexar the biggest town in Texas. There are almost eight thousand of us!"

"Why on earth are you telling me all this?" she asked.

"I suppose, my dear, to impress on you the fact that we are a primitive, backwoods place. Our largest towns aren't much more than villages. We don't make anything. Look at us. In Bexar, we trade in hides, we supply the army, we broker trade with Mexico and California. We're merchants.

"I was just thinking about what Sam Houston said the other night. That we couldn't endure in a fight with the Yankees. In east Texas, where the plantations and the slaves are, they grow cotton. But there are no cities or industries. Planters and farmers and slaves. And what they grow, most of the profit goes to the cotton factories in Galveston.

"And you know, because most of our people live east of the Colorado, those people dominate the legislature and sometimes are concerned with plantations and slavery, when neither is in our best interest."

"That's how it's supposed to work, isn't it, this democracy thing?" she asked.

"Yes. But it's hard," he said. "Do you know what Juan Pardo said? He said I'll have to face what he once did when the War for Texas

Independence was coming. He was a Texas-born Mexican who had to choose between his own country and his local neighbors."

"So he fought with his neighbors, even if he didn't agree with everything they did," she said. "So is this leading to your telling me what you would do if there is trouble here?"

"I suppose so," he said. "I'm too old to start over someplace else. I'd like to be neutral, but that's not really an option in the kind of mess we're getting into. There are no neutrals! So I suppose we'd stand with our neighbors from east Texas against the Yankees. It won't mean we approve of everything east Texas does, but the Yankees will make no distinction between us. We'll be slavers, too. Actually, I suppose we're lucky."

"From all you've said, I really don't think we sound very lucky."

"Compared to others. Listen, do you know the Juan Sequin story? In the War for Texas Independence against Mexico, he faced the same problem. He fought with the Gringos. He was brave. He led troops at San Jacinto. After the war, he was honored, here in San Antonio. He was *alcalde* once. Then, certain land-hungry and unscrupulous men. . . ."

"Judge Belcher. Prosecutor Booth Jenkins. Marshal Shirley. That kind of unscrupulous?"

"Exactly! They began to circulate stories about spies for Mexico ready to help Santa Anna retake Texas. They voided Spanish grants and took the land of many loyal Texas Mexicans like Sequin, who had fought for Texas, and sold the land at auction. They beat some Mexicans in the night. They killed some in fake robberies or fake Comanche raids. Juan Sequin had to flee for his life to Mexico, where Santa Anna promptly threw him in jail."

Oscar Schiller was there when Ulrich Silesia told that story, and the boy was so furious Elizabeth thought he was having a mild convulsion.

And after Oscar left for home, because on that night it seemed he was anxious to go there, Ulrich told Elizabeth she might understand now why there was so much concern about Oscar Schiller's property.

"But he's not Mexican," she said.

"No, but what he holds on that property is a Spanish land patent.

Which makes him fair game for anybody ready to take advantage of hatred for Mexicans around here among certain Anglos."

"Belcher, Jenkins, Shirley again? And maybe the entire Bat Club?"

"Maybe not everybody among those politicians and lawyers, but certainly those three you named and a few suckerfish that swim around them. But it only takes a few, because among most white Texans— German, Anglo-Celtic, Swiss, whatever—when Mexicans get spit on around here, they won't have any part of it. They don't approve of such shenanigans, but they let it go. They don't rear up in wrath. The ones doing the spitting are usually the authorities, and it's not worth anybody's time and trouble and maybe life to oppose them just for a few Mexicans!"

"I tell you, Oscar is not a Mexican."

"No but his papa was, and that land-grant was as Spanish as old Isabella's garter, and besides, even if he's half German, Oscar's a bastard, after all, with a mother who flew the coop."

"Oscar's deed is still in Hausmann's safe, isn't it?"

"Yes. But it may not stand up."

Oscar Schiller wanted to be at the Silesias' whenever there were guests and the talk was about the problems in the East and all this slavery business. Listening on the street, all he could get was a lot of shouting and hand waving from the Anglos and more questions asked than answered from the Germans. Mexicans just shrugged and tried to stay clear of even a discussion of it.

There was a new guest at the library-table gatherings. He was the commanding officer of the U.S. Army's Second Cavalry Regiment stationed in Texas. He was from Virginia, and Oscar Schiller thought maybe he was the handsomest man he'd ever seen. Certainly the ladies of San Antonio thought so.

His name was Robert E. Lee, and he spoke elegantly about his home and about his hope that the men from Virginia now in the city of Washington trying to negotiate a compromise on the growing crisis would be successful. He was opposed to human bondage and said it had to be done away with, but he hoped this could happen without bloodshed.

Oscar Schiller felt a glow in his chest when he heard such things from Lee's lips, and he remembered Sam Houston describing other men, fanatics from both the North and the South using the vilest, cruelest rhetoric, as though they were goading an already furious beast, intentionally encouraging blind hatred and fear.

Lee spoke to Oscar and shook his hand, and generally treated him as though Oscar was a full-grown man. When they were on the street and met, Lee always acknowledged Oscar with a smile and a touch of fingers to his fine hat.

Oscar Schiller began attending church at the new Saint Mary's Episcopal, where Lee appeared each Sunday morning in mufti. This always disappointed Oscar Schiller a little, because he thought Lee looked so magnificent in uniform, with the double row of shiny brass buttons.

Lee rented a small riverside house. When he wasn't riding to an outpost with his troops, he often sat on the Menger veranda for morning hot chocolate. Oscar would see him and imagine Lee was looking at the old Alamo mission and thinking about all those men who had fought and died there.

It was here one morning that Lee asked Oscar to join him and he bought a second cup of the thick Yucatan chocolate for the boy and told him of places in Virginia where there were miles and miles of great forests and clear flowing streams and where the color of summer was green, not tan.

Oscar Schiller never told Lee about his real mother, but he talked at length of the Tonkawa, recognizing Lee's interest in Texas Indians. Lee was impressed and said he'd like to meet this unusual woman someday.

Oscar Schiller showed Colonel Lee the pendant finger he wore under his shirt at all times now, taking it as a good-luck charm. Lee touched it and was very impressed.

On one occasion, when a party of the Silesias' salon members was planning to attend a performance of a play at the Casino Club, Colonel Lee suggested that Oscar Schiller come, too. Thus, after the Tonk worked him over with soap and water and braided his queue and brushed his best serape, he saw his first and only San Antonio high-society repertory stage play.

It was Albert Lortzing's *Der Wildschetz*, or *The Poacher*, an ambitious effort which Oscar Schiller found dismally bad, unimpressed with the astonishing fact that a German opera was being done in its original German on ground where, if the wind was right on certain days, you might hear Comanche war chants.

Many of the army officers assigned to Texas, far from home in the East, took Mexican mistresses, and most of those who did not availed themselves of the professional ladies of San Antonio. Oscar knew all this in some detail, having been the agent for many *asignaciós* between local señoritas and lonely bluecoat soldiers.

But Lee was never involved in such things. He flirted with the ladies of the church and with wives of the visiting planter aristocracy, but despite his obvious delight in the company of women, he never broke the faith between himself and his sickly wife, some of whose problems he confided to Elizabeth Silesia. Hence, Oscar Schiller was well aware of these.

Although generally Oscar Schiller might have been amoral, Lee's faithfulness to his wife and to his ideals of justice and fair play carried a great weight with him, and it was soon impossible for him to entertain any thought of Lee without a surrounding glow of nobility and goodness. It was almost like the halo of a sacred trust, to be held forever inviolate.

This was, in fact, an effect that Lee had on a great many people.

Often, Oscar would bring Lee's horse from the Menger stable and wait at the front of the hotel until the colonel appeared and mounted to ride off on an inspection tour or some such thing. Oscar refused to take any money for this.

Lee was the only person to whom you'd ever see Oscar Schiller doff his hat when they met on the street. In fact, when Oscar waited with Lee's horse, he always stood there holding the reins in one hand, his hat in the other, as Lee came striding out.

Encouraged by former Ranger Buster Lloyd, Oscar Schiller learned to ride. With money he had earned in the hotel business, as he put it, he bought a blue roan and kept him in one of Gunther Roth's livery barns.

"You get good enough on that little gelding," Roth said, "me and

Johnny Pardo'll hire you on with the other vaqueros to trail a herd of longhorns to Gila Crossing one of these days."

He named the horse Blacky, in memory, he told his friend Jesus Montez, of a certain dog they both had known who traded his life for one last hang-up with a bitch in heat!

Jesus Montez thought this was so funny he told his older brother Ramon about it, and Ramon beat hell out of him for saying anything aloud about that dog because it had been Ramon who'd helped the Tonk in her canine assassination and he was still afraid of what might happen if the Jenkins bunch ever suspected he could tell them anything about that dog's last moments of ecstasy.

One of Juan Pardo's tack-wagon men rebuilt an old Mexican saddle for Oscar. It had one of those high, flat-topped horns that had distinguished Spanish saddles in the Southwest for three centuries.

The saddle was what they called a Spanish rimfire rig, with a single cinch, which was deemed adequate because it wasn't expected that Oscar would be doing any cattle roping, an activity that made the second cinch a requirement.

The foundation wood for the fork and horn and cantle was mostly exposed, showing finely polished cypress. All the leather covering the rest, and hanging as latigo, stirrup leather, and skirt, was old and well-cured bull hide, tough but glistening. *Tapaderas* hung from the wood bow stirrups to protect the feet from cactus and thorns. Set in each fender was a Mexican silver dollar.

To go with the saddle, the wagon men made Oscar a woven horse-hair bridle with a split-ear headstall. It was one hell of an outfit, and a drover from Gonzales offered Oscar ninety dollars for it. No sale.

It had been a late discussion at the Silesias'. Afterward, nobody could recall everyone who had been involved because subsequent events washed out the memory of such incidentals.

But no matter the participants, it had apparently been a pretty good shouting match, good enough anyway to keep Oscar Schiller hanging on every word until the end. By which time it was so late that roosters had stared crowing somewhere in Barrio del Sur.

They didn't crow long. A sudden high southwest wind and rainstorm hit, water and hailstones coming down so hard and thick that all the oil lamps on the posts around Main Plaza were knocked out.

Not many people were on the street at this pre-dawn time of day. A few farmers were in town for market, crawling from beneath wagons, yawning, stretching, urinating on wagon wheels, munching cold tortillas, and generally making ready to set up their produce stalls so that the town's restaurant and hotel and mission cooks could come for daily shopping.

A woman at the far end of Main Plaza came to her door and threw the contents of a chamber pot onto the street.

A brown and white and black dog slowly walked from the south side of Military Plaza to the north side, which he did every day. Nobody knew where the dog came from or where he went, but he made the trip each morning when it was so early there weren't many people around to kick at him.

All of this was barely visible in the wan light of street lamps, and then the storm broke with the sudden fury of west Texas storms, and the lamps were gone. But the storm brought its own light, a kind of weird red glow that such storms seemed to generate, which marked the Second Coming of Jesus, according to some Baptist evangelicals, when they saw the phenomenon for the first time.

Everyone skittered for cover, like water bugs, but Oscar Schiller stayed under the front veranda cover along Mrs. Wolf's Commerce Street front, huddled against the wall.

Upstairs, Elizabeth Silesia stood for a long time at one of the windows, watching the storm lash the trees around San Fernando Cathedral. She was hoping Oscar would return to the Silesia rooms and spend what was left of the night under his usual serape in the corner near the library table.

But downstairs under the awning, Oscar Schiller was waiting for even a small lessening of the storm's fury so he could make a break for Armador Street. Time had slipped away from him while he was unaware, and he felt some kind of dread and apprehension about not being in his house on this night.

Well, this was no longer night. A gray light was creeping through the town, as though each bolt of lightning was pushing the darkness away. Even through the downpour, Oscar could make out the details of buildings across the plaza by the time he finally decided to run for it.

Even where the surfaces had been cobbled, mud seemed to have seeped back up through the cracks, and each running step Oscar took splattered a red gummy paste on his legs and the bottom hem of his cotton smock. He dashed across Main Plaza and across the cathedral garden and jumped the back stone wall and was in Military Plaza then, and running through a maze of Gunther Roth's parked wagons.

A whole family of Mexicans—man, woman, and half-a-dozen children—was under one wagon, jabbering, waiting to come out and set up their chili stand for those Bexar residents who enjoyed frijoles and chilies for breakfast. As Oscar rushed past, the children squealed and shouted at him and laughed.

On the far side of Military Plaza, under the porch awning of Felipe Valasco's saloon, he saw two vaqueros. They were leaning against the wall, dry under the overhang, smoking long, crooked white cigarillos.

They recognized him and shouted, waved their sombreros, and laughed.

"Hey, keedfrido, *mi* amigo, my little runt friend, who's after you so early in the morning?" one shouted.

This made him feel a little better, a little more secure, as though everything was in its right place.

The Mexican cowboy had shouted a nickname by which Oscar had become known among friends since the morning he'd helped Ulrich Silesia in his dining room, the morning Sophia and Heimel Uttegard flew the coop.

The Mexicans started it, pronouncing Oscar Schiller to be San Antonio's *pequeño huevo frito*. This roughly translated as fried eggs kid.

Like most sobriquets, this one went through a good many evolutionary phases. It was *muchacho de los huevos* for a while. The Germans made the name *Eierkind*. Then stage drivers and stable people and customers he'd served as the Bag Boy and most of his Celtic friends made a mixed, half-breed name of it, as they did so many times in Texas, and it settled down permanently to Kid Frito.

When the Mexicans said this, it sounded like "keedfrido."

At that moment, it was a good thing for Oscar Schiller to hear.

Oscar ran diagonally to the far corner of the plaza and into the end of Armador Street and along it. The rain was slackening as suddenly as it had begun, and the light was chasing close behind the rain. So a long time before he came to the *casa*, his throat began to close. For in the light of the gray, wet dawn, he could see that the front door was open and hanging crookedly on one hinge.

He knew another kind of storm had come to the inside of his *casa*. He had no idea what he would find there, but he stopped in the street, the last of the rain beating down on the brim of his hat, and looking at the gaping dark opening where the door was supposed to be closed, he ground his teeth together and willed himself to move very slowly, very deliberately.

And no matter what he found, to control his temper and be cold and detached and, if called for, murderous. Of course, Oscar Schiller didn't think of any of this in such terms.

What he thought was, I will be a man no matter what it is, I will be a man like Colonel Lee would be.

And with that, he stepped inside.

Chapter Twenty

Alex Mesero's bed had been pulled away from the wall, and the expensive mattress had been slashed at many places with a knife. Cotton batting was scattered about the room like wadded puffs of dirty yucca blossoms. There were shredded pillowcases, one an embroidered gift from Elizabeth Silesia.

Blankets and quilts were scattered about, the comforters ripped open, and serapes and ponchos and coats tossed everywhere, linings torn out of anything that had linings.

A lamp was broken, and the fish smell of whale oil hung like smoke in the thick humidity of the room. A small pottery vase where the Tonk kept her medicinal wild flowers had been smashed with a boot heel, it appeared, and the shards lay in the red and purple and green pulp of the plants.

Every pan and dish and knife and fork was on the floor, and all the sacks had been emptied, so there was cornmeal and salt and coffee beans and dry pinto beans everywhere. Jars had been broken, sugar and ground chilies dumped, tomato paste splashed across the floor. One taste proved it was not blood.

And in one corner was the box that had held the Tonk's special things. Some items of clothing like a silk scarf and a red-and-black-striped woolen shawl Paco Salazar had given her.

And her medicine bag, in which she kept the secret symbols of spirituality known only to herself and her own personal gods.

These were the connections between her earth self and the supernatural place of dreams, which to her was the only true reality. She'd never told Oscar this in so many words, but she'd told him enough for him to know it was true.

Oscar Schiller had never seen the contents of the medicine bag before. He knew with a deep trembling that there would have been a monumental resistance to anyone seeing these things, especially strangers, and a struggle to prevent this from happening.

Everything had been dumped without ceremony in the wooden box where the Tonk kept such things. There was a small leather pouch to hold everything, which Oscar Schiller knew she carried with her no matter where she went, just like the men of the wild tribes, between the legs under a loincloth or apron.

There were a few tiny bones; a number of colored, shiny stones; the delicate skull of a very small bird, maybe a cactus owl with its cruel little hooked beak; a bun of human hair the size of a chicken egg, tied with horsehair; what appeared to be a blue-jay feather; and the dried skin of a sidewinder rattlesnake, complete with three rattles.

That someone would defile this thing—the Tonk's earthly representation of the supernatural power in which she believed—made Oscar Schiller so furious he slid off Alex Mesero's ruined bed, where he had been sitting, and writhed like a hoe-cut worm, pounding the floor with his fists, trying to control his furious rage.

Slowly becoming rigid, still lying there among all the debris, eyes shut, teeth clenched, he began to think again with some semblance of reason. And that's when the realization came hard, and he started to sob and call the Tonk's name.

He crawled and scrambled around the cluttered room, scattering everything still further, being sure. When he finally rose, he knew. The Tonk's big knife with the green cowhorn handle was gone.

He knew without even thinking about it what had happened. Somebody had come to find the Spanish land patent. And they'd tried to make her reveal its hiding place, thinking it was most likely in this house.

And if the Tonk had told them it was in somebody's safe, they would not have believed her. They would have tried to force her to tell them where it really was.

And Oscar Schiller had a pretty good idea of how the Tonk would react to somebody trying to force anything from her. They must have caught her in her sleep, and there must have been a half dozen of the bastards. He couldn't imagine the Tonk being subdued by any fewer.

Where was the blood? For them to hold her while they ripped her house apart seemed impossible without them seriously wounding her, killing her. How, without any bleeding? But she was gone.

God, that was the bad part. She was gone.

He stumbled out into the street and found the rain had stopped. And he stood a moment, uncertain about where he was, for his reason had now begun to leave him, and his will to be controlled melted and his thinking grew muddled and confused. He had a sudden sense of being left alone, and he had to jerk himself about to keep his mind on what he should do next.

Oscar Schiller began to run. He ran along Armador Street to Laredo Street and along that to the alley that led to the Montez *casa*. Jesus and Ramon and Señora Montez and the four younger children were eating their breakfast, tortillas and beans.

They all stared at the wild appearance of a muddy, dripping, and glassy-eyed Oscar Schiller gasping out German words they didn't understand. It took him three starts before he could get his questions into Spanish.

It didn't matter. They hadn't seen the Tonk.

He didn't wait to explain, and Ramon was clearly upset and hissed at Jesus, "It's that damned dog business again!"

Oscar cut back east to Flores and ran until he came to the army arsenal. There were a number of low buildings, lines of canvas-top wagons, a mule corral, and a two-story structure before a parade ground, where a storm flag hung limp on the staff, the breeze not strong enough to move the wet bunting.

Later, the soldiers laughed about it.

"What did that Mex young-un in the big sombrero that run in here want?" the corporal of the guard asked.

"He ain't no Mex," said the charge of quarters sergeant. "He's that German kid rings the bell for stagecoaches at Wolf's. They call him Kid Frito. Wanted to see the colonel."

"The colonel? He wanted to see Colonel Lee?"

"What he said. Said he knew Colonel Lee and needed to see em."

"What'd ya tell em?"

"Well, hell, I told him the truth, that the colonel rode out of here before daylight with a detail headin for Fort Davis. That's a wild-lookin little devil. I ain't ever seen a kid that young wearin them eye-glasses. Looks like a damned ole owl, you know it?"

Oscar Schiller went back by his *casa* in Armador Street. Nothing had changed. He hadn't expected it would. But he was calmer now and paused long enough to rummage in the scatter of clothing and find a dry smock and pantaloons and a serape, because it was a little chilly with clouds still hiding the sun.

He ran back toward the plaza area. As he came to Via Dolorosa on Military Plaza, he saw three figures standing close together at the foot of the outside stairway at the Bat Cave. They saw him, too, and stopped talking to watch him.

Oscar Schiller could see the shine of their eyes, like a pack of dogs under the shadow of a wet bush, he thought. He wasn't close enough to see their features clearly, but he knew them.

It was the prosecuting attorney, Booth Jenkins, the city marshal, Dubb Shirley, and that county clerk man, what's his name, Ernest Kilpatton.

Oscar Schiller felt a chill go up his back, and not from the cold wind blowing from the west, chasing the storm. He hurried along Dolorosa until the cathedral cut off his view of the Bat Cave, then went straight across to the Death Corner sidewalk, along Soledad to the alley, and into the back door of Mrs. Wolf's Cafe.

He went along the back hall and into the small room where his mother had lived. It was being used as a storage room again. The Mexicans working in Ulrich Silesia's kitchen now lived in Barrio del Sur.

But the bed was still there, simple chicken-wire springs on a raw pine frame. There was a straw mattress rolled at one end and he undid the string around it, flattened it on the springs, and flopped down, throwing his hat aside, feeling completely undone.

It would be late in the morning before Elizabeth Silesia found him there, sleeping a hard, exhausted sleep. His glasses had come off and fallen on the floor, and she took those in her apron pocket for safe-keeping, pulled a large cotton bean sack over him, and left him to sleep.

They knew the Tonk had disappeared and the Armador *casa* had been ransacked, and they assumed what Oscar Schiller had. That somebody was looking for the deed.

Señora Montez had gone to the Silesias' a short time after Oscar Schiller had interrupted her breakfast. While she spoke with Ulrich

Silesia in the cafe, Elizabeth came in from the post office, and they all figured something was wrong at the Armador house from the way Oscar had been jabbering at the Montezes'.

At the moment, Oscar Schiller was in the back room sleeping, but they didn't know that yet.

After he went upstairs to ask the former Texas Ranger to accompany him, Ulrich went to see for himself, with Buster Lloyd beside him stride for stride, the grip of a big Colt six-shooter showing at his waist.

They found nothing to make them change their minds about what had happened and why. Next, moving at a rapid pace, they went to Frederick Hausmann's mercantile, crossing Military Plaza to Commerce Street, a short distance away from the courthouse.

By now, the plaza was filled with traders and chili stands, but as they wound their way through the wagons and dogs and women with market baskets and umbrellas, in case the rain returned, two men came out of city hall at the top of the outside staircase, and despite the general confusion and milling crowd in the plaza below, specifically picked out Silesia and Lloyd and watched them cross the plaza.

"We've got some *hombres* hangin on that high roost at the Bat Cave mighty curious about us," Buster Lloyd said.

"I see them. Who's that slender one?"

"Our grease-butt marshal and it looks like that kid, that snotty high-toned Jenkins kid, what's his name?"

"Jesus Christ! John David? They've started him mighty young in this sorry business, haven't they?"

"A young Gila monster is still a monster," Buster Lloyd said. "Should I wave to em?"

"No. To hell with them."

At the mercantile, they asked for Hausmann, who opened the safe himself. The Spanish patent was there, of course. After a long discussion, they decided to leave it, warning Hausmann once more to protect the document every time the safe was opened.

By the time they returned to Mrs. Wolf's, Elizabeth had discovered Oscar Schiller. While they waited for him to wake, they sat around the library table, trying to think of the best thing to do.

First, Ulrich Silesia decided they needed to report the Tonk's disappearance and the ransacking of the Armador Street *casa*. A detail of interest to a prosecuting attorney, he figured. And one look at Oscar Schiller when he came upstairs was enough to convince them that he should stay out of sight and out of harm's way.

One moment, Oscar seemed as calm and unconcerned as though they were discussing the arrival of the next stagecoach from Austin, and then when someone mentioned the Tonk or anything that might remind him of her, his eyes grew glassy hard and his anger choked him so much he had trouble making any sense when he talked.

Ulrich Silesia's rage and frustration really began after he and Lloyd went to the Bat Cave, reported what they knew about the Armador Street business, and got the official view of how things were in Bexar when land was involved, especially Mexican land located where money might be made.

"No more than you can expect," Jenkins said. "A cannibal Indian who's been nothing but a squatter on public land, an embarrassment to the Christian community, hiding behind a bastard kid whose mother was a German harlot who run off when she found out this town wasn't gonna put up with her kind anymore, for there was this Christian who desired to get the real estate in proper hands for progress, like Providence expected, and her sort no longer to be put up with.

"Can you beat that? A savage infidel claiming to be the guardian of this kid, using this little child as an excuse to stay in this place after some Mexican spy for Santa Anna who claimed he owned it died, and the German harlot comes up with some crazy claim about a Spanish land-grant like this Mexican traitor to the state of Texas was some kind of a big aristocrat and had this land and now give it to the German harlot and she give it to this kid, all the while with their pet cannibal sitting pretty, high and dry and not hungry either, you can bet.

"And so now finally the land commission has gotten around to getting that land into some citizen's hands, some Texas white Christian citizen—and not a damned papist—who will improve it, as Lord God ordained, and make some progress in that part of this town.

"Go see Judge Belcher, Silesia. I'm not wasting any of my time on this thing. The damned Indian wandered off someplace with a drunk vaquero and decided not to come back. And if you think the great

state of Texas is going to award that property to some weak-eyed bastard kid on the basis of a silly piece of paper anybody, even you, could
have written, you're crazy!"

Ulrich Silesia was stunned and shocked that Booth Jenkins knew
so much about the tangled relationships between Sophia, the Tonk,
Oscar, and Salazar. He allowed himself to be led out of Jenkins's office
by one of Marshal Dubb Shirley's deputies.

It was only some time later that he began to recall all the vicious
and slanderous things Jenkins had said about Sophia and her child and
the Tonk, and most of all the incredible accusations against Salazar,
and then he frightened his wife with what she supposed were the symp-
toms of a violent stroke before he could be calmed enough to discuss
the next step.

Oscar Schiller had spent a short time with Buster Lloyd, cleaning pistols, and then he was out and away before anyone could stop him, doing
some of his own investigating. But he didn't go near the courthouse.

Silesia did. But taking an obviously armed man into the chambers
of a circuit judge seemed a little bellicose, so when he visited Judge
Belcher in his back office of the Bat Cave, he took his wife and Frederick
Hausmann.

The judge, behind the fortress of a massive desk, had two of Dubb
Shirley's deputies in the room with him, men who could have been
cut from the same hickory stick. Rake-skinny and raw-boned, long-
fingered and wolf-eyed, smelling of old sweat and tobacco juice.
Showing the signs of their office with any number of pistol butts stick-
ing out of their clothes in the appropriate places.

Later, Elizabeth Silesia remarked that either deputy would be a
hazard in a civilized parlor, sure to bump and scar the furniture with
any move they made, what with all the metal that stuck out from them
in every direction. And near a China closet, they would be a disaster.

They'd brought the old Spanish land-grant, and Ulrich Silesia
unfolded it on the desk. Belcher scarcely glanced at it.

"I see hundreds of these every month," he said.

He was getting pretty old, and he was dyeing his gray hair now
with walnut-hull stain, but he was always a little behind so the gray

was still obvious. A lot of the juice got on the bare skin of the judge's forehead, making a greenish-black smudge.

"Hundreds, hundreds," he said, tossing it aside. "It's worthless. I'm sure the circuit clerk would have told me if there was any credence here. Nothing has been executed before a notary public."

"Judge," said Frederick Hausmann, "Spaniards didn't use the same system we do."

"I'm not going to sanctify some scrap of paper," the judge said. "It's worthless. I never heard of a Salazar family in that neighborhood. Never heard of any land transfer."

"Your Honor, it's a matter of record," said Silesia. "I personally had it entered on the tax rolls in this county when Paco Salazar died."

"None of that's credible. What business do you have in this, anyway? What profit do you expect from all your interest in this property?"

"Profit? Profit?"

"Stay calm, my dear," Elizabeth whispered.

"I did it to help a woman whom I employed and then a child whose welfare was my concern as a caring citizen. I had supposed that such things. . . ."

"Yes, yes, yes," Belcher cut him off. "Very, very commendable, all this love of illegitimate deformed urchins and their unsavory mothers who brought the manners and morals of bordellos in some pumpernickel city like Hamburg right in here amongst good American wives and children. And why bother me with it? This is a situation the land commissioner makes decisions on, so go see him and stop bothering me."

Now it was Ulrich and Frederick Hausmann restraining Elizabeth Silesia and trying to get her out of the judge's office before the deputies grabbed everybody and took them upstairs to jail.

"Morals of pumpernickel bordellos?" Elizabeth screamed. "Who are you to be slandering your betters, you intolerant buffoon, sucking the blood of good people, you slimy leech! You insignificant boil of corruption! You ignorant piss ant! You uneducated loudmouth bumpkin!"

They had her out by then, Ulrich on one arm, Frederick Hausmann on the other, out into Military Plaza, Elizabeth screaming over her shoulder. People at the chili stands and along the Commerce Street sidewalks stopped and stared.

"You lying, walnut-colored, pus-eyed bigot!" she shouted.

"All right, dear, all right," Ulrich was gasping, pulling her along toward the cathedral and Main Plaza.

Hausmann was tugging on her, too, and laughing so hard tears ran down his cheeks.

"The piss ant part," he said. "I liked that best. The piss ant. *Ja! Ja!*"

Some of the pins in Elizabeth's hair had come loose, and there were tendrils hanging alongside her flashing eyes. Her hat was askew, and they had pulled so hard getting her out of the Bat Cave that two buttons had popped off the front of her blouse.

Before they reached Mrs. Wolf's, a number of men along the sidewalk under the awning of Miller's taproom began to applaud. Onlookers later claimed that by the time they came to Death Corner, half-a-dozen Mexican children were following, laughing and waiting to hear more cussing from the well-dressed Gringo lady. There was a number of barking dogs as well.

Street hangers-on said it was a better show than when King Fisher killed those two Mexicans who got drunk and tried to knock his hat off with a stick at the chicken fight during last year's Independence Day celebration.

In their rooms, Elizabeth sat panting, anger still putting little pinpoints of red in her cheeks.

"I'm sorry I made a scene," she said.

"My dear," he said, bending to kiss her, "I was proud of you."

"Best I didn't have a pistol. I would have shot the filthy pig!"

So the representative of the land commission was next, Mr. Ernest Kilpatton, also circuit clerk, secretary-treasurer of the Royal Order of Bats, and vice president of the Balcones Ridge Development Land Company.

Ulrich Silesia didn't dare take his wife near any government office again. So he asked Buster Lloyd to accompany him on this last act of a bad comedy, sure that nothing was going to get any better and wanting someone as witness so that when he told the story, people would believe him.

Among his ledgers and barricaded behind his high wooden counter, Kilpatton reminded Silesia of a fugitive weasel expecting a visit from a pack of hounds.

"Of course I know the property," he said. "It was put up for sale last week as public domain after processes of warrant found it abandoned."

"Abandoned?"

"Circuit court judgment."

"Bullshit!" Ulrich shouted. "People were living there. All right. You've got to announce public sales."

Kilpatton yanked a page of newsprint from beneath his counter as though he'd hidden it there, waiting for this very moment. It was a sheet of the last week's edition of the *West Texas Star*, a weekly newspaper published by one of Judge Belcher's brothers-in-law that had the county contract to print official Bexar announcements. This particular sheet showed pages three and four, meaning it was the last half of the edition.

With an ink-smudged finger, Kilpatton pointed to a small item with three property listings, each posted up for sale on call at the circuit clerk's office.

Ulrich's face turned purple, and he was starting to shout something when Lloyd touched his arm. Looking back, Ulrich saw Marshal Dubb Shirley lounging in the doorway and one of his gangling deputies just behind him in the hall.

Shirley was picking his teeth with the straw from a broom, it appeared, grinning and watching the two men at the counter with what Elizabeth always described as "those little squinty pig eyes." One hand was hooked with its thumb in his belt, an inch from the butt of a pistol.

"All right," said Ulrich Silesia, his voice shaking. "I'll buy that lot."

Kilpatton made an elaborate face, and Dubb Shirley laughed.

"Oh, that property's been sold."

In the ledger margin was a short entry in black ink indicating that the lot was now the property of the Balcones Ridge Development Land Company, Booth Jenkins, President.

"Why would they go in that house and tear it apart looking for the deed, ready to drag off a woman and a boy or kill them, God forbid, when they knew they could get away with stealing the lot as they did? By public sale after the judge said the patent's not binding? Why bother with making a mess in the middle of the night? Not to mention committing at least two felonies?"

"Elizabeth," said Gunther Roth, "these are cruel men. They wanted to rub somebody's nose in something rotten and nobody can do anything about it. The next one on their list will remember that when they think about resisting."

"It's more than that," said Frederick Hausmann. "They knew they could buy that place without anybody being able to stop them, since they are themselves the authorities here. But they figured it would be nice to take that Spanish deed out of the hands of anybody who sometime in the future might bring the case before the supreme court over in Austin."

"Hell!" Roth spat. "That supreme court's so buried in all this slavery and secession business, they won't be looking at any land-claim cases for a long, long time."

Somehow, it didn't surprise Elizabeth Silesia that Oscar Schiller had no interest in that Armador Street house where he'd grown up. While Ulrich was trying to establish the Spanish land-grant, Oscar Schiller was scouring the town for clues to the Tonk's whereabouts.

He made a nuisance of himself at every Catholic mission in town, whether they had young women living there or not. He was just as persistent at the plaza markets and on the river where the Tonk had done her washing each week.

In Barrio del Sur, he talked to the housewives and the old men who sat on the sunny side of the alleys all day. He spent time quizzing the Mexican children who played around the plaza chili stands, and he questioned all the drovers and wagon drivers who worked for Gunther Roth.

He rode his horse along Laredo Street to the south pastures and spoke with Juan Pardo's vaqueros, who were forming up a herd for a drive to Bayou San Patricio, crossing the Sabine and going on to Natchitoches.

That night he sat behind the stove in Mrs. Wolf's Cafe, and when Elizabeth came to him with extra bedding so he could more or less settle into his mother's old room, he said Pardo's vaqueros had teased him about being a cowboy now and asked him to join their drive.

"And you almost went, didn't you?" Elizabeth asked.

He looked up at her sharply, his eyes a little grotesque behind the thick glasses.

"Yes. They said a drive going to Louisiana was better for me to start with than one going west. No worry about Comanches or Apaches going to the Sabine."

"Why didn't you go?"

His head dropped, his eyes hooded, and after a moment he shrugged, just a faint movement of his shoulders.

"I'll never be big enough to be a cowboy. Besides, if she comes back, I'd want to be here, wouldn't I?"

Elizabeth Silesia thought there might be more, so she stood silently, arms folded, listening to the cookstove flue puffing and the clatter of plates and the loud chatter of the cooks, in Spanish. Her kitchen smelled Spanish, too.

Well, this one did, she thought, but her private kitchen upstairs still had the solid German odor of apples, cinnamon, sauerbraten, and goose liver.

"I just don't have any business runnin off to Louisiana," Oscar said softly. "She may need me out there someplace."

Two days after the ransack of the *casa* on Armador Street the sun was bright even in the first hour after its rising, as though more joyful things were in prospect. But it was time for the dark side, and somehow, Buster Lloyd said, he had the expectation of evil winds.

He was on the balcony porch above Commerce Street when he saw Jesus Montez running furiously from the west end of town, past the horse pickets on Military Plaza, past San Fernando Cathedral, past Soledad Street, and into the rear of Mrs. Wolf's Cafe, almost directly beneath Lloyd.

This was strange, because Jesus Montez wasn't noted for running anywhere, much less at this hour in the morning. But Lloyd had little time to ponder such a novelty when there was Jesus Montez again, running back in the direction he'd come from, and running just behind him was Oscar Schiller, running so fast the tail of his serape flew out behind like a German frau's wash hung to dry on a windy day.

Later that same day, Ulrich Silesia and Elizabeth held Buster Lloyd hostage in their rooms, so to speak, until he related chapter and verse of what had happened that morning.

"It was a feelin, something bad wrong somewheres," he said. "Those two runnin like scalded cats. I didn't even have on my boots yet. But I didn't want to lose them, so I just vaulted over the banister and into the street and pert near bust my legs, but they held up, and I taken in after those two.

"There's a little grove of pin oaks where Commerce crosses Pedro Creek. I see a crowd of people there and the kids bustin right through. By then I was close in behind em. Gimme a glass of that lemonade of yours, would you, please, Miz Silesia?"

After he drank, he lit a cigar, the Silesias making no effort of to conceal their impatience.

"They'd made a circle around the body. The body was naked—a woman. Face up. There wasn't no doubt it was the Tonk. She didn't have a mark on her cept around her neck, which was swollen and black. And she'd been scalped.

"I heard Oscar make a little animal cry. I couldn't see his face, but I can imagine. I tell you, the sound he made woulda sent a shiver into your very heart, Miz Silesia.

"He runs over right quick and flips his serape off and covers her and pats it down and tucks it in all around like he was puttin some-body in bed at night, then he glares around at the crowd, mostly Mexicans, and it was as hard a look as you'll ever see, Oscar ready to kill them for lettin her lay there naked and everybody gawkin at her.

"I went over to him then and squatted with him, just to let him know he wasn't by his self, and pretty soon a couple of Dubb Shirley's deputies come and talk to this Mexican farmer who found the body that mornin out west of town and brung it in on a burro. They wasn't all that interested.

"They had a wrangle then with the farmer because they wanted him to haul the body to the southside graveyard and he wanted pay. I finally went over and paid him a dollar, and that's how we got the body to the burial ground, and I paid a couple kids, town kids, to dig a grave, just put her in with Oscar's serape. I mean, hell, we needed to get her in the ground quick, Mr. Silesia. It was over two days, and we just couldn't stand on no ceremony. She was already gone swollen and soft."

"I understand," said Ulrich. "I'm amazed that Oscar just stood aside and took it without protest."

"Hell, I'm not," said Lloyd. "He understood. He told me later that wasn't really her. The real her was gone someplace else. He understood the rest of it too. I didn't say anything, he just understood."

"Understood what?" Elizabeth asked.

"You know what's being said on the street," Lloyd said. "That it was a Comanche raiding party, come in close to town, and she was out gathering some of her medicine flowers and plants. That she went too far. So they caught her and did this, and scalped her. It's all hogwash, of course. I seen right off no Comanches done this."

"How? What did you see?" she asked.

"More what I didn't see, maybe. First off, Comanch' war party take a likely lookin woman like this, especially a Tonkawa, they ain't gonna just kill her right off and leave her lay. They're gonna ride off and keep her for maybe two, three days, doin what you'd expect, as they move. Until she's dead—then they'd drop her body and ride on. Next off, I got a fair to middlin look, and I'd lay odds this woman wasn't taken advantage of in that way. Excuse me, Miz Silesia, for talkin indelicate."

"God, Buster, don't be absurd! You mean she wasn't raped!"

"Yes'm," Lloyd said, his face flushing red. "And then next, I never heerd of a Comanche killin somebody by stranglin em, which that Tonk definitely was. No other mark on her. No wounds, no bruises I could see. And they usually do a little knife work on a prisoner, and they sure would on a Lipan or a Ute or a Tonkawa, all of them tribes they do their best to kill off. As I say, wasn't a single cut that I seen."

"So what it seems," said Ulrich Silesia, "is that this wasn't a Comanche war party. And somebody scalped her to make it look like it was."

"And a pretty sloppy job of scalpin it was, too," said Lloyd. "Folks, I'd bet my life no Comanche had anything to do with it!"

"Well, that's what Marshal Shirley and his mob are saying on the streets right now," said Elizabeth. "That the Comanches did it."

"Yeah, despite the fact that nobody's heerd of any Comanch' raiders near Bexar at the time. When they're around, you usually hear about somebody or other losing a few horses or mules from their corral at night. Which we didn't."

"More than that, too," said Ulrich. "They say that somebody passing the house on Armador saw nobody was home and went in to van-
dalize it. Mexican kids, they're saying."

"And I'll tie your wedding bow if Oscar Schiller hasn't figured all
this out, too."

"Has he said anything?"

"No. Not to me. Not to anybody I know of. All he's done is just
sit and look glum one minute, glassy-eyed the next. Except for one
thing."

"What?"

"He took those two Salazar six-shooters with him, and he's keepin
em in his room downstairs now," said Lloyd. "I expect he may think
somebody might try visitin him in the night."

"What for? The bastards have already got his house and lot," said
Ulrich.

"Remember what Gunther said. There are cruel people out there
who like to rub your nose in the wickedness you can do nothing
about," Elizabeth said.

"I don't see the connection," Ulrich said. "I don't think he should
have those things in his room. He's liable to shoot a foot off."

"No, he won't do that. He can handle them six-shooters as good
as me," Lloyd said. "And I'll tell you, I knew Paco Salazar, and I imagine Oscar's got a tad of his pappy's blood runnin in his veins. So don't
ask me to go in there and try to take those pistols away from him!"

Part Four

—▸●◂—

Oscar

Chapter Twenty-one

The world was crashing down and all the old leaders with it. Sam Houston, savior at San Jacinto, president of the republic, governor of the state of Texas, United States senator, Oscar Schiller's hero, was being branded traitor in all the Texas newspapers and in all the sidewalk conversation around Ulrich Silesia's cafe.

"I assure you, fine citizens," preached Judge Belcher, "our sterling Texas legislature will never send him back to Washington as a senator."

"Such comments are heard in shouted speeches and harangues from men who suddenly find political wisdom bubbling about in their heads," Ulrich Silesia said. "Wisdom they think needs to be revealed to the ignorant citizen on such subjects as slavery, black Republicans, the United States Constitution, and other things an ordinary citizen can't figure out for himself. To save us all, you see, from the evils of Abraham Lincoln, in case he wins this coming election."

And the most popular stage in town was the front balcony of Mrs. Wolf's Hotel and Cafe. The balcony elevated the speaker and overlooked a wide area, Main Plaza, where a lot of people could congregate to listen and cheer and sometimes shoot off pistols into the air, although the carrying of firearms in the town was supposed to be against the law.

None of this made Ulrich Silesia very happy because he obviously was not in sympathy with the ideals of most of these speakers. You would call him a Jackson Democrat or maybe even a Whig. He had no more of a moral problem with slavery than he did with prostitution, gambling, or a lot of other things. But he was against it because of the social disturbance it created and because of his strong sense that bringing people into the country as slaves weakened the whole ideal of a great American republic. He got all that from Sam Houston.

And he had a terrible problem, as did Houston, with anything that might destroy the Union.

"Of course, we've got to get rid of black slavery," he told Elizabeth.

"But we have to do that as a strong nation working to a solution that hurts the least people. In other words, within a strong Union."

Well, it mattered not that those balcony orators were from the fire-and-brimstone-Union-be-damned bunch. Marshal Dubb Shirley would appear in Silesia's cafe's kitchen and inform him that there would be a speech today and that he should keep his central staircase to the second floor clear so that the speaker and his guests could get to the balcony without undue disrespect and congestion.

"That son of a bitch," Ulrich would say. "When he tells me that, knowing it is like pouring hot soup in my trousers, he grins like the fox of literature, eating the tender grapes, and I have this mad desire to yank the broom straw from his mouth and stick it up his. . . ."

"Ulrich!" Elizabeth would cut in, knowing her cue exactly. "Your feelings do not need such graphic illustration!"

Anyway, Houston's stock was very low in Texas. Understandable in east Texas, cotton country, but sad along the western Indian frontier.

Houston had voted against the Kansas-Nebraska Bill. It abrogated the Missouri Compromise, he said, which it did. Compromise was dead and so was any chance of a peaceful solution to the burning question, he said. Union at any cost, he said.

"He's joined the abolitionists," said Booth Jenkins.

And Houston: "Damned Calhoun Democrats will destroy this nation! Why are we listening to that madman?"

But then the real madman stepped to center stage, in Kansas where the savage fight for squatter sovereignty was tuning up. John Brown, former preacher and self-proclaimed savior of the black race, butchered a half-dozen men in cold blood at Pottawatomie, then collected a small group of sons and other fanatics and seized the federal arsenal at Harper's Ferry, Virginia, killing a few there, too, in his ardor for doing the right thing.

Brought to bay and into a court of law, John Brown was tried in Virginia for murder and treason; he was found guilty beyond any shadow of doubt, was convicted, and hanged.

Naturally, he issued statements claiming he had divine instructions to slaughter the folks he had slaughtered, and unfortunately for any chance of cooling regional tempers, such statements were widely published, and when the Calhoun Democrats in Texas heard about the whole sorry mess, they equated all Yankees with this demented felon.

Astonishingly, this equation got plenty of support from the intelligentsia of New England. Reading some of the reaction to the Harper's Ferry episode, Elizabeth Silesia said, one got the idea that maybe all the people in the North *were* as crazy as John Brown.

"It is incredible," said Silesia, reading his New York newspapers. "There are people making this madman a saint. I mean important men. Horace Greeley says he can find nothing wrong with anything Brown did. Is he mad, too? Can just anybody get one of these messages from God and go kill somebody and then have a good chance of being freed? Can I do that? I've got a couple of victims in mind."

"I see that people like Longfellow and Lowell say it doesn't matter that he pulled off these bloody crimes," said Elizabeth, "because it was decreed by God. It was ordained from eternity. Sounds very Calvinist to me."

"Well, I don't like slavery even a bit, but I'm above going into a moral frenzy," said Frederick Hausmann. "Here we have Emerson and Thoreau telling us it was too bad those women and children had to die, but that Brown was divine in his motive. Divine! How do you like that?"

"I don't like it worth a damn," said Gunther Roth. "I'm like Ulrich, I'm no slave man. But my back goes up a mite when I read in one of those newspapers that William Lloyd Garrison says that every slaveholder has forfeited his right to life. And that all us others living south of a certain latitude share the blame and that John Brown is a blessed martyr. Who the hell is this Goddamned William Lloyd Garrison anyway? Who gave him the right to brand my calf and tell me who's sainted? Does he pick the Pope, too?"

The day they hanged Brown, so it was reported in Silesia's newspapers, church bells were rung from Boston to Chicago in tribute. And at Albany they fired a hundred-gun salute, the cannons' boom raising ripples across the Mohawk River.

"My God," gasped Ulrich. "I've never heard of any king or minister or chief of state getting a salute with that many guns. I've never heard of a president of the republic being so honored. This maniac who receives messages from God to kill innocents gets a hundred guns! Our country is going to destroy itself with mindless stupidity."

After John Brown, every time a farmer's barn was struck by lightning in Texas and caught fire, it was reported that the abolitionists were trying to burn up the South.

"I don't really know who's silliest," Ulrich said, "our friends or our enemies."

And Elizabeth asked, "Which is which?"

Not much of anybody had time to worry about a bastard kid and a piece of property acquired by a local *empresario* combine. Especially when the kid was a crossbreed between a Mex Gringo whom rumor was now making a traitor and a pumpernickel seen as loose in her morals, and when the property was one of those Spanish land-grant things that most Anglos thought of as not much more than a perpetual nuisance to be liquidated with all possible speed, either under the law or otherwise.

And nobody gave a second thought to an *indio* squaw butchered by Comanches. No matter that her people had pitched in from the start to help the white man against the Lords of the Southern Plains.

"These lazy, sluttish Tonkawa cannibals are a blight on any Christian community," proclaimed Booth Jenkins.

Oscar Schiller was busy, too. There were more stagecoaches running between Bexar and Austin than ever before, mostly full of politicians who wanted to come to the biggest town in Texas.

And speak from my balcony, Ulrich Silesia fumed.

So Oscar was doing a lot of running up and down the cathedral steps and hanging over the cast-iron railings at Mrs. Wolf's Hotel and Cafe, ringing the arrival bell. But now and then he still had thoughts about the other.

Sometimes, when he was on Military Plaza for one reason or another, he saw people watching him from the city hall steps or sometimes from the shaded sidewalk under the awnings of the Miller Dentist Office and Drug Store on Dolorosa.

At first, he gave this little thought. Then he noticed that the person watching was always one of the Jenkins bunch, which included John David, who was now almost six feet tall and one of San Antonio's fancy dressers.

Then Oscar figured out that this clique at the prosecutor's office was maybe concerned that somebody was likely to bring out that

Spanish land-grant at any time, take it to Austin, and challenge the disposition of the Armador Street lot. And who better to do such a thing than Oscar Schiller?

His only intention regarding that transaction was to forget it. And as soon as he could, to get on with a new plan he'd devised to leave this place and go east to see some of that country covered with green Colonel Lee had talked so much about.

No matter. The watching made him nervous after a while, so he began avoiding Military Plaza, which was a little inconvenient when he wanted to ride, because his horse was stabled at one of Gunther Roth's barns at the west end of the plaza.

Maybe the measure of his discomfort at being watched was that when he went to the stable, he detoured around the north of Commerce Street so he could come into the livery from the back side, without setting foot in Military Plaza.

No matter how hard he tried to keep it from his mind, now and then there came a bitter twitch when he thought about the Tonk. It was still hard for him to believe she was dead. But what had been a blinding, savage rage when he'd first realized she was gone had settled into a deep, molten hatred.

His hatred had no finely defined target. At times, when it rumbled near the surface, the heat was directed at one or the other of the Bat Club people. More usually it was general, an anger at the club itself, or sometimes at all Anglos, or all lawyers, or all public officials.

Except for Sam Houston, who, along with Buster Lloyd, was Oscar's strongest connection with a past in which his father had played an important role. And R. E. Lee, who was Oscar's most important sounding board to the future.

Anyway, on one of those afternoons when there were no coaches due to arrive or depart, he walked into Barrio del Sur, avoiding Military Plaza, coming to Armador street from the Camino de Laredo side. There was some kind of urge to see the *casa* again, to stand on the patio and look at the place where his Tonk mother had cooked his tortillas.

The unhinged door had been carried off by somebody. He peered inside and saw that all the furniture had been removed. On the rear patio, everything was the same, except that weeds were now high where the goat or the Tonk had always kept them cut back.

There was no indication that any work had started on tearing down walls and fences and raising a commercial building that would open toward the plaza. Along one wall was a stack of rough lumber, but nothing more.

He turned toward the small alleyway that led alongside the house. And then he saw them, standing in the opening that led to the street. Dubb Shirley, grinning, his pistol butts showing, a broom straw in his mouth. And one of his lanky deputies. And John David Jenkins.

John David was wearing a plug hat, tilted over one eye. In his hand was what appeared to be a walking stick of green willow with a knob at one end. He wore a tight vest, with bright silk embroidery showing designs of roses, under a short coat of tan cotton, plus trousers they would have called riding britches in Virginia, and button shoes with leather, pointed toes, and gray felt uppers. He was altogether an apparition as out of place in west Texas as a polar bear would have been.

Oscar Schiller was caught dumbfounded for an instant, staring, standing stock still, his reaction that of a grown man caught with his finger in the sugar bowl and compounded by the extraordinary vision of John David in his gloriously incongruous get-up.

At that instant, John David stepped forward and swung his stick, and it made a soft little whistle. And then he swung it backhanded, and there was the little whistle again and this time a gasp of pain.

The first slash had knocked off Oscar Schiller's sombrero, and the second cut his cheek and sent his spectacles flying. Dimly, Oscar Schiller saw Dubb Shirley crush the glasses under a boot heel on the patio floor, dimly aware of the marshal grinning savagely, dimly aware of John David's snarling face and the willow stick drawn back again.

He tried to duck, but it caught him across the top of the head, and as he tried to dodge and get to the alley, the skinny deputy grabbed him and Marshal Shirley laughed and shouted, "Get the little whelp bastard! Burn his ass good, John David!"

Then John David was in front of him, the plug hat fallen off, the cane thrown aside, and pummeling Oscar Schiller's face with his fists as the deputy held him.

"You runt bastard," J. D. Jenkins was panting as he struck, time after time, the sound each time like that of a slab of meat slapped on a cutting block. "You best run to Mexico, you four-eyed midget goat turd. You ain't got no Tonkawa whore to stand in front of you now, have you, huh, have you, little fart head?"

Oscar Schiller could see his own blood splattering the silk-embroidered roses on John David's vest.

"Lemme have a little taste of that half-breed piggie," the marshal yelled, and the deputy shoved Oscar forward and as Oscar stumbled, Dubb's massive fat palm slammed across the side of his head and sent him sprawling.

He tried to get his feet under him, and John David kicked him in the groin, once, and then again, with Shirley yelping about flattened gonads. Shirley grabbed the back of his collar and stood him up against the adobe wall of the house, and John David was spitting on him and kicking and cursing him.

The deputy had moved back away from them and was watching, and through the red blood haze, Oscar Schiller saw his look of discomfort and tried to think of the deputy's name, because he had often helped Oscar unload luggage at Mrs. Wolf's and the Menger. He was the only Bat Club member who'd ever said a civil word to Oscar.

And now John David was panting, his arms hanging at his sides, too dried out to spit anymore. Too spent to hit any more.

"We're gonna fix you," he gasped.

"Whoa up, John David," Marshal Shirley laughed. "You gonna scare this poor blind dwarf who ain't got no mama no more."

John David kicked Oscar in the groin, then kicked him a second time, and Dubb Shirley made his same gonads joke again and released Oscar, and Oscar collapsed in a kind of ball, doubled up with his arms holding his belly. John David kicked him in the kidneys.

But Oscar's eyes were open, and although everything was blurred, he watched the marshal retrieve John David's plug hat. As he handed the hat to the younger man, his jacket, incredibly, swung open, and Oscar Schiller saw Dubb Shirley's pistol belt.

In the belt beside the six-shooter holster was a knife, the handle clear and plain to Oscar's view. Green cowhorn! Oscar knew he'd seen that knife at least a hundred times while he watched his Tonk mother cutting a melon or slicing a beefsteak.

For a moment, Oscar tried to rise, but John David kicked him under the ear with one of those fancy button shoes, and he almost lost consciousness, but not quite. He could taste and smell his own blood, and he opened his mouth and three teeth fell to the ground under his face.

Then he began to listen to them. They were in the alleyway that led to the street, and Dubb Shirley was the only one he could see. But he could hear them talk, enough to know what they were planning.

"Your daddy never said do that yet," Dubb Shirley was saying. "Are you sure we want to do it? Is this runt so important? This here was just a little chance we seen for fun when that Mex kid told us he was comin along this way."

"He's that important to me. And Papa won't care," John David said. "We got him this far. Let's be done with tryin to scare him off. Let's do him up right and have it over with."

"It's too damned light now," Dubb said. "I guess we could leave Grover here to watch him and come back after dark and do it, then haul him off downriver. But you gotta talk to your daddy."

There was a lot more. But Oscar Schiller had heard enough to know what was in store. But when he tried to rise, he wasn't able. His insides felt torn away from all their foundations, and any move sent a stab of pain all the way to his heels.

"He moves, bust him with a pistol barrel," he heard John David say. Then Grover was back on the patio, squatting along one wall, and Oscar Schiller lay motionless.

He wanted to lie perfectly still. Maybe, he thought, Grover would think he was dead and leave. It wasn't much of a hope, but it was all he had.

To help him stay motionless, he concentrated on Grover's last name. Oscar had the feeling he'd heard this string-thin man's name somewhere, and it was at least something to keep his mind off the thick blood taste in his mouth and the pain throbbing up his back.

Lying bruised, still bleeding, some of his teeth on the ground, he managed to stay still for over two hours, but he still couldn't remember Grover's name, if he ever knew it.

It took a long, long time for the sun to pass along the western sky and the dusk to come on. Twice Oscar had to relieve his bladder, and he did it lying right there without moving. Grover apparently wasn't aware of this. Once, the deputy went to the privy at the fence corner, and twice he just stood against the rear wall of the house. Oscar figured he'd been at the beer keg in Goshen Steiner's pool hall.

By the time Grover started getting impatient and went to the alleyway and began peering up the street, Oscar Schiller felt he could move. Maybe not too fast, but move anyway.

Then Grover was back, squatting close, so close the rowels on his Spanish spurs looked large as silver dollar cartwheels. Oscar figured that before this was over, he'd likely get some gouges from those, too, before Dubb Shirley finished him. Because by now, he'd decided it was the fat marshal who was Jenkins's hatchet.

"Kid," the deputy said, "I wanted you to know, I ain't too all-fired delighted with any of this here kind of hawg stompin."

Oscar Schiller lay for a moment, trying to decide if he'd heard correctly. Then, without moving his head, he spoke. His words bubbled around the clotted blood in his mouth.

"What's your name?"

Maybe the deputy thought this was a damn fool question for the situation, but there seemed to be something about it that he liked, because he chuckled. Not the savage giggle of Dubb Shirley while John David Jenkins used his fists on Oscar's face, but just a regular, ordinary chuckle.

"Grover. Grover Fulton."

Oscar struggled up to a sitting position, groaning. Grover Fulton didn't help him, but he looked as though he wanted to.

"You're not no longtime Texican, are you?" Oscar said. He found that even a slight movement of his lips hurt his mouth. The thick, salt taste of blood was nauseating. He hoped he wouldn't vomit.

"No. Me and my woman come here from Arkansas two years back to get shed of all this nigger trouble, but we never went far enough, I expect. Are you all right?"

"No," Oscar Schiller gasped, rubbing his sides. "I guess I'll feel even better when your friends get back."

"Yeah, well listen. I'm gonna go watch up the street like I was waitin for them others, and if you can make it, I'd say you orta hit fer that fence back yonder by the outhouse and light outa here."

"What'll happen to you, then, Grover Fulton?"

"They's lots a stories I can make up. They figure I'm thick as a post anyway, so iffen I drop the bucket they gimme, they'll figure it was their own fault givin the bucket to a big dumb ox in the first place. It works ever time."

"Lord, I can see you got a wonderful job."

"Yeah, well listen. I ain't gonna shoot nobody if I see em crawlin over that fence yonder. You understand?"

So as Grover Fulton went to see if his friends were coming through the gloom, Oscar got up and over the privy fence, through the chicken coop of Señora Flores and out into Laredo Street and along that to the old Governor's Palace and beyond that to Soledad and into the back door of Mrs. Wolf's Cafe.

Since he'd been dispossessed and had come to live at Mrs. Wolf's, Oscar Schiller had established no pattern. Ulrich and Elizabeth Silesia were satisfied to allow him to come and go as he pleased, to eat in the cafe kitchen when he liked, to sleep any time he felt the need.

So it wasn't unusual for a few days to pass now and again without their seeing Oscar at all, except when he rang the coach bell. And then without being near enough to see something like blackened eyes and swollen lips.

On the evening of the day he was beaten, he had the Mexican kitchen helpers in Mrs. Wolf's Cafe help him clean his wounds with saltwater and bandage his head. It was painful to walk or to stand on his feet, his kidneys and groin protesting sharply.

The Mexicans slipped some of Ulrich Silesia's precious ice from the taproom and applied a cold compress to Oscar's back. They brought some whiskey from the taproom, too, and Oscar gagged enough of it down to give him a swirling head and a terrible urge to sing.

Heat seemed to work even better than the ice, and they heated flatirons and wrapped them in newspapers, and Oscar lay with these hotpads for hours, waiting for the musk taste of blood to leave his mouth and trying to blow the red clots from his nose and fingering the empty spaces on his gums where teeth had been.

It was Buster Lloyd who finally came looking for him. It was a speech day, with the Calhoun Democrat bunch sending an orator to Silesia's balcony pulpit, so Lloyd and Oscar had planned an outing for riding and turtle shooting downstream, along the San Antonio River.

When Oscar didn't show up at the stable, Lloyd came looking for him, and when he saw the damage to Oscar's face, he swore a vile and mighty oath.

This was the beginning of the long and determined attempt by the Silesias and Buster Lloyd to find out what had happened and the equally determined and stubborn resistance of Oscar Schiller to giving any details whatsoever.

Everybody had their own ideas, of course, and each of these ideas included one or more villains from the Bat Club, with Booth Jenkins most popular among the suspects. When Buster Lloyd said he couldn't picture Booth Jenkins doing such work with his hands, Elizabeth said probably not, but he could always be blamed as the power behind the one who did.

At which point somebody would say maybe Judge Belcher ought to be considered for the role. But Ulrich said he figured the judge was an old tag-along who added nothing but the name of his office to the ring of actual miscreants.

As all the others guessed and fumed, Oscar quietly went about his coach-watching duties. But they all noted that after the beating, he no longer went across the river to hustle baggage for any of Joe Menger's guests at his hotel on Alamo Plaza.

They started unraveling the mystery through the time-honored way, waiting and listening, and within a week, Buster Lloyd saw Deputy Grover Fulton catch Jesus Montez in a doorway of Hugo Schmeltzer's Wholesale Store and bend down to talk vehemently to the boy. Ten minutes later, Buster Lloyd was holding that same Jesus Montez and asking questions just as vehemently.

"I don't know, Señor Buster," said Jesus. "He just say if Kid Frito my amigo, I best tell him stay out of Barrio del Sur."

"Why? Why should he stay out of there? *Por que?*"

"Who knows?" Jesus Montez shrugged elaborately. "*Quien sabe?*"

But when she heard that one of Shirley's deputies knew there was danger for Oscar Schiller in Barrio del Sur, or anywhere else for that matter, Elizabeth Silesia said she knew why. The Bat Club bunch knew what was happening because they were the ones initiating everything, she said, and she grabbed her hat, announcing she was off to city hall.

Ulrich Silesia sprang into headlong motion. He barred his wife's way, trying to explain the obvious. That the worst possible thing they could do was complain to the very people who were basically at the bottom of Oscar Schiller's problem in the very place where on her last visit she had upbraided Judge Belcher.

But after twenty minutes of discussion, much of which could be heard in the street below, Ulrich agreed to make a case for assault and battery without naming any suspected person, but with a demand for the law to look for somebody.

Walking to Military Plaza and the city hall/courthouse, Ulrich Silesia muttered about the hopeless situation he faced. Marshal Shirley took care of arrests for petty crimes around the city, but everybody understood his main function was to enforce the land deals of the *empresarios* around Bexar and collect taxes and rents.

For serious things, like horse stealing, cattle rustling and murder, the Vigilance Committee put on their black suits, took the culprit in hand for long enough to explain how he had disrupted the peace and dignity of the great state of Texas, and hanged him.

The serious pistol fighters—and San Antonio had more than its share—generally killed only one another, and the Vigilance Committee pretty much ignored them unless some of their shooting resulted in injury to innocent bystanders, in which case the shooters got the same treatment as horse thieves.

Any matter dealing with gunmen was left entirely alone by Dubb Shirley and his clutch of deputies. Disrupting *pistolero* activities could be dangerous.

Surprisingly, Booth Jenkins was nicer than Ulrich had ever found him.

"I understand. I've had to raise a boy, too," he said, coming around his desk and placing an arm around Silesia's shoulders. "Boys will be boys. We can't really go chasing around after every young-un who gets involved in one of these schoolyard fistfights. It usually looks worse than it is."

"This was a serious beating," Ulrich said, "and my wife is concerned for his safety."

"I'll mention to Marshal Shirley that he should keep his eye open," Jenkins said, now having expertly guided Silesia to the door and through it. "Thank you for coming by, Silesia."

And before Silesia could say anything else, there was Dubb Shirley beside him, nudging him toward the stairway, and the marshal wasn't smiling. Ulrich thought that the marshal's fat face looked particularly evil, with its huge, loose lower lip and those tiny little eyes glinting in their puffy folds.

"Let's go along outa here, now, Silesia," Shirley muttered, and his fingers on Ulrich's arm were surprisingly strong. "You know that little half-breed runt would be better off if he went on back up there to New Braunfels, where his old lady come from. You know that, don't you?"

Ulrich Silesia jerked his arm free of Shirley's grasp and started to respond in a heat of temper, but he couldn't think of anything to say.

Oscar Schiller's face had lost most of the traces of his beating by then, and his back had stopped hurting each time he lay too long in one position. There had been blood in his urine for almost a week, but that had stopped. His jaw still ached, but at least the new eye spectacles Frederick Hausmann had given him didn't hurt his face each time he put them on.

After Ulrich Silesia's trip to the prosecutor's office, Buster Lloyd went into Oscar's room late one night after Oscar had blown out his candle and in the dark explained what had happened, and when Oscar asked why anybody bothered, Lloyd said their friends wanted to bring somebody to justice for that assault on the Armador Street patio.

"They won't do nothin," Oscar said, and later Lloyd would report that Oscar's voice had sounded grim and unlike a kid's, coming out of the darkness. "They know who did it, but they won't do anything to theirselves, will they?"

"You've never told anybody who did it," said Buster Lloyd. "Will you tell me now?"

"The same ones who killed my Tonk mother," Oscar said.

Even though he'd suspected all along who the culprits had been, in general, it was a shock to hear it stated so firmly, so matter of factly. For a long time, Lloyd sat on the edge of Oscar's bunk, and the only sound in the room was of their breathing.

"Well, maybe we can do something about it," Lloyd finally said.

"You may as well leave it be. And I'm sleepy now," Oscar Schiller said, and Lloyd felt him turn on his bunk and pull a blanket over his head. Then muffled, from beneath the blanket, Oscar said, "It'll be took care of in good time."

When Buster Lloyd reported all this upstairs, Elizabeth Silesia asked what that meant, that it would be taken care of in good time.

"I truly don't know," Buster said. "Brought up like he was, by that Tonk, he's just like an Indian his ownself. I can't figure out what's in his head."

"He sounds a little like one of these hellfire preachers," Ulrich said. "Sinners get their just desserts through all eternity."

"I can't quite see Oscar being satisfied with retribution in some other world," said Elizabeth. "In fact, I can't quite see him even believing there is such a thing as another world, much less a place where a score is kept on foul deeds so revenge can be taken for them, one by one."

"I never coulda said it like that," said Lloyd, "but if I could have, I would."

"And it doesn't make me too happy. Maybe we should think about sending him back to New Braunfels or Fredericksburg."

"I think maybe he's gotten too old to be shuttled around like one of those packages he's always unloading from the stagecoach," said Ulrich. "We make the mistake here of still thinking of him as a young child. He's not very big, but he's no child anymore, and he's probably old beyond his years, at that."

"That's what I'd say, too," Lloyd said.

Chapter Twenty-two

"And now it's all coming undone," Elizabeth Silesia said.

It was true. The political parties had held their conventions, had split and shattered and split again, and the country was looking at four candidates for the office of president. And everyone was talking secession.

At about this time, a couple of visitors came up from Brownsville, both respected men in their communities, both strong Unionists. They always stayed at Mrs. Wolf's Hotel and had often attended sessions of Elizabeth's evening salon, with Colonel Lee as a guest.

Oscar Schiller was always in attendance at these meetings. He understood only a small part of what was said, but there was something compelling about it. These were not gatherings where you'd see such people as Buster Lloyd or Gunther Roth or any of the book-chitchat crowd of ladies. These sessions were always serious, with a lot of frowning, Oscar noticed, and a feeling that there were things being discussed that were confidential or even secret.

Yet Lee himself had once said that he minded not at all having the young man with the thick glasses and the strange necklace hear his conversations. This was a point of great pride for Oscar.

So on this visit of the two men Oscar always called the Brownsville gentlemen, Oscar came into the Silesia parlor for the first time since that savage beating he'd taken. Elizabeth Silesia looked at him closely, trying to make it appear that she was not doing so. The only signature of that violent incident was a little white scar beside Oscar's eye, and it was pretty much hidden by the rim of his spectacles.

Well, his nose was not the same as it had been. Now there was a definite slant to the right, and the left nostril was larger than the right.

Oscar Schiller settled into his usual position on the floor, beside and somewhat behind a small marble-top table with a vase and huge fern. From here he could peer out between the long green tendrils like a glassy-eyed frog.

The conversation was quiet and rather short. Toward the end, one of the Brownsville men abruptly asked Lee what he intended to do, under the assumption that the Union would be divided. He expressed at the same time a strong appeal for Lee to remain with the federal army.

For the first time Oscar had ever seen, Lee became rather agitated, rose, and paced back and forth, his face working with emotion. Finally he stopped pacing and said something Oscar remembered for a long time.

"Mr. Ellis, I dread seeing our country torn asunder. Secession is a complete and utter calamity that we are brought to because of fault on both sides. Our situation is somewhere between anarchy and civil war. I love the army, and America is my country."

He paused for a moment and drew a deep breath and looked up at the ceiling, and watching him, Oscar was holding his breath. It was that kind of moment.

"Virginia delegates are now sitting in a peace conference with the members of the American government, trying to find a peaceful compromise. I pray to God for their success," Lee said. "For myself, I have sworn an oath of allegiance to the United States, and I have honored it. It is sacred to me. But if the final test comes, I could never draw my sword against my Virginia neighbors.

"I have been taught from childhood that my first allegiance is to the older sovereignty. I must remain loyal to Virginia, and if it comes to that, I will become a farmer and grow my corn. And will draw my sword only to defend an attack on the Old Dominion."

Then Lee explained that he had to go, for he was riding early the next day to join a squadron of his regiment at Fort Mason.

For a long time after Lee left, Oscar Schiller remained squatting behind his fern. And he heard Elizabeth say, "Well, if you come to think about it, there was indeed a Virginia almost 150 years before there was a United States of America."

And the day came when Ulrich Silesia said, "Remember what Houston said? The South Carolina Calhoun radicals don't care that Virginians might work out a compromise. Damn their eyes!"

"You got plenty of Texas Calhoun Democrats, too," said Gunther Roth. "They may not call themselves such, but they be."

"And not all secession people own slaves," Jerome Falsworth said. "Most of them don't, in fact. A lot of people just plain don't like the Yankee Union tellin em what to do."

It was true. You needed to walk only ten feet along any street outside the Mexican barrios to find it was the same.

"We joined their Union," people said, "and what did we get? Customs officers at Galveston to collect duties for the central government, all our New Mexico territory and Santa Fe took away from us, but damned little protection from Mexicans and Comanches along the escarpment or along our stagecoach lines and cattle trails. To hell with it. It wasn't nothin but a confederation anyway. We joined, and now we aim to unjoin!"

"Such statements leave out a lot of things," Frederick Hausmann said. "We got paid for that New Mexican land. They sent as much army here as they had to send. And like Houston said, anybody is empty headed who thinks them northern people are just going to say go ahead and leave, it's voluntary."

There were telegraph lines from east Texas to New Orleans, as there had been since the California gold rush. Now there was a line to west Texas, too, so news from the rest of the country could come to Main Plaza almost as it was happening in places like the national capital or Virginia or Charleston.

Ulrich Silesia would have preferred the old system of getting news that was six weeks old from his papers and magazines, because that way you didn't have to worry so much about what was going to happen because sometimes it already had.

Just as everybody had suspected, as soon as Lincoln's election was assured, South Carolina passed an ordinance of secession. That was in December. Most people in San Antonio heard about this on Christmas Eve.

A lot of folks went a little crazy with joy, so they said. There were a lot of firecrackers going off, which is one way people celebrated Christmas, especially people who'd come from places like the Carolinas or Georgia. But now, nobody knew if all the banging and popping and sparkle and stink of black powder was in celebration of Yuletide or of South Carolina's raising the war hatchet.

And the big question was, What do we do now?

Well, by one of those crazy quirks of history, Sam Houston had been elected governor of Texas despite his being called a traitor for his anti-slavery stand. He'd stumped the state, and folks voted for him because he was still the hero of San Jacinto.

But now, when he said secession was a terrible thing, everybody in the legislature ignored him and called a convention to consider pulling out of the Union.

People were running up and down the streets, even in daylight, firing off handguns and shouting about the dirty Yankees. Or about going back to Republic of Texas days. Or about making a friendship pact with the English.

Not all of these people were drunk, either.

There was a virtual parade of speakers on Ulrich Silesia's balcony. Only a few of these were calling for moderation, and they were hissed and tomatoes were thrown at them.

After the first of the year, there was a parade of states following the lead of South Carolina. Mississippi, Florida, Alabama, Georgia, Louisiana.

"My God, the Virginians are still trying to talk a compromise to avoid war," Ulrich Silesia said. "May destiny be with them!"

They were organizing Texas militia units. Some of the leaders were former Rangers with a lot of experience fighting Mexicans. Militiamen wore a red patch on their sleeves. They paraded in the streets of San Antonio and stood in formation along Soledad Street in front of the army depot.

The American soldiers sat inside their compound and talked with the Texas militiamen in the street. It wasn't a very hostile situation. Everybody said that there'd be a little war, just for appearances, and that that would be the end of it and that the Union would go their way and the brand-new Confederate States of America would go theirs.

Then, in February, the Texas convention voted an ordinance of secession, and another wild party broke out on San Antonio's streets. Mexican citizens watched from a distance. As much distance as they could find. Some of the Germans did the same. But a few of the friends of Ulrich Silesia joined the rebels, and most of the Anglos and Celts were whooping it up for the Confederacy.

You couldn't allow a foreign government to have troops and weapons right in your midst, of course, so the Texas militia moved into the American army's installations and held a little talk with the man in command of all U.S. forces in Texas, a man named Miegs or Twiggs or some such thing, and decided the soldiers could march to Indianola and take ships out of Texas. It was all right, the militia said, if they took their individual weapons with them. Which was good, because the Comanches had decided it was time to start some serious raiding again, and they might run into a war party on the long walk south.

All military stores, like artillery and ammunition, livestock, and vehicles were seized for the Confederacy and put in a park at the Alamo and guarded by men with those little red patches on their sleeves.

"Thank God nobody started shooting," Silesia said, after watching the whole takeover of Union stores and weapons. "Maybe there's a chance. Just maybe the Virginians will work something out."

Oscar Schiller was trying to find out what he could about Robert E. Lee. He was at the telegraph office each morning, the Silesias noticed.

"It's the first time he's really been out of the hotel since he took that beating in Armador Street," Elizabeth said.

And finally the operator told him Lee had orders from the army to report to Washington. He'd be coming from Fort Mason to San Antonio in a few days on his way to the coast. He needed to pick up some of the personal belongings he'd left at his old Bexar quarters.

Lee came in an army ambulance, mule drawn, and the day it approached Bexar from the north along the road from Austin, Oscar Schiller was in the bell tower of the San Fernando Cathedral. There was a sharp wind that afternoon, and even though there was a harsh February sun, it was cold in the high perch where Oscar waited.

He saw the plume of dust, and then Jesus Montez, who was there because it was said he had eyes like a red-tail hawk, announced that it appeared to be an army ambulance like Gringo officers were always riding around in. Taking that as proof enough, they ran down into Main Plaza.

Arriving well before the army vehicle, Oscar dispatched Jesus into Mrs. Wolf's to alert the Silesias that Lee was about to arrive. Then he waited under the porch awning, a little apprehensive that there were so many men with red sleeve patches in the plaza. But apparently the Texas militiamen were there by chance rather than design.

In that moment, Oscar Schiller began for the first time to appreciate what a confusion of errors and miscalculations a revolution or civil war can bring. Here were two agencies who were his friends — the Texans, who would shield the state from invasion by whomever; and Lee, who was a great hero to Oscar, and whose mission was to protect the entire country, Texas included until now.

Suddenly, because of something that had happened hundreds of miles away, these two had opposing objectives rather than complimentary ones. They were, in fact, possibly deadly enemies to one another.

Booth Jenkins had been named the Confederate state's local commissioner until elections could be held for such positions as delegates to the congress at Montgomery, Alabama. But Buster Lloyd was a captain who commanded a company in the militia! For God's sake, Oscar thought. Where am I supposed to stand?

The ambulance first came into view as it crossed the Commerce Street bridge and came on toward Mrs. Wolf's. There were no escort riders with it. The driver reined his team in close to the sidewalk in front of the double doors that led into the lobby and cafe.

As Lee stepped out, in full uniform excepting saber, Elizabeth Silesia ran out onto the sidewalk to greet him, and Oscar Schiller moved without any instructions to the vehicle and pulled out two leather traveling bags.

He was delighted to see Lee in uniform, the dark-blue coat making the highly polished brass buttons in two rows shine like newly minted double eagles down Lee's breast. Oscar obviously expected a happy greeting from the officer and, carrying his bags onto the sidewalk, was waiting for it.

But no happy greeting came. Lee's face was stern, and he was perplexed as he looked around at the crowd of Texas militia. It seemed that there was no one else on the street but these civilian soldiers. And now that they had seen who was in the ambulance, the militiamen moved close around it and the team of mules, and the two soldiers on the box looked very nervous.

Lee took Elizabeth Silesia's hand and nodded briefly in Oscar's general direction, but after only a few words he asked, "Who are these men?"

"They're Ben McCullock's militia troops," she said. "This morning, General Twiggs surrendered all stores and units to Texas. All United States troops are prisoners of war."

This stunned Lee. By then Ulrich Silesia had arrived, along with a few of Lee's other San Antonio friends, including two who were longtime secessionists. They guided him into the hotel, Oscar Schiller bringing up the rear with the bags and upset beyond any reckoning, because when Elizabeth Silesia had said to Lee that they were prisoners of war, Oscar had seen tears in Lee's eyes.

But if Oscar was left out at first, once Lee had a room and had moved up to it, all the others left him to himself, and Oscar was there alone, still holding the bags.

"Come in, come in. I'm glad to have a friend to talk with."

As was almost always the case, Oscar Schiller was close-mouthed about the short time they were alone in Lee's room. The only thing he ever mentioned was that Colonel Lee had said he was still an officer in the United States Army and would continue to be such until he saw what Virginia would do.

"I said he ort to touch my necklace for luck," Oscar said. He never told if Lee touched the pendent finger as he once had.

In less than an hour, Lee appeared in the lobby in civilian clothes, and there he learned that his ambulance and the mules had been commandeered and were already in the militia's wagon park across the river in Alamo Plaza, his drivers marched away to the army depot and placed with the other American soldiers making ready to march to the Gulf.

Then with Oscar Schiller and Ulrich Silesia beside him, Lee went to city hall to ask the Confederate commissioner to give him proper transport to the Gulf so he might fulfill his orders and return to Washington.

"It was ghastly, a man like Lee standing before the likes of Booth Jenkins and pleading a case," Silesia said. "Of course, Jenkins said Lee was like the others, a prisoner of war.

"But he told Lee that if he would resign his commission and take an oath stating his loyalty to the Confederate States of America, he would be given a general's commission and all the privileges of that rank in going about his business.

"It was difficult to say who was more furious, Lee or Oscar," said Ulrich with a small laugh. "That cretin trying to bribe a man like Lee. When we walked out, Dubb Shirley slid along behind Oscar like a Gila monster."

"Yes," said Elizabeth. "Dubb Shirley the Gila monster. Very apt, my dear."

"And he was wheezing practically in Oscar's ear that Lee was not going to be exchanged or allowed to leave but thrown into the pen at Huntsville because he's a dangerous Yankee who was plotting the destruction of Texas all the time he served here."

"The slimy pig!"

"And I began to realize something," said Ulrich. "Oscar had heard these things, or worse, from Shirley before. Yet he was so angry, it was as though he was hearing them for the first time. And I understood. It wasn't the current obscenity that infuriated him. It was the memory of the older abuses that Oscar now calls up whenever any of that Bat Club crowd does anything untoward."

"Of course," she said, a little impatiently. "They stole his property. They brutalized him, starting with that bully schoolboy and his vicious dog, and that horrible beating he took just recently. And before that, they smeared the honorable name of his father. Made a lewd slander about his German mother at every opportunity. And we're sure they killed his Tonkawa mother, and what's more important, Oscar believes they did. So naturally, when anything happens, his mind jumps back to those crimes."

"And all along the line, they've made a public joke of his physical misfortunes. The weak eyes, the stunted stature."

"And point out that he's a bastard!"

"So it doesn't matter what they do, does it? All of it only serves to remind him of the original reasons he despised them in the first place," Ulrich said.

"And they never fail to continue turning up ways to infuriate him. But I doubt seriously that they worry too much about upsetting a very young man they consider to be a crippled dwarf," Elizabeth said. "We can only be thankful that all the men at Austin running the government are not such dreadful, arrogant monsters."

Well, Oscar soon found that he was not Lee's only admirer in

Bexar. With the exception of Bat Club members, who seemed to be programmed to follow the Jenkins lead, most people in San Antonio were helpful, and happy to be.

Seeing that taking his belongings out might create problems, Lee asked that someone take his considerable furniture in hand and ship it later, and half-a-dozen men came forward to do this.

Although he was in a hurry to leave, Lee would not go until he'd made a formal farewell to many friends. Now that his United States Army mount was no longer available, he used a horse borrowed from Gunther Roth's livery stable, where they would accept no pay, and Oscar accompanied him about town, riding Blacky.

Lee at one point complimented Oscar's saddle, and those who were near said it was the only time they'd ever seen Oscar blush and duck his head beneath the wide slant of his sombrero brim to hide his self-conscious grin.

So even though Lee received no official help in leaving, nobody tried to stop him. In fact, Ben McCullock himself issued an unequivocal written field order to his troops stating that no one was to harass or forestall Colonel Lee.

On the final morning, before mounting his enclosed coach, which had been provided by Gunther Roth and included two drivers and three outriders, Lee stood for the last time in the library-table room. And when he finished his goodbye, it was Oscar Schiller's eyes that had a film of moisture.

"Oh yes," said Ulrich Silesia. "Every misfortune and embarrassment Lee had in Texas, Oscar put on the Bat Club bunch. Everything, including the man's terrible decision about how he would respond to war, even that, Oscar blamed on the Bat Club. They had no part in that, but no matter. To Oscar, they were the source of all evil in matters of heartbreak for those people he loved."

"My friends," Lee had said, once more in uniform, complete with saber, "if Virginia stands by the old Union, so will I. Though I do not believe in secession as a constitutional right or that there is sufficient cause now for revolution, if Virginia secedes, then I will follow my native state. I know many of you feel very differently, but I can't help it. These are principles I must follow."

"It was a powerful goodbye," said Elizabeth.

"Yes, and then Oscar spent the next week pacing through the kitchen and along the porch, so long as somebody wasn't making a speech. Finally, when we heard Lee was safe at Indianola and away on some ship bound for the East, he went to bed and slept for two days."

"And rose quietly, but angry," she said.

"Then everything changed."

"Yes. Everything changed. Again."

In the harbor of Charleston, South Carolina, all hopes of peaceful solution disappeared on what Elizabeth Silesia later would call the darkest day in southern history. Forces of the new Confederate States of America fired on Fort Sumter when a Union vessel was attempting to resupply the federal garrison there.

Naturally, Lincoln called for volunteers to suppress the rebellion. Southerners logically assumed that to get to the rebels, the federal army would have to invade the southern states, and hence Virginia and North Carolina bowed their backs and seceded, along with Arkansas.

This put a new complexion on everything. Booth Jenkins had taken to making a daily patriotic speech from Ulrich's porch balcony, urging men to join up for a glorious fight against the villainous Yankees.

Beside him always stood his most cherished recruit, John David, in some kind of uniform featuring a plumed hat that might have been copied from a portrait of Santa Anna, cascades of gold falling from the point of each shoulder, knee-high cavalry boots. and a sword with a bejeweled hilt that could have been brother to the one Herr Meuller had given the Comanches years before as part of that famous peace treaty.

And behind the two of them stood the man who apparently was growing more and more powerful, the pudgy marshal Dubb Shirley, who was no longer being taken as a fat joke, but rather as a man it was best to stay on the good side of. And now, quite openly, Shirley wore in his pistol belt the knife with the green cowhorn handle.

Buster Lloyd said he saw Oscar Schiller watching a couple of these performances, standing far away along the porch, hidden in one of the full-length French windows that looked out onto Main Plaza. He said the glare in Oscar's pale eyes was almost a heat to be felt, like holding your hand close to a cheery red branding iron just out of the fire.

"He hates anyone, I still think, who makes Robert Lee and men who have similar opinions the wicked ones in this play," said Elizabeth Silesia.

"I don't think so," said Lloyd. "It's not Lee. It's not politics. It's that knife. Every time he sees it, he's reminded of everything that's happened."

"Can you imagine anyone like that pig?" asked Elizabeth. "Displaying the thing right out there for everyone to see. Everybody in town knows where that knife came from. Advertising what he did to that poor Tonkawa woman."

"Sure," said Lloyd. "He's proud of it."

"Of course," Ulrich said. "The ultimate bullies. John David Jenkins and Dubb Shirley. What a pair. Proud of victories the victim can't resist. Never having fought anyone who could hit back."

"Someday, they'll meet somebody who can," said Lloyd.

"I fervently pray I will live to see that day," Elizabeth said.

After one of Booth Jenkins's most violent speeches from the porch balcony at Mrs. Wolf's, condemning all Unionists and fence-sitters as traitors to Texas liberty, Ulrich Silesia found Marshal Dubb Shirley in the kitchen of the cafe, looking at pots and pans, opening oven doors, running his fingers over various pieces of china, and generally acting for all the world like an army surgeon inspecting a troop mess.

"I beg your pardon, marshal," Ulrich said. "Perhaps I could help. For what are you looking?"

"Oh, I expect you'll help a lot by keeping all this stuff clean and in good trim," Shirley said, and he laughed and moved toward the door. Oscar Schiller had come into the far end of the room and was standing with the two Mexican employees.

"We always keep our kitchen clean," Ulrich said, and his voice shook a little from obvious nervousness. Which wasn't helped any by Shirley's display of weapons as he elaborately pulled back his coat so that the butt of his revolver was revealed.

"You just better do," said Shirley. He was grinning, and in the heat from the kitchen stoves, he was sweating, and drops of clear liquid hung under the bulb of his nose for an instant before falling. "Because right quick now, we'll come in here and confiscate this place on account of you bein one a these disloyal pumpernickels with the Union itch in your britches. Us loyal Texicans gonna start takin everything away from you traitors to Texas liberty."

"What are you talking about?" Silesia said. He was finding it difficult to breathe, maybe because he was aware that the Bat Club bunch could do this and he would have little recourse. "We're Texans, too, for God's sake. We stand with the will of the people."

"Oh, you make a real nice speech," Shirley said. "You pumpernickels are all such nice talkers, ain't you? Well, you're about to. . . ."

Whatever he was going to say went unheard, because in that instant there was a shriek, and a large porcelain pitcher flew across the kitchen and shattered against a row of cast-iron pans hanging from wall hooks. The white shards showered Dubb Shirley's back and neck and bounced off the brim of his hat as he ducked and half drew his pistol.

"Get out, get out, you slimy pig," Elizabeth Silesia screamed, reaching for more crockery as she came further into the kitchen from the dining-room doorway. "Go away and leave us alone! Go away, you murdering swine! Go back and wallow with your friends in all that Bat muck!"

By then, Ulrich had her in his arms, but she was struggling to get her hands free.

"Help me, help me," Ulrich called, and the two Mexicans ran across the room and tried to find a handhold, which wasn't easy, because Elizabeth Silesia was thrashing and grasping for something to throw and cursing the marshal now with the language of a wagon yard.

Oscar Schiller stood rooted to his spot near the outside door, and Dubb Shirley went within a few feet of him on his way to the alley doorway. The marshal was giggling.

"We ain't forgot you, either, you four-eyed dwarf bastard," he wheezed. "Ole John David gonna have his self a big chunk of your hide to pin on his wall."

Oscar Schiller still waited, unmoving, watching Ulrich Silesia and the two Mexicans get Elizabeth under control and out into the hallway, where the stairs led to the rooms above. She was sobbing now, uncontrollably.

Outside, he could hear the people celebrating Jenkins's speech still, with shouting and some singing and a few pistol shots into the air. In a little while, the local marching band started playing, missing some of its German members, but not all. A parade was being organized.

There was elation now, because word had come that Texas troops had marched north into the Indian Territory and captured three federal forts there. Somebody was already building a rack of wood in the middle of Alamo Plaza for a bonfire.

More men mounted the back stairs of Mrs. Wolf's to appear before the cheering, progressively drunker multitude in Main Plaza and shout the slogans that brought cheers and the popping of pistols. They were even chanting, "Remember the Alamo," and there were a great many people, much older people, at the fringes of the crowd, who felt a chill at that cry. When they first heard it they had been young and sure of what Texas liberty meant. Now, they were not so sure.

But one of those rushing up Mrs. Wolf's stairs was not an orator. Dr. Edwin Luther had been summoned when Elizabeth Silesia finally collapsed and fainted and lay white and motionless on the bed, hardly breathing. The day wore down to night, and it was long after sundown before the doctor left.

Having been in the library room all the while, unsure of what to do, ignored by everyone as they hurried in and out of the bedroom with hot towels and pitchers of drinking water, Oscar heard the doctor say something about a stroke as he was leaving. What was a stroke? Sensing that it was a serious thing brought on by Dubb Shirley's arrogance, Oscar stomped down to his room to brood in the dark.

Finally, he collected a few things, went upstairs to Buster Lloyd's room, found it dark, stayed a moment, then went downstairs and into the darkening streets and toward the Roths' stable, where he kept his roan.

The things he had selected to carry from the hotel were very heavy.

When Buster Lloyd returned to his room, he found that a pair of his Colt revolvers had been stolen. For a moment Lloyd stood in the darkness, and he recalled earlier in the evening having seen Oscar Schiller standing in a corner with a forlorn expression while everyone ran in and out of Elizabeth Silesia's bedroom.

He ran downstairs, buckling on his remaining pair of six-shooters as he went.

He found Oscar Schiller's room empty, and he quickly checked for the Paco Salazar revolvers in their usual place. They were gone. Then he saw the empty peg on the wall where the fancy bridle normally hung. Oscar always left the saddle at the livery, but he always brought the bridle to his room. It wasn't there now.

Lloyd made his way to the west side of Military Plaza and Gunther Roth's livery. He ran most of the way, reminded once again that nothing is more awkward than trying to run in a holster with a heavy revolver on each hip. There were still a few drunken celebrants on the street, and a band continued a discordant playing somewhere.

In the stable, there was a lighted whale-oil lantern in the middle of the barn, and by its flickering yellow light Lloyd saw Oscar Schiller tightening the cinch on the blue roan. Oscar looked up, startled, his eyes wide behind thick glasses.

"You take two of my pistols?" Lloyd asked. He had no idea why he was speaking in hushed tones, almost a whisper. Oscar replied in kind.

"I borrowed a pair of .44s," he said. "I planned to get them back to you before morning."

He was wearing the Paco Salazar revolvers in holsters at his waist, and they looked gigantic on his slight frame. A belt with Lloyd's two guns was hung on the saddle horn.

"What are you about, this late at night, prowlin around here with four loaded cannons?"

"I aim to pay some old debts," Oscar said quietly.

Buster Lloyd and Oscar Schiller stood silently in the dim lantern light, staring into one another's eyes for a long moment. Lloyd took off his hat and scratched his head.

"Well, maybe you better take me along," he said.

"If you don't get some idea about changin my mind."

"No. I expect maybe I feel like maybe I owe something to the same people you do."

"You're welcome to come."

Chapter Twenty-three

The men who organized it hadn't called it anything at first. It was just a group of land speculators who were also lawyers, and they joined together so that they might coordinate with one another in skinning land-hungry immigrants.

As San Antonio grew, a good many men who were members of the lawyer and land *empresario* clan became politicians with offices or bases of operation in the city hall, which came to be called the Bat Cave because of the hairy little creatures who roosted upside down in the attic as aforementioned.

It was only a matter of time before somebody like Booth Jenkins brought this distinctive name and the lawyer and land-grabber group into a formally organized outfit called a fraternal order.

There were a great many such organizations. And each was established in an attempt to copy the oldest, best known, and most powerful of the fraternal orders, the granddaddy of all men's clubs, the Freemasons. Each organization had its own objectives and secret handshakes and blood oaths and other such things, which men who enjoyed fraternal orders always seemed to believe were essential.

They drew up a charter, which was secret, of course, but the essentials of it had to do with the club's furtherance of Texas freedom, which meant freedom from participation by such people as Catholics, Mexicans, blacks, and other "foreigners," which had to mean Germans.

That pretty much narrowed it down to Anglos, which all the lawyers and most of the land speculators were anyway, as were the politicians. The club showed a definite lack of interest in issuing invitations to such people as Jerome Falsworth and Randall Reed, or to others in the cattle or hide business, because these Celtic people, like the martyr Davy Crockett, were famous for not holding still while somebody told them what to think. And telling people what to think seemed to be a major chapter in the Bats' charter.

But not all the Anglos in politics were a part of the Bat Club either. When Jenkins started calling meetings in city hall, county and city men who were not members raised such a stink about that, the Bats had to find another roost.

The idea behind all of this was to get land, by fair means or foul, and to control county and state elective offices in Bexar. In the legal government, the Bats were a strong force, but they didn't make much headway in another important place, the Vigilance Committee.

As already noted, the members of this committee were not elected by anyone, but when their leaders observed what was obviously a men-ace to the public dignity, they could put a lot of armed men on the street. These were not ruffians but respected and very substantial citi-zens, so the Rangers or local lawmen or the militia never tried to inter-fere with them.

"Hell," said Gunther Roth. "A lot of the officers in the militia and some of the past Ranger captains are the best vigilantes we got on the committee."

The Bats were doing quite well when you consider that Bexar probably had more Germans than Anglos. The Bats had a municipal judge, a circuit court prosecuting attorney, and the city police force, as it were.

Booth Jenkins leased an old stable west of Military Plaza, on the far side of San Pedro Creek, and spent a lot of somebody's money sprucing up the inside.

The stable was a rectangular structure, sixty-five by thirty feet, approximately. One end was adobe, since the structure was started as a house for some long-gone *alcalde*.

The building had been extended with rough-cut cypress logs to make a stable some time in the distant past. The whole thing was roofed with thatch, an indication of how old it was, and although they had talked about getting good tile on the roof, the thatch remained in place.

There were small windows along each long side and two doors, wide enough for horses to pass through easily, at either end. Along one wall inside, stalls had been left to form little tête-à-tête booths.

Women were never brought into the clubroom, but the cubicles served for private plotting or perhaps a closed game of bluff. A platform was built in one cubicle, where three or four Mexican musicians could play for everyone's pleasure.

At the back, where the old stalls took up one side of the room, there was a bar or counter and a backbar with bottles of various spirits and all the equipment for serving food and for cooking on a big cast-iron stove and an earthen oven, which was just outside the door in the alley. It seemed that a major reason for all Bat gatherings was to eat and drink.

The remaining space was covered with tables and a few horsehair couches and chairs. It had the atmosphere of a deep cave because it was so dark and gloomy. This effect was produced by all the black cheesecloth.

The cheesecloth had happened by accident. Early on, some of the members complained about scorpions and bugs and dirt falling into their drinks and frijoles or onto their heads, so they dyed a bolt of cheesecloth black, in keeping with the bat idea, and hung it below the thatch to form a droopy ceiling.

Many of the members began to think that the cheesecloth, undulating gently in whatever currents of air happened to be moving in the place, produced a mood of deep darkness and secrecy, so cheesecloth had been hung in various places around the room, creating billows of blackness.

The windows were curtained in black cheesecloth. The ceiling posts down the center of the room were wrapped in black cheesecloth. The walls of the stalls and the front of the bar were festooned with black cheesecloth.

They had created half partitions with cheesecloth hung from the ceiling to within a few feet of the floor. This gave an impression of many rooms in the long hall. But you could see through the walls. In fact, you could walk through them, leaving the cheesecloth swinging gently.

There were members of the Bat Club who found this rather sophisticated. Those who felt thusly, you would suspect, had once been impressed by hanging strands of beads in interior doorways of New Orleans or Natchez whorehouses.

This black, undulating cave gave a sense of the utmost intimacy and intrigue, of a true bat cave cut off from all who were not initiates, unknown to any who could not give the secret handshake, beyond the reach of anyone not of the blood oath.

This strange place was about to be named the William Barret Travis Chapter of the Bat Club of Texas. This name would have been apt, because not only was Travis a local hero and martyr, commander of the fight at the Alamo, but he had also been a lawyer and a land speculator. For some reason, the name never caught on, so it was just called the Bat Club.

Other than a few Mexicans hired for music, special clean-up, and cooking occasions, the Club's only employee was Grover Fulton, who had been taken off Dubb Shirley's city police force and made manager and bartender and chief cook of the club.

The reason for this demotion, of course, was that Grover had shown an ignorance of the required urgency in complying with instructions given by his betters. As example, the day when J. D. Jenkins had returned to the house on Armador Street, expecting to find a battered victim helpless to resist the final blow, but finding only an empty patio.

Grover had a pretty good job, with always plenty to eat and drink at hand and the prospect of lying late in bed with his wife in the home they'd made in the hay shed across the alley from the Bat Club. Almost nobody ever came in for a jolt of mescal or a stein of German beer until after noon.

Grover Fulton had not missed the irony that here among the Bat Clubbers, Mexican and German beverages were popular, despite members' loud and frequent disparagement of both Mexicans and Germans. And the food was almost exclusively Mexican, except for the occasional beefsteak dinner in honor of somebody's birthday or some such thing.

Anyway, he had some interesting responsibilities. Somebody who had friends in Pennsylvania had received a five-gallon can of coal oil, but the Bat Club only had lamps designed for whale oil, and instead of trying the new oil in the old lamps, they decided to wait until they had real coal-oil lamps from New Orleans or some such place, so the five gallons of coal oil sat almost forgotten under the bar.

Forgotten by everyone except for Fulton, who made it known all over town that he had a can of coal oil at the Bat Club and that anyone who could put him onto a good lamp for it would be given more than considerable recompense.

His most cherished role was that of anvil man. There was an old anvil in the alley behind the Bat Club, and on any proper occasion, like Independence Day when Texas was still a part of the United States, black powder was poured into the hole found on the top of all anvils, fused with a string dipped in whale oil, and fired. It made a huge explosion and raised a cloud of dense white smoke, better than a score of ordinary firecrackers.

This was called "shooting the anvil," and Grover Fulton was the official anvil shooter of the Bat Club.

Naturally, this was an honor he was happy to relate to all who would listen, so it is hardly conceivable that anyone in Bexar over the age of seven was unaware of Grover's job with the anvil, when the time came, or of the fact that the black powder was in a five-gallon oaken cask kept under Grover's bunk in the outhouse.

Also, at the time of Dubb Shirley's threat to the Silesias' real estate, red tiles for the roof had been ordered and lay stacked against one wall of the old stable, and inside, behind the backbar, were a number of closed cans of tar and turpentine for sealing the tile once it was in place.

Grover Fulton would supervise this work, the anticipation of which became a part of his almost daily conversation at the billiard parlor of Goshen Steiner, where Grover went during that time between midmorning and noon before he might expect the arrival of the first Bat at his own dark and gloomy cheesecloth-festooned saloon.

In fact, had Grover Fulton been a soldier on duty in wartime, he would have been an intelligence disaster, because he could not resist bragging about his importance by displaying his knowledge of intentions and hidden materials in the very presence of people who might be enemies.

In fact, that's about the way it worked out.

Presenting his evidence after the disaster, part of what Grover Fulton said in response to the investigator's questions can set the scene as well as anything.

"Ever'body been outside lookin at them fireworks we set off to celebrate all them Texas militia takin Yankee forts in the Indian Territory," said Grover. "So they was blinded a little with them bright explosions, and that club was dark as hell inside anyway, so you couldn't see much.

"The boys, they come back inside and was all yellin and workin up to a fine time and drinkin good. I never even seen nobody at the end of my bar, back close to the door into the alley. I never even seen nobody. All of a sudden, they was this blast loud enough to bust your eardrums and a big sheet a orange fire shot acrost the bar, and they was smoke so thick an sticky it was like wet sheep wool.

"You ever see a big .44 Colt shot in the dark? And inside a room, too. You ain't never seen such a long, mean-lookin streak of fire and sparks and smells like the door to hell has been throwed wide open, and the racket's like to loosen your teeth.

"The next one come right after, then another one. I thought right off it was just one shooter, but then I figured it had to be two, because I didn't see how one man could thumb back a hammer that fast. Then the shots was comin one right on top of another, and I knew they had to be more'n one.

"Hell, I was flat on the floor by then. I never seen who they was. I was just tryin to crawl out of that damned place, and the noise was like to make a man puke, and them muzzle flashes one after another, orange lightning, and they was yellin and screamin and glass breakin and furniture bein busted up with the boys tryin to get the hell outa that one door at the other end and it was just one hell of a mess.

"But no, dammit, I tell you, I never seen who they was!"

Nobody else had seen who it was, either. In the ghastly red roar of the first fusillade, most of them had started a mad scramble for doors or windows. Later, all who admitted to being in the place said they figured it was a full squad of Yankee Unionist traitors who had infiltrated the South to do just such terrible work.

Of course, Red River and the nearest Yankee were over three hundred miles away, in a straight line, and the only route to Bexar was either through settled country full of a newly mobilized militia or else through Comanche country, where the war parties were out singing again.

The next favorite culprit was local traitors, banded together in secret, armed, and bent on the destruction of all peace-loving, liberty-cherishing Texicans.

But if there was no consensus on who, there was general agreement on what. It had been fiery bedlam, flaming chaos, those long tongues of muzzle flash licking out like the searching, hunting lick of Old Nick's very tongue, setting fire at first to cheesecloth and then to clothing, and then the sputtering blue flames of burning tequila, and then of course, the sudden sweep of flame across everything, as the cloth ceiling exploded in a blanket of fire.

"You could hear them big lead slugs hit the walls and sometimes whine around. You could hear em hit them peeled pole pillars in the middle of the room, sounded like a big steer dumpin a ten-pound wet cowpie in a washtub!"

The smoke was choking and blinding, and some caught near the center of the room lost their bearings and were running into others trying to escape, and they clawed and scratched and screamed, striking each other with fists and bottles and kicking at one another, shoving and pushing in a panic at the prospect of being engulfed by the flames.

Somebody started screaming, "Comanches! Comanches!" And another screamed, "Get outa the way, God dammit, get outa the way!"

A few of the Bat Club members didn't make it out before the coal oil exploded and threw liquid fire over all the room, and with this, even the wooden rafters and the slat pine lumber of the old horse stalls began to burn. It appeared as though the can of coal oil had somehow rolled out from under the bar to the middle of the floor.

The can was found later with .44-caliber holes in it.

It was rather mangled when found, but the holes were there nonetheless.

The reason the coal oil can was mangled was that shortly after the real fire started, the keg of black powder in the outhouse across the alley mysteriously found its way into the Bat Club, and the last escapee claimed he had seen the powder keg rolling slowly down the center of the room, surrounded by burning tables and fallen and still-flaming cheesecloth. Then, as he dove out into the street and scrambled toward his fellow club members, who had preceded him and now stood wide-eyed across the street watching, the place went to pieces in a mighty red and yellow and blue roar!

Flaming debris was sailing about west San Antonio like a flock of insane lightning bugs. Luckily, the only other building ignited was one of Gunther Roth's feed barns near his largest livery stable.

By this time, the San Antonio Volunteer Fire Company Number One was on the scene, and the feed barn was saved, but the Bat Club was no more.

"All that was left to do," said Ulrich Silesia, who was a member of the Volunteer Fire Company Number One, "was to clean up the battlefield and account for the casualties."

Well, more than that.

If the Bat Club was effectively made ineffective, not many people other than old Bat Clubbers were unhappy about it. Although the Bat Clubbers had tried to put themselves across as Bexar's big leaders in the secession movement, this wasn't true.

There were a lot of ideologies around. There were pro–state's rights ideologies, and pro-slave, pro–southern defense, pro–Texas Republic, and pro-Confederation, plus an anti for each one of these pros.

And everybody understood, whether or not they could explain it, that social pressure was more powerful than ideology. So you went along with your neighbors, no matter what you really thought. You might be dead set against slavery, but with the dangerous temper of the times, if your community went for secession, usually you did, too. It was a matter of survival.

And the Bat Club didn't represent any of the ideologies. The Bat Club was an outlaw band organized around lawyers with the common objectives of land grabbing and amassing some political power to do so, and if jumping over the moon was the community answer to a problem, the Bat Clubbers would make it their answer, too.

So when the Bat Club got grabbed by the ears, that didn't make too many people sorry, no matter where they stood on the questions of the day. In fact, most people saw what happened as just fine, because the fire smoked some rotten bats out of San Antonio's belfry, as some of the saloon wags said.

So maybe Austin's reaction to the San Antonio fire wasn't so strange after all. Francis Lubbock, governor of this brand-new Confederate state, wasn't going to just let the fire be accounted for by the rumor mill, which said it had been the Mexican bandit Juan Cortinas, it had been Comanches, it had been Yankees.

That last point stuck in the governor's craw. He wanted to be sure nobody could seriously suppose that a Yankee outfit would come right into the middle of *his* state and shoot hell out of a nice little social club. So naturally, there had to be a state investigation. Mostly to prove it wasn't a Yankee raid.

And who better to investigate than a former Texas Ranger?

So an official courier came down from Austin with a commission, an executive order, and a badge. All of which were given, under oath, to the new Texas Special Inspector General, Buster Lloyd.

It wasn't until history revealed a lot of things later that the irony of this appointment became clear. Of course, the irony had been clear earlier to Buster Lloyd himself. And it would have been clear to Oscar Schiller, who incidentally had not been seen or heard from by anyone since the night before the attack on the Bat Club, and who quite possibly never knew of the appointment anyway.

At the time, Buster Lloyd must have enjoyed many moments of pleasure thinking how he and Oscar Schiller might have talked quietly and laughed about that appointment, with Oscar's eyes glinting behind his thick glasses.

And Oscar might have said, "They sure brought the fox back into the chicken coop, didn't they?"

The report submitted to the governor by Special Inspector General Lloyd has been lost to posterity. Maybe there were some people in the capital who found the whole business an embarrassment and conveniently misplaced it.

It would have been an interesting document if for no other reason than that Texas Rangers like Buster Lloyd were not noted for their high literary style in written communication. Except that Buster Lloyd didn't write it. Ulrich Silesia wrote it.

You might expect that Elizabeth had a great hand in the composition of that paper, but she didn't. After the fuss in the kitchen with Dubb Shirley, she never recovered from her seizure and was almost totally paralyzed and unable to speak.

There was a Mexican woman who cared from her, and Ulrich sat beside her bed each night and recited everything he could remember of the day and swore to Buster Lloyd that he could see from her eyes that she heard and understood. Sometimes he remained at her bedside, bent over with his head on the pillow beside her, holding her hand, sleeping there the whole night, and rising in the morning from the chair aching and bent and red eyed.

Oscar Schiller, before he disappeared, had come twice and stood looking at her, and had once reached down and touched her limp fingers lying above the comforter. When Oscar Schiller left Elizabeth's room, other visitors said his eyes had that ghastly, inhuman shine.

Later, when Buster Lloyd asked for assistance in doing the report he supposed they expected in Austin, Ulrich leaped at the chance to strike some sort of blow against the Jenkins bunch. Useless as he figured such an attack would be, it might at least provide a safety valve for his agony.

"But if we write what I know to be the fact," Buster Lloyd said, "we put Oscar at the risk of arrest and trial."

"Where is he?" Ulrich asked. "Nobody knows. And surely you don't think he'd do something like this and expect to come back here. He's gone. Who knows where? *Quien sabe?*"

"I won't put my name to anything that puts him at risk," Lloyd said. "I won't incriminate myself, either."

"All right," said Ulrich. "Let me think about it. In my youth, there were those who said I could be devious if the situation required."

So the final report indicated that it was impossible to name the perpetrators of the heinous Bat Club fire and all that went with it, but it also allowed light to be shed on various heinous activities of Bat Club members, activities which might account for a motive.

In other words, Ulrich Silesia rather ignored the question of who it was that had committed the Bat Club attack and persecuted the victims instead. In fact, a few people who were allowed to read the document before it was carried back to the state house in Austin, like Gunther Roth, said it was as good a piece of crooked lawyer fancy footwork as he'd ever seen, making everybody forget who was directly responsible for the fire and explosion and casualties and start hating the ones burned, blown up, and shot.

"Although it is impossible to determine the person or persons who actually attacked the Bat Club building on the date specified," Ulrich Silesia wrote, "those disposed to mount such an attack could be legion due to many well-documented grievous wrongs and yes, even atrocities that the leadership of that same Bat Club has committed against various law-abiding citizens of San Antonio de Bexar in the interest of personal gain, enrichment, and aggrandizement!"

If that paragraph didn't make the state's attorney general and Governor Lubbock sit up in their chairs, the next paragraph certainly would. For therein, Ulrich, over the signature of Special Inspector General Lloyd, of course, detailed such things as turning a vicious dog on children, peace officers holding the arms of young boys so that they could be beaten, threats of seizing property from loyal and patriotic citizens unhappy with Bat Club practices, illegal seizure of real estate, sale of confiscated land and buildings without proper prior public announcement, and torture and murder of citizens who refused to vacate illegally seized premises.

Not to mention circulating foul slanders against men celebrated for patriotism and valor in gaining Texas's independence and whisper campaigns attacking ancestors and belittling the constitutional right of freedom of religion.

"That's good, that's good," said Buster Lloyd, reading over Ulrich Silesia's shoulder. "Throw in anything, even if it ain't true. If that Jenkins bunch ain't done it, they probably thought about it."

"No need," said Ulrich. "The record of what they've done is black enough without coloring it."

"Yes, yes, by God, it is," Lloyd said. He took the paper and read those first paragraphs again. "Yes. I sure write good, don't I?"

Obviously, with words like that, the powers at Austin could see that if such a report came to light, the public would clamor for indictments. So the only answer was to lose the inspector general's report and hope that everybody forgot about it in the frenzy of fighting a war with the Yankees.

Surely the powers that be in Austin at the time knew. the citizens of Bexar could not have forgotten the consequences of the Bat Club disaster even if they hadn't seen the inspector general's report. Because the consequences were right under their noses, to the endless delight of many.

On that fateful night, with the first burst of firing from the back end of the room, Judge Hiram Belcher had made a waddling dash for the front door, which was also the objective of everyone else in the room, including the Mexicans in the band who had been retained for entertainment that evening.

In the congestion and confusion, the pushing and shoving, the rudeness and panic, the judge received a blow across the top of his head with a cornet which knocked him down. On rising in the bedlam of noise and the stench of black powder, the judge's sense of direction was impaired, and he dashed face first into one of the side walls. Beginning now to wail, His Honor scrambled along the wall until his frantic fingers found a window, through which he thrust his body.

Unfortunately, the window was not of sufficient width to accommodate his girth, so he remained for some time, his upper half squealing on the outside, his lower half kicking on the inside, until the ceiling burst into flames and fell on the judge's rear, lighting his trousers and underwear.

Fortunately, at this exact moment a pair of Mexican boys, who had run up from Barrio del Sur to see what the shooting was all about, saw the judge's plight and, each taking an arm, pulled him like a cork from a bottle out of the window and onto the ground, where his clothes could be extinguished.

None too soon. A moment later, the powder keg exploded inside the club.

It took a long time for the judge's burns to heal, being as they were in such a delicate and tender part of his anatomy. He lay on his back for weeks, naked, legs apart, a doctor and nurse applying salves and powders, the judge cursing and vowing vengeance on all enemies of the state.

But when he announced a leave of absence to allow his burns to heal, it was his last official act. He never sat on the bench again.

It was reasoned that most of the shots from the rear of the room had been aimed high, as though this was just a random shooting, maybe even a sort of Texas-style practical joke that got a little out of hand with the fire and the explosion.

But most folks began to say the practical joke idea, although not beneath the sense of humor of any number of barroom stalwarts, was a pail that didn't hold water, because the casualties in that Bat Club were too specific to have been coincidental.

Booth Jenkins was the Bat Club's High Potentate or Exalted Wizard or Grand Wing Flapper, or whatever it was the Bats called their leader. And according to the testimony of Grover Fulton, the first shot, before the room was shrouded with smoke and filled with the flashings of muzzle blasts and trembling under the concussions of explosions, sent a leaden slug smashing into the pilsner-style stein sitting on a table directly in front of Booth Jenkins's face.

Cheeks and forehead lacerated by glass shards and drenched in beer, His Royal Bat Highness screamed and leaped backward and was immediately knocked down by the stampede of his loyal Bats, including his own son. In a panic, he scrambled on hands and knees toward the front door.

A more embarrassing posture and deportment for such an eminent Bat could hardly have been conceived. This was the man that very evening had been shouting the virtues of battle against the Yankees, death- before-dishonor kinds of phrases, now being frightened by a bullet striking a beer glass and crawling like a squealing pig out into the middle of the street before gaining control of himself.

So then, in front of some townspeople who had gathered on the sidewalks to watch, he rose and dusted off his clothing and marched away from his followers still trying to escape the Bat Club. He hardly could have missed the most dreadful sound a proud man can hear. Scornful laughter.

The next day Booth Jenkins resigned from his public office. This was not due entirely to his humiliation at what people were calling the Bat Club crawl-away. It was also something his wife, Lucretia, had insisted on his doing for the sake of their son, John David.

For John David had suffered a grievous wound from one of those shots that perhaps were not random at all. A large-caliber slug had struck him in the face, taking away a considerable portion of his chin and all his teeth. Obviously, there was no medical help in Bexar that could accomplish much with such a wound, so he had to be taken to New Orleans at once.

Maybe wanting to show that the quality of mercy is not strained, Gunther Roth provided a well-upholstered coach with leather-strap suspension and a wheel team, swing team, and lead team of fine bay horses, all at no charge.

On the way out of town, the coach paused in front of the Menger Hotel, and leaning from a window curtained with loose canvas, Mrs. Booth Jenkins made her first and, so far as is known, only public pronouncement. "I earnestly pray," she shouted, "that as soon as I have my dear husband and my beloved son over yonder ridge, this filthy town and all its detestable people will sink twelve miles into the hottest pit of flaming hell!"

It was astonishing, but only one fatality was reported in the Bat Club disaster. The body was found well toward the back, between the bar and backbar, on its back, hardly burned at all. A badge of office was clearly visible, and a pistol was held in the body's right hand, gripped tightly, all cylinders exploded.

Apparently the fat, foolish, butt-of-jokes city marshal, Dubb Shirley, was the only man in the Bat Club with the courage to charge the enemy guns once the shooting started. He didn't make it, of course, and was shot down with any number of wounds, from throat to groin.

But most apparent was something perhaps intentionally left as a kind of reminder of what this whole thing had been about. A long knife was buried in his body so that, just below his ribs, the handle protruded like a slightly bent finger pointing at the charred remains of a cheesecloth ceiling.

Anybody could see that this was what remained of a cowhorn handle. A green cowhorn handle.

Down the line, the property on Armador Street went on the block for delinquent taxes. It was bought by Juan Pardo. Maybe with his cattle-drive partner Gunther Roth—nobody ever knew—he established a large Mexican-goods mercantile store that extended to Military Plaza. Gringos could buy anything there that otherwise would have meant a trip south of Laredo, so naturally the store became instantly popular.

In fact, as the Yankee naval blockade more and more shut off anything coming along usual routes of supply, Mexico became the primary source for almost everything. And if something was available in Old Mexico, Johnny Pardo had it in his shelves.

There were other more immediate results of the Bat Club's demise. Jesus Montez took Oscar Schiller's place as coach bell ringer. Although the war cut off all the Butterfield runs from Saint Louis, and the California runs were suspended, too, there was actually an increase in coach traffic inside the state and back and forth to cross the Sabine.

Jesus liked the bell-ringer job. The Gringos treated him good, too. But even better than the job was telling the story.

Now that Dubb Shirley was gone, and the Jenkins family was, too, Jesus Montez didn't have to worry about somebody retaliating against his brother Ramon for his part in the massacre of John David's vicious black dog. Now Jesus could relate to his friends all the wonderful details of that night.

This was a very popular story in the Barrio del Sur because a lot of boys there still bore scars from that black dog's teeth. And there were many whose pigeons had been stolen by John David on his threat of turning the dog loose on them.

Jesus didn't tell the story to Gringos, of course. He told it to Ulrich Silesia because Silesia was *un alemán,* a German, just like Oscar Schiller. And Señor Silesia said that it was a very fine tale and that it was good to know for sure what had happened that night, and he told Elizabeth the story, sitting beside her bed, holding her hand. He didn't know if she understood. But he pretended she did and that she enjoyed it, too.

Still, Jesus Montez missed Oscar Schiller. And sometimes when he was in the San Fernando Cathedral watching for the dust cloud of an approaching stagecoach, he hoped that he would see the blue roan coming back with a rider who wore spectacles that shone in the sun like little mirrors.

Almost every day, Jesus hoped Oscar Schiller would come. But he never did.

Epilogue

They decided to hold a big treaty council with all the Southern Plains wild tribes. They found a nice little basin near the river where the Kiowas were always holding sun dances. The white men called the river Medicine Lodge Creek. The Indians called it Timbered Hill River.

This was after the Civil War, in 1867.

The white men brought their usual entourage. There were half-a-dozen uniformed army officers, an escort of troops from the Seventh Cavalry, and high-ranking civilians representing the Department of War and the Department of the Interior.

There were a long string of army wagons and ambulances, an abundance of food and gifts for the tribesmen, and the personnel to do all the camp work. There were stenographers to get down every word spoken, a platoon of interpreters, and something that was becoming standard at these meetings: a white woman saying she represented one of the chiefs.

Such ladies normally were part of the tribal retinue, riding, eating, and lodging with a chief's tribe. Many stories were told regarding their relationship to the chief or maybe some of his retainers. They claimed to be experts in the chief's language, a point of some considerable doubt among those present who really were experts, people like trackers and army scouts and Indian traders.

Maybe as important as anyone were the newspaper and magazine reporters. There were a lot of them. Their stories and drawings appeared all across the country.

There were large contingents from the various tribes. The Comanches, the Kiowas, the Kiowa-Apaches, the Arapahoes, and the Cheyennes. But many bands among these tribes sent no representatives at all.

There were colorful chiefs. An Arapahoe who lay on his back crying so hard his tears washed away his face paint. The infamous Satanta, who said the white man's corn hurt his teeth and now and again blew the bugle he always carried with him. A stern Cheyenne who told another chief of his tribe that if he didn't behave, he would go out and kill all his horses.

Maybe the one the news reporters liked best was the Comanche, old Ten Bears. Because even though he was illiterate, Ten Bears wore steel-rim eye spectacles.

His hair was docked at the shoulder, except for a single scalp lock down the back. He wore no feathers anywhere, although other Comanches said he had earned many in battle. He had the usual Comanche bandanna around his neck, a white man's collarless gray linen shirt, a woolen vest, woolen pants with the seat cut out, a loin cloth and knee-high buckskin moccasin gaiters, with long fringes.

He was about fifty, pretty ancient for a Comanche. He'd been many places, seen many things. He spoke fairly good English, and he had a fine sense of humor.

"Yes," he said. It was evening at the fire before his lodge, and he spoke with a circle of perhaps nine reporters squatted around him. "I can tell you all about the nose glasses. But you have to have some patience. I am not so old that I have forgotten how impatient young men like you can be, but I am too old to give my words the swiftness your interest deserves."

It was the season, he said, just before the start of your big war. The one where the Texas white man and the bluecoat white man fought each other over the black man.

I never understood why anybody would have a war over such a thing. But much of what the white man does is strange, especially the Texas white man.

We had started a few little raids again. We'd been quiet for a long time. Now we rode the forks of the Brazos and along the Balcones Escarpment and took a few horses and if it looked right, set fire to a few ranches. Some of the Texas white men were already gone off some-where to fight the bluecoat white men.

The Texas white men called these bluecoat white men Yankees. I suppose that's the kind of white men we have here at this treaty meeting.

I enjoy treaty meetings. I like to talk to the white man and make speeches. Not to the Texas white man, but to the bluecoats. The Yankees. Of course, they never listen to what I tell them. They could save themselves a lot of trouble if they did.

So we were out riding the Brazos. I think we were far up the Salt Fork.

Our leader for this raid was a man much admired among our people, Rides the Rain Storm. He was the son of Wolf's Road, who was famous among my people for making the treaty with a new tribe that came to Texas many years ago. The tribe they called *los alemáns*, the Germans.

It was a good treaty. It still works. The Germans on the escarpment pledged friendship and gifts from time to time, and the Penatekas pledged land for the Germans to plow so that they could grow things to eat.

The Germans are the kind of people who like to plow in the ground and grow good things to eat. At least, they think these things are good.

Wolf's Road gave the German chief, a man named Miller or some such thing, a talisman so that he and his people would not forget the treaty. It was a sacred object, Wolf's Road said.

It wasn't, actually. It was just an old dried finger some Comanche brave had taken off an enemy he'd killed. After he dried it nice and neat, he had one of our old spirit men weave a lanyard for it so you could wear it as a necklace.

The German chief didn't know all this, so it was only as sacred as Wolf's Road wanted it to be, but it sealed the promises made and bound both sides to them.

Everybody in the tribe knew about it. It was a nice joke on the German, but it made the treaty work, which showed you how smart Wolf's Road was.

I never saw the thing at the time, but I knew about it, and I knew that at the treaty meeting, Rides the Rain Storm had given the necklace to the German on behalf of his father. So you can see that Rides the Rain Storm, who we just called Storm for short, had a lot of prestige in the tribe, and when he wanted to go out on a raid, he never had any trouble getting men to go with him.

So we were riding along in the hot dust one day, just under a ridge, and one of our outriders signaled a white rider near. I rode to the ridgeline with Storm to see, and there was a single man on a blue roan horse.

It looked like a young boy. He wasn't very big on that black horse.

So we rode right in on him, not so fast, but we had a couple of riders on his flanks so he couldn't run. He was smart enough to see that, so he just stood and waited. If he'd tried to run, our riders would have killed him right away with their lances.

He wasn't so young after all, just a small man. And he had these glass things on his nose. I'd seen them before, when we had meetings with the bluecoat white man. Until that day, I never trusted a man who wore them.

While Storm tried to talk with the little man, I flipped those glasses off with the tip of my lance and leaned down and took them off the ground and put them on my own nose and everybody laughed.

They made me lightheaded. They made things look large.

But now, Storm had found two six-shooter pistols under the man's serape, and he took them and asked the young man what he intended to do with such weapons here in the land of the Nerm.

Now all the others joined the fun. We were slowly undressing the young man while he still sat on his black horse. He was very brave. He didn't say anything. He didn't beg or make lies about being a big friend of the People. He just sat there and allowed our men to strip him down, as though we would not be able to strip his dignity.

I liked this. Storm liked it, too. This was a brave, tough young man. It was going to be interesting to see how brave he would be when we used the knives on him, how much courage we could expect to be given to us when we defeated him at last.

You don't understand such things, so it is useless for me to explain.

But we never got to the knives. For as the shirt was torn off the small body, we saw something swinging across his chest from a rawhide cord around his neck. As soon as I saw it, I knew what it was. And of course, Storm did, too.

It was a powerful medicine suddenly before us, and all fell back amazed and only Storm could find a voice, and he asked the small man if he was *un alemán*, a German from the Balcones Escarpment. That's when the small young man amazed us all again. He spoke for the first time, in our own tongue, saying he was a German from that area.

Storm pointed to the talisman around the little man's neck and said he had given that pendant with his own hands to one of the German fathers as a proof that there would be peace so long as it was worn.

So the little German man said his father had died. And Storm said his father had died as well. And the little German man said the pendant had come from his father, as well as the two big pistols we'd taken from him.

It was like finding a brother lost a long time ago. It was a very happy thing.

So we were glad to share our camp with the little German man, and we named him Comes with Glass Shining on His Eyes, and called him Glass Shining for short.

We made a fire. It was a good fire, too, not a fire lit in a trench hole to conceal it from enemies far out on the plain who might be looking for us. We stopped the raid for a little while. We got acquainted with our newfound brother.

We cooked some antelope meat we had from a hunt the day before. We had some good pemmican, too. My best wife had made it with pinecone nuts and wild cherries. She was the best pemmican maker in the band.

Glass Shining said he was trying to leave Texas. But he had to stay out in the plains away from the Texas white man settlements because the Texas white man was likely looking for him so they could put him in one of their iron houses for a while before taking him out and maybe hanging him.

He said he had shot a lot of Texas white men in Bexar and set their council house afire and blown it to pieces with gunpowder, and he figured they were pretty upset and unhappy.

It made Storm and the rest of us laugh and slap Glass Shining on the back because we said it was revenge for the time the Texas white man had massacred a group of our chiefs who had come into San Antonio to talk peace back before the Germans ever came to Texas.

So after a few days, we guided Glass Shining north to Red River and into the land of the Chickasaws. We had sold a lot of captives to the Chickasaws and knew many of them and they said they would help our friend on his journey east to see mountains with green trees on them.

We never heard from him again. I suppose he traveled as he planned to do and saw what he wanted to see. He appeared to be a young man who was determined to get what he wanted.

Before he rode away, he gave one of those big pistols to Storm to repay him for his hospitality. Storm gave him a horse so Glass Shining would have more than just the blue roan to make his journey.

And then he gave me these eyeglasses. He had two or three of them. And when I told him that looking through them made my stomach rise up and quiver like a hummingbird wing, he said just take the glass out and you won't have any trouble like that.

But maybe, Glass Shining said, if you leave that glass where it's at, someday it will surprise you.

Sure enough, I left the glass where it was at, and when I began to get old and my eyes began to itch and burn and things looked fuzzy, I put on those nose glasses and things looked all right again.

Well, there was still itching and burning, but I could see good anyway.

How do you like that? I tell you, Comes with Glass Shining on His Eyes was a smart little man. I wonder what ever happened to him. I hope those Texas white men didn't catch him.